The hot, wet heat of her tongue sent a fire through me. I could feel liquid seep from deep inside, soaking my panties. Her tongue and teeth pleasurably tortured one nipple as her hand played with the other. I groaned, feeling like my insides were melting.

❧

My name is Luce.

Way before I loved the woman I love now, there was a woman I will never forget, even though when I think about her I sometimes see her unclearly. Her features and body and dress appear drenched in such bright sunlight that the details are obscured.

❧

Crack. She's just smacked my ass hard, and the sensation is only a little less scorching than my embarrassment.

"What are you doing?" I glare at her. "People can hear."

"Isn't that the point?"

"I don't want to be escorted out of here by store detectives!"

She grasps my hair, pulling my head back, and hisses in my ear, "Then ask nicely next time you want something." Her breath is a fever on my cheeks.

"Please," I pant. "Fuck me."

❧

"You look very pretty sitting there, Jennifer."

When Judith's voice comes over the PA system, the audience relaxes a little, seemingly relieved they don't have to worry about what they are supposed to do regarding the blindfolded naked woman in front of them.

"You'd look even better if were touching yourself."

Visit

Bella Books

at

BellaBooks.com

or call our toll-free number

1-800-729-4992

Fantasy

UNTrue Stories
of Lesbian Passion

Edited by:
Barbara Johnson and
Therese Szymanski

Bella
BOOKS

2007

Bella Books, Inc.
P.O. Box 10543
Tallahassee, FL 32302

Printed in the United States of America on acid-free paper
First Edition

Editor: Barbara Johnson & Therese Szymanski
Cover designer: Stephanie Solomon-Lopez

ISBN-10: 1-59493-101-1
ISBN-13: 978-1-59493-101-7

To all lovers—past, present and future.

Acknowledgments

We would like to especially thank Bella's incredible proofreaders, Ruth Stanley and Deana Casamento, as well as all of Bella's truly wonderful and talented staff!

Oh, and, of course, a big thank you to Linda Hill for again letting us follow through on our lusts!

Contents

Fantasy:
The realm of vivid imagination, reverie, depiction illusion, and the like

In our never-ending quest to please you, dear reader, we challenged writers from around the world to share their steamiest stories of Sapphic sensuality. After exhaustive and exhilarating nights of one-handed reading, we handpicked the hottest of the hot to create *Fantasy: Untrue Stories of Lesbian Passion*.

What is it that makes untrue stories so enticing? Simple: truth has consequences, fantasy does not.

Case in point . . . In reality, sex in the workplace can lead to office gossip, lowered productivity and termination. In fantasy, you can get away with a lot more on the Xerox machine than just copying your ass.

In fantasy, you can make love on the beach for hours and the water won't turn you into a prune, the sand won't irritate your pink bits, and you won't be accosted by the shore patrol or lifeguards (unless, of course, you want to be).

In fantasy, one-night stands never show up at your door with a U-Haul or a meat cleaver. And mind-blowing sex doesn't lead to restraining orders or a visit from the EMTs (unless you want them to join you).

By letting you play your way, fantasies can push boundaries that you may not be ready, willing or able to cross in real life. You can cheat without cheating. Be who you are or who you want to be. Do what you want, but are afraid to ask for. And don't be surprised if your mind takes you farther than the words on the pages of this book, because that's exactly what we're hoping will happen!

So, lie back, relax and take an erotic journey with us through the greatest bedtime stories never told.

Barbara Johnson

Reese Ryan

All About Her
Karin Kallmaker

"Tell me a fantasy," she persisted, pressing me down into the soft easy chair in the sunny corner of her study. "I'm out of ideas and I have a deadline."

It wasn't the first time she had made that request, but today, with afternoon shadows already heavy with winter cold, I didn't feel like talking about the flash and fire of something fast and heady. I could come up with a hundred bar fantasies and a few true stories, but the comforting aroma of the hot apple cider she'd poured for me had dark and smoky rooms far from my imagination.

I watched her settle at her desk, her back to me. One hand lifted blonde tendrils so she could briefly cup the back of her neck. It had taken me years to realize that the gesture was meant to warm her fingers before typing.

"You just talk and I'll quietly type, and I'm sure there'll be something that'll spark a story. I promise I won't even look at you."

The chill of the season seemed to be seeping into my bones more this year and my fantasy thoughts—to my chagrin—turned not to sex but warmth. I didn't want to disappoint this lady, never her, so I hoped if I just got going I would find something that would amuse and divert. My day wasn't right if I didn't hear her laugh or make one of those appreciative "I love you to bits, Jac" noises of hers. It was usually followed by a sigh of contentment that meant "You're a good friend." My head heard that part; it was my heart that didn't want to accept it.

"Well, last night when I was at Tammy's get-together I didn't know anyone much. Just Tammy and she's so married."

"I like her girlfriend, but I sure wish Tammy was single," she said. "With a physique like that I could use her for fodder in a hundred stories. Which would get me into big trouble with the missus."

I laughed. "You can say that again."

"A woman with native blood and blue eyes—but there are too many Amazons running around in books these days."

"Yeah, whatever happened to stories about cute little imps of dykes?"

"Oh, so this fantasy is about you?"

She didn't turn around which was good, because I blushed. "I prefer to fantasize about taller, curvaceous womanly types—"

"Yeah, but you're in the room with them."

"Of course. Whose fantasy is this? Do you want to hear it or not?"

Her fingers were poised over the keyboard. "Go ahead. You were at Tammy's last night for the party and you didn't know anyone much."

"No, so I nursed a glass of a very nice red wine for a while. Everyone else was a couple, and you know how that goes."

"Yeah, tell me about it."

"I chatted a bit. Whenever anyone sat down for a while we'd

talk about Tammy's coffee table."

I rested my head on the back of the chair, closing my eyes. "The color has deepened since she finished it. I still can't believe she made it. I mean, I know that she did. She's very creative and has always loved woodworking, but every time I see it I think how beautiful it is, and how useful—and sturdy too."

She made a pleased little noise. "Ah, now we're getting somewhere."

I had to grin, but I tried to sound stern when I said, "Stop interrupting."

"Sorry."

"They had a fire and that felt really good. I sat on the table while I warmed my wine a little, and it felt like summer in spite of the snow yesterday." My eyes still closed, I said softly, "I noticed how warm the wood was under me and I thought to heck with bearskin rugs in front of a roaring fire. A warm satin-finished wood table under a voluptuous woman who was under me . . . that works, big time."

She wanted a fantasy and I didn't know why, but today I was tired and cold. My guards were down as I looked at her silhouette, knowing from those so friendly full-body dyke hugs she gave how she curved, how we fit. I shouldn't tell her my deepest fantasy, *the* fantasy of fantasies, the one that ran in high-definition digital surround sound whenever I indulged myself. Between the wine and the warmth last night, I'd not been able to curb it. I couldn't tell her or she'd know the last of my secrets.

Maybe, I told myself, since she was in her analytic, creative mode at the moment, everything I said she would hear using the writer parts of her brain. And that did fascinate me. She would chop my story into kindling and pick the best pieces for her fire. The heat that resulted was all hers. She'd treat this story no differently than the first one I'd shared. Why would she?

It had been three years ago that I'd told her about a somewhat quirky tryst with a woman whose name I'd never learned. It wasn't all that typical of me, which had been part of the fun. I'd had a bad relationship to kick over—getting picked up by an aggressive dynamo in high heels had proven an excellent cure. When I'd finished my little story she'd grinned at me over our hot cocoa and asked if she could use part of it for a hot little short story. I agreed, expecting a fictionalized version of that night. A couple of days later she'd e-mailed me the file, and I'd found nothing of the kind. It was another scenario entirely, but I recognized the high heels, the effective knots and raw excitement of uncomplicated sex. There were little pieces of me in her work. And I liked that. I liked that a lot.

After reading her story I couldn't help but ask, of course, if the ropes had been the thing she'd really wanted to write about and she—blushing and giving me one of those laughing, I'll-never-tell looks—had said, "Maybe. Maybe not."

After that, I had shared more thoughts and ideas, enjoying the pleasure of finding them scattered here and there in her stories. And I learned a lot about what intrigued my best friend. I reread everything of hers, hunting for clues, learning to split the creative fantasy muse of the writer from the fantasy life of the woman. It was the writer I was talking to right now, I told myself. It was safe to share what I'd imagined last night.

"Anything is possible in a fantasy—you told me that yourself. You can have full-on, naked sex in a crowded room and nobody notices. Or they notice and watch. That can be part of the fun." I opened my eyes at the sound of keys clicking and watched her fingers move over the keys, supple and sensuous. "So, I am feeling that warm wood and thinking how it gives off the kind of heat you feel in your bones, and she walks in." I studied her sleek hair where it lifted in short curls, some shot with silver, then continued. "She walks in and we're all alone. There's the party in the next room, but nobody will look our way. She's dressed for me."

I had to breathe for a moment, thinking back to that

Thanksgiving dinner party with many of our mutual friends, when she'd arrived on the arm of what's-her-name, now six months out of her life. "Her sweater is almost off her strong shoulders and my eyes trace that wide neckline several times as she walks toward me. She says to me, softly, 'I'm so glad you're here,' and I can smell her perfume. Her body, as she stops in front of me, is warmer than the coffee table, giving off that same kind of bone-deep heat."

I heard the little chime from her laptop that meant she'd saved her notes so far. "She's wearing a soft linen skirt and the kind of shoes that make no sense in the snow. The most natural thing in the world is for me to move to the nearby chair as I slide my arms around her waist. I pull her down onto my lap. I tell her I've been missing her all day."

I realized I'd cupped my arms around empty air as I'd spoken. With her back to me I felt free to mold where a full, rounded breast would be and I tipped back my head, imagining the lips I would gaze at before softly covering them with my own.

"She settles into my lap and we're kissing as I slowly pull that wonderful sweater farther off her shoulders. I don't know what the fabric is, but I love the contrast as my fingers travel between her smooth skin to the soft, brushed texture. She murmurs my name and her shoulders drop back. She won't ask, not at the beginning. I know it's up to me to read her, so I bury my lips in the hollow of her throat. She makes the first of the noises that mean 'don't stop' and my fingers ease the neckline down until the upper lacy edge of her bra is exposed. I start to purr inside because it's one of the ones she told me weren't about support or comfort, but designed solely to keep things looking high and firm when laying on her back."

Her fingers stilled on the keys and I wondered if I'd gone too far. Could I take it back? Was her neck flushing? How could I be telling her this story, revealing that her own shy but bawdy admissions over time had become permanently carved on the inside of my fantasy rooms?

She didn't say anything, however, and so I went on, thinking I was totally screwing up the best thing in my life, that I was going to lose everything I valued, but the release I felt at finally letting it out was too good to stop.

"I slip the straps off her shoulders and peel the bra down as well, little by little, until my fingertip can brush the swelling roughness of her nipple. I love the shudder that runs through her as she arches against me. She won't ask, not yet, but again I know that she means 'don't stop.' And in my fantasy," I say very quietly but distinctly, "I know what she wants. There's very little she doesn't like—her menu of options has an amazing range. We've talked about them all. I *always* know what she wants. Tonight . . . dressed like this, moving against me like this . . ." I swallowed hard. "Tonight she wants me to decide what she'll get."

I realized she was backspacing and clicking, fixing a typo maybe, or already editing something that will later be a few words in the story. I felt safe again, not so exposed, but my voice sounded tight and strained to my own ears.

"I brush her nipple again and then squeeze it slowly between my fingers. She gasps and I stare into her eyes, which have gone the deep blue-green that always means she's very aroused. Her brows arch as I continue to squeeze and pull more of her breast free from her clothes. I whisper to her that yes, that's how it's going to be tonight. I give her an impish smile as I study her shivering body. Her legs have parted for me, and I like that." I had to swallow again because I have pictured her this way a thousand times. Imagined her so aroused that I was the only person in her world at that moment. Craved knowing that the look in her eyes was for me, about me, and what she knew and trusted I would do—which was take care of her, take care of both of us. All night. Every night.

"She's so sexy like that, her breast half exposed, her skirt up around her thighs. I release her nipple and let my hand drift to the hem of her skirt. I want to shove it out of my way and bathe my fingers in the swirl of wet I know must be there, but instead I slip my hand under her skirt to cup her hip, feel the line of her body. She shivers and parts her legs more. She's not going to ask, not yet, but still, I know she means 'don't stop' which is good, because I'm not going to. It is time for my words, though, and I tell her that I planned ahead, that I knew she was in one of her sexy, wanton moods. The panties she has on have no functional purpose but to make my fingers feel naughty as I slip them under the lace of one leg and trace it around to her ass. She lifts herself as if to give me more room to touch her. I squeeze the full, lovely shape of her, then run my fingers back over the front of her thigh until the soaked lace wets my finger. She's breathing hard. Now she can speak. Now the eager, sensual woman is ready to play. Finally, she says 'yes' and then she says 'please' and she moves my hand between her legs and for just a moment I'm struck dumb at how hot and how wet and how much I love touching a woman there. God, there's nothing better."

More roughly than I intended, I rushed on with, "I push the lace out of the way and tease her slippery folds, dipping inside just enough to open her. All the euphemisms about flowers make sense when the curls and ripples of her beautiful soaking cunt unfurl and I'm inside her, my lady, my siren, and all her sexiness is just for me. I kiss her throat and feel her tightening already. I'm so torn. I want to feel her melt and hear her sharp little cry and know I brought her over the edge in under a minute. But if she comes I know she'll be a little less driven and I like it when she can't think about anything but me and what I'm going to do to her."

The afternoon light had faded to gold and orange, and I couldn't tell now if the curve of cheek I could see was tinted with pink. I was not usually this explicit but now that I'd started I wanted her to know. I wanted her to know that I *know*.

"I say into her throat 'don't come' while still moving my fingers. She shudders and I whisper it again into her ear. I can feel her muscles shifting as one part consciously tries to stop the very thing my fingers are bringing on while the rest of her continues to flood and open and respond. I say 'don't come' one more time and ease my fingers out of her. She moans and her hand squeezes my shoulder so tight I can feel her nails. She says my name. Her eyes are dark with lust. I tell her I want her on her back, on that gleaming, satiny warm coffee table."

My heart was pounding against my lungs as I pictured her obeying me. I couldn't stop now. I had to tell her everything. "I taste my fingers and make no effort to hide that it makes me a little dizzy. Standing over her, I look at her beauty—one breast exposed, her skirt up around her waist, the sodden panties askew and her long creamy legs spread open for me. There is no party anymore, just us. The coffee table is more than solid and I plant my hands on the warm wood to either side of her ribs. My teeth find her swollen nipple and I bite down softly just to feel her writhe. Her hands are in my hair and I shake them off. One at a time I move her hands to the edge of the table, curling her fingers around it firmly. And I tell her, 'Keep them there or I'll stop.'"

She stopped typing. She had to know. She had to realize it at that point. I had paid attention to everything she'd ever said. I don't know where I found the courage to say, "Keep typing or I'll stop."

She made a little noise, and it was one of the ones I'd fantasized about hearing. After a moment, her fingers moved on the keys.

"What are the right metaphors for how edible she looks? How desirable she is? I want to devour her, feast on her. I tell her what I know she has to hear before she will completely abandon herself to me, and it is the absolute truth. That I am so unbelievably turned on by her. That she makes me crazy hot. That I want to feel every inch of her. The kiss we share is deep and wet and she's lifting her hips to brush against mine and I know she's craving my weight on her. In this mood she wants me to enjoy myself playing with her body, to do whatever will make me even hotter. I bare her other breast and roughly tug her nipple, then suck it between my teeth to flick it hard with my tongue. She's a ripple of motion under me. I slip my hand behind her neck and look at her through a haze of red lust. I say 'You need to get fucked now, don't you' but it's not a question. I'm not asking, I'm taking. I don't need her to say 'yes' but she does, oh she does. She says it over and over, with her voice, with her body, with her hard, red nipples filling my mouth."

Maybe it was just my wishful thinking, but her fingers seemed to be shaking on the keyboard. I imagined those fingers dancing on my skin and I almost lost my train of thought. She made a little sound of frustration, and it broke my reverie.

"Her eyes go wide as she hears the sound of my zipper. I am so ready for her. I've spent all day planning this moment. I've chosen the toy that nobody else knows she can handle. I remind her that she can't let go of the table and she groans out a very long, sexy 'yes,' the kind I want to hear for the next couple of hours." I paused to laugh a little. "Because this is my hottest fantasy, I have no trouble balancing on one hand while I rub the tip of my toy against her clit. She shudders and tries to wrap her legs around my waist but I'm still not close enough to her for that, not yet. I open her cunt with the toy, rubbing it up and down her swollen and slippery lips. For a moment I consider stopping long enough to get my face all wet with her, but she twists under me and the toy slips just inside her. I can't stand it anymore and I press firmly forward, not fast, not slow, but forward. Into her. She lets out a surprised, strangled cry as I fill her. I ask her if this is what she wants and she can say it all now. The rest of the world is gone. It's just me and the sexy woman of my deepest fantasy, and she can say all the sweaty, heavy, needy things I long to hear. And she begs, never letting go of the table, begs for all of it, and

I give it to her. She needs this, I need it, we're both getting what we want, getting fucked and fucking with all of our strength. She is crooning my name, and I love that."

I realized then that she had stopped typing. She appeared not to be even breathing, but then I saw the ragged movement of her shoulders as she took a deep breath, before hurriedly putting her hands back on the keyboard.

Leaning forward in the chair, my voice husky with the desire to finish, I said, "I am lost in moving on top of her, in enjoying her straining abandon and the broken cries of pleasure she seems helpless to stop. I take everything I could want, over and over, listening to the slide of us merging, the wet slap of our bodies. I'm fogged with passion and don't know how long she's been saying 'please, Jac, please' and I know it's not her wanting me to stop. I suck her nipple hard into my mouth and her legs shake uncontrollably. I say what she needs now, awed that she could wait when I'm so close myself and I'm not the one being fucked. 'Come now,' I tell her."

She stopped typing, and this time I could see that her hands were shaking.

"She comes, screaming, wake-the-neighbors loud. I am holding on to her bucking body in a place of my own that I've never been before and then I feel her soaking me. She's hot and wild and still coming. When I feel the heat of her climax flooding over my clit I can't stop myself from coming too, and she groans out my name, over and over."

The orange and gold of the afternoon had eased into the blues of twilight. The only light is from her screen. The silence felt cold suddenly, and the heat of my fantasy faded away, the way it always did, leaving room for intrusive, unwanted thoughts of reheated soup for dinner and the unwelcome echoes of my empty life.

Finally, because I was starting to shiver, I said, "Did I inspire a story—"

"Don't Jac."

Surprised, I could only think to say, "Don't what?"

"Don't pretend."

She cupped the back of her neck with her fingers and I wondered if she was feeling the cold too. Rising quickly, I crossed the room to press my lips to her fingers, as I had wanted to do a thousand times. She pulled them away and I kissed the nape of her neck, and it was as warm as I had always known it would be.

I rubbed my lips across her satiny skin until they brushed her soft lobe and the delicate ring that pierced it. "Is this okay?"

She shivered. And then said, simply, "Yes."

I was never going to be cold again. I went on nuzzling along the beautiful arch of her neck, inhaling the scent of her skin.

Her voice soft and choked, she asked, "How did you know?"

I knew she could feel my impish smile against her throat. "That you had a fantasy about getting well and truly fucked on a coffee table?"

"No silly. That my deepest fantasy wasn't about a time, a place or a scene. That it was about being with someone who loved me enough to give me what I wanted without me having to say it or write it first. Someone who just *knew*."

I turned her desk chair slowly so I could finally look into her eyes. "Someone who enjoys knowing—no, not just enjoys it, but takes absolute pleasure in it."

She nodded and her shoulders dropped back as she arched into me. "You never told me your fantasy woman's name."

I moved as close to her as I could get without actually pressing my lips to hers, waiting for any sign at all that I shouldn't kiss her now. "Karin, honestly, what do you think?"

Nick of Time
Radclyffe

When the phone rang, I knew I shouldn't answer. Part of me craved a diversion, and that's exactly why I hesitated. I didn't have time to be distracted. Zero hour, D-day, the Moment of Truth—whatever the phrase for "the clock is ticking and you're running out of time"—was written in big, bold letters across the blank screen of my computer monitor.

Second ring. I clenched my jaws, determined to be strong.

Third ring. I ground my teeth.

Fourth ring. I pressed both hands hard against my thighs.

Fifth ring. Sweat broke out on my forehead.

Sixth—I snatched up the phone.

"Hello?"

"Did I catch you in the middle of a workout?"

"Nope, I'm at my desk."

I leaned back and closed my eyes, picturing my best friend Carly. At ten o'clock at night, she'd probably be curled up on the sofa with a book, her long, runner's legs bare and her riotous red curls disheveled because she unconsciously twisted the long locks around her finger as she read. We'd met on our first day of college at freshmen orientation and had been practically inseparable ever since. We'd pledged the same sorority, ended up sharing a room and throughout most of that year shared pretty much everything, even dating the same guys, although not at the same time. All that changed one night in the middle of commiserating about the unsatisfying state of our love lives because neither of us had been able to find anyone who could kiss, or do anything else to our satisfaction. We were sitting cross-legged on her bed, facing each other, wearing what we usually wore to bed, big, long, loose T-shirts and nothing else. I can't remember which guys we had been complaining about, but I distinctly remember Carly stopping in mid-rant and staring at me as if she'd never seen me before. Or maybe seeing me for the first time.

"You know, you have a fantastic mouth."

"What?" I said stupidly.

"Your lips," Carly murmured, leaning forward so our knees touched. She braced her hand on my bare thigh as if she needed to keep her balance and traced my bottom lip with the index finger of her other hand. "They're a beautiful color and so full." She dipped her finger ever so slightly inside, and without thinking, I caught it with my teeth. She made a little sound of approval in the back of her throat, and I felt weak and hot, as if I'd been running for hours.

I'd seen her naked. I'd touched her casually hundreds of times. I had told her things I'd never told another human being. There were things I didn't know about myself, or hadn't yet admitted, but Carly—Carly, I *knew*. But until that moment, I had never noticed there were tiny flecks of gold around the edges of her hazel irises. I hadn't imagined that her fingertip running along the inside of my lip could feel as if she was stroking me deep inside. I had never once dreamed that the heat of her body could consume me when we weren't even touching.

"Carly, what—"

"Shh," she whispered. "You know."

Her lips were hot and wet, and when her tongue slipped gently into my mouth, I whimpered helplessly, wanting things I had no clue how to express. She took my hand and guided it beneath her T-shirt to her breast. Her nipple tightened against my palm, and she shivered and gave a little cry. That tiny, vulnerable gesture gave me the courage to follow my desperate desire.

I guided her back onto the bed, following until I was lying on top of her, my thigh between hers, my hand traveling from one breast to the other, squeezing and fondling, exploring her with breathless wonder. I kissed her and lost myself in her softness, in the sweet taste of her mouth—too lost to realize what her breathless cries meant until she clutched my shoulders and arched beneath me, her legs twisting around mine.

"I think I'm coming," she gasped.

I remember holding my breath, my heart pounding so fiercely I thought it might burst and not caring if it did, so long as I lived long enough to watch her face while she came. She kept her eyes open and I couldn't have looked away if someone had held a gun to my head. She let me see everything in her eyes— her need, her fears, her pleasure. I've never known anyone braver, before or since. I didn't take a breath until she started to laugh.

"Oh my God," Carly half-laughed, half-sobbed. She wrapped her arms around my waist when I tried to pull away. "Oh my God, that was unbelievable."

My leg was still between hers and she was wet and hot and beautiful. I was—I don't really know what I was, because I'd never felt anything like that before. Terrified, exhilarated, aching, in awe. Carly nudged me with her knee and I shuddered. Grinning, she turned her hand over and slid it between us, down my sweat-slick belly and between my legs. My head snapped back when she closed her fingers around me, and I thought I might pass out.

"Just hold on," Carly whispered, as she held me and stroked me until I couldn't hold on anymore. Then she held me and stroked me as I lay quivering in her arms.

"Do you think this means . . . ?" Carly whispered after a long time, and I answered, "I don't know."

I wasn't ready, but Carly was, and I'd never known Carly to run away from anything. So she ran toward her truth while I stumbled along behind. I took too long and she found a girl-friend. There have been a lot of girlfriends in the six years since then. For both of us. But the one constant in my life has been Carly.

"You don't sound like you're working." Carly's voice called me back to the present. "You sound breathless."

I hadn't been before, but I was now. I concentrated on sounding normal. "Actually, the correct term would be *trying* to work."

"You're stuck?" Carly asked incredulously.

I never suffered from writer's block, and she knew it. It wasn't writer's block precisely, it was . . . boredom. "Not exactly. I'm just having trouble getting motivated."

"What are you writing?"

I sighed. "I promised Vanessa a selection for her next anthology."

"The fantasy thing?"

"Yeah, that's the one."

"When is it due?"

"Uh . . ." I glanced at the time on my computer. "In about two hours."

Carly burst out laughing. "I can't believe you waited this long. You always get everything done weeks in advance. It's disgusting."

"I know," I said miserably. "I've been putting it off."

"Why?"

I shrugged and then realized she couldn't see me. "It's weird. Every time I sit down to write, my mind goes blank."

"No fantasies, hmmm?" Carly teased.

I laughed. "Oh, I've got plenty of fantasies. But this isn't supposed to be true confessions."

"You just need to get primed. Do a spinoff of one of yours." Her voice held a note of challenge. "Come on, let's practice. What's your favorite fantasy?"

"Forget it, Carly. I don't do autobiographical erotica."

"I didn't say *write* it. I said tell me. Or are you chicken?"

"Chicken?" I heard a muffled sound as if the phone had been dropped. "What are you doing?"

"Getting comfortable on the couch. Stretching out so you can tell me a story."

I'd sat on that couch dozens of times, watching television with her, eating popcorn and sharing a bottle of wine. Sometimes she fell asleep. Sometimes we both did and woke up leaning against each other, as comfortable in each other's space as a long-term couple. I pushed back my swivel chair and propped my feet on my desk. I always worked in sweats so I felt pretty relaxed too.

"Maybe I should write about one of *your* true life adventures," I goaded.

"Like you'd know."

I'm not sure exactly why I said what I said next. I could tell she wanted me to do something, *say* something, but I wasn't sure what. She was always a step ahead of me, and I was tired of trying to catch up and always getting there too late.

"Well, there's the night Lucy Carmichael went down on you in the middle of a pledge party."

I heard a gasp, then total silence, and I started to worry.

"Carly?"

"How did you know that? I never told anyone."

I suddenly realized I'd made a big mistake. As close as we were, there were still secrets between us. And I had just told Carly that something she thought had been a secret, wasn't. I searched for a plausible story. But this was Carly, and though there might have been things I hadn't told her, I wouldn't lie.

"I watched you."

"Where?" she whispered.

I closed my eyes, picturing the dark room with a bed in the middle piled high with coats. There was just enough moonlight to see my way around the furniture as I crossed toward the bathroom. The party was in full swing downstairs, and when I'd finally gotten fed up with watching Lucy fall all over Carly, I decided to take a break upstairs. Just as I reached a hand inside the bathroom, feeling along the wall for the light switch, the bedroom door behind me banged open and two women stumbled in. Almost by instinct, I ducked into the dark bathroom. And then I recognized Carly's voice. I peeked around the corner and saw she was with Lucy.

"Whoa, hey, in a hurry?" Carly laughed as Lucy threw her down on the bed.

"God yes," Lucy gasped, tugging at Carly's jeans. "I've wanted to taste you all night long."

Carly twisted her fingers in Lucy's hair. "Come on up here and taste some of this, first."

Lucy climbed up Carly's body and attacked her mouth. I considered trying to sneak out while they were groping each other, but I was afraid they would see me and I was embarrassed to admit I'd been watching this long. I was even more humiliated that I couldn't look away. I knew what Lucy was tasting as she plunged her tongue into Carly's mouth, how good Carly's body felt moving beneath her. I imagined the heat and the small sounds Carly made in her throat and I couldn't stop staring, desperate for some glimpse of her face, terrified I would see her look at Lucy the way she'd looked at me once. With such stark honesty I'd wanted to weep.

"I can't wait," Lucy groaned, pushing away and grabbing Carly's legs. She twisted them until Carly was laying half on top of the pile of coats with her legs dangling over the side of the bed, and then she knelt, forcing Carly's legs apart.

When Lucy buried her face between Carly's thighs, Carly pushed herself up on her elbows and looked down in the moonlight, watching Lucy make her come. I hid in the shadows and saw Carly shiver with each small movement of Lucy's head. I clenched my hands, my body rigid, listening to Carly's sobbing breaths, her broken moans of pleasure, knowing from the sounds that she would come soon. She struggled on the edge for long minutes, her chest heaving, her legs trembling.

"Oh, I can't get there," Carly groaned, "and I need to so bad."

I'll never know why I slid into a sliver of silver light, but she stared across the chasm into my face, her mouth opening wide in a silent scream of pleasure as her back arched and she came instantly. I slipped out of the room, her cries following me into the night. That night and every night thereafter.

"I was in the bathroom," I confessed.

"You were really there?" Carly whispered.

"Yes."

"I always thought I'd imagined it. Seeing you. You never said."

"Sorry," I muttered. "I thought you might be mad."

"How could I be mad when you made me come?"

"I wish," I whispered.

"You wish what?" she said, sounding confused.

There was still time for me to laugh it off. There had always been time enough for that.

"I wanted to be the one making you come." I took a deep breath. "In fact, it's one of my favorite fantasies when I want to get off."

"You think about me when you make yourself come?"

"Sometimes, yeah. A lot of times, actually."

Carly laughed, a lazy, throaty chuckle. "Wanna tell me what you think about when you're rubbing your clit? Is that how you do it? You rub it until you get all wet and it gets stiff and you come?"

"Mostly." I was already wet and stiff, and hearing her talk about it made it impossible for me to think of anything else. I slid my hand into my sweatpants and touched the top of my clit with one finger. A jolt of pleasure shot down my legs, and I started a little tiny circular motion, just enough to keep the feeling going.

"I like a vibrator myself," Carly said. "Do you ever use one?"

I flashed on an image of her lying on her bed, her legs spread wide, her head tilted back, making herself come on the vibrator. I rubbed my clit a little harder. "Not too often. It makes me come too fast."

I heard a thunk. "What was that?"

"I'm getting out the vibrator I keep in the end table," Carly said. "Sometimes when I'm reading and I get turned on, I need a quickie."

I groaned and switched to squeezing my clit.

"So tell me what you think about me when you're coming."

"When I first start getting my clit hard," I said, "I think about you naked and about us kissing. I think about the way your tongue fills my mouth and me sucking on it." I pushed a finger lower and stroked between my lips and over the underside of my clit. It ached in that need-to-come way. "While we're kissing, I'm playing with your nipples."

"I love when you pull on them," Carly whispered, her words slow and careful, as if she was concentrating very hard.

"Are you teasing your clit with the vibrator?"

"Uh-huh. Just for a second . . . every now and then."

I leaned my head back and masturbated my clit faster. The pressure was building in my pelvis, but I was good at holding off. I could push myself to the edge over and over, backing off each time until my whole body twitched and I'd come no matter how hard I tried to stop. "Don't come until I get to the part where I'm licking you."

"I'll wait," Carly gasped. "Tell me what you're doing to me."

"I'm playing with your clit until it's as hard as it can get—"

"You make me have to come so bad . . ." she whispered.

"I pull your legs over the side of the bed and kneel on the floor between them." I hooked my thumb over the top of my clit and held it with two fingers underneath, starting to jerk it slowly. "And then I swirl the tip of my tongue around the end of your clit."

Carly whimpered and I knew she had the vibrator right on her clit.

"You sit up to watch me make you come, and I push my tongue lower where you're sweet and hot. I want to stay there, inside you, but you can't wait."

"Oh, soon."

"You rub against my face and tell me to lick . . ." My clit started buzzing and I knew I only had a few more seconds. "I usually come as soon as you tell me to lick . . . oh, fuck Carly . . . I—"

"Lick me . . . lick me hard . . . lick me so I come in your mouth."

I held my breath and stopped moving, every fiber focused on Carly. I saw her eyes, wide and stunned with pleasure, felt her body shudder, heard her voice catch on a cry of pleasure, and another, and then another. I forgot to breathe for so long, spots of light danced behind my eyelids, but still I waited. Waited for one more thing.

Carly laughed. "Oh my God, that was incredible."

"Yes," I whispered, caressing my clit until my hips rose and I flooded my hand with come, "it was."

"So," Carly said teasingly. "Was that better than the fantasy?"

"Oh yeah," I said, stretching my cramped legs. I toyed with

my clit, keeping it hard, and wondered if I could get off again so soon.

"You're not the only one who's had that fantasy, you know."

"Really?" I sat up and forgot about wanting to come again. She had that serious note in her voice and I needed to pay attention.

"Really. In fact, there's a whole other part to it we didn't get to yet. The part about what I do to you."

I waited for her to say more, and when she didn't, I realized it was finally time for me to go first. "Maybe I should come over and you can tell me all about it."

"Maybe you should come over and I'll show you."

I grinned. "What about my deadline?"

"Vanessa will cut you some slack. You can write about all of this first thing in the morning."

"Yeah, but it's supposed to be a fantasy, not real life."

"So? Who's to know?"

At the Strip Club
Victoria A. Brownworth

Her name was LaVergne.

Of course it was. Later—much later—I would discover her real name, but that first night it was LaVergne.

LaVergne was a stripper. She worked at a little club on a side street in the French Quarter in New Orleans in the days before Katrina. She was tall and curvy, with burnished olive skin that looked slightly shiny all over. Her hair was black and sleek and fell to just below her shoulders. On her left ankle wove a tattoo of snakes, their heads biting into each other. On her left wrist, five teardrops the color of blood. At the base of her throat, just to the left of the hollow, a short, bent branch, stuck with thorns and one more blood-colored teardrop.

Her lips were thick and full, made fuller by a slick, purplish lipstick. Her eyes were the color of martini olives and just as densely unreflective. Her breasts—well, I'll describe those later.

LaVergne was what some would call exotic. I simply found

her ravishing.

Ravishing. One of those words from Victorian literature. Ravish—from the French word "to seize." It has a consonant sexual undertone—ravishing—implying something illicit. To ravish is to enrapture, to seize with delight. Or, to take by force.

I was interested in taking her, but not by force, although I would not have been averse to pinning her to a wall or a bed, or having her do the same to me, her lovely long fingers covering my mouth, stifling the cries of desire from her touch.

How was it that I came to be in a strip joint in New Orleans when the city was still the town that time forgot?

I could say I was in town for a conference—the MLA perhaps? I could say I was doing research at my alma mater, Tulane. Or perhaps I merely wanted a long weekend of jazz and dancing among the little clubs of the French Quarter.

Or was it that I still lived in New Orleans and had just finished my dissertation, but had run out of money, needed work and had stepped into the little club with the handwritten sign posted in the doorway: Dancers Wanted.

LaVergne was onstage that afternoon, nearly naked by the time I entered the club. It was a raw, wet day like most January days in New Orleans. Mardi Gras was still weeks off, and the streets were cold and more empty than usual.

The little club—we'll call it *The Hot Spot*—was dark and somewhat gloomy, despite the throb and pulse of the music and lights. The winter damp clung to the patrons and hung in the doorway like a persistent drunk. Everything—except LaVergne—seemed a little lackluster.

Clients peppered the room, none seeming terribly interested in the woman writhing around the steel pole in the center of the stage dressed in five-inch, white patent leather heels with white, lace-topped stockings that reached mid-thigh. LaVergne also wore a white, fringed thong that was stuffed at each side with bills. Her breasts—full and high with dark, plum-colored nipples—were luscious.

It's difficult to know if I would have stayed and actually applied for the job, were it not for LaVergne. Perhaps, perhaps not. I wasn't eager, just desperate. Money was supposed to come with hard work and I had surely worked hard this last year and a half, my research—it doesn't matter into what, not for the purposes of this story—detailed and arduous and assiduous. I was deeply committed to my work. But the grant had run out before my dissertation committee sat and, as a consequence, I found myself at *The Hot Spot* on a raw, wet January afternoon staring at the dark woman with the white accoutrements slithering around the pole the way I hoped she might slither around me.

I had no business being there, really. I had done this work before, some years back, while an undergraduate. I was one of those girls putting herself through college with a combination of academic grants and cash stuffed into my bra and panties by men who just wanted to remember what a twenty-two-year-old looked like close-up: fresh, smooth-skinned, nubile, anonymous. Girls like I used to be didn't sell sex so much as remembrances of things past. We were fictions and figments, but oh-so-necessary to these men being able to go on with their lives once they left the club. Because what I learned from that work was that desperation is palpable. I never wanted to be that desperate. I hoped I never would be.

Yet there I was, on a wet January afternoon, sunset nearing, ogling LaVergne as I filled out the application that was mere formality. I'd already been judged—and approved—on my tits and ass when I walked in the door. I'd dressed as much for the occasion as I could muster—tight black pants; short, black stiletto boots; tight, lacy and low-cut black shirt; snug denim jacket. I looked the part of either a would-be stripper or a woman on leave from her ordinary life looking for something extraordinary in a dark alley somewhere off Bourbon Street.

Given the fact that I really was no longer a sex worker, but was instead a shopworn academic, I seemed to fit Dancers Wanted well enough to be hired. Which was good, as I was now the desperate one, just differently so from the men I had danced for in years past or from the men LaVergne was dancing for while I watched.

The fact of who I was now wasn't the only reason I should not have been contemplating the job or LaVergne. I was also married. Well—nearly so. Sylvie and I had been lovers for more than three years. Monogamous lovers. We didn't live together—my fault, I'm not good at coziness—but we had recently agreed to trade in our individual flats for one together and have a commitment ceremony. The day I went to *The Hot Spot*, Sylvie was gone—out of the country doing her own research and due to be gone for six more weeks.

Six weeks was a long time for me to be within proximity of a woman named LaVergne in a place called *The Hot Spot* when both of us would be naked, or nearly so much of the time. Of that I was certain the instant I walked through that dank entryway and saw her silken body, her hair whipping out behind her, twirling around the pole that I would soon share with her. Was this my last hurrah before taking the plunge into the formalized monogamy of marriage? Or was I really just that ordinary woman looking for a little something extraordinary? Just a taste, a quick, fleeting taste.

I couldn't start dancing that night—I had work to do, plus I had to get enough money together to pay for my spot on the pole. What? You didn't know the girls pay to strip and then hope to make it back in tips? Yes, that's the way the game is played for those who think it's not *really* prostitution. The men may be desperate, but the women are always more so. The house—like a pimp or madam or casino—always wins.

I had stayed a few minutes after getting my schedule and securing my times for the pole. "Just check out the place, get the feel," Stan, the guy with the slight Russian accent who hired me said. "That's LaVergne up there now. Quite a hooch, that one." He'd nodded appreciatively in her direction and when I had turned to look in her direction, I felt my clit pulse and throb like a back-beat to desire. She was indeed ravishing. I moved unobtrusively—as unobtrusively as a woman in clothes can move in a club where all the men are dressed and all the women are naked—toward the stage. I was in time to see LaVergne slide down the pole and deftly slip the bills that lined her thong into a little white bag on the floor. Then she slid back up, danced backward, her dark hair whipping from side to side over her bare shoulders, her ass swaying and pumping. Then she bent forward, her ass protruding up in a perfect rounded arc toward the suddenly appreciative audience.

The money shot was in reach. I slipped into a seat right in front of her and watched as she smiled back over her shoulder at the middle distance of the audience and then snapped the little white thong away. She spun around and the room saw her Brazilian-waxed pussy, a series of small silver rings piercing the labia. She squatted down on her haunches, exposing her clit briefly and incredibly sexily. The men scattered through the club applauded and whistled. As jaded as they had seemed when I had entered, they were now enthralled. They were not alone. I wanted LaVergne as much as anyone else in the room. And likely had as little chance with her as they.

"I told you she was quite a hooch!" Stan had sidled up behind me and put his hand on my shoulder. I stifled the urge to slap him away.

"She's good," I agreed, trying to sound noncommittal and like I knew I could do better. Perhaps I could, but I wasn't looking forward to it. LaVergne seemed to enjoy what she was doing—and that was always the key. Getting into the game of the dancing, the voyeurism, the exhibition. I needed twenty-four hours to pull that off, as well as twenty-four hours to try and remember I loved Sylvie and had been monogamous for nearly the whole time we'd been together. I was being swept into the same fantasy as every man in the place—that the beautiful vixen on the stage had a place for me in her heart, her bed, her cunt.

I rose to leave, but Stan's hand was still on my shoulder. Another woman had come out onto the stage, this one smallish and blonde with outsized breasts.

"Come on—I'll introduce you to LaVergne. She's been here a while. Likes to meet the new girls. Show 'em the ropes. You know—you done this before." Stan didn't actually wink at me, but his voice did.

"Okay." Again, I feigned a hint of boredom. I wasn't ready to meet LaVergne. I wasn't ready to discover that she was not the fantasy I had already built around her. I wasn't ready to try and woo her, no matter what she really was, because something came off her—it wasn't the tattoos or the hair or the eyes, it was something else. And I wanted to taste it, smell it, hold it, roll it around on my tongue.

Backstage was just as ickily claustrophobic and dirty as every other club I'd ever been in, no more, no less. Clothes everywhere. Small lockers jammed with costumes and the smell of makeup, hair gel and sweat. A perfume medley smacked you in the face the minute you went through the doorway. LaVergne was sitting, sipping a bottle of water and re-applying eyeliner. Her martini olive eyes took me in from the mirror, but were unreadable. My heart and clit were throbbing in unison. I could barely breathe, I was that close to her.

"Hey, babe—I want you to meet Tamika. She's the new girl." Stan had his other hand on LaVergne's shoulder now. She seemed not to notice.

The new girl. I was going to be thirty-five in another month—fortunately a youthful thirty-five or I'd never have gotten the gig—but we were all girls here.

LaVergne turned toward me, the eyeliner still in her hand, elongating her slender fingers that were lacquered the same purplish color as her lips.

"Hey, Tamika. Why you want to be workin' here?" Her voice was thickly smoky, like a jazz singer, and her accent was pure bayou—she was a girl from the swamplands. You could hear the primordial chord of the Atchafalaya in her voice. I could see her lying in a hammock outside one of those cypress shacks that pepper the bayou and swamps, Spanish moss hanging all around, the slap of alligators in the water nearby mixing with the low, long drone of insects. I could see her hair falling over the side of the worn hammock and her hand trailing down, fingers massaging the scrub grass beneath. I could see her like that, through her voice that told of dark, prehistoric canals filled with alligators and lizards and hawks and owls looming above, all waiting to kill something. I knew where she came from, could see her skimming the dank waters in a pirogue. I wanted her even more.

"Gotta pay the rent, ya know," I said, suddenly back in the bayou myself.

Some people are like mockingbirds—they mimic accents. They don't do it maliciously—they just can't help themselves. Like the grey birds mocking the cats who want so desperately to eat them. My aunt had always called me a mockingbird—catbird, actually. But that's what catbirds are, mockingbirds. I picked up accents wherever I went. Sylvie often said she wasn't sure what my real voice sounded like.

I was a catbird, all right. And before me sat the pussy I was meant to tease.

"Ain't that the truth, ain't that the truth." LaVergne looked at me, still unreadable. I tried for inscrutability, but knew I failed.

She laughed a little, the sound thick and dark, then said, "Well, have a seat then. My tips better not go down when you let that tight little ass out on the floor." She leaned back a little and slapped my ass lightly with her left hand. My nipples hardened involuntarily. She seemed not to notice.

Stan was bored—whatever he'd hoped for when we met

hadn't happened, even after the pretend slap. Or he hadn't caught it, at least, because I was fairly sure he was onto me. "I gotta get back out there," he said and was gone, leaving me with LaVergne, leaving me wanting to have her touch me again.

When Stan left, the room was suddenly far too close. As chill as I had been when I'd come in, I was now overly warm. And next to the near-naked LaVergne, overdressed. I slipped off my jacket. She watched me, unmoving.

"When you start, Tam?" She'd already shortened my name. It was New Orleans, after all. Who has time to say more than one syllable, possibly two? I inhaled slowly and then said, "Tomorrow. Afternoon shift."

She was back to the mirror and the eyeliner, but she was watching me, not the makeup. She finished and continued to stare at me from the mirror. Her lips were beautiful and lush and I wanted to reach out and put my finger to them, touch them, then slip that same finger between her lips and have her lick and suck it. I could imagine her on me, those lips on me, those lips on my neck, my nipples, my clit. Those long, elegant fingers stroking the lips of my now very wet cunt. Meeting her had indeed been a mistake. I was too ready for her. And knew I wanted her—badly. And just as likely would never have her, even once.

I needed to turn myself into one of the men in the audience. Distance myself from the ache between my legs and my lust for this woman I knew nothing about except that she was ravishing and her voice was the voice of desire and primeval swamps.

Suddenly, she stood.

"Well, Tam, I gotta get ready. I'm up next. We're short a girl, today, and it's not even Mardi Gras." She laughed that throaty laugh again and I felt a hot twinge in my cunt.

"You know how to do this, right? You done it before? Or do I need to show you anything?" She had moved past me into a little bathroom off the dressing room. The door was open and I turned toward her voice, not realizing that she was about to piss.

I read once that Havelock Ellis, the famous sexologist, had been impotent for years until one day—at sixty—he discovered that he was aroused (that's the word all the books use) by the sight of a woman urinating.

I had never actually watched a woman pee before. Sylvie and I had a rule about closing bathroom doors. Privacy maintains intimacy, I believe. I'd certainly never thought about watching a woman urinate, although I'd read an autobiographical short story by Dorothy Allison in which the butch lover pees on the femme while they make love. It was a hot story, but I had still thought, *how messy.*

Now I stood, transfixed as Havelock Ellis must have been, while LaVergne stood in the little bathroom and spread her legs over the toilet. All she wore was a black silk kimono, black stockings to the thigh and black stilettos. She hadn't finished dressing for the stage yet. I could see her breasts through the open robe. I could see a glint of the rings in her labia. She seemed to intuit what I suddenly had a desire to see.

I had to get out of there.

She saw me watching her. An eyebrow lifted ever so slightly and I knew, instantaneously, that she was about to give me a show. She knew how much I wanted one.

Outside the room the music pulsed and throbbed and inside my clit was stiff, my cunt wet. I might as well have been one of the men out there in the room beyond us, erection bulging in my pants. There was no visible sign of the intensity of my excitement, but my lips had parted involuntarily, and my breathing had become more shallow and rapid. Could she see my heart beating beneath my flimsy shirt?

Was it only seconds since she had moved from the little chair in front of the grimy mirror to the bathroom? It seemed so much longer; the intimacy of the claustrophobic space pulsing around us.

I wanted to know what she would do next. Did she want me to come closer? Did I dare to come closer? I took a step toward the bathroom. She stood there. I took another step and she spread her legs wide over the toilet and put both hands on her shaven cunt. She opened the lips and I could see her vulva, dark and beautiful, like a ripe plum. The silver rings—one at the top of her clit, three others along her labia—glinted in the dim light of the small bathroom.

Was this what Stan had meant about LaVergne showing the new girls the ropes? Did she give each one an introduction to fantasy sex before they ever hit the stage?

She began to rub her index finger, with its long, lacquered nail, along the tip of her clit. She pulled at the ring above it and her mouth opened just a bit. I moved closer. Now I was in the bathroom with her, the music enveloping us. I stood with my back against the wall, facing her, watching her. I put my hand between my legs. My pants were damp at the crotch. I ached to come, ached to have her make me come.

Her other hand went to her nipple, twisting and rubbing. It hardened immediately. She kept the other hand fingering her clit, slipping in and out of her pussy. I stepped away from the wall and she didn't stop. She still stood, legs straddling the toilet, one hand massaging her breast, the other working her cunt.

Did I dare to touch her? Did I dare to touch myself?

I stepped close to her. I could see this was no game now. She was fully aroused. I reached for the hand that was playing with her hardened nipples and put it inside my shirt, onto my breast. Then I pulled her other hand away from her clit and pulled her toward me, against the wall. A small sigh escaped her now fully parted lips. I pulled my pants down just enough to expose my own cunt. I put her hand between my legs. My pussy was incredibly wet, my thighs damp. She slid her long fingers onto my clit, and I felt it throb and pulse as she twisted my clit the way she had her own. I was trying not to make a sound and, as if she knew, she took her other hand away from my nipple and put it over my mouth—lightly, but firmly. I can't remember ever hearing myself make the sound I made then.

I wanted to fuck her. I wanted to touch and taste all of her. We didn't speak. I didn't dare kiss her—she had to go on stage in minutes, there was no time for more outlining of eyes and lips. I put my arm around her and put one hand on her ass to steady myself. The other I slipped between her legs. My fingers pulled on the little rings, and this time it was she who made the sounds. Then I slid first one, then two, then three fingers into her pussy and began thrusting into her. I felt her cunt tighten around my hand. I rubbed her clit hard as I fucked her faster and faster. She was breathing heavily and her skin was damp against my thighs. "Hurry," she whispered near my ear. I felt faint, the excitement was so intense.

It wasn't long before I felt her come. I let myself be taken over by her then, my clit exploding in three separate waves of orgasm as she fucked me again and again.

And then it was done. We were both spent. I wanted nothing more than to take her in my arms and lie down on some soft bed and go to sleep.

I stepped back and pulled my pants up over my wet and still-throbbing cunt. She walked to the sink and washed her hands, then turned to me, her beautiful face still flushed, her lush lips still slightly parted.

"I see you do know what to do," she said, in that smoky voice redolent of the bayou. "I don't need to teach you at all. But maybe next time I'll do that thing you wanted me to do."

Had it all been a lure? Was this what LaVergne's specialty was—discerning the forbidden desire and playing to it, hard and fast? She had enticed me with her exposed and luscious pussy, with that exotic jewelry, so unexpected. And I—I had dived in with alacrity.

She left the bathroom and quickly put on the rest of her costume—a black thong, black leatherette vest and miniskirt, black cowboy hat. She turned toward me before she left to take the stage.

"Save the last dance for me!"

I heard her laugh as the door shut behind her. I leaned toward the mirror through which she'd first seen me. My face was flushed, my eyes glittery. I could have been any one of the men out in the audience now, the ones watching her tease them.

She had teased me, but I had teased her back. Or so I thought. Perhaps I didn't know the ropes after all. Perhaps LaVergne knew more than I would ever know, from how to shake a jaded audience out of its torpor to how to find the fantasy not yet fulfilled.

I wasn't sure I'd be back the next day. I knew LaVergne was more temptation than I could handle. I'd had my little bachelor party there at the strip club. I'd been that otherwise ordinary woman looking for a taste of the extraordinary and I had found it with the ravishing LaVergne. But then there was Sylvie. And six weeks of LaVergne was far too dangerous, that much I knew.

I licked my lips, turned toward the door and left the club.

It was a raw, wet, late afternoon in January. A typical winter day in New Orleans. I'd been working the better part of the day at home, trying to complete the final chapter of my dissertation. I knew I had to get a part-time job; my grant money had run out and I was desperate. I dressed for an interview and left the flat, walking through the cold mist toward the French Quarter. When I reached my destination, I turned off Bourbon Street and toward the little strip club. The street was nearly empty, but music pulsed from behind the doors of the club. A small sign tucked in the window of the door said, Dancers Wanted. I wondered about the women on the other side of the door, the women on the stage.

I would soon be one of those women—or so I hoped. I needed the job, a job that wouldn't interfere with my real work, a job that was all about fantasy and provocation.

I shook my hair to fluff it, unbuttoned my shirt to show my cleavage and licked my lips. I pinched each cheek to flush them. Then I opened the door and walked in, the music wrapping itself around me like an insistent, eager lover . . .

Garters and Boxers
Nairne Holtz

She's waiting for me on a public bench, just outside the lingerie store. Punctual, which is always auspicious. Manners, not
charm, tell a girl what she can expect from someone. It's our
second date. On the first we talked about jobs we'd held. She was
intrigued to learn I once worked in a lingerie store. When I told
her the male customers had us model the lingerie they wanted to
buy for their girlfriends, a practice encouraged by management,
she said, "That's outrageous." Then she said she would love me
to model sexy clothes for her. But that night she fled without so
much as a good-bye kiss. She's a curious mixture of bold and
timid. Our first date, with its advances and retreats, reminded me
of the children's game Snakes and Ladders.

With her muscular build, short, gelled hair and handsome
features, my date is unmistakably butch, a woman who makes no
attempt to soften or disguise her masculinity. I hope her butch
image is grounded in some reality: if she can't replace a car

engine, let her at least be able to put up a bookshelf. But I also hope she is capable of surprising me by doing or liking something girly or sissy.

"Hey, stranger," I say.

My date lifts her head. She's wearing black jeans and a dark jacket, whereas I have on a black cashmere sweater, a gray A-line skirt and black high heels. My look, aided by glasses and long, dark hair, lies somewhere between librarian and dominatrix. She stares at me and grins. When the wind ruffles my skirt, exposing my knees, a pink scar from childhood on the left one, she pats my hem down. Her fingers are on my bare skin for only a second but the impact of them—and of her knowing smile—sends a ripple of pleasure through my entire body.

"Bare legs. Must be cold," she says, referring to the chilly fall air. "We better get you some stockings."

At the entrance to the lingerie store, she hesitates, her arch demeanor evaporating. This is girly-girl land, not her territory. It is mine though, so I take her hand and lead her into the airy, upscale boutique with its polished wood floor and scent of Chanel No. 5 wafting through the air. The place is moderately busy; a dozen or so women are sorting through racks of flimsy apparel. Near the back I find rows of stockings, along with racks of garter belts to hold them up. I thumb through the garter belts on their plastic hangers, searching for something dark and silky.

I hold up a black velvet garter. "Do you like this?"

She nods weakly. She is slouching in the middle of the aisle, trying not to stare at or touch anything or anyone.

I begin picking out stockings. There are some cute striped ones, but they aren't sexy. I finger some fishnets, contemplate tight-weave versus fencenet. Consider a pair with the ass-cheeks cut out. Too tacky? I look up to consult her, but she's disappeared. Perhaps she's discovered some men's boxers somewhere.

She reappears just as I decide upon a pair of fishnets.

"Ready to go?" she asks.

"Go?" I wave several garter belts in the air. "I have to try these on." I motion her over and then stride to the change rooms at the back of the store. Outside the rooms is a table heaped with sports bras. I pick up a gray cotton one in what I would guess to be her size and thrust it into her arms.

"I don't need a bra," she says.

"But I want you to come into the change room," I reply.

She blushes. When she reads the tag on the sports bra, her flush deepens. The femme has discreetly checked out the curves of the butch and correctly estimated her bra size.

The change rooms are bustling with customers. I can hear a susurration of women slipping into camisoles and bras, strutting before mirrors. After we've waited in line for a few minutes, a middle-aged clerk leads us to two change rooms side by side. She unlocks the doors and then eyes us uncertainly. "Let me know if you need another size," she finally says to me.

"Sure," I reply, but she's off assisting another customer. My date is already in her change room with the door shut. I knock, the garters and packages of stockings bunched in my arms. She yanks me into what turns out to be a spacious room with a luxuriant taupe carpet.

"This is insane," she mutters. "I thought we were just buying stuff."

I open my eyes wide. "We are. I just need you to help me unbutton my sweater." The buttons on my little black sweater go up the back. I turn around so she can undo them. Her hands tremble as she pulls each round pearl button through its hook of thread. When she slides the sweater off my arms, she discovers I'm wearing a full-length vintage slip. Elizabeth Taylor in *Cat on a Hot Tin Roof*. Except my slip is black, not white.

She wrenches me to her. What I had in mind was showing myself off, teasing us, but when she kisses me, I can't bring myself to do anything except let her loot my mouth with her deft, teasing tongue. Her hands clasp the small of my back, making me feel cherished and protected. I also feel a pang between my legs. When she grabs my ass and squeezes me against her hips, the pang floods.

The stall next to ours is opened for another customer. The braying voice of the clerk makes both of us freeze, like playing the childhood game of Statues. My date whispers, "Maybe this isn't such a good idea."

"I just want to try on some things," I reply in a normal voice. The women around us are too busy worrying about whether their husbands or boyfriends will think their asses are too big. They won't notice us.

I sit down on the cushioned bench to the side of the mirror. My date watches as I undo the snap on the side of my skirt, draw down the short zipper and pull my skirt off. I hike my slip above my waist to reveal my panties, a sliver of black fabric now utterly drenched. From a hanger I remove one of the garters, gird my waist with it, and join the hooks in front.

My date crouches before me. "You're beautiful."

I experience a flutter in my chest. It isn't her words, but the way she said them, like she'd just unwrapped a gift, and it was even better than she thought it would be.

She gathers me up in her arms. Kisses—no, make that bites—my neck while brushing her hands across my breasts. She stops, takes a breath, as if she is struggling to get herself in hand. How far are we going to take this? *I dare you. I double-dare you.* Her fingers draw figure eights over and around my nipples. Soon the tips are stiff, visible through the satiny smoothness of my slip. I can barely keep myself from moaning when she withdraws her hands, picks up a package of stockings and rips it open.

"No!" I cry. "You can't try stockings on. You have to buy them."

She laughs. "I already have."

Ah, so that's what she was doing when I thought she was looking at boxers. Thoughtful of her. A fistful of feathery chiffon is draped across my bare thighs. The stockings are black and seamed.

"Put them on," she says.

I remove my heels. I scrunch up a stocking, guide my foot into it, and slowly inch the material over my long, slender leg. Then I put on the other one. I'm reaching for the snap on my front garter when her hand covers mine.

"Let me do it," she says.

"Wait." If she fastens the garter without first letting me take my panties off, she won't have access to me. Are we going to fuck in here? It isn't smart. But the thin crotch of my panties is so wet, is digging into me, which isn't comfortable . . . I tug them off.

She raises an eyebrow.

I say, "We don't have to do anything."

When she laughs, it's edged with harshness. "Don't even try and get out of this now." She picks up one of the fasteners and looks at it quizzically, but I don't dare say a word. Fumbling at first, she soon figures it out and attaches my front garters to my stockings. Standing on her knees, she parts my legs, exposing me for a long moment, making me squirm with desire and vulnerability. I watch her as she spreads my lips open, an act both raw and delicate. She bends her head down and I feel her tongue swim along my glistening crack, then dart across my clit to settle into a steady lapping. The sensation is splendid—I clutch her hair. Should I warn her I'm the female equivalent of a premature ejaculator when it comes to cunnilingus? Then again, a quick orgasm might not be so bad in the present, slightly perilous, circumstances. When her finger plunges inside me, I'm lured to the brink of . . . my God, she stopped!

Before I can complain, she tells me in a low voice to "stand up and bend over."

With my need only barely overcoming my resentment, I get up and lean forward so my hands are flat on the bench, my ass is in the air, and my slip is billowing down my back. I look in the mirror to my side where I can watch her pulling down my right back garter in order to snap it onto the top of my seamed stocking. Then she does the left one. Rising from her knees, she stands back to examine the effect. Noticing that the seams aren't quite straight, she frowns and fussily smoothes the stockings this way and that before readjusting the snaps. It seems as if she is deliberately taking her time. I want to order her to continue eating me, but she's in charge at the moment. The idea of begging irritates me, but I'm considering it. At last her hand reaches under my ass. She slowly caresses me from front to back while I streak her palm with my wetness. Then she drops her hand.

"You're torturing me!" I grab at her wrist but she wriggles her hand free.

Crack. She's just smacked my ass hard, and the sensation is only a little less scorching than my embarrassment.

"What are you doing?" I glare at her. "People can hear."

"Isn't that the point?"

"I don't want to be escorted out of here by store detectives!"

She grasps my hair, pulling my head back, and hisses in my ear: "Then ask nicely next time you want something." Her breath is a fever on my cheeks.

"Please," I pant. "Fuck me."

Her fingers penetrate me, their bones much harder than the so-called real thing, and I gasp.

"You're so tight," she murmurs. "Play with yourself." This in as stern a tone as she can manage while whispering.

Moaning gently, I reach down and touch my clit. I can't come standing up, but I rub anyway, my pussy a spinning top around her fingers and mine, sensation wobbling down to the soles of my feet. There are rules and then there are exceptions: I *am* about to have an orgasm. If I do, I'll make noise and we could get in trouble because I can't help it—I'm loud. But she must be able to read my mind as well as my body because suddenly one of her hands is covering my mouth. All of my thoughts alchemize into sharp heat and gluttony. Biting her hand to keep from crying out, I start to orgasm in a long chain of bliss.

When I finish, I sink onto the bench, overcome with voluptuous exhaustion. She sits beside me and brings her fingers to my mouth. I slowly suck off my juices, lick her fingers clean, and as I do so, I feel my energy level rise. The smell on her hands is great—it makes me want to go down on her. But I don't know what she likes. Butches are *so* unpredictable. They might want to be touched in a certain way, in a particular order; they might not be able to let someone else make them come so they sprawl on their back, vigorously jerking off; or they might wryly observe your strap-on isn't big enough for the hard fuck they require.

"What can I do for you?" I whisper.

She glances nervously at the door. The sounds of the other customers drift in. "We should go."

"Is that an excuse?"

"No." But she won't look at me. "I think this little game has gone far enough." She moves to get up from the bench, and I grab at her pant leg. She scrambles out of my reach but not quickly enough—I have a firm grip on her thigh. But then she slips on the dense carpet, and we both topple onto the floor with me landing on top of her. I can't resist taking advantage of the situation: I pin her hands to the floor. She struggles, but we're about the same size and strength.

"Say 'uncle,'" I tell her.

"I guess that's better than 'daddy.'"

We both laugh, but her amusement goes on too long. My childish request is ignored. I swing my knee over and release her arms. Kneeling beside her, I wait for her to tell me what she wants.

Silently she sits up to unclasp her heavy brass belt buckle and unbutton her jeans. Then she reaches over to give my hair a tug.

"Do you like long hair?" I ask. "Do you like it across your thighs?"

No reply, but there's a little smirk on her face, which causes a rush to shoot between my legs.

I ease her jeans down to her ankles. She's wearing boxers, no surprise there. But they're black silk. Someone has put on her special boxers; someone is wearing her lingerie for me. The crotch of her boxers is a darker black, is wet from her juice. I place my fingers upon her dampness, letting her feel the tender pressure of a small, cool hand against her moist heat. There's a sharp inhalation of breath from her.

Knocking my hand aside, she hurriedly shoves her boxers down and kicks free her tangle of clothes and shoes. Naked, she stretches out onto her back. I lie between her bare legs, breathing her in for a moment, soap and girl. Then, with my chin pressed against her hole, I begin to lick. I don't fool around, don't try to tease her or toy with her—I just suck the swelling part of her until her face is red, almost angry with need. Taste her until her cunt is sweating, streaming, until she slams it against my face, then, gasping, releases me.

As we scramble into our clothes, there's a knock on the door. A female voice asks us, "Everything all right in there?"

The words take a moment to sink in. I suppose our crashing and writhing about on the carpet has attracted attention. I answer, "No, we're fine, thank you," although in fact my date looks stricken. I reach over and give her hand a squeeze. She bites her lip.

"Thanks," she murmurs.

Leaving the garter belt on, I snap off the price tag to take to the register.

When we slink out, a female security guard who is unmistakably butch is waiting for us. Her mouth opens but no words tumble out. An expression of disbelief crosses her face followed by a faint grin.

Lewd conduct in a public place—looks like we're going to get away with it.

As we stand in line to pay, I smile as I feel my lover's fingers tracing the outline of my garters through my skirt.

Contrary to Fact Present
Nell Stark

The sun is warm and the wind is soft as it caresses new leaves. From its perch on the windowsill, my cat chatters at birds. I am curled up on my futon, trying to study—to distract myself from wanting you so damn much.

It's not going well.

I am tired. I am bored. I am listless, restless, breathless because my hand has slid under my sweats and I am stroking myself lazily. Gently—I am not very wet. Not yet. But I know that I want to come, long and hard, forever and over and over. I know that in a few minutes, when I finish this chapter, I will go to the closet and then to the nightstand and then to the bed. That I will strip and lie down on the sun-dappled bedspread and run my hands over my breasts, my stomach, as I inhale deeply and long for you.

What if, just at that moment, you appeared in the doorway, one eyebrow arching as you watched my fingers tug at my nipples?

Yes, I can see you, now—one hand in your jacket pocket, your shoulder resting against the frame and your head cocked to one side.

"Who are you thinking about?" you would ask.

"Who do you think?"

That smile would curve your lips—the one that's predatory and possessive. The one that reminds me of every sensual promise you used to whisper in my ear. Once upon a time.

"Want a hand?"

"Only," I would say, "if that hand is yours."

You would shed your jacket, the leather cascading from your shoulders to puddle at your feet. I would watch your elegant fingers curl beneath the hem of your shirt and the ripple of your stomach muscles as you pulled the fabric over your head.

"Everything," I would say. "I want to feel you—all of you." And you would bow in mock obeisance and do my bidding because, for once, you'd be unable to resist me.

Naked, you would approach my bed, taking in the objects on my nightstand as you survey the scene. Your expression would get harder, somehow. Hungrier.

"I'm going to fuck you with that," you'd say, nodding at the black double-dildo resting next to a bottle of lube. "But not right away."

And then you would spread my legs with your hands and settle fluidly onto the mattress, kneeling between them. I would gasp as your hot palms came to rest on my stomach—as you traced the dips and curves of me, moving steadily toward my breasts. When you cradled them, I would sigh—but then you'd take my nipples between your thumbs and index fingers, and I would cry out as you rolled and squeezed them.

This is how you would banish the words from me—all but one. "Please," I would say, and again when you lie down on top of me. "Please."

Your breath would be warm against the shell of my ear as your tongue flicked my earlobe until I was writhing beneath you. You would pin me down so easily, your breasts pressing against mine. And I would hold you to me—one hand between your shoulder blades, the other resting lightly on the back of your head.

"Please—"

You would begin to move down my body then, retracing the paths of your fingers with your tongue. My hips would buck as you first sucked at my nipples, then scraped them with your teeth. The tiny twinge of pain would rise over the tide of my pleasure like a descant, and I would groan.

There is nothing you can't take from me, I would think as your mouth left my breasts and pressed a line of sucking kisses down my torso. You would nip lightly at the skin just above the apex of my thighs, and my hands would fall from your body to grasp the blanket.

"Please."

You would spread my folds open with your thumbs and look at me, and I would tremble beneath your gaze. Your warm breath would tease me for what felt like hours until finally, *finally*, you would touch me with your tongue.

Your tongue—the essence of warm and soft and wet—would lick me so lightly that I'd strain against you, struggling to find some measure of control. But you'd deny me even as you fulfilled me, backing off and returning, forcing me to lie quiescent under your sweet torment. Only when my thighs began to quiver would you lick me more firmly, dipping inside before curling your tongue around my clitoris.

My body would be so full, supersaturated with the pleasure you coaxed from it. The ecstasy would leave me in quiet moans, like solar flares bursting from the molten surface of the sun. And when you finally buried your face in me, taking my clit between your lips and milking it so gently with your mouth, I would . . .

become . . . Supernova—my true nature—light and heat spilling over the edges in wave after wave. Because of you.

"You needed that, didn't you?" you'd ask as you rested your chin on my stomach. And I'd look at you through dazed eyes and smile and reach one hand down to stroke your hair back from your face.

"Yes," I would say. "Need you. Just you."

Your face would soften a little then, and you would rub your cheek against my skin. I'd love that tiny gesture of intimacy just as much as the sensation of coming so hard beneath your tongue. And your silent affection would only make me want you again.

I would reach for the dildo on the nightstand, and you would lift your head to bare your teeth at me. That look would make my throat go dry. "I want to put this in you," I'd say hoarsely. "And then I want you to fuck me with it."

You would roll over onto your back and spread your legs, and I'd be held captive by the sight of you—dark hair swirling around the deep crimson of your softest skin. I'd lean down to kiss you hard and slide one hand down your body, and you'd gasp as my fingers found you. You'd be so wet, and I'd dip briefly inside, anointing my fingertips before moving back up to massage your clit. I'd watch your heels dig into the sheets as your back arched involuntarily, and I'd love that I could make you feel so damn good.

I'd alternate the pressure of my touches—first firm, then barely glancing—and I wouldn't stop teasing until you told me you were close. Then I'd sit back and watch you try not to tremble while I coated one end of the dildo with lube.

"Nice and easy now," I would murmur as I rested the head against the opening to your body. I'd reach up to gently twist one nipple, and as you exhaled, I'd push the toy into you, so slowly. I'd lean down and nip at the skin of your belly, and you'd breathe deeply as I filled you.

I'd return my attention to your clit, taking it between my fingers, massaging you until you growled low in your throat and pushed me away. "Lube," you'd say, and I'd eagerly coat the other side of the toy as your hips shifted restlessly. I'd twist it slightly, of course—just to tease you even more. And then you'd grab my waist, positioning me above you, and I'd guide the dildo so the head was pressing against the base of my clit. You'd thrust against me shallowly, and I'd toss my head and groan.

But I'd be aching inside for you, so finally, I'd lower myself down inch by inch, until I could press my slick forehead to yours. You in me and me in you—no top, no bottom, no giver and no receiver. Just us. One.

Maybe you would move first, or maybe I would. But we would find a rhythm together, and as we shifted against each other, I'd reach down to stroke you. You'd mimic my touches with your own fingers, and I'd groan as I leaned forward to close my lips around your earlobe. You'd be so sensitive there, and I'd love how your hips would jerk as I licked you.

You would talk to me while we fucked each other. "Beautiful" and "hot" and "I love you"—a waterfall of words mingling with my come. When you kissed me—or maybe I'd kiss you—our movements would grow sloppy. I'd press down more firmly on your clit, and your thrusts would become faster, choppier.

"Come inside me," I'd whisper. "And feel me come inside you."

Your body would go rigid against me then, just before you shouted wordlessly and shuddered in my embrace. And as I felt your release, the rising pressure in me would spike, and I'd clamp down hard around the dildo as the pleasure slammed through me.

I'd collapse against you, burying my head in the dip between your shoulder and collarbone, inhaling your scent. You'd play with my hair while I listened to your slowing heartbeat, and I'd know you were smiling even though I couldn't see your face.

♥

That's how it might happen. If. But you're not here, are you? My doorway is empty and my body is aching. I have tried so hard to bring you back, but all I can hear are my memories.

Are you proud? Even the fading echo of your voice can make me come.

Topping from the Bottom
Cate Lawton

My favorite moment onstage is when the spotlight goes on and I hear the audience take a collective inhalation so strong that I can almost feel the air brush across my skin. The sash blindfolding me is made from the same shimmering scarlet silk that only moments earlier Judith had skillfully used to bind my legs to the chair upon which I am sitting. The audience sees me as naked and blind. But I see them through a crimson veil, and I never tire of watching them watching me.

Our act is very unlike what the other women do in the club. It is atypical enough that finding the proper venue was a challenge, even in San Francisco. Most clubs offering adult entertainment by women for women are regular weekly events that have an arrangement to use a location such as a lounge or club that leads a far less interesting life the rest of the week. Actually, that describes me pretty well, too. Diligent monitoring of various Internet sites and chat rooms led to an ever-increasing and evolving list of potential locations for our act. Going to the clubs and watching the women perform as we evaluated where to approach management about offering our entertainment proved to be a delightful process. Judith and I spent countless evenings enthralled by the women who found pleasure in dancing for other women. Remembering to observe aspects of our potential venues other than the seductive bodies undulating before us was an enjoyable struggle. We would go home after the night slipped by us in the darkened rooms and still be electrified by the feeling of ourselves as sexual beings. Hungry for each other, we'd walk to our flat, hand in hand, hoping for a red traffic light so we'd have an excuse to kiss while waiting to cross. Our more passionate street corner embraces were often accompanied by honks and whoops from passing motorists. While Judith found the attention mildly amusing, I was invigorated—writhing in Judith's arms and quite willing to enjoy several more cycles of the light alternating between a flashing red hand and a white gender-amorphous pedestrian.

"Hey Jen, has anyone ever told you that you're a hopeless exhibitionist? And, I might add, a very naughty girl." Her teasing would be followed by a quick swat on the butt that left a slight sting. If I was wearing jeans that night, she'd slip her fingers into my back pocket and we'd finish the walk home with her hand deliciously cupping my ass.

In our apartment, Judith and I would make love as feverishly as we had when we first met more than nine years earlier. The press of our mouths together inevitably gave way to trails of kisses winding down our bodies. While I generally struggled to slow myself down in my need to taste her wetness, she managed to maintain composure, licking and gently biting at my nipples with the base of her palm resting on top of my mound as her fingers pulsed in and out of me. When I'd get desperate for release, I'd arch my pelvis up, trying to increase the pressure while urging her fingers deeper inside of me. Sometimes she'd let me use her hand this way, but other times she'd smile, her steel blue eyes shining as she pulled back just enough to tease me into a state of arousal where nothing existed but the oneness of us. When I finally felt Judith's lips and then her tongue brush across my clit, the orgasm would wash across me in a series of waves. Judith would keep her fingers inside of me so she could feel me pulse and contract around them. Only after our breathing had slowed would she take her hand away and curl up against me. Our arms intertwined, we'd fall asleep to the booming of our heartbeats.

Morning would bring the smell of coffee and an often feeble attempt to impartially list the pros and cons of the club we had visited the night before. Talking about the club experience usually served to recharge the air with sexual electricity. The choice between being late to work and spending the day regretting the chance to enjoy each other was easy. For me, at least, spending the hours sequestered and unnoticed behind the faux walls of my office cubicle allowed many of my tardy entrances to slip through the bureaucratic cracks. Judith simply began driving to her office a lot faster.

When we visited the weekly venue that dubbed itself Sappho's Salon, we both knew we had reached the end of our search. Housed in what used to be a jazz club, the mahogany booths and tables speak of a time when every meal was preceded by a martini and the women serving the drinks would have been wearing seamed hose and offering to sell cigarettes tableside. The crushed velvet scrolls decorating the wallpaper are worn in spots, but the club is clean and inviting. Small round tables float like lily pads in a pool of burgundy chairs that cover the club's floor. But my appreciation for the retro-era charm of the building is surpassed by the feature that I appreciate most—the stage.

Unlike a stereotypical theatre, this club features a relatively small stage that rises only three feet off of the ground. The obligatory black curtain hiding the comings and goings of offstage life hangs in the back, compressing the usable stage space to about fifteen feet. A pole, which was probably once considered an eyesore necessary for structural integrity, has been recovered in a shiny, brasslike metal, and many of the Sappho's Salon women use it to show off their enviable strength and agility. Because the engineer who originally designed the stage did not anticipate the pole as part of the entertainment, it is slightly off center and about seven feet from the front of the stage. We always place my straight-backed chair directly in front of the pole. This means that during performances, I am close enough to my audience that if I want to, I can read the names and phone numbers that have been scribbled on the paper napkins littering the tables of especially lucky dykes.

The period of time when Judith and I were developing our act and working out the logistics was a blur of overwhelming nervousness, overcome only by perpetual horniness. The weeks leading up to beginning the act also brought about an emotional growth period that would have emptied my bank account if I had pursued similar results from a therapist. From the safety of our bedroom, the idea of bringing a part of our sexuality to life in front of an audience was exciting. Because Judith would not be appearing onstage and would play her role from behind the black curtain, at least she could hold onto her anonymity. I would have the opposite experience. I would be physically naked except for my not-so-blinding blindfold and the silk swathes binding my legs to each side of the chair. In a very real sense, I'd be open and exposed. Physically. Emotionally.

In order for my audience to be aroused by me, I knew I'd have to accept who I am, and that meant not only the public persona witnessed by the people I encounter at the grocery store or on the train, but also my sexual side. I'd need to drop the body issues echoing in my head that told me that I wasn't pretty enough or sexy enough or perfect enough to excite a roomful of women who came to see performers whom I perceived as the ones who really were pretty and sexy and perfect. I also knew that to face an audience, I would have to acknowledge my sexual fantasies were a positive part of me. The fact that I enjoy role playing and some mild bondage isn't something that I needed to be cured of or hide. Whether or not mainstream America feels guilty at the thought of anything beyond missionary-position intercourse in a darkened room is irrelevant. I did not have to buy into the concept that sexuality is shameful—something to be condemned or restrained. It was not my shame, and I did not have to accept it.

I learned to embrace the fun, daring, erotic side of me—the side that reveled in my sexuality and was fueled by the ability to arouse others. Reaching this level of acceptance was an ongoing process facilitated by long, late-night discussions with Judith, as well as some of my closer girlfriends. Beginning to perform and experiencing my audience's reaction helped cement what I had theorized and crystallized it as reality. Now that Judith and I have been incorporated into the Sappho's Salon lineup for several months, I don't worry about my old doubts coming back, which means I can more fully enjoy the experience of arousing, and being aroused by, my audience.

I think that the moment when the spotlight explodes on, illuminating me partially restrained in the chair, is so powerful because it stands in stark contrast to what the audience has seen up to this point. Our act is strategically placed about two-thirds of the way through the evening's entertainment. The audience has slipped into the comfortable routine of the club's DJ thanking the departing dancer, extolling the virtues of the next performer, and then blasting a song laden with pulsing bass. The performers before us provide a fun exhibition of smiles, flashes of skin and lust-inducing hip rotations, often delivered within inches of the drunkest woman's face. This is all done with the promise that at the end of the song, the performer will give one last broad smile and a wave while gathering her tips and bounding offstage. On the heels of this comfortable, sexy frivolity, the audience sees me. No music. No dancing. Just me involving them in my intimacies.

Judith and I have perfected the logistics of my entrance. After the act preceding us ends, our DJ announces, "Stay in your seats ladies, because the lights are going out for a moment and we don't want you tripping and falling into the lap of someone who will get you in trouble with your girlfriend. When the lights come up you're gonna see something that will certainly get you in trouble with your girlfriend."

As soon as the club is plunged into darkness, Judith and I scurry onto the stage. We align the chair on pre-placed pieces of glow tape so it is in position, its back pressing against the pole. Naked, I sit on the simple silver chair while Judith ties each of my legs to the chair legs. She ties the sash gently over my eyes, then places three boxes, each one stacked upon the other, on the floor in front of me. Judith kisses me with her soft lips, filling my mouth with the taste of her. She cups my breast with her hand, her fingers finding my nipple and rolling it gently as our lips part further to deepen our kiss. A quick pinch from her fingertips makes me stifle a squeal.

"Show time, my love," she coos in my ear. She slips offstage, my nipple still feeling the effects of her manipulations.

The spotlight bursts on, illuminating me, making my pale flesh look even whiter and emphasizing the burst of color provided by my short dark bob and the three scarlet silk sashes. I am facing the audience, my hands holding onto the pole a little above where my head rests against it. With the thrumming of the bass stopped and no music playing, this moment is undoubtedly the quietest the club has been, and will be, during the night.

"You look very pretty sitting there, Jennifer."

When Judith's voice comes over the PA system, the audience relaxes a little, seemingly relieved they don't have to worry about what they are supposed to do regarding the blindfolded naked woman in front of them.

"You'd look even better if were touching yourself."

I take my right hand off of the pole and reach down. I only have contact with my pussy for an instant when Judith's voice stops me, "Not there. Not yet. You're in too much of a rush." I pause, waiting to hear her order. "Put your hand back."

My hand goes back to the spot above my head on the pole, which realigns my body, bringing my shoulders back and pushing my chest out.

"There are three boxes in front of you."

Since I'm blindfolded, I'm not supposed to be aware of this rather obvious fact, so Judith announces it. Repeat audience members know there are always three nondescript, gray shoebox-sized containers that play a role in our act. However, the content of each box is as much a mystery to me as to the audience. Judith takes great care to place an item in each container when I am not present, and she is the sole proprietor of the boxes until the moment she steps offstage.

"Open the top box and take out what is inside." Reaching out my hands, I bend forward to lift the lid off and remove what I recognize from the shape and feel as a bottle of my favorite massage oil. "I want you to rub the oil over your body."

I place the box on the ground next to me. Flipping the cap open rewards me with the luxurious smell of sandalwood, bergamot and rose. I fill the palm of my hand with the rich liquid, setting the bottle down before rubbing my hands together and releasing more of the scent. I begin with the front of my left shoulder, pushing my hand up and then sliding it down and around the outside of my breast. I cup the underside of my breast, hesitating so I can feel the weight of it in my palm. I move my hand around, gently kneading the oil over the entirety of my breast, taking extra time to savor the moment when my nipple slips in and out between my fingers. I slowly spread the oil over the other side of my chest and find this nipple erect even before my fingers get there. Reveling in the feeling of the warm oil, I lift the bottle and dribble a generous line of oil across my chest. Using both hands to rub and squeeze my breasts, I feel the oil oozing between my fingers. Taking a lesson from Judith, I pinch my nipples and make a quiet moan when they make a slippery escape from between my fingertips. I spread the excess oil over my abdomen, applying more pressure when I get to the spot below my belly button and above my pubis.

The next palm full of oil I use on the tops of my thighs. I start above my hips, push my hands to the point where they almost touch my knees, and then work my way back up by drawing my hands along my inner thighs. My body feels hot and slick, like my pores are filled with sex. Just as I am reaching the pounding area at my center, Judith's voice interrupts me.

"You can put the massage oil away. Everything appears to be nice and moist."

Obediently, I close the lid and slip the bottle of thick golden liquid back into the box next to me. I can almost hear a collective exhale from my audience as many of them discover they have been holding their breaths.

Taking my hands back up to their resting position above my head, the fragrance of the oil is mixing with the smell of my arousal and I can't help but squirm in my chair. The heat from the intense stage lights is making me perspire, and now that my chest, stomach and thighs are awash in oil, every part of my body seems to be wet, slippery and hot, especially the area between my thighs. I become hyperaware of body sensations—the tautness of my nipples, a wisp of loose hair tickling my shoulder, the pressure of the ties around my ankles, the rise and fall of my chest as I breathe. And though I'm centering myself on what my body is feeling, my eyes are watching my audience. Through the thin blindfold I am aware of their excitement and curiosity. Sitting forward in their chairs, they are directing their glances between my still squirming form and the remaining boxes in front of me.

Judith lets me savor the moment briefly before directing me again.

"Open the next box." Judith pauses while I reach for the box lid. I can almost hear the mischievous laughter in her voice as she says, "There's a plastic baggie in there and in the baggie are several pieces of the same kind of item. You just need one, so only take one of the items out of the plastic bag."

My stomach gives a nervous flutter. I've never heard this introduction to an item before. Puzzled, I root through tissue paper until I feel the plastic. I am so startled that I have to stop myself from reflexively pulling my hand back.

"I think that it's time to cool you off a little." Even though Judith is hidden behind the black curtain, I know she is wearing an expression I have dubbed "brat face." She loves her brat face moments. I love those moments, too. Sometimes.

Careful not to let it slip between my oily fingers, I pull an ice cube out of the baggie. Although it is not huge, I surmise Judith must have made the ice specifically for the act because the cube is noticeably bigger than what floats in our drinks at home. The larger size has the benefit of being more visible to the audience and less likely for me to drop it. However, I am painfully aware this mega-cube will also take much longer to melt. While this is a good thing in the sense that the stage lights would have dissolved a normal ice cube to a small puddle in short order, as the person whose warm body will be subjected to this chilly treatment, a quickly melting ice cube has its appeal.

Sounds of nervousness emanate from some of the audience before Judith's voice breaks me from my thoughts. "Don't worry. We're not jumping in quite yet. Put your right hand back on its spot on the pole." I comply, aware of the ice quickly chilling the fingers of my left hand. "Don't touch yourself with it. Just hold the ice over your chest."

Judith's plan for an erotic form of water torture is now clear. I hold the ice about eight inches above my right breast, and brace myself for the first drop of cold water to hit. Although every moment that passes seems like both an eternity and a nanosecond, I do not have long to wait. I inhale sharply as my skin is shocked out of the comfort of its oily warmth. It seems almost incongruous that I'm not hearing the sound of sizzling as the icy droplets hit my spotlight-baked body. Even though no actual steam is rising from the drips, I can hear several in the audience make sympathetic noises. I'm amused to discover the anticipation of having the ice water hit had so thoroughly consumed me, I had momentarily forgotten about my audience. Their murmurs remind me of their presence, and I take joy in knowing we are all wincing at the fiery cold together.

Since one of my hands is bracing the pole, there is no sheltering my right breast from the onslaught of icy droplets. My trembling provides just enough movement for the water to hit slightly different places on my breast. As each drip lands in an unanticipated spot, the shock of the cold continues to feel fresh and new. The first drop that lands directly on my nipple elicits a high-pitched sound of surprise. It is almost painful, but whatever hurt there is quickly dissipates and leaves me with a very sensitive, erect nipple. My mind flashes on how delightful it would be to have Judith's warm mouth wrap around my rapidly cooling breast, her tongue lapping up the water that is beginning to stream down the swell of my bosom and onto my torso. However, my fantasy is interrupted by her directive to essentially torment the left side of my chest in the same manner I had done my right.

I change hands so I can hold onto the pole with my left hand while my right is in charge of delivering the delightful torture to my unsuspecting tit. When the first few drips hit and roll down my chest, I experience the same shocking sensation as before. However, my body has cooled off substantially since this icy treatment began, so this breast accustomed quickly to the cold water. Judith must have sensed my growing immunity to the ice, either that or my ADD girlfriend was growing tired of water torture.

"I want you to rub it on yourself."

Normally, when I hear her give the go-ahead to touch myself, my first reaction is to bring my hands to my nether region. Clutching the ice and feeling the warmth radiating from between my legs, I feel no such compulsion. Instead, I press the ice cube against my chest and begin making quick circles around and across my breasts. As I grow more confident, I slow my motions down so I can experience the difference between the warm skin the ice approaches, the spot where it delivers its cruel coldness, and the cool trail it leaves in its wake. Grasping the cube like a child might hold a large piece of sidewalk chalk, I experiment with drawing it across my nipple. I focus on how that sensitive skin reacts as the ice passes over it and then on the sensation of the evaporation as the hot stage lights cook away the water.

"Jennifer, you're stalling." Her voice has a hint of amusement as she tries to sound annoyed. My considerable streak of stubbornness emerges as I hear her reveling in her "brat face" moment. I try to look confident as I move the ice away from my chest and prepare to show that I can meet her challenge.

Arching my neck back, I inhale deeply, my chest rising as I fill my lungs. I place the rapidly melting ice cube at the base of my throat and exhale while slowly tracing a line down my center, between my breasts, over my rib cage and down to my abdomen. Water runs from where the ice cube is making contact, trickling down my torso and, ultimately, pooling onto my chair. Despite my growing arousal, I prolong the anticipation of the ice meeting my pussy by taking a detour when I reach the top of my hairline. Changing my grip on the cube so its full length is exposed, I choose a part of my inner thigh that is only a couple of inches above where it meets my knee. I press the ice against the inside of my leg vertically, maximizing the amount of skin that the ice will touch. The initial contact between the ice and my soft inner thigh causes both my legs to jerk. My ankles strain against the silk ties that are keeping my legs spread apart. As I draw the ice up the length of my leg, the water pooling against the oil I rubbed there a lifetime ago, I realize this sensitive area has been thirsty for the bitter cold that the ice delivers. I guide the ice over the roundness at the top of my inner thigh, lifting it only a whisper before it would have touched the growing wetness that is at the center of me.

The journey up my other leg is filled with the anticipation of the pulsing area I am heading toward. The melting ice cube is growing smaller, so I move up this thigh more rapidly than the last. As the squirming of my hips increases, I can tell my audience is matching my arousal. My pubic hair is neatly trimmed, so there isn't much of a barrier between my skin and the ice, but as I glide the ice cube across the top of my hairline I am grateful for the scant protection it gives. More than the direct contact with the ice, I am aware of the extraordinarily cold water that is running down the lips of my pussy. When the water goes between my folds, I am electrified. I move the ice cube lower, using only light pressure as I venture farther down between my open legs. I moan as the water drips into my opening and mixes with my hot moisture. I linger momentarily in this spot before drawing the ice cube back up my mound. I use the cube with more confidence, pressing more firmly against my skin and thrusting my hips upward. Little shocks of cold hit me at seemingly random moments. I experience a certain level of sexual frustration as I balance my desire for stimulation with the intense cold that increasing the pressure creates. As I try to reposition the sliver of remaining cube, it slips, falling into the puddle on the seat of my chair. I try to retrieve the ice. My fingers, stiff and insensitive from holding it for so long, cannot grasp the slippery surface.

"It's okay, Jennifer. We'll get you something new to play with."

I stop trying to pick up the tiny ice shard and resign myself to the last of it melting against my ass cheek. I am warming back up quickly. The oil and water mix feels sticky, and I know that I must be glistening under the lights.

"Open the third box."

This box is so light, I would have assumed it was empty, had I not heard something rolling around. I reach in, feeling around until I touch something small and rounded. I smile, pulling out what I call my "itty-bitty finger vibe." One of my favorite toys, it is a small vibrator with a ring-shaped base reminiscent of the kind of ring you get in little plastic bubble for a quarter from a vending machine. This grown-up girl's version slips over the finger like a ring, but it also has a rubbery textured pad about the length of a finger that attaches to the base. The pad positions to rest under the fingertip, allowing the wearer to have a surprising amount of control over the "where" and "how hard" of the vibrator.

"I know how much you love your finger vibrator. Since you did such a good job with the ice cube, I will let you play with your toy. But you might want to go back into the box. I think you missed one."

Pleased at this turn of events, I thrust my hand back into the box and retrieve my other prize. I slip the rings around the first finger of both of my hands, the pad of each vibrator positioned like an extension of my fingertip. The vibrators are controlled by a single wireless remote, which is in Judith's enthusiastic hands. She turns them on without warning. Startled by my hands suddenly coming alive, I jump slightly. With toys on both hands, the vibrations seem especially strong. They also create an impressively loud noise for something so small. The women in the back of the audience can undoubtedly hear the tell-tale buzzing. But unlike the classic "embarrassing moment" tale of the dildo in the carry-on luggage suddenly singing its song while passing through an airport magnetometer, I love that my audience can experience the sound with me.

Knowing that Judith will probably stop me, I immediately put one hand to my pussy. I enjoy a moment of feeling the rapid movement against the top of my slit before I hear her disapproving voice over the speakers.

"That was a rather presumptuous move."

The vibrators go dead. The silence is broken only by the sound of frustration coming from the audience, as well as myself. Knowing that my audience is invested in my sexual release excites me. The pulsing in my core continues even after I remove my hand from the forbidden area. The vibrators spring to life again as I cover both breasts with my hands. The game is on. To keep the vibrators alive, I must not do more than Judith will allow. However, finding that line and pleasing her sufficiently so she allows me to cross it is my quest.

Starting safe, I touch my nipples. They are fully erect, and when I gently touch my fingertip pads against them, a sexually charged tickle shoots down my body. I hold my hands as quiet as possible, losing myself in the sensation of my nipples just barely touching the vibrators, the pressure against them changing slightly with each inhalation. In contrast to the stillness in my hands and chest, the rest of me is squirming—my hips perform an erotic hula, my ankles strain against their ties.

Lightheaded from my self-induced torment, I massage both breasts before sliding my hands over my stomach and then down my thighs. I lightly brush the insides of my thighs as I move my fingers toward my center, my skin tingling as I go. When I reach the spot between my legs, I take a fleeting dip into my flowing wetness before tickling down my inner thighs again. At the conclusion of the second trip up my thighs, I linger a bit longer, not wanting to move, but uncertain if staying will displease Judith to the point where she turns off my toys. I fall into a pattern of surreptitiously touching myself this way. Eventually, I become confident that I have been given freer rein. I push part of my vibrating finger slightly up and inside of me. As my warm juices wet the end of my finger, the vibrators stop, leaving an eerie silence that is quickly broken by the noises coming from my audience. The sounds of groans, of anxiety, of excitement fill the club.

I pull my arms away from my body, letting my hands drop open—a showing of submission to the woman holding the key to my stimulation. Mustering patience, I place my hands back on my breasts. The vibrators buzz alive. Eschewing delicate tickling, this time I pinch my nipples, pulling and twisting them, my hands betraying the strength of my desire. Dropping my hands, I press against the muscles of my lower abdomen with my left hand and inch my other hand lower. I move back and forth almost gingerly over my mound, afraid that Judith will use her power to turn off the vibrators. Jolts shoot through me each time I skim over my clitoris. I inhale sharply as I increase the pressure, feeling my desire rise. I hear murmurings in my audience and watch them through the silk blindfold as they fidget in their chairs. My left hand slips down to take over the duties at my throbbing clit while the index finger of my right hand presses into my opening. A wave of wetness drenches my finger as the pulses echo through my body. The vibrators go dead again.

If Judith wasn't hidden behind the curtain, I think some audience members would be throwing rotten fruit at her, or at least wrestling the remote control from her hands. Their reactions to the vibrators stopping show they have aligned with me, accepting that their own pleasure rests with me achieving mine, forgetting, or perhaps unaware, that having them enthralled like this is my desire. Unlike my audience, I am not upset by Judith's latest exercise of power—I think that I understand the line I am not allowed to cross without her permission.

The vibrators turn on when I put my hands back on my chest. Keeping my left hand on my breast, I take a calculated risk by pausing only briefly before trailing my other hand back down my body. Although I have a goal, I still enjoy igniting my skin with soft touches before I arrive there. When the textured tip of the vibrator rubs against the top of my pussy, warmth radiates from within me. I push my hips up to meet the stimulus. The vibrator slips up and down over my clit effortlessly, my wetness mingling with the remnants of the massage oil. I dare to make bolder movements with my hand, exploring my engorged folds while cautiously avoiding my opening, hoping this strategy will keep the vibrators alive. My breathing shallows, and I find myself unconsciously pulling at my nipple. Continuing my movements, I struggle to focus on my audience through the scarlet filter covering my eyes.

There is a dichotomy of reactions to me. Some audience members lean forward, their necks stretched like racehorses, willing me to cross some imaginary finish line. Others are more relaxed, leaning back in their seats, lost in fantasies they are commingling with mine. I study their faces, relishing their excitement while I am touching myself. Like a scientist measuring the reactions of her human subjects, I experiment with how they respond when I alter my movements. I try using only my finger to deliver a light vibration to the top of my clit, taking a break from my lap and stroking my body, making sounds of pleasure. Each of my actions elicits a different response from my audience. However, the more I observe and manipulate their arousal, the more I am losing control of my own. Although I don't want it to end, I am hopelessly compelled to fuel their excitement.

Despite willing myself to linger on safer parts of my body, my hand keeps heading to my pussy—stroking the swollen region up and down, quickening my motions with each passing moment. If Judith would stop me, I could reengage my analytical side, but she is remaining silent, allowing the sexual momentum to build. The vibrations, which once had felt so powerful, are now just part of my natural rhythm. My hand is slick, my juices covering my fingers and the palm of my hand. Passing the point of concern for consequences, each time I push my hand down, I venture closer to my opening. My pelvis unconsciously undulates with every sweep of my hand. The idea of touching the vibrator to the forbidden spot holds my mind hostage. The next down stroke of my hand brings the nubs of the rubber pad to the edge of my vaginal opening. The down stroke that follows allows the slightest bit of my fingertip to press inward. As I move my hand back up to tickle my clit, a fresh river of moisture flows from me. My breathing sounds loud to me, and unless Judith intervenes, I have lost the will to stop stroking my pulsing center. I can barely feel the self-inflicted pinches on my nipple, but what I do feel makes me want to cry out for lips and teeth to be sucking and biting at it.

I watch my audience. They can sense I am getting close. I am looking them in the eyes, although they are unaware of it. I feel the world narrowing as my breathing increases. My left hand wills itself from my breast and resumes its starting point back on the pole. The vibrator makes a ridiculous noise as it bounces against the metal, but my grip doesn't loosen—the pole feels like the only thing keeping me from flying away. My hips in constant motion, I continue to stroke my hand over the length of my soft mound, dipping a millimeter more boldly into myself with each caress. Keeping my eyes fixed on the women caught up in watching me, I am repeatedly sweeping my hand down my swollen pussy, pressing my palm firmly against my clit and covering my opening with the vibrator before sliding up again. On the verge of climaxing, I can only run my hand down the length of my pussy one final time before an uncontrollable desire makes me halt my near-frantic movements and revel in having my body strain against my own hand. Pressing my palm against my throbbing parts, I allow the pillow softness of my vagina to envelope my vibrator-clad finger. I gasp as my body produces waves of contractions. My back arches and my legs strain against the ties. I hear someone moaning, and recognize my own voice. A moment later, the toys stop. All I feel is the pounding coming from my lap and my heart. My breathing is still fast, but as it starts to slow a light-headed euphoria surrounds me. I drink in the view of my audience, their reactions, their arousal, their energy. Then the lights go out.

No warning is needed by the DJ this time. No one has ventured from their seat during my entire time onstage. In the darkness, I hear Judith make her way to me. Although the blindfold is intentionally ineffective, the ties do their job. Judith carries a seatbelt cutter—the same kind that firefighters and paramedics carry to free crash victims trapped in their cars. She slides the device over the silk sashes, quickly freeing me from the binds. I rise on trembling legs. With one arm around my waist and the other carrying the chair, she helps me backstage.

When the lights come up, the stage is bare. There is an audible restlessness in the audience as the DJ spouts the usual drivel about the next dancer. The other acts hate following ours. The mood in the club is invariably altered, and I have a hunch the tips don't flow as freely after I have been onstage. Because Judith and I aren't doing this for the money, we never solicit tips. I get from my audience what I want without anyone touching her wallet. While the pulsating bass starts up for the unlucky dancer entering the stage, Judith and I head toward the backdoor.

"You were topping from the bottom again," she says, invoking the BDSM phrase used to describe when the "sub" or submissive partner tries to call the shots and control the encounter. I disagree. I haven't had any transgressions against Judith's control. The situation is more accurately described as me being her sub, while I simultaneously have a roomful of women who are my subs. However, I'm not going to argue the point with her.

I turn and face her, giving my most playful grin, "I guess you'll just have to deal with me at home for that."

Judith returns a smile that outshines mine. The club's door closes with a solid click as we step into the brisk night air. We intertwine our arms and begin the stroll back to our apartment.

Bringing Her Through
Eva Vandetuin

She wasn't my student, okay? This is not me fraternizing with the students—whatever that means when classes are mixed grad/undergrad half the time anyway. We did meet in a class where I was a teaching assistant, though. She was in one of the other sections, but her TA was gone that day and she came up to me to ask a question. I liked her immediately, an intellectual-looking girl with wire-rimmed glasses, a shock of curly brown hair hurriedly pulled back, and blue eyes seemingly too big for her pale face. There was a hunch to her shoulders that suggested too much time spent with books and computers. She was dressed to blend in, but she asked her question assertively enough, and I liked that too. *Bet she's an A student*, I thought as she walked away.

After that we had a few conversations after class here and there, and I forgot about her until the following year, when she showed up as a one-year master's student in my program. At our first symposium of the year, we smiled at each other, then struck up a conversation about modernist literature. We're both fans of Virginia Woolf's novel *Orlando*, probably the most literary book about a sex change in the English language. And doesn't that say so much right off?

So we go to see a movie, and movies lead to tea, and tea leads to going over to each other's houses for late-night study sessions. She's five years younger than me and I feel a little bit like a mentor toward her still, but the gap is small enough to cross. One night we drink a bottle of wine together and she tells me shyly that she's a virgin. I'm a little tipsy and I lay my hand on her arm, saying, "Honey, there's no shame in that. It's smart to wait for somebody who you know will be good to you." And because the wine makes talking easy, I tell her all about my first time, and some of the times after that, and about how I was in my mid-twenties before I admitted I liked girls more than boys, and all sorts of things that are easier to confess in dim light with a little artificial courage. And maybe because I'm tipsy, I don't notice how carefully she looks at me, how she watches my lips forming the words.

Is she pretty? Not in a purely conventional way, maybe, but she's beautiful to me. She's my height, but more angular, with narrower hips and smaller breasts, a certain lingering athleticism from a more active period of her life giving her lovely, lean muscles under a layer of student fat. I'm a little bit in love with her and doing my best to hide it, I don't even know why. Because I'm older, maybe. Because I want her to feel safe talking to me. Because she's just a little fragile and she brings out my protectiveness.

After that we start to talk about sex much, much more. We trade favorite erotica, send each other links to particularly juicy slash fanfic, shriek with glee over Harry Potter BDSM genderfuck threesomes with Extra Special Sex Magick. When we're together we don't study anymore, we just eat and watch movies and talk talk talk. But somehow I'm still not expecting it when on another tipsy evening some months later, she puts her hand on my knee and says, "I'm tired of being a virgin. Do you think I'm attractive?"

I'm so unsure of my own desirability that for a moment I don't know what she means, and so I say, "Of course, yes, of course, I think you're beautiful," and then my mouth drops open as she moves her chair closer, presses her knee into mine, and looks me dead in the eye. And she says to me, "Well, I think you're someone I could trust to be good to me." In a flash I see how hard this is for her, something in the line of her mouth is full of hope and intense fear. Her bravery and bluntness excite me enormously. An eager, tender smile moves over my face, and I lean forward to kiss her soft lips, free the wavy mass of her hair from its tie and let it fall over her shoulders.

"Oh my dear," I whisper to her as I find the hardness of her nipple through her shirt, "I would be *so* honored."

We don't do much that night—just kiss and stroke each other for a while, give each other long massages, talk in quiet voices. I want so much to do everything right for her, and I tell her so. There's a busy week of classes coming up for us both, so we continue the flirtation online. I ask her to make a list of everything that turns her on, all the things she'd most like to do, and give her my own list. We shop the Good Vibrations Web site together, oohing and aahing and occasionally shrieking with self-conscious laughter at dildos as thick as our forearms. I even pretend I'm not a poor grad student, and I spend about two-hundred dollars on sex toys and lubricant, including the leather harness I've been lusting after since before I knew I wanted to fuck a girl while wearing it. I have everything shipped next-day air, and we make a weekend date. I can barely teach, I am so distracted; I keep thinking I smell her perfume.

Soon it's the appointed night and I'm emptying my closet, trying to find just the right thing to wear. Femme or butch? Is texture more important than the way things look? She likes the smell of leather. Should I wear a jacket?

My straight roommate shakes his head in bemusement and tells me, "Sweetie, it doesn't matter that much, you're just going to take it off anyway." I throw a fuzzy red bra at him and tell him he has no concept of the sexual importance of fashion. Then I put on a garter belt, stockings and a simple, brown velvet dress. I feel like me. And I have a bulging bag of sex toys, which is even better. I wave good-bye and my roomie gives me an exaggerated wink. He's teasing me again, but this time I only smile.

I take public transportation to the little flat she shares with another student (who is conveniently out of town for the weekend) and all the way I rehearse scenario after scenario, fantasizing about her pleasure but also reminding myself to make sure she's okay at every step. Does she trust me enough to let me know if she's uncomfortable? The last thing I want to do is hurt or scare her.

I get off the bus and walk the short block to her door. Through the windows I can see the room beyond is dimly lit with flickering candles. A tiny quiver of nervousness skitters across my consciousness, and I push it firmly away, say a prayer to Aphrodite, and knock softly on the door.

She must have been waiting nearby, because she opens the door almost immediately and draws me inside with a tremulous smile. Seeing her nervous like this, just a little bit schoolgirlish, makes my own mild attack of nerves melt away. I put down my bag and cup her face in my hand, running my thumb over her cheekbone. Her blue eyes widen behind her glasses as I back her up against the door, lean into her gently, and give her a long, thorough kiss. Her tongue flickers into my mouth and she embraces me, her body relaxing against mine. After a moment I pull back and give her a reassuring smile, which she returns. She's wearing a red silk dress, and I step back and hold her hands out from her body to admire her. "You look terrific," I tell her.

"So do you," she replies, and there's a hint of restrained

eagerness in her voice that makes my pulse quicken.

Picking the bag back up, I take her arm with a silly wink as I try to shift the mood to something more like our usual, comfortable companionship. We go into the kitchen to get fruit and glasses of water while I ask her about her day, her papers, her cats. It's small talk and we both know it, but soon she's chattering away like usual, relaxed and familiar. We take the food to her bedroom and sit on the bed, drawing the little conversation to its natural close.

"Time for show and tell?" I ask, and when she nods I open the bag and start to take out the contents one at a time. I've brought more than I plan to use, including some things I don't think she'll be ready for tonight, but I have to admit, I'm hoping to pique her curiosity enough to make sure this becomes more than a one-night stand. There are silk scarves for blindfolds or for bondage, lengths of rope, feathers, fur, and metal claws for sensation play, my trusty leather cuffs, a vibrator, some condoms, several kinds of lube, a leather flogger. I hand each item to her as I pull it out, watching her reactions—still eager, still a little nervous, her eyes flickering between my face and the objects in her hands.

Finally, I reach into the bottom of the bag and pull out what I hope will be the main course—the brand-new leather harness and a slim dildo. Closing her eyes, she raises the harness to her face to inhale the strong scent of leather, and I wait until she's put it (somewhat reluctantly) aside before I hand her the dildo.

"Look, it's even nonrepresentational, for extra political correctness," I tell her, and she giggles, running her hand over the toy's smooth lines.

After a moment I take the dildo from her and lean in close, sliding a hand under her dress. Her legs are bare, and I make my touch light to stir the tiny blonde hairs on her unshaven thigh. She shivers, then leans her head against my shoulder, and I smile. I tell her we can use any of these toys tonight, or none, whatever she wants, but I have something in mind I think she will like. She assents quietly, and I kiss her ear, her neck, her shoulder. She smells faintly of jasmine, subtle but exotic, and underneath I catch her natural scent, warm and female.

Under her dress, I move my hand farther up and run my fingers over the curve of her hip. No panties, how delightful. She cooperates when I lift the dress over her head, then sit back to give her a long, admiring look. A faint blush rises to her face as my eyes drift over her high, small breasts, the graceful bulge of her belly, the triangle of curly hair between her legs. Blushing a little more deeply, she shifts back against the headboard, letting her thighs fall open to reveal the pink slit of her cunt. I put the dress aside and meet her eyes again, touching her face, her breast, her belly.

"You are absolutely lovely," I tell her. "I am so lucky."

I kiss her for a few moments, letting her feel the velvet of my dress against her bare skin, and her hands move under my skirt, tracing the straps on the garter belt and caressing the skin just above where my stockings end. She helps me off with the dress, unclips the stockings and rolls them down slowly. "Let me look at you too," she says, and so I mirror her, and as my legs part I catch the familiar spicy scent of my juices. She looks vulnerable and I want her terribly, but I am patient. I let her take her time, enjoying being looked at as much as I enjoy looking.

After a few moments, I pick up one of the silk scarves and ask, "May I blindfold you?" She nods with a mixed look of excitement and apprehension, and I take off her glasses, then tie the scarf around her eyes and ease her onto her back. Kneeling, I let my calf rest against her side as I sweep most of the toys back into the bag, leaving out the few that I want. There's a CD queued in the player, some trance-inducing world music that we picked in advance, and I press play and turn the volume down low. Now we begin.

I run my hands lightly over her, pausing to massage the deep knots in her shoulders and neck, then kneading down her arms. She relaxes under my touch, her breathing slows. *Good.* Leaving one hand resting on her belly, I reach for a feather, letting it brush lightly over one of her nipples; it brings a shiver, a sharp intake of breath. I tickle her ear, her jaw, trace a line between her breasts and over her belly, her waist, her thighs, drawing her attention to the sensations of her skin. Her breathing has quickened again, and I sense her tensing slightly, though not with nervousness now. Anticipating. Listening.

I take an ice cube from a glass of water, letting the warmth of my fingers make it drip on her nipple, then her lips, then her exposed clit. She shudders deliciously. I tease her with the claws, rake them lightly down her thigh, prick her throat. She whimpers faintly, and I ask her, "Doing all right, sweetheart?" Her voice is husky as she answers, "Oh yes."

I put the claws aside and lean down to warm her ear with my breath and trace the delicate edge with my tongue, and am rewarded with a quiet moan. She is almost ready, I think, but to make sure I start to cover her torso with light kisses, pausing over her nipples to suck and nibble. Her hips lift to meet me as my breasts brush her belly, so I move lower to kiss her abdomen and her thighs, which fall open at my approach. She's more swollen now, and as she shifts I am surrounded by her scent: Jasmine and the unique smell of her cunt, crisp and a little acidic like a freshly cut green apple. I breathe in deeply, then open my mouth and exhale hotly on her exposed labia. She shudders again.

"You smell wonderful," I tell her quietly. "Is this all right?" I'm stroking her thighs, and perhaps she's gone a bit nonverbal now, because all she manages is "Mmmm-hmmmmmmm."

I take another deep breath to recall the memory of the best oral sex I've ever been given and do my best to reproduce it on her body, first tracing her labia with my tongue, then lightly stimulating her clit through its hood. She gasps and I reach up to hold her hand, moving my tongue a little faster, dipping down to stroke her labia more firmly, then moving back to her clit. And oh, she's moaning regularly now, squeezing my hand, moving her head distractedly from side to side, and so I wet a finger with her juices and slide it inside. Her hips push upward, forcing her clit deeper into my mouth, and I suck on it gently as I penetrate her. She thrashes a little, gratifyingly.

She's told me she's orgasmic, but slow, so when I begin to tire I leave my fingers inside her and switch to stroking her clit with my thumb. Carefully, I move to lie down beside her and tell her she can take off the blindfold. Slightly glazed, blue eyes emerge and stare into mine, and we smile at each other. She kisses me, tasting herself on my lips.

"And what can I do for you now, beautiful girl?" I ask her, nuzzling her neck playfully. She pushes against my hand again and I move my fingers in and out slowly, producing another shudder. Her breasts and the skin on her chest have flushed, giving her a rosy glow. A wave of arousal moves over me. I move closer to her, hooking my leg over her knee and pressing my clit against the bare skin of her thigh.

She sighs, eyes closed, and then turns to me with a look of determination. "I want you to fuck me," she says, and then her resolve wavers slightly. "Um, I think." She blushes a little, embarrassed, and we both chuckle, leaning our heads together.

"We can go slow," I tell her, "and stop at any time, if you want to try." She takes a deep breath, and nods.

I remove my fingers from her with some regret and stick them in my mouth, quirking an eyebrow at her as I do. She blushes again, and smiles. "Why don't I give you something to play with while I get ready," I tell her, and dig in the bag until I find the vibrator, a cute little multi-speed device with a pleasantly lumpy head. I switch it on, letting her feel it on the inside of her thigh and her outer labia before touching the tip to her clit. She gasps, and I take her hand and wrap it around the device. "Let me see where it feels the best to you," I tell her, and watch while she changes the angle, rubbing the shaft across her clit and inserting the tip into her vagina. Her eyes close again and her hips lift as pleasure buzzes through her, and I can't resist bending down again to suck on one hard, red nipple. "Don't come without me, sweetheart, I don't want to miss it," I tease, and she laughs, adjusting the vibrator again.

I've practiced putting on the harness until I'm fairly fast with it, but I'm distracted tonight by watching her masturbate, and I fumble a bit with the buckles. Finally I've strapped it on and I look down at my brand new cock with a faint sense of surprise. She looks into my face and laughs, resting her free hand on my erect, lavender phallus. "Honey, it is so you," she says, her eyes dancing, then glazing over with pleasure as she moves the slim vibrator against her clit. She is too far along to blush now, her cunt beautifully open and red, and I roll a condom onto the dildo hastily, frantic to get inside her, increasingly desperate to feel her hips grinding against mine. I switch the mini-vibrator in the harness on, leaving the one intended for my clit in the off position— I want to spend all my attention on her. Then I kneel between her legs and position myself over her, kissing her gently as our faces come close. My tongue slides wetly into her mouth, probing, and when I feel her turn the vibrator in her hand off, I rest the tip of my cock against her opening and look deeply into her eyes. "Ready?" I ask, and she takes a deep breath, blinks, then nods.

It is so much easier than I expected. The long period of foreplay seems to have done the trick, because as I apply gentle pressure, my cock slides easily into her. She groans, her eyes wide, and when I ask her, "Still all right?" she nods rapidly and wordlessly. I slide in almost to the hilt, resting the tiny vibrator on her clit, and just stay there for a moment, letting her get used to the sensation of being filled. She is breathing shallowly, her lips parted, and I feel tender as I watch her. I smooth her hair back from her forehead and kiss her jaw as her arms snake around my neck, gripping my shoulders, my hair. Our breasts touch lightly. "More," she says.

I start to rock inside her, slowly at first, but she thrusts her hips firmly against me and I meet her rhythm, my cock sliding wetly in and out, the strap of the harness pressing against my vulva. Her eyes open and close as she writhes beneath me; her lips part, soft sounds come from her throat. I watch her with increasing intensity. God, she really is beautiful, even more beautiful than I'd thought, her curly hair spread out on the pillow, her pale skin delicately flushed.

I have forgotten the music, but it pops suddenly back into my awareness. We're listening to a track with a heavy drumbeat and we are moving to the rhythm. My nipples are brushing her sweet, soft flesh and sending pulses of hot fire directly to my clit and she is moaning, alternately clutching at me and the sheets. Minutes are passing, and with each one she seems to grow more splendid, more shiningly glorious. Her skin glows softly in the candlelight; the tendrils of her hair writhe like snakes. She opens her eyes and I am looking into the endless blue of the sky, her pupils shining voids that I could fall into, forget myself. There's a lump in my throat from looking at her, she is so, so beautiful. I had no idea, I didn't know I would be so moved.

And then, oh goddess, I think she's coming, and I am whispering her name, urging her on. She is leaving teeth marks in my shoulder as she bites down on a scream, her hips are bucking under me and I'm almost there myself just from feeling her, just from watching the pleasure that turned her momentarily into something more than human. My astonishment must show because as she recovers, she looks into my face and laughs. In my peripheral vision I think I see her hair curl sinuously. Her luminous eyes and a red, red mouth seem to take up her entire face. Oh, glory. So beautiful, I didn't know.

And maybe I have fucked all the shyness out of her, because in the next moment she is kissing me, her tongue pushing aggressively into my mouth, and we are both awkwardly releasing the buckles of the harness, tugging at the straps. I pull the dildo out of her gently, but hardly a moment passes before she is taking it out of my hand and tossing it aside, pushing me down on the bed beside her and thrusting her fingers into my wet cunt. She may have been a virgin a few hours ago, but her fingers are knowledgeable enough and when she lowers her mouth to my nipple I come almost immediately, crying out and tangling my hands in her wild hair. She raises her head and looks at me with a crooked smile I've never seen before. And then she licks her lips.

Some hours later, exhausted and having eaten our fill of fresh strawberries and grapes, I pillow my head on her breasts as she sleeps. It was not what I expected, not at all—I came to deflower a girl and ended up nearly ravished myself by the person I— we?—*she* brought through. I wonder, in the morning will my timid, blushing friend have returned? And if not, who has been left in her place? I tilt my head to look at her face again, and she shifts in her sleep; her hand moves up to stroke my hair, then tug on it gently. I think she means to keep me.

And now I'm the one who feels shy.

The Boss
Ren Peters

It was dress-down Friday at work. I was wearing Levis, a red turtleneck, my favorite black leather blazer and black pant boots with two-inch heels. I liked the elevation and the smart click they made against the hardwood floors. The sound made me feel confident and in charge as I strode deliberately down the empty hallway to the stockroom. I felt particularly in control that day—I was the boss.

I was also packing. It was nothing really obtrusive, and not for any particular reason except that, when it was there, I felt good. I always marveled at how a little bundle could make me feel so powerful. And today, with the possibility of a big job on the line, I needed all the power I could muster.

We were preparing a presentation for a potential new client—ideas for brochures, fliers and a TV ad campaign. My job didn't usually include getting supplies from the stockroom, but because my secretary Millie was working through lunch preparing the text for the brochures, it was the least I could do to get the paper samples for the client to look at.

As I rounded the corner, I saw Chris, the latest hire in the graphics division, standing next to the stockroom door at the end of the hallway. She leaned nonchalantly against the wall, her legs crossed, her arms folded at her chest, her small, slender athletic body very much at ease while she stared directly at me.

Momentarily uncertain, I slowed my steps, but then quickened my pace. After all, I was the boss; I belonged there. I looked at her as I approached and she, almost insolently, continued to look back at me, at my every move, at my package. That was a little unnerving.

I decided on the casual approach. "Waiting for someone?"

"Yeah. You. And if that's your pickup line, I'd get a new one." The edges of her lips turned up in the hint of smile as her eyes traveled down my body and settled, once again, on my crotch.

That was even more unnerving, but I was the one in charge; I decided to ignore it. "Well, then, if you're waiting for me, what can I do for you?" I slipped the key into the lock.

Pushing herself off the wall, she gestured toward the stockroom. "I need some stock for the storyboard. I'd get it myself, but you keep the door locked now."

"You know we have to since the theft. Just call my secretary and she'll open up for you." I pulled open the door and gestured for her to enter.

As I followed her into the stockroom, the door automatically closed and locked behind us. Just inside, she stopped and turned so suddenly I almost walked into her. We stood face-to-face in the narrow, shelf-lined room. Soft light streamed through the window at the far end and everything seemed to slow down. Everything, that is, except my heart, which was hammering to beat the band. Her face was mesmerizing as she looked up at me.

Softly, in a husky voice, she said, "And if I call you, Boss, will you do that for me? Will you open up for me?"

Did time stop? Was my mouth dry? I looked into clear blue eyes that held just the slightest hint of a challenge. I looked down. Not a good idea. Her nipples were clearly erect under that rather tight silk T-shirt. Farther down. Her hips were rocking ever so slightly. Better get back up to the face.

Since the casual approach obviously wasn't working, I decided a shift to the business approach was necessary. In my most officious voice, I said, "Well, yes. If Millie's busy, of course . . . and if I'm not busy . . . of course I'll help you." I started to move past her.

"Boss," she whispered, "do you know how sexy you are?"

I froze. I was the boss, but I was clearly losing control of this impromptu staff meeting.

"Do you, Boss?"

She leaned into my side and I felt the slightest pressure of her hand on my stomach, then felt it move hesitatingly down to the package between my legs. Her mouth was so close to my ear I could feel her breath. "Is this equipment just for effect, or do you know how to use it?"

Taken aback at the challenge, I turned my head to face her and suddenly all I could see were her lips, slightly parted, soft, and so inviting. I was going to say something, honest I was, but my rule against fraternization between employees left my head. All my thoughts were bundled in a knot of nerves between my legs, and I just closed my eyes, dipped my head, and met her lips with mine.

Oh, sweet Jesus, what a kiss! So I leaned in for another, slightly more possessive. She moaned, or did I? No matter, enough of this kissing over my shoulder; I turned to face her and she came willingly into my arms. The kisses, at first so gentle and sweet, became a hunger. She was ravenous and I wanted to feed her. I placed my hands around her waist and walked her the few steps back to lean against the workbench along the rear wall. I felt her hands drop lightly to my hips. Her mouth opened to my tongue, and my hunger matched hers.

"Stop!" She pushed me away.

I was startled. I thought she had . . . No! I know she had started this. Why stop now? But my confusion was answered in an instant as she reached down and pulled her T-shirt off, then quickly unclasped the wispy piece of lace that held her breasts captive.

Oh my! That time I know it was I who moaned as she pulled my face down to her small, firm breasts. I cupped them with my hands, sucking first one nipple, then the other. She tasted so sweet and her scent hinted of corn silk and musk. I was fast losing myself in the soft warmth of her body.

Arching her back, she pressed her chest to me as she fumbled with the buttons on her jeans. I felt her tugging on my belt. Then I felt her pulling down the zipper and easing the cock out of my boxers. Before I lost total control of the situation, I took her hands and placed them on my shoulders as I leaned toward her, kissing and taking little nips up her neck and around her ears and finally to her mouth.

I worked her jeans and panties off her hips in one smooth maneuver. As I lifted her onto the workbench, she kicked off her shoes and let her pants fall to the floor. My hands were all over her. Her nipples and breathing were hard, matching my own. I slipped a hand between us and down through her soft curls. She moaned through my kisses as I ran my fingers the length of her and dipped into her wetness. Oh, she was so wet my knees went weak, but I had no time for that. I was the boss here—I had work to do! With my thumb rubbing her clit, I teased her with my fingers. Just once she whimpered "Please" and pulled me closer. I held the cock against her then, slowly leaning forward into her as she wrapped her legs around my waist and pulled me deep within. We both moaned and our lips met again as I gently did the in-and-out.

She lay back, so vulnerable, so lovely, and looked up at me

through half-lidded eyes clouded with desire and longing. I had to make her come; after all, I was the boss! I lifted her legs to my shoulders. Then, cupping her ass, I drove home the final thrusts that brought her over. Her body went rigid; I heard her gasp; then I felt her shudder and relax in my hands. Her body was so supple and her skin so hot, I couldn't stop from rubbing and massaging her breasts, her hips, her thighs. I was insatiable for the heat of her against my hands. The smell of her arousal filled the air and I craved more. When I eased out of her, she looked up at me through eyes still heavy with desire. As though understanding my own unspoken need, "Please," she whispered again, and reached down with both hands to hold herself open for me. With her legs still over my shoulders, I lifted her hips and buried my face into her wet heat. I savored the salty taste as I licked and sucked and pulled her to another deeper, stronger orgasm. Spent, I collapsed forward on her and held her close as I caught my breath.

In the stockroom, everything was still. I could hear distant talking and laughter as people returned from lunch. And then I was aware of a movement beneath me. Chris was shivering.

"Are you cold?" She shook her head, but her trembling increased.

I quickly stood, climbed onto the workbench beside her and pulled her into my lap, cradling her shaking body tenderly in my arms. I was suddenly very afraid. What had I done? I know she had come on to me, but there in my arms, she seemed innocent and vulnerable. Her shivering had become so violent that I could hear her teeth chattering. Where was that brazen, sassy attitude?

I think I whispered sweet nothings, but it was an awkward moment. My MBA classes hadn't exactly covered this scenario—I had to improvise. I cradled her head to my chest, kissed her forehead and pulled her closer to me as I gently rocked her in my embrace.

She murmured something against my chest I didn't quite

hear.

"What?"

Again, but a little louder, "I'm sorry."

"Pardon? Why are you apologizing?"

"I've been trying to get your attention since I started working here five months ago. Then I figured you weren't family because you never noticed me. This morning, when I saw you come in, I knew you were packing, and I just had to have you. But now I think I ruined everything."

"Shhh. Don't say that. Everything will work out. I promise. We'll be fine. I know it."

She turned in my embrace and put her arms around my neck. My heart ached to see the anguish in those beautiful eyes.

"Are you sure?"

She clung to me as I placed gentle kisses on her eyes and nose and cheeks. "Of course I'm sure. I promise. We'll make it work."

She didn't look convinced, but then I had a sudden moment of managerial brilliance. "We'll do it by starting all over again. The right way. With a date."

I looked into her eyes and gave her my most charming smile. "Chris, would you like to have dinner with me tonight?"

At my words, she hugged me tightly and laughed through her trembling. "Would I? You know I would! Oh, I'm so relieved."

I was too. All I had done was step into the stockroom for supplies and, before I knew it, all hell had broken loose in my life. I clearly had lost control, but it seemed I was recuperating quite nicely.

There was one question niggling at the back of my mind, though. "How did you know I'd be in the stockroom?"

"Easy," she said, grinning. "I called Millie to come open the stockroom for me and she said you were on your way. It was the chance I needed for you to notice me. I just made sure I got here before you did."

Hmmm. I had been ambushed . . . waylaid as it were. But she

was so lovely and warm in my arms. And her perfume and her eyes and her sighs, all so beautiful, so perfect in my arms. I held her closer and kissed her gently and again and again.

She sighed. "I think I should get back to work. My lunch break is way past over." She moved to get up, but I held her close.

"Don't worry. I'll walk you back to your division. It's okay if you're late." I grinned. "After all, I am the boss."

Mother's Day
Joy Parks

I want to lose all your demons and ghosts . . .
I want to tear off your chains 'cause I know . . .
All the way to Heaven is heaven. *

"Are you two celebrating Mother's Day early?"

The waitress's voice takes me by surprise. The booth in the diner has dissolved beneath us, the menu under my hand is written in an unknown language. I'm looking at you. I don't see or hear anything else. I have forgotten that we are in public, that there are people around us in the restaurant, walking outside on the street, driving past us on the their way to or from wherever it is they go. I am lost in you. I often am. More specifically, I am lost in the lines of your face, the soft slight wrinkles that fan out from your eyes, now lit hard in the sun streaming through the

*"All The Way To Heaven" — Written by Melissa Etheridge
© 1995 MLE Music (ASCAP)
Used by permission. All rights reserved.

diner window. Eyes that had seen much before I was even born. I follow the soft rise of your cheek, still smoother, sleeker than most women your age. You're beautiful, but I know you'd never tolerate me saying that. Your face, your eyes, your skin, your index finger gently tapping inside my palm. You are holding my hand. And I am shamelessly lost in you.

Mother's Day. I think of my own mother, remember that she is playing quarter slots and eating buffet in Vegas, on one of what we secretly refer to as her pastel polyester pantsuit tours. For a split second, I think of the day I told her about you, her fear for me, of what I was now up against. My father had been twelve years her senior. My sister married a man fourteen years older than her. I joked about carrying on the family tradition. Mom didn't find it funny. I think of her disbelief when I stopped in the middle of what she had come to expect of my life, moved a country away, changed everything. I think of her unspoken fear that you might somehow replace her, a worry we can't talk about because of her refusal to admit it exists. Sunday is Mother's Day. I'll call her.

You gently squeeze my fingers to bring me back. I look up at the waitress, confused. Then I realize what she is saying, her mistake. Still hazy, I open my mouth to protest, but before I can say a word, your leg jogs mine, you order a coke for me and tea for you and send her on her way. You have that conspiratorial smile on your face. I've seen it a thousand times, this is how you make me your ally. You gently shake your head, raise your eyelids, give me that look. *Play along* you're thinking, aligning us against them. You do this all the time. But why?

Why do you want me to let them think you are my mother?

When I was fifteen, you were twice my age.

You like the fact I was born in the year you came out. As if I came into the world just for you, custom ordered. On one of our more savagely honest nights, when we laid beside each other talking until it was nearly light, you told me that you wished you could have brought me out, took me on, as you said, when I was fifteen. You would have been thirty. The thought of you wanting this should have disturbed me. Instead it made me hot. Technically, biologically, physiologically. Yes, it could be possible. I suppose if we count from the day you got your first period, then yes, I am in love with a woman old enough to be my mother. But then again, it's not possible at all, never, not in the world in which we inhabit; not in the women we are. Not possible at all in ways only you and I could understand.

You could never think of yourself as mother, not even to the pets. The cats look to you as their "Daddy," a term I use when I want to make a flash of wildfire rise in you. How you grab at me when I tease you with that deviant term, how this simple word makes you feel like we're breaking even more of the rules. How it makes you pull me down onto your lap, where I wrap my arms around you, lay my head on your shoulder, trail my lips across the nape of your neck. How it changes you, makes you fierce. I call you Daddy when I want you to know this is possible, that despite everything, we are possible. To remind you that you can have this anytime, as much of me as you want or need, in all the ways you need it. I call you Daddy to prove that I understand exactly who you are. That I know how you need to feel.

Impossible, because by the time I was born, you were already beyond boys and babies. I imagine you sailing through the streets on your bike, flying toward the bubblegum-scented kisses of a young girl, propelled by your rebellion and your bravery. I see you young and strong and full of yourself, numb with fear at times, but still defiant and determined to be exactly who you knew you were.

Not much later, just before I learned to write my name, you would learn how to live half in the shadows, discover ways to earn your independence without spending your days wearing heels and typing correspondence in some gray office, ready to spring into who you really were when the darkness came. At night, while I slept tucked in safe with my dolls and teddy bears, you were navigating the bars and the street and the world in your boots and your jeans, learning how to satisfy a woman, how to love and how to drink to push down the pain. You would learn, as I learned to tell time and count and tie my shoes, how to live as butch, the word itself bristling with sex and danger. Forbidden and rebellious and full of desire. I think of how I learned to love the sound of that word from your lips, that one solid syllable, this label you learned to love as you learned to love yourself, finally.

Sometimes I think of your life unfolding like the pulp novels I read when I first came out. The ones I read as history. The stories I wanted for my own.

You knew from the start that this is what I wanted from you. That it was your stories that drew me close. The badness and the secrets. You knew this is what I was seeking from you on the nights when we talked till dawn, nights when you would tell me how I made you feel younger and stronger and ready to believe again. Your words were like a gift, something I had wanted for a long time without realizing it and had finally been given. Later, when I first pulled your cool, dry hands to my breasts, when I pressed my wetness against your fingers, you knew I was straining to be filled up with your history. When I spread my legs and my heart and my mind wide open to you, I was learning all that you had felt, touched, tasted, loved. I wanted to feel your knowledge, your honor, your hurt and horror in every sweet thrust of your magnificent, skilled hands. I longed to feel the true butch of you; the what had never really felt wanted-ness of you. Take it in. Inside me.

I remember how I talked about my secret attraction to older women, dropped more hints than ever should have been necessary. It took so long for it to occur to you. Did you know that your talk and tea made me whole again, after two loves that left me broken and bruised and one where the neglect grew like a cancer inside me? You were my mentor, guiding me back into the world I had abruptly left, the one the pain forced me from. I needed you more than you needed me. And I flirted with you beyond the point of return.

"Be my girl," you whispered on the phone, when you finally admitted your loneliness was colder than the January night around us, when what neither of us ever thought possible seemed inevitable.

But it wasn't quite that easy, was it? You fell in love with my understanding of butch fears and sorrows. You told me they didn't make women like me anymore. Too good to be true. And how that frightened you. How you wanted it almost too much to let yourself take it, believing it was better not to love at all, than to give in and live with the fear of losing it. I still remember the pain of the waiting. The anticipation. The confusing days I stayed home from work, not able to trust myself to not cry in public. I couldn't think of anything but you—you swinging blindly at me with desire you couldn't contain, throwing love like a bomb and then running for cover from the impact. I think of the times I had to slow you down, start again, make you wait and walk and court me. And stop you from fleeing every time you let me near. Later, you wondered if another woman would have had this patience with you. I knew what I was waiting for.

Can you believe that? Young stuff. Young piece. Robbing the cradle. Jailbait. Old enough to know better. Second childhood. Too much of a good thing. At least she'll go with a smile on her face. What a waste.

We both heard those thorny phrases; they cut you far more than they did me. Made it sound like you were the one doing the pursuing, some leathery old butch chasing something you were no longer worthy of. Too private and shy to let on that I, this younger, uninhibited femme, chased you until you caught me. That I pursued you relentlessly, refusing to stand down to your fear. And waited so long for your first touch, that first sweet kiss. Wanting you so much that the unbelievable miracle of being in your arms made me teary for days.

You touched my hair, and whispered, "So this is what my hair felt like before it went gray."

The intimacy of that. And in your touch, the acceptance that it was possible you could love a woman my age. Without fear.

Do you remember when it finally happened? When what had been became something new, the gradual slowing orbit of our emotions? You had always been there, I had always noticed. And oh how you praised me, raised me up, made me soar, circle, risk falling on my face just to brush against your wings. That's how it began. "She's quite the treasure," you said, speaking of my talents, my potential, not me. But the praise and the phrase wouldn't leave me alone, your words following me for days, wrapped around me warm as a coat. Playing your words over again and again. Dreaming of hearing you whisper "my treasure" in the dark, my naked body cradled into yours, your arms wrapped tight around me, possessing me. Your treasure. Yours.

Friends ask me if it's different because of our ages. Of course it is. Different in ways I cannot speak of, don't have words for, only understand through your hands and your mouth. Different because we live in a culture that wants us to believe that women past fifty are no longer valuable, no longer sexual, no longer needing of touch. Nothing to give. I know better. Different because to want you; to yearn for you is to rebel once again. A new kind of coming out. It's one reason why my desire for you is precious, obsessive, necessary. Not only do I give my love to a woman, I give it to one few assume has the right to have it. You are my own private revolution.

I know what worried you the most. That I would leave you for someone younger, less complicated. You had nothing to fear, but how hard you made me work to prove this. How you came to me with tentative steps, then darted back for cover. How I fought your fears, how I kept my distance without letting you push me away. I remember, too, the first time you didn't retreat, but raced forward without restraint. The welcome heat of your mouth, how your voice dropped low and how you clung to me, your hands caressing me as I had dreamed they would. And afterward, me staying wet for days just thinking about the possibility of your passion. I had finally worn you down. And I loved you even more for your surrender.

If your greatest fear was my future, then mine had to be your past. At first, I listened intently to every detail of your love of every woman you'd ever been with. It was part of your stories, and I was trying to learn you through them, because I loved what you had become. But there seemed to be so many, you had so many more years than I to fill with lovers. I began to see these women as a long line that stretched between us, with me at the end, the farthest away. Then, in the middle of a dark spring night, in the middle of your sixth decade, you woke me to tell me that you've been longing for your own virginity. You want me for your first and your last. You whisper of how much pain that could have saved you. But since that's not possible, you want to find some way to love me that's new, only ours. Something to give me that you never gave anyone before. I realize they're not between us anymore, they're behind you now, each one of them pushing you forward, pushing you closer and closer to me.

It's not always easy. I told you once that I would want to live with you even if we weren't lovers. It made you burst into tears, get angry, get sad. I was trying to tell you that I would stay even if there came a day when we could no longer make love. You heard me say there would come a time when I wouldn't want you.

And the first time I said "forever," how difficult you found that word. How hard it was for you to admit your fear that I had so much more forever than you.

But most days, none of that matters. What matters is the sweetness of the names you call me and the silliness and the fact that you are far more the teenager in love than I know how to be. It is you who writes my name on the steamy windows in the car, you who guilelessly wraps your arm around me in the movies. It is you who beckons me to slow dance with you in grocery store aisles. You who whispers my name like a litany when you enter me. Your tongue that traces I love you on my belly. It is you, only you, who can love me so well. It is you.

I think about the mornings I wake up with your hand moving slow between my legs. You whisper something about dew on the morning rose. I laugh because at times you are so corny. And I feel my wetness rush to flood your hand.

And there are the nights when you lie behind me, your chin resting gentle on my shoulder, the way you stroke the extra belly I should lose, the way I curl against you and beg you in the dark to tell me one of your stories. You tell me about the days when you were young and just figuring things out, how the straights used to hang out on the streets in the Village so they could look at queers. And I think how brave you must have been, how tough and full of yourself and full of belief that this, that to have a woman in your arms in the dark, was worth the toll it took from you every day.

And when you stop talking about who did what to whom and who said what after, when you start to talk about what the pain and shame was really like, I want to comfort you with my willingness and skin, draw the hurt away like a sponge, ease your fear with my wetness and sheer raw want of you. I want to love the pain away from you like a charm, wrap my legs around your still supple and muscular thighs to guard you from your past. I want to be your shelter and your rest.

I was in love with you long before I could tell you.

This secret kept me going. And slowly, you realized just how good I was for you. And even though you ran hard and fast and almost wore us out, I knew that, eventually, you would run back to me. Then both of us could rest. I knew it was just a matter of time.

And when you finally took me to your bed, we didn't leave for nearly two days.

My biggest surprise was the ferocity of your passion. The fierceness of you, just minutes inside the room, how you backed me up against the wall, my arms above my head, your hands moving over every inch me, the sound of your yearning low in your throat and your leg between mine, parting me, how I ached for you and arched my back. I think about how your lips never left my mouth, how you undressed me like a present, how quietly we made love, with no words, just sighs and cries of pleasure, and how it was different, somehow deeper and sweeter than ever before. Then falling asleep in the gray afternoon, our bodies tangled, and me thinking, *so this is how it should be done.*

I remember waking warm next to you, your fingers stirring up fresh want, desire trembling in my gut, pinching my skin with light. How you looked down at me and whispered, "You're mine now," and the raw shaking longing it unleashed in me, a new kind of need I didn't know was possible. How I began to writhe on the sheets, how I pulled you down to lie on top of me, wanting you to engulf me, wanting to be taken under by the sweet force of you, loving your possessiveness, a reminder that this is what we would be from now on.

That we would belong to each other.

And the tenderness after we were both spent, how you kissed a line down from my breasts to my belly, how you looked up at me helplessly, almost pleading with me to stop you. How little you believed you deserved all this, a surprise at a time in your life when you considered all the good things long past. You call me your reward. Your miracle. You tell me I am what made everything worthwhile.

"Why did you do that? Why did you let her think you were my mother?" I ask.

You give me the look that says I still have a lot to learn. "You think she got that impression?" you ask. Then you grin.

I roll my eyes.

I don't know what you're up to. I have never needed to learn these subtleties. But then, what difference does it make? If she thinks I'm your daughter, then she'll think nothing of the fact you're sitting here, holding my hand in a busy little dive in a small town somewhere in New England, some sleepy little place we'll never pass through again. I don't need you to be brave right now. I just need you to be exactly where you are, here, across the table, holding my hand. So I smile.

You look behind, see that the waitress is tables away, out of sight and earshot. You sit up, your fingers circling my wrists, you're moving toward me and I notice as you come closer, as always, that the faint wrinkles near your eyes disappear, the deepening laugh lines around your mouth fade. I don't see your age or the years that lie between us. I just see you, my love. You tug me closer; my body follows. You press your forehead to mine like you would if we were at home. I hear you laugh, low and soft, in my ear; you're happy, like a kid getting away with something. I close my eyes and feel your lips brush mine, gentle at first, then a little more urgent. I hear your breathing change. I squirm slightly in my seat, the unexpected intimacy and the brazenness of you kissing me publicly in some small-town diner exciting me.

You've never done anything like this before. You look at me, your eyes gentle, a soft, dark blue. You want me. You whisper, "doubt she thinks I'm your mother now" in that low hard-edge gravel and velvet voice that made me fall in love with you. I slide back into my booth, too aroused by the kiss and surprised to feel anything else. I wonder where your courage came from.

The waitress is standing beside our table, motionless and silent, the hand holding her pen stuck in midair above her pad. She looks embarrassed. But you don't. You sit up straighter, butch pride welling up in your chest, making you look taller than you actually are, somehow more solid, more present. Just more. You look sure of yourself, defiant and brave, still ready for anything. With one swift, definite move, you close your menu, look at the waitress who won't look you in the eye, and then ask me, "So, do you know what you want?"

Then you smile.

And I'm laughing too hard to answer.

Because we both know that I do.

Senior Skip Day
Anna Watson

My gay-boy buddy, Patrick, convinced me to skip that day—
me, such a good young person, someone who deplored the crude
pranks and stupid drunken parties that were going on all over the
place our last semester of high school. Patrick swore we would
have a great time, though. The whole freaky gang of us from the
Gay/Straight Alliance (at that time, I thought I was in the
"straight" part of our little group), were headed out to the new
sex store that had just opened up. I may have been a good girl,
but I was no prude, and already had a little stash of Black Lace
novels and a few Playgirls under my bed, so I thought it would
be fun. Wrong. I should have known I would hate it—all those
disembodied penises for sale, all those magazines like PHAT
ASS BLACK CHICKS and LEGG SEXX. It turned my radical
feminist, anti-racist stomach, and I couldn't wait to get out of
there. I left my friends shrieking and daring each other to stick
their fingers into the "Try me!" display of a really disgusting

looking cyberskin vagina that said FUCK PORN STAR CINDER MCBRIDE'S SHAVED SLIT! and rode my bike over to Darcy's.

I'd been spending more and more time at Darcy's lately, ever since my mom had started acting like a pod person. Darcy and my mom were best friends, but Darcy was a lot cooler about everything, and she never asked too many questions when I came by and wanted to hang out, to escape from the home front a bit. That had been happening a lot lately. Earlier that month, I'd been accepted to Stanford—my first choice—and I guess my mom was having a hard time thinking about me moving out. It was like now that I was almost grown up, she wanted to turn me back into a baby again, and she was clingy and nosy and all up in my business all the time. I'd be coming out of the shower, or getting something to eat, and all of a sudden I'd feel her looking at me, this really insane goo-goo-ga-ga expression on her face. It was freaking me out, and the less I was around her, the better; although, ironically, I could already tell how much I was going to miss her.

Darcy lived right downtown on Main Street, in an apartment above a jewelry store. I loved sitting and looking out the window at Ann Arbor's finest, a mix of townies, druggies, old punks, students—freaks and jocks—professors, visiting celebrities. The only problem was, I didn't feel entirely comfortable at Darcy's these days either because her new girlfriend, Kit, was usually there, and she could be really bitchy to Darcy. Just the other day, I walked in on them fighting—Kit, all red in the face, looking like she wanted to cry, but screaming horrible things at Darcy, with Darcy, her eyes big and pleading, just trying to get a word in edgewise. I loved Darcy so much—she said I was like the daughter she'd never had—that it really upset me to see Kit screaming at her like that. But when things were calm, the three of us would sit around smoking and playing Hearts or just watching dumb shit on TV and laughing. It was such a relief not to have my mom's voodoo messing with my head.

I carried my bike up the fire escape and propped it next to Darcy's kitchen door. That was another cool thing about the apartment—you could get in from the fire escape, even though you weren't really supposed to, and in the summer, you could sit out there and use it like a little porch. No one was home, so after fixing myself a snack, I laid down on the couch with my iPod and dozed off, listening to some crazy mix Patrick had put on there for me.

I don't know how long I slept—it must have been past five, because the sun was setting—when I was startled awake by a big crash. I heard a bunch of giggling, and realized that Darcy and Kit must be coming in from the fire escape. I started to sit up and say hi, but something made me stop.

"Is Tess here?" Kit asked, sounding kind of out of breath. "I almost killed myself on her fucking bike!"

"Nah, it's Senior Skip Day. She and her little pals went off on some sordid outing." They laughed and then I could hear them kissing, Kit moaning all dramatic. After a while, I heard a smack and Kit gasped and giggled. Darcy said, "Get your sweet ass in there!"

"Yes, Daddy!" Kit said in a little girl voice. I almost laughed out loud. "Daddy"? Sure, Darcy was butch, that was no secret, but "Daddy"? I didn't even know what it might mean, but it was obviously about sex. Yes, of course—they thought the apartment was empty, no pesky teenager hanging around—they were getting ready to do it. I don't know what came over me. I held my breath and didn't move. I decided to spy.

Kit walked to the bedroom—right next to the kitchen—and shut the door. I could just barely hear her moving around in there, high heels clicking.

I peeked carefully around the edge of the sofa and saw Darcy standing in the kitchen, lighting a cigarette. I'd known her all my life, but tonight she looked different. She looked good. She's tall and curvy, with red-brown hair and hazel eyes, and she's really careful about her appearance. She has a kind of 1950s men's hair-cut, and she goes to the barber every two weeks. She always smells really good, like some kind of upscale Old Spice thing, and her clothes are impeccable. Today she was wearing ironed 501s and shiny polished loafers, and I knew her breasts were bound down beneath her blue-and-white striped men's shirt. She'd shown me her binder once, when she was explaining about being butch. I didn't really care at the time—just something from an older generation, kind of weird, whatever—but tonight I felt a lot more interested. She shook out the match and threw it into the sink. I could smell her cigarette, and it made me want one. My mouth watered.

"Come an' get me, Daddy!" Kit called out in that silly voice, and Darcy took a deep drag, half closing her eyes against the smoke. She looked so cool in the dim light, so handsome. She walked slowly down the hall, not even glancing into the living room, which was good, because she might have seen my back-pack. When I heard her open the bedroom door, I peeked out again. I realized I had a really good view, right across the hall to the bed, and I felt a thump of excitement in my belly. Sleazy as it might have been, I was too curious, and, if I was honest with myself, too turned on, to stop now. Sex was such a mystery to me. Nothing I'd ever done with the guys I'd gone out with had been as exciting as some of the stuff I read about in my Black Lace novels, where sex seemed to come as easily to the characters as breathing and always be seamless and exciting. I told myself this was an opportunity to see how grown folks got down to it, and for a little while, was able to convince myself that I was watching for purely scientific reasons.

The light in the bedroom was dim and sexy—candles, I saw, that Kit had lit and put around the room. Kit was kneeling on the bed, her head bowed, looking demure and slutty at the same time in a leopard-spotted slip that rode up her thighs. She looked great, with her straight, dark hair swinging over to cover her face. Maybe everyone looks great when they're about to have sex. I thought about how the whole time I'd been crashing at Darcy's apartment, I'd never heard the two of them in bed, and had only seen them kiss a few times. Darcy was gentlemanly like that, of course, and private to boot. But now I was getting to see this hot connection between them. I was having a little trouble breathing.

"Hi, Daddy," purred Kit, looking up at Darcy, who stood beside the bed, her loafers planted firmly on the bedside rug. Keeping her eyes on Darcy, Kit raised her arms over her head and stuck out her chest. I could see her bouncy, dark-tipped breasts through the sheer material, and Darcy's eyes were riveted on them. "How do you like my new nightie?"

"I like it very much, baby," Darcy said, low and gravelly. Her voice was different from usual; this was how she sounded when she was horny and turned on. I settled myself more comfortably on my belly, my chin on my folded arms. I was pressing my pelvis into the couch, and when I caught myself doing it, I made myself stop.

Darcy took a last drag on her cigarette before putting it out in an ashtray on the bedside table. "Daddy thinks his baby girl looks like a royal princess tonight."

I didn't feel like laughing now, and I didn't even feel like I was doing anything creepy anymore. My body was tingling; I felt flushed and happy. The sexy love between Darcy and Kit was reaching out to set me on fire. My hand found its way under my T-shirt to my hard nipple. I rolled it gently between my fingers.

"My girl wants to get fucked tonight, isn't that right?" said Darcy, moving closer to the bed. Kit smiled and wiggled. Her red lipstick made her lush, full lips look unbelievable. I pinched my nipple harder.

"Yes, Daddy! Oh, Daddy, I've been thinking about your hard dick all day!"

Darcy chuckled and moved her hand to cup her crotch. "Is that right, Princess? Couldn't keep your mind on your work for thinking about Daddy's meat?"

Kit was breathing hard—she sure liked this Daddy stuff. "That's right, Daddy," she said. "I kept thinking about how much I like to suck your cock, Daddy, and I was getting wet right at work, and I thought, well, maybe I should go into the ladies' room, and well, you know, get a little relief, but then I thought, no, Daddy wants that for himself. I can't take that from Daddy!"

"Good girl," crooned Darcy, reaching out to stroke Kit's shiny hair. "Daddy's best girl. You've been such a good girl, and you look so beautiful tonight, all wrapped up in a pretty package for me. You watch, sweetheart, Daddy has something nice for you."

Darcy started to undo her belt, while Kit watched greedily. I'd never seen Darcy looking so fine, her features suffused with a masculine energy. She moved firmly and decisively, opening her jeans and stroking the bulge in her boxers. If I hadn't just seen a whole bunch of them for sale at the sex boutique, I might have been totally shocked, but instead, another thump of excitement hit me in the belly. Darcy grabbed one of Kit's hands and placed it firmly on her crotch, thrusting as Kit moaned and stroked. I moved my hand down to my belly, playing with my belly button.

"Please, Daddy?" asked Kit, and Darcy nodded. Kit moved eagerly forward, reaching under Darcy's waistband and taking out the dildo. It was a Caucasian one, maybe a bit too pink, but Kit started licking and petting it like it was the best thing on earth. Darcy was breathing heavily, saying over and over in that low voice, "Yeah, that's my good girl, take my dick, girl."

By this time, my hand was down my jeans and playing with the soft hairs guarding my pussy. I hiked my butt up to give myself room so I could go a little farther inside. I felt puffy and slick; I couldn't believe how wet I was. I felt a pang of guilt—that was my mom's best friend in there!—but by then I was too far gone, and all I could think about was how good I was feeling, how turned on I was by the raw sexual energy in the next room.

"Show me how wet you are!" growled Darcy, and I couldn't stop myself from moaning just a little. I don't think they heard me. Letting Darcy's dick slip out of her mouth, Kit moved reluctantly away, sinking onto her back and moving her legs wide apart. She lifted her ass, raising her slip up over her belly. She wasn't wearing any panties. I'd never seen another woman down there, turned on like that, and I wished I could get closer. I was sure she looked like I felt—gorgeous, swollen, glistening.

Darcy moaned, her hand on her cock. "Look at that hot little snatch, waiting for Daddy's big, hard dick. Tell Daddy how much you want him to fill up your hole with his cock, Princess. Let Daddy know how much you want it."

As Kit began a low string of dirty talk about *fuck me* and *plug me* and *take what you want from me, Daddy*, and *use me*, I became more and more involved in taking care of my own arousal. I plunged a couple of fingers inside me, just as Darcy lowered herself onto the bed and started doing it to Kit. I watched their groaning, sweaty lovemaking, thrusting right along with them, using my other hand to rub my clitoris, just the way I liked it. I came hard, grinding into the grungy couch cushions and biting my forearm so as not to make any noise. Not like Darcy and Kit would have heard me, they were so loud themselves. Blushing like crazy, I rolled quietly off the sofa, did up my pants, grabbed my backpack, and sneaked out the front door. As I was leaving, I heard Kit scream out, "I'm coming, Daddy, I'm coming!" and my pussy clenched in sympathy as I ran down the stairs and out onto the busy street.

Later that evening, Patrick and the rest of the crowd found me where I was sitting at the Town Diner. I was drinking coffee and trying to write in my journal without much success. I didn't even know what to put. I felt like the biggest Peeping Tom pervert of the universe, but I was still turned on. I didn't know what to do with myself.

Patrick scolded me for leaving them earlier and then started telling me some long story about how the owner of the sex store had thought they were trying to steal something and it was so funny and ridiculous, blah, blah, blah. I was barely listening. Everyone tried to convince me to ride over to the quarry to go skinny dipping, even though it was kind of chilly, but I wouldn't. My bike was still at Darcy's, and anyway, the last thing I wanted was to be naked in public. I decided to go home. When I got there, Mom was waiting for me and I let her hug me and fuss over me and make me hot milk and go on at me about what kind of clothes I was going to need for college. It was annoying, but when I looked at her, so concerned and worried and loving me, I forgave her, and just sat there, nodding and agreeing with everything she said.

Domme's Games
Rachel Kramer Bussel

When Dana told me she was a dominatrix, I almost spit out my rum and coke. We were on a first date at a classy French restaurant, both of us dressed in elegant outfits. She had on a sheer white blouse, black velvet pants and heels; I wore a low-cut white shirt, a deep-purple silk skirt and CFMPs. We'd been set up by my friend Eliza, who figured that femmes looking for other femmes were so rare, we'd surely hit it off, but Eliza had told me Dana was a trainer at a local high-end gym.

"Well, I am a trainer, in addition to being a domme, and the two jobs are kind of similar—I get to yell at people and watch them squirm. It's a total power trip, and I get off on both of them. But my real passion is women; with the guys, it's like a warm-up," she said, her dark eyes glinting. She was gorgeous but had a dangerous vibe, not like she might hurt me, but like she knew things about me and could see inside me in ways even my longtime friends couldn't. It didn't seem like an act, either, the way she gazed at me so intently, like we were the only two people in the whole city, let alone the whole restaurant. I felt my face flush and my body twitch slightly as I waited for her to continue. Her hand reached under the table, stroking my bare knee beneath my skirt. The delicious warmth of her fingers traveled up my leg. She massaged just my knee, but with such intensity I could barely breathe. "Do you like to be dominated, Julie?"

"I don't know," I answered, only semi-honestly. Nobody had ever actually so much as laid a hand on me or spoken in a harsh voice in bed . . . except in my head. In my fantasy, I'd been naked in a room full of powerful women, crawling around as ordered, bending over so they could spank me and spread my ass cheeks and order me to do all kinds of depraved acts that made me blush there at the table just thinking about them. In my head, I'd taken a fist in my cunt and a butt plug in my ass, all at the same time. I'd been shared by two women, tossed between them like a rag doll, "made" to have orgasm after orgasm while clamps set off heat waves in my nipples. But fantasy and reality were very different creatures. They were about to meet, and I wasn't totally sure how I felt about that.

Dana's grip tightened, then she pinched my inner thigh before replacing her fingers with the sole of her foot. She'd slipped it out of her shoe and was pressing her foot flush against my pussy, with none of our fellow diners any the wiser.

"Really? You have no idea how you'd feel about being stripped down, tied up and told exactly what you could and couldn't do?" She smiled at me, a victorious grin, her lushly painted lips curling up at the sides. "Open your mouth," she said, the sensual tone gone in favor of a clipped, brisk command, made even more imperious by her faintly British accent. She'd been living in the States since she was a teenager, and had actually lived in more of them than I had, both of us winding up in New York in the last year or so. My lips parted slightly, just enough to make me feel the breath emerging from them slowly seep out . . . and allow her fingers to slip inside.

They were short, with nails polished a gleaming bright red that had glinted in the restaurant lighting, teasing me with its brightness, and I felt their shiny surface against my tongue as she turned her fingers this way and that. She curled them against my teeth, claiming me in the process. My nipples hardened as I felt her possess me, fantasy giving way to an even hotter reality than I could ever have imagined. I gave myself over to her in those moments as my tongue melted against her. I wanted to do anything she wanted me to—pleasing her was suddenly all that mattered.

"For the rest of the night, you're not going to talk unless I tell you to. You will follow my orders and you will not protest. I'm going to show you what a real dirty girl you are and you're going to love it, I can just tell," Dana said, pulling her wet fingers from my mouth. I missed them the moment they were gone, but they soon found their way to my lips, toying with my fat bottom one as I wet my panties with pussy juice. I had no sooner thought about the state of my underwear when Dana said, "Give me your panties, Julie." She sensed my question before I could utter it. "No, not in the bathroom, right here, and hurry up about it."

Before I could stop to think or worry or look around, I was discreetly slipping my hands down below and pulling them off, trying to pass them off to her under the table.

"No," she said, her voice short, clipped, and efficient. "Roll them into a ball and pass them to me across the table, like you were giving me your napkin."

My cheeks felt on fire, and I started to wonder if this was a very good idea. It was fun, and totally hot, but what if we somehow got caught? I'd be mortified if anyone else at the restaurant knew that I had instantly become Dana's slave, that I would've practically walked around the restaurant naked if she told me to. Blushing furiously, I attempted to ball the black lace into my palm and pass it off to her between our plates. As our fingers met, though, she made sure my flimsy underwear shook loose from our grasp. The black lace was gone in an instant, but I grabbed my water glass and drained it in a futile attempt to quell my beating heart and flushed face. I couldn't bear to look around to see if anyone had caught on.

I stared at my plate, knowing I'd never be able to finish what was on it. I wasn't queasy, but I craved something more than food. I looked up at her, expecting us to exit quickly, so she could continue to order me around. Would she make me bend over and get spanked? Wear certain kinds of embarrassing clothes? Order me to masturbate? My mind swirled with naughty possibilities, but Dana managed to flip me around without us ever leaving the table.

"Eat up, Julie. You won't get any dessert if you don't finish your dinner . . . and I know you want your dessert. It's your favorite," she said, transforming into Mean Mommy before my eyes.

Her tone was gentle but had an undercurrent of force, like if I didn't do as she said she'd walk up behind me and shove my face into the plate—and make me like it. I still wasn't hungry, but with a shaky hand I picked up my fork. Each bite, no matter what was on the end of the tines, tasted like sex. That's the only way I can describe it; the food melted on my tongue and seemed to plunge me into another world. I ate each bite while staring back at her, knowing my cheeks were red, and feeling my pussy getting wetter and wetter.

"Very good," she said, leaning across the table to pat my head. The gesture was so completely condescending, clearly designed to put me in my place, even though we were the same age, that just as I was about to get indignant, I realized I was still soaking wet. As in, I wasn't sure I'd be able to stand up without it being obvious. Dana must have sensed something was amiss because she smiled at me sweetly.

"Julie, would you be a dear and get up and go ask the waiter for some decaf?"

I was amazed at how her requests and commands, though seemingly nonsexual in nature, were making me feel like I was going to come right then and there, like she had some invisible pointer aimed at my pussy and was ready to shove it inside me. I could feel my skirt sticking to my body, but hoped my arousal wasn't too visible. I was trembling when I found the waiter, feebly tapping him on the shoulder, then haltingly getting out my request. In less than an hour, Dana had transformed me from my usual assured self into a simpering nitwit, but I didn't mind. I wanted to see what was going to happen next.

"Thank you, Julie. You follow orders very well," she said, giving me an appraising look. "What if I ordered you to get down on the ground next to me and put your head in my lap? Would you do it?" she asked, gazing at me intently.

I stared back at her, wondering for a moment what I'd gotten myself into. Could I really do it? Should I? I had no one to ask, no lifelines to call, but I followed the source of all my biggest dating decisions: my pussy. It was telling me to do it, diners be damned, so I slid gracefully to the floor and rested my head against her silken thigh, doing my best to arrange my skirt around me so not too much skin showed. She sipped her coffee while looking down at me with a now-wicked grin as she entwined her fingers in my long, sleek brown hair and gave short, subtle tugs. I gasped, then shut my mouth, not wanting to call even more attention to us.

Dana calmly finished her coffee, then loudly flagged down the waiter, calling out and even snapping her fingers. The spectacle unnerved and aroused me simultaneously. I could tell people were starting to wonder what was going on, but Dana calmly kept a firm grip on my hair, sending sparks of arousal straight down to my cunt. When the waiter walked away, she leaned down, her lips brushing my ear and said, "Are you ready for me to fuck you yet, Julie?" Then she tugged hard on my hair, making me gasp loudly. She let go immediately, and I stared up at her in awe. "What are you waiting for? Get up, we're leaving!" she barked, her tone morphing from seductive to stern in seconds, her voice certainly loud enough for others to hear.

I popped up, grabbed my coat, and was ready to go. By then, my skirt was really glued to the back of my thighs, thanks to my cunt, sticky with need. Dana pushed me ahead of her as she steered me toward her car. "We'll leave yours here," she said, and by then, there was no arguing with her. I'd do whatever it took to get her to fuck me. As it turned out, that didn't technically happen, but I'm getting ahead of myself.

She drove, keeping one hand on the wheel and one hand on me the whole time. I was so turned on I was tempted to fidget, but I made myself sit still. She made conversation even as her fingers crept up my leg, but when I tried to clamp them together and trap her hand next to my pussy, she immediately pulled it away, making a tsking noise.

"If you try to get me to touch you, I won't. Wait your turn, little girl," she said. And it was those two words—little girl—that really set me off. I waited, seething not with anger but with pure, raw lust. We got to her place but she didn't let me out of the car. "I think I want you right here," she said, her voice trailing off as she got a vision in her mind. "Strip!"

This was something else entirely. Her street was fairly deserted, but still. "I don't think I can," I said, my voice trembling, not with fear but with the underlying knowledge that I was really getting off on her orders.

She reached between my legs to fondle my wet pussy, pressing her fingers against my sex. "Oh, really? It seems like maybe you protest too much, my dear."

I knew she was right even as I shuddered half in horror, half in pleasure. But still, I began to take off my few items of clothing, starting with my shoes, then lifting my blouse over my head and wriggling out of my skirt, while heat suffused my entire body. I pretended I really had no choice, even though I knew Dana well enough to know she'd respect my wishes should I politely request we go inside. I also knew I could "blame" her if anything went awry.

I settled down wearing just my bra, having already given her my panties, then turned to Dana expectantly, but she looked like I'd bundled up instead of stripping down. She cleared her throat, the noise loud in the confines of the car. "The rest . . ." she demanded impatiently, and I squirmed as I unhooked my bra, freeing my large breasts with their already hard nipples.

"Now I want you to come for me," she said, her voice gentle and seductive. "And I'm even going to help you." With that, she reached into the glove compartment and pulled out a pocket rocket vibrator.

By then, I was too far gone to protest anything she wanted me to try; I'd have pressed my breasts up against the windows for passersby to ogle, I was *that* horny. This request was more intimate, though—and more arousing. Performing for Dana's eyes alone gave a new nuance to my exhibitionism. Instead of worrying what anyone else thought about what I was doing, I simply wanted to please her with my pussy. I turned on the vibe, which had a much lower intensity than what I'm used to, but I was so turned on, it didn't matter. I leaned back against the window, spreading my legs as best I could so she could see exactly how aroused she'd made me, then went to town. Whenever I had the urge to close my eyes, I reminded myself that not only was I displaying myself for her, but I could watch Dana as well, enjoying the pleasure of her watching me in my wanton state. Soon I was moaning, soaking her car seat as I shoved three fingers into my pussy while the vibe hummed against my clit, my hips rocking back and forth.

I let the shudders subside as I turned off the toy and looked up at her, suddenly embarrassed. We barely knew each other but she'd managed to strip me, in more ways than one, removing any armor I might have been wearing to expose the girl who just wants to be told what to do.

"Come here," she said, pulling my head into her lap and stroking my hair.

I was naked, but I wasn't cold or embarrassed as she held me in her tight embrace. She stroked my head, her fingers dancing along my scalp until I felt that heat inside me begin to rise once again. Whereas normally I'd have been quick to let my lover know that I was ready to go again, this time I just nestled deeper into Dana's lap.

She'd let me know when it was time for sex, and I had no doubt it'd be explosive when she did.

That Was Then, This Is Now
Jean Rosestar

Friday, 9 April 1976
Fort Devens, Massachusetts

What does someone wear to a gay bar? I looked inside the army-issue metal locker that served as my closet. I had no idea. I'm straight, but agreed to go out with two friends, Pam and Donna, who may or may not be on their first date.

I put on my favorite bright red sweater over a pair of blue jeans. My light blond hair hung just past my shoulders with bangs that barely managed to stay out of my eyes. I added a bit of makeup. *This is as good as it gets.* I shrugged at my reflection. Sighing, I closed my locker just as Pam and Donna arrived at the door to my barracks room.

"You guys look good," I said, opening the door to let them in. Donna had on blue jeans and a striped turtleneck sweater, whereas Pam, also in blue jeans, wore a starched white cotton shirt. Pam showed me the tie hidden in her pocket, which she planned to put on once we got to the bar. She could not wear it on post for fear of exposure.

"Leave your military ID here," Pam said. "Bring just your driver's license."

"Why?" We were always supposed to have our military ID with us, even though we didn't need it to get back on post. Fort Devens was an open army post, with no guards or gated entrances.

"Sometimes the MPs come to the bar and check IDs. You don't want them to see yours."

"Can they do that?" It didn't sound right.

"I don't know if it's legal, but they do," Pam said.

"Being at a gay bar doesn't mean you're gay."

"Right, but the bar is on the official list of off-limits places. You get in trouble for just being there. Are you sure you still want to go?"

"Yes." I removed my ID from my wallet and put it in a drawer. Safely stripped of my military identity, I followed them out the door.

As we stood outside the parked car, Donna helped Pam get her tie in place. The building had no special markings or lights to indicate there was even a bar inside. It was well off the main road, and the isolation gave patrons a sense of privacy.

Once inside, it took my eyes a few moments to adjust. For a gay bar, it looked a lot like most other nightclubs: dark, loud and smoky. Dim neon lights illuminated the bar, tables and a small dance floor. The only difference was, there were no men.

Pam led us to a table where several women, most of whom were friends from the barracks, were already seated. They knew I was straight, so I'm sure they were surprised to see me. There were still a few empty chairs at the table. Pam pulled out a chair to her right for Donna. She turned to pull out my chair, but I had already seated myself. Realizing my error, I shrugged and mouthed "sorry" to her.

"Do you want me to get you a drink?" Pam asked me.

"Bourbon and coke," I said. Getting a ten dollar bill from my purse, I handed it to her. She took the money and walked over to the bar.

I looked around to see if I could spot anyone else I knew. Linda and Karen sat at a table to my right. They were nurses at the army hospital where we all worked. Both were E-5 sergeants, so I guessed them to be about twenty-five or twenty-six, a couple of years older than the rest of us. My heart skipped a beat when I saw the other woman sitting with them. I had noticed her at the hospital, but didn't know her name. In fact, I often looked for her. I didn't know why, but she fascinated me.

Tonight she was obviously out of uniform. She sat with her long, blue-jean clad legs stretched out before her. Her short, dark brown hair was in its usual comb-backed style. Oh yes, she fascinated me. As if feeling my gaze, she turned to look at me.

Even in the dark, I could feel her predatory eyes check me out. I was used to that look, having often encountered it in straight bars. When men looked at me like that, I felt dirty. This time, however, I felt an unexpected electric current surge through me. Embarrassed, I looked away. But I couldn't help my pleased smile, nor the feeling of warmth that flowed through me.

The evening progressed, and it was obvious things were going smoothly for Pam and Donna. I soon started feeling like a third wheel. To entertain myself, I searched the dance floor for my mystery woman. She moved with a sensual rhythm and grace. I couldn't take my eyes off of her. Slow dances made my pulse race. Observing her, I imagined our bodies rubbing together, her thigh pressing between mine. The unfamiliar longing left me confused, yet I couldn't stop thinking about it. Faster songs allowed me the pleasure of seeing her body move to the music. An unexpected twinge of jealousy swept over me whenever she danced twice with the same woman.

I felt the music tempo shift as the fast-paced "Don't Go Breaking My Heart" gave way to the slower "All By Myself." Someone's joke diverted me from watching the dance floor. A tap on my shoulder jerked me to attention. I turned to find myself looking up at the woman I had been perusing all evening. Trying to keep a blank face, I felt my heart throb in my throat.

"Would you like to dance?" She held out her hand.

"Sure," I replied with a calm I didn't feel. I took her hand, allowing her to lead me to the dance floor. I tried to maintain an air of casual indifference, a difficult endeavor because my insides had turned to mush.

"You haven't danced with any of your friends," she said. "I was worried that you don't like to dance."

"Oh, I love to dance, but they all know I'm straight."

"You are?" She looked surprised.

"Yes," I answered. *I think so*, my mind continued.

"Then why have you been spying on me all night?" she asked with a grin. I hated the confidence in her tone, because we both knew it was true.

"Have I?" Answering with a question is good.

She pulled me tighter. "Mm-huh. You have." My body flushed with heat as I wished her leg would move between mine. *What's happening to me?*

"I don't know," I said, answering both her and the voice in my head.

"I'm honored." The predatory gleam left her eyes, and she smiled. Something about her smile was more powerful than the predatory look. My heart skipped in panic. I suddenly realized how much I wanted her. I've never wanted anyone. *My God! What am I doing?*

We continued to dance in silence. *You idiot! Think of something to say. If you don't say something, she'll never want to dance with you again. I want her to dance with me again, to hold me close, to touch me, to kiss me. I want her hands to roam my body.* Admitting it was difficult, but I knew it was the truth.

Silence made seconds seem like minutes. "I'm sorry," I said, pulling away. "I didn't mean . . . I mean . . ." I rolled my eyes. "Okay, I'm a complete moron."

She laughed and pulled me back to her. "It's okay. I'm often a complete moron myself."

"No. Not you." I looked at her and shook my head, laughing.

"Yes, me."

"Okay, maybe we could start over. I'm Sally Joyner, it's nice to meet you." I looked into her eyes.

"I'm Cheryl Taylor, but everyone calls me Taylor. It's very nice to meet you," she said, grinning.

The rest of the evening went by faster than I wanted. Taylor and I danced several more times. After each dance, she returned me to my table and rejoined her friends. When she danced with someone else, my heart sank.

It was getting late, so Donna and Pam decided it was time to go back to the barracks. I reached down to pick up my purse. When I turned back, I was surprised to see Taylor standing next to me.

"Are you leaving?" Though she looked at the three of us, I knew she was talking to me.

"Yeah, they're ready to go and I came with them." I wished I hadn't.

"I can give you a ride back to the barracks, if you want," Taylor said.

I hesitated. I didn't know her, but I wasn't ready to leave yet.

"I'm safe," she said. "My friends will vouch for me." She nodded toward Karen and Linda.

"Are you sure?"

"Sure that I'm safe, or sure about giving you a ride?" The predatory gleam sneaked back into her eyes for a second.

"I'm sure," I said with a sudden conviction. She graced me with a devastating smile. *What? Are you crazy?* I blocked out my inner voice.

"Sally, are you sure?" Pam's expression matched my internal voice. I assured Pam that I would be all right. Pam gave Taylor a warning look before leaving with Donna. Taylor led me to the table she shared with Linda and Karen.

Almost immediately, she took me back to the dance floor. Her soft breasts pressed against me, making my head swirl. My hands itched to feel them. She moved her leg between mine and I wanted to grind myself on her thigh. Just that contact instantly made my clit throb with need. *Behave*, I promised my body, *and I'll take care of you later*. I'd never felt this kind of desire for anyone before tonight.

Taylor pulled back, causing me to lift my head. *Did I do something wrong? Oh god! Tell me I didn't hump her leg.*

"I really want to kiss you," she said. It was almost a whisper. I wasn't sure I'd heard correctly, or even if I'd heard anything at all. My heart heard, or maybe it was my libido.

Whichever one heard, my lips answered. "Yes," I said.

Tenderly, I felt her soft mouth pressing against mine. I surrendered myself to her. I could no longer resist pressing against her leg. Our tongues danced in unison with the music. A moan escaped from between us. I felt the wetness flow between my legs. Had I really moaned? *Please don't let it have been me.* Her glazed eyes told me it could have been either of us.

"Would you like to go to my apartment?" she asked.

Unsure if I could speak, I nodded. *What am I doing? I'm not gay.* I was terrified. I was excited. When she reached out to hold my hand, my world tumbled, yet everything felt right.

"This is it. What there is of it, anyway," Taylor said as she opened the door and we entered her apartment. It was small and simple, almost Spartan, and furnished with inexpensive furniture that appeared to be several years old.

"Not big on decorating, are you?"

"Most of my stuff is still en route from Korea. You know the army—they put it on the slowest boat they can find," Taylor said. "This place was cheap, and it came furnished. Can I get you something to drink?" She looked inside the refrigerator. "Let's see . . . I've got milk, Pepsi or beer."

"Pepsi is fine." I hoped she didn't hear the nervousness in my voice.

She handed me a can and set another on the nearby kitchen table. I took a quick sip, trying to calm myself. In her kitchen, under the stark lighting, I realized what was about to happen.

Taylor reached out to take the soda from me and, with her other hand, she pulled me to her. Setting the soda on the table, she pushed my hair away from my face. "It'll be okay." Her words calmed me. She pulled me close and wrapped her arms around me. "We won't do anything you don't want."

My eyes closed when I felt her breath on my throat. I trembled as her tongue left a trail of wetness from my neck to my jaw. Her hand came up to hold the other side of my face. I opened my eyes to find hers questioning. Mine answered, *Yes.* Taylor broke off the kiss and stepped back. Taking my hand, she led me toward the bedroom. I followed, my desire overpowering what little was left of my earlier panic. I had no more doubts.

Like the rest of the apartment, her bedroom was barely furnished. My gaze was drawn to the double bed. It was next to the wall, a nightstand beside it. Leading me to the bed, Taylor used both hands to push the hair away from my face. Her eyes, concerned, looked deep into mine. "Sally, are you sure?"

"Yes." Suddenly sure, I pulled her close, opening my mouth to kiss her. Our tongues met as our bodies pressed together, my hands exploring her back and roaming over her muscular shoulders. As if I'd been doing this forever, I reached down to squeeze her tight ass. At the same time, I could feel the heat of her hands exploring me.

Our kisses deepened. My body was being overloaded with sensations. The smell, warmth and feel of her overwhelmed me. Her hands moved under my sweater to caress my breasts through my bra before she reached behind me and unclasped it. I gasped at the smooth warmth of her hands as she massaged my naked breasts, moving her thumbs over the peaks of my nipples, already erect with desire. When she used her thumb and forefinger to tweak them, I almost came. Pulling off my sweater, Taylor moaned and bent forward to suck one of my nipples.

The hot, wet heat of her tongue sent a fire through me. I could feel liquid seep from deep inside, soaking my panties. Her tongue and teeth pleasurably tortured one nipple as her hand played with the other. I groaned, feeling like my insides were melting.

With her mouth and one hand playing with my breasts, her other hand went for the zipper of my jeans. Automatically, I spread my legs to give her access. God, how I needed her. She caressed me through my jeans, making my clit throb almost painfully.

As her hand continued to caress me, I nibbled her neck and played with the rippling muscles across her back. Emboldened by her answering moan, I moved my hands to cup the round smoothness of her breasts. Feeling her nipples rise and harden through her thin bra, I began unbuttoning her shirt.

"Just a minute." Taylor stopped and stepped away from me.

My heart leapt in fear. *Did I do something wrong? Was I not supposed to touch her, too? Please don't let that be true.*

Smiling, she quickly removed her clothes, while I did the same. We fell naked to the bed, with her on top of me. I put my leg between hers, moaning with pleasure as I felt her wetness on my skin. Feeling my own flow begin, I ground against her thigh. Our slick bodies slid together while we kissed and she continued to play with my breasts. I reached between us to caress her full breasts. Loving her hardened nipples, I teased and tugged on them. I ached to taste them, to suck them, but I had to wait.

Taylor moved to suck my nipples. My hands roamed across her back and shoulders. Almost painfully slow, her hand meandered down the outside of my leg. I opened my legs as wide as possible. Her hand moved down to my knee before it began its trek back up the inside of my thigh. We moaned in unison when her fingers reached the apex between my legs. Teasing me, she brushed through the top of my hair. Arching, I quietly pleaded for her to touch me, then jumped when her fingers briefly stroked my clit.

"Oh yes, please." I begged.

Chuckling softly, Taylor ignored me as she moved below my clit to my hot, wet opening, letting her finger circle around before sliding inside. My hips rose to meet her hand. Then a second finger entered me, making me moan again. Her thumb circled my throbbing clit, leaving me groaning in frustration. She moved her fingers in and out, and when her thumb finally slid over the top of my clit, my body trembled.

"You like that," she whispered.

"Oh yes."

Taylor edged down my body until she hovered just above me. Blowing lightly on my pubic hair, she stopped her hand. Her thumb moved away from my clit, her fingers still inside me. Squirming in frustration, I clutched at her hair, willing her to do more. I gasped when I realized what she was going to do.

With her free hand, she separated my labia. I could feel her breath hot against my clit. My body arched to meet her. Her fingers resumed filling me. Her tongue flicked lightly over my clit. Hoping to encourage her to ease my torment, I bent my knees and reached down to hold myself open for her.

The hot, moist heat of her mouth engulfed me. Her tongue swirled along the sides of my clit as her fingers increased their speed. I lost control. My hips bucked furiously, her fingers matching my pace. When she sucked my clit, my world exploded. Darkness, brightness . . . I was floating, I was falling. I was consumed.

"Oh, Taylor," I cried out.

Slowly, I returned to the real world. A warm, comfortable glow surrounded me, us. I looked down to see her smiling with a Cheshire grin. As she moved up along side me, I felt the wetness of her on my leg. Kissing her, I tasted myself.

Feeling her wetness anew caused a new wave of desire in me. I wanted her. I needed to feel her, to touch her, to taste her, just as she had with me. Pushing her onto her back, I climbed on top with my leg between hers.

"You don't have to do this, Sally," she said.

"I want to." I looked in her eyes for permission. I didn't know how this was supposed to work. "Please?" Her answer was to pull me down for another deep kiss.

I knew from years of self-experience what I liked and what she had done to me was still fresh in my mind. I pulled myself up so I could use both hands to explore and massage her breasts. My leg pressed into her wet, hot center. Cautiously, I lowered my head to one breast while my hand played with the other. Moaning, I first licked her nipple, then sucked it. She whimpered. I released it. My tongue circled the rippled bumps of her areola before I took her other nipple into my mouth and sucked hard. As she began to squirm beneath me, I moved my hand down to explore between her legs. Moving my fingers through her hair and into her wet folds, I slowly edged my fingers toward where I knew she wanted me. Taylor moaned and lifted her hips, letting her legs fall open to allow me access.

"Yes, that's it," Taylor said.

I inhaled her sweet aroma, finding her as wet as I had been. I could feel my own wetness flow again. Both of us moaning, I continued to explore her as I ground my pussy against her leg. My fingers circled her clit. She pressed up to meet my hand, but I continued circling without touching the swollen peak. I positioned myself so my clit rested against her leg, feeling a fresh jolt as we made contact. My left hand took over circling her clit. Occasionally, I let my fingers cross over the top of it, barely caressing its peak. My right hand moved to her hot, soaked opening. She clenched the finger I slipped inside her and thrust her hips upward, pushing my finger deeper. I continued to tease her clit as I added a second finger, moving to her rhythm. I followed her lead and matched her tempo.

Increasing the pressure around her clit, I plunged deeper and deeper inside her. I could feel her clench and unclench around my fingers. I ground against her leg, keeping time with my hands. I sensed her urgency as she began her climax.

"Please, Sally, don't stop."

Her hands grasped my shoulders. The muscles inside her contracted around my fingers. I continued moving in and out, and began rubbing directly on her clit. Her body trembled with her orgasm, as mine did as I came against her leg. We both cried out, saying each other's names, before collapsing together.

I relaxed against her, my head on her chest. I could hear her rapid heartbeat, and knew my own must be just as fast. Taylor pushed her legs tightly together, trapping my hand between them. Her hands on my back gently caressed me. I shivered with pleasure.

As we lay entwined and our passion abated, she relaxed her legs. Slowly, I removed my hand and then propped myself up so we were face to face. Worried, I looked into her eyes.

"Was that okay?" I asked.

"Oh yeah," she replied with a smile. "Definitely okay." She pulled me close and wrapped her arms around me. In comfortable silence, we rested in each other's embrace.

As I lay wrapped in her arms, the realization of what just happened hit me. *I just made love with a woman. I should feel strange, but it was wonderful, natural. Am I a lesbian or is it just because it was Taylor? What happens now?* I couldn't stop the grin from spreading across my face. *I'll worry about that tomorrow. Tonight I'm just going to enjoy this feeling.*

After a while, the coolness of the room reminded us it was spring. We got under the blankets. Snuggled together, we fit perfectly in the cocoon Taylor made around us.

Sunday, 9 April 2006
Boston, Massachusetts

As I walk down the church aisle, past friends and family, all I can focus on is the woman waiting for me at the altar. Handsome in her tux, her dark brown hair streaked with gray, she is the woman I love. I thank whatever powers made me go to that secret lesbian bar thirty years ago. Times have changed. In the past, we had to keep our love secret and hidden. On this spring day, Taylor and I formally and legally proclaim our love in front of our families and friends.

Act I
KI Thompson

I rushed to my seat just as the houselights dimmed, arriving in time to give my eyes a chance to adjust in the darkened theatre. The tuning of the orchestra began to subside and a hush fell over the audience as the anticipated opening night performance got underway. Sitting in the box seat stage left, I hastily retrieved my opera glasses from the balcony's rail and scanned the stage right box directly across from me. I was not disappointed. She was there, but unlike other occasions, this time she was alone.

I've had season tickets to the San Francisco Opera for nearly twenty years, but it was only this season that a newcomer to that box had appeared, always wearing black and always sitting opposite me. Her hair was usually swept up in an elegant French twist, and jewels often glittered at her throat. She was, in a word, breathless. During intermissions I would seek her out in the lobby and watch as heads turned when she passed by. She never seemed to take notice of anyone other than her female escort, and even then seemingly with dispassionate interest. She had a cool, remote air about her that served to both attract and repel her admirers. I found it challenging, drawing me to her like a moth to a flame. Once, I was certain she caught me staring. Our eyes locked for a brief instant and I felt the flame ignite, only to have her turn away seemingly indifferent to my notice. I tried in that moment to convey my desire for her, but was unsure the fleeting glimpse communicated anything meaningful.

My attention was drawn back to the Kabuki-like figures parading onstage and the entrance of Madam Butterfly. I have attended several Puccini operas over the years, but this one was my favorite, even though it makes me cry every time. Mirrored in Butterfly's face and lyrics are my own tragic relationships, my last one almost as devastating. Evidently, however, I am more resilient than she, because I feel myself emerging from my chrysalis whenever I glance at the woman in black.

The first act was a struggle for me. I have waited to see this particular soprano for years, but even her magnificent voice cannot hold my concentration long. At one point I sensed I was being observed, but when I looked across to the other box, the object of my desire seemed absorbed in the production. So while her attention was elsewhere, I gazed longingly at her exposed shoulders and the plunging neckline of her gown. The diamond choker at her throat flashed when she moved, reflecting star-like patterns across the swell of her breasts. I wondered what it would feel like to trace that pattern with my tongue, following its journey to where it disappeared beneath the fabric of her dress.

Drawing my eyes upward from their lascivious perusal of her décolletage, I was immobilized by the penetrating stare she had fixed on me. Unable to move or avert my eyes, I watched as she raised a finger to sensuously outline her moist, red lips. My breathing stopped when she inserted the finger into her mouth, and even from this distance I could see she was sucking on it. She leisurely removed it and began a slow, deliberate path down her cleavage, leaving a damp trail that glistened in the reflection of the stage lights.

The opera, all but forgotten, continued on, but I was immersed in the music being played by the woman in black. I could no longer see her hand as it continued on its way below my line of sight, but soon her head tilted back slightly and her eyelids became heavily hooded, barely able to keep contact with mine. Her arm moved slightly, and I realized she was touching herself where I most wanted to be and my clit reacted in sympathy. With her every motion, I imagined it was me touching her, my fingers separating her lips to expose her swollen clit, and my mouth enclosing it, drawing it inward and feeling its rigid softness. I crossed my legs in exquisite agony, curling my toes under as I clenched my thighs together.

It was excruciating for me to sit still, and I began to squirm from the ache that was developing between my legs. Finally, when I could stand it no longer, the voyeur within demanded closer scrutiny, and I rose from my seat and exited into the hallway. Walking rapidly from one end to the other in an attempt to relieve my distress, it dawned on me that I could see her better if I were closer, so I headed down the stairs, crossed the lobby and went up the stairs on the other side to arrive at the rear of her box. I peered through the curtains and observed her from behind, the urge to walk in and lick the back of her bare neck almost overwhelming, and I had to physically restrain myself.

"Excuse me ma'am, but you'll have to return to your own seat," a voice behind me whispered audibly.

I swung around to see an usher urging me away, and then, sensing a presence behind me, I slowly turned back and came face-to-face with the woman in black.

"It's all right," she whispered to the usher, "she's with me."

Taking me by the hand, she led me to the vacant chair next to hers. My pulse was racing and my heart was pounding with such ferocity that I thought she would be able to hear it, but after a moment we casually resumed viewing the singers onstage until I could no longer resist the temptation. Using the age-old and not too subtle ploy of stretching my arm, I encircled her back, allowing my hand to rest lightly on her shoulder. Since she didn't seem to object, I rubbed my thumb against her skin, confirming its silky softness, and I leaned into her, feeling the warmth amplified between us. Immediately her hand found the cuff of my pant leg, and she slipped it up my calf, stroking me with the tips of her fingers. The dull ache inside me rapidly increased to a sharp pain, and I wished she would reach farther up my leg. Taking a quick look to ensure privacy, I drew the side curtains just enough to block the view from the box seats next to ours.

While one hand caressed her neck, I reached across with my other and slipped it under the hem of her dress so I could fondle her right leg. Reaching her thigh, I dissolved in ecstasy when I discovered the garter holding up the lace top of her stockings. Going higher still, I was overjoyed to discover there was nothing to obstruct my access to her very hot and deliciously drenched center. My fingers found their way into the slippery folds, tracing the outer lips with a delicate massage, and although her focus was onstage, she reacted by slowly writhing under my touch.

"Mmm, yes," she hissed, "put your fingers inside me."

With that pronouncement, she spread her legs more accommodatingly and I eagerly complied, effortlessly gliding into the welcoming heat. Her attention never left the stage, as though nothing out of the ordinary was happening between us, and I marveled at her self-control. The only betrayal of feeling was physical when her muscles contracted fiercely, drawing me in deeper until I perceived she needed more than what I had offered. Withdrawing my index finger, she gasped noticeably until I quickly inserted two fingers. She sighed and her eyelids fluttered as she struggled to keep them open. Leisurely, I slid in and out of her and then, with each thrust, gradually increased the pace. Her breathing became shallow and rapid as she braced herself against the back of the chair. I knew it was just a matter of time.

Suddenly conscious of the melody, I glanced up quickly and noted that Cio-Cio-San and Pinkerton were getting married, signaling the end of the first act. I intensified my efforts, not wanting the houselights to interrupt her concentration. Then out of nowhere, she found my fly and unexpectedly unzipped me, reaching in to find me soaked. I was wearing boxers open at the crotch and she snuck her hand in, cupped me and then expertly thumbed my clit. I nearly collapsed forward at the sensation, but I managed to hang on, not even disrupting the rhythm of my own stroking. In fact, I found us both plunging in and out of one another in tempo with the soaring music as the couple onstage sang of their love in a moonlit garden.

"Oh God, keep doing that and I'll come," she panted as the chair she was sitting in rocked slightly. I could not help but smile knowing I was finally getting through that layer of ice, and the thought made me melt.

"Don't worry, I'm not going to stop. Come on baby, let it go."

I was on the edge myself as her thumb had found just the right cadence that really gets me off and that heavy weight that infuses me right before orgasm began to permeate every recess of my body. I couldn't hold on much longer, but I also didn't want to upset the delicate balance I'd attained with her body, so I held back and applied more speed and pressure.

"Yes, that's it, that's it, yes, please, a little faster." An intake of breath, and then, "Ahhh . . . I'm . . . coming—"

Her body jerked convulsively, followed quickly by several tremors that caused her to shudder back. If music could be seen as well as heard, her body would have been a sublime crescendo—all instruments building to a furious zenith and then spilling over gently into the soft soothing sounds of the violins. It would take one of the great Russian composers of old to express the majesty of her climax.

Knowing I have been left on the edge, she somehow managed to bring her thumb down hard on my clit, then stroked and teased me until I felt my insides clench with anticipation. Tugging relentlessly, the rush was exquisite and I tumbled into oblivion, collapsing against the armrests of my chair. I lay helpless, waiting for my breathing to return to normal and for the hum of my body to dissipate. Utterly spent, I felt like a marionette whose strings have been yanked hard, only to have them cut, leaving me limp and useless.

The sudden burst of applause and shouts of "Bravo!" startled me out of my languorous state until I realized it was the first act of the opera they were cheering. Sheepishly, I withdrew my fingers from inside her, and she gave a slight grunt as they popped out. I fumbled to close my zipper while she reached down for her pocketbook and retrieved a tube of lipstick. I watched fascinated as she touched up her lips. After smoothing her gown with her hands and tucking an errant strand of hair behind her ear, she took my hand and we left our box.

In the lobby I acquired two glasses of champagne at the bar and we stepped outside into the unusually warm evening. Sipping gratefully at the chilled liquid, I let it flow over my tongue, allowing it and the evening air to cool me off, and I began to feel refreshed as well as sated. We drank in companionable silence, occasionally stealing furtive glances at one another, smiling intimately whenever we made eye contact. When the interior lights began to flash, I downed the rest of the contents of my glass and turned to lead her back inside.

"Well," she inquired, pausing to slip her arm in mine, "are you ready for act two?"

The Watcher
Marie Alexander

I felt like I was in a scary movie as I walked down the block to my building, key in hand, the fallen autumn leaves scurrying across the sidewalk and rustling in the gutters. The wind blew a plastic bag across the lawn on my right, and the streetlights flooded the street sepia. *If this was an episode of CSI, I'd totally be about to bite it*, I thought as I walked faster, my heels echoing loudly on the sidewalk. People who said that this city never slept had never been on this street after ten. I could hear the cabs speeding along the avenue behind me, and I could faintly detect the thrum of the city in the background, but my block was deserted and the only other person I could see was my doorman. Even he was resting his head against the door frame, his eyes halfway closed.

He snapped to attention when I finally reached the door.

"Good evening, Miss Winters," he murmured as I stepped past him into the lobby. With one white-gloved hand, he gestured to the marble counter that stood in front of the row of locked mailboxes. "There is a message for you."

"Oh, thank you, Benjamin."

"Of course, Madame." He turned his attention back to the street, his posture now straight and alert.

I saw on the counter a cream-colored envelope with my name swirled across the front in a familiar, elegant handwriting. I picked it up and pressed the Up button for the elevator, then carefully popped open the envelope. Inside was a single page of matching stationery, folded in half. A chill of excitement ran up my spine as I unfolded the sheet and read, 58th Street, through Simone's and up the steps. Nine on Friday.

I smiled to myself as I slipped the note back into the envelope and stepped onto the elevator. I pressed the 27 button and calculated in my head. It had been three months since the last note. I had thought there wouldn't be another; that she had moved on or grown tired of the game. By the time I reached my floor, I was hot with the memories of our previous encounters. I pushed them to the back of my mind with effort as I opened my apartment door and snapped on the lights.

Dropping my briefcase and bags in the foyer, I locked the door behind me and headed straight for the bathroom, where I ran hot water and dropped capfuls of lavender bubble bath and baby oil into the tub. This was my favorite room. The tub was set into a marble alcove with a huge window overlooking the lower buildings on the block. Leaving the tub to fill, I stripped out of my suit, the silk camisole, my hose and bra, leaving them scattered on the Travertine floor as I headed to the kitchen. I grabbed the bottle of red wine on the counter and a wine glass. I was practically shaking by now, and the throbbing between my legs was getting stronger with each moment. The anticipation of Friday was as overwhelming as my memory.

The bath was ready, and I turned the water down to a steamy trickle, lit the scented candles that were scattered around the tub, and poured my wine. I stretched my naked body like a cat, allow-ing the memories to fill me, before stepping down into the tub, feeling the hot water pleasantly stinging my skin, the oils swirling around me as I sank into the froth. The hot water sent shocks of pleasure through my already pounding clit. As I parted my thighs and my fingers found a rhythm, I was lost in the memory of our first encounter.

I had stopped at Simone's on my way home from the office to have a drink and maybe bump into one of the girls. I'd spent the last three months basically holed up in my apartment, having sex with Lynne and nesting, ignoring the outside world. But she had moved out now, and I figured it was time to reconnect with my drinking buddies. Unfortunately, it seemed like everyone was somewhere else that night, so I practiced flirting with the bar-tender, a skinny redhead with spectacular breasts that strained to escape her tight, black tank top. I figured she must have started working here since I'd been preoccupied at home, as I'd never seen her before. Four glasses of wine later, I was just drunk enough to consider asking her to step into the ladies' room with me. She was bent over the bar, leaning in close to whisper in my ear how much she liked to eat pussy, her breasts almost fully bare and just inches from my face by now, when the phone at the end of the bar rang.

She sighed heavily and moved away to answer it. She sashayed back to me, holding the cordless phone out to me. "It's for you." She smiled. "Your girlfriend?"

"Uh, I don't think so." I smirked at her. "Hello?"

"Hi, beautiful," a low voice purred.

"Well, hello." I was stalling, trying to put a face to the voice.

"Don't bother, you don't know me." It was as if she had read my mind. "I just have to tell you, I'm watching the two of you, and it's making me really hot."

I glanced around the room. It was half filled with women, some dancing, others in groups at the tables and some couples gyrating in the dark corners. None of them seemed to be paying the least bit of attention to me.

"Where are you?" I don't know if it was all the wine, or the foreplay with the bartender, or the sexy voice, but I was feeling a deep tingle starting between my thighs, and I wanted to see who was on the other end of the line.

"It doesn't matter," she whispered. "Just don't let her leave!"

I turned back to see the redhead laying her towel on the bar and smiling at a brunette in hot pants who was filling beer mugs and setting up tequila shots. The redhead ducked under the bar and headed toward the back of the room.

"Wait!" I called to her. "Don't leave yet."

She turned and walked back to me, smiling and placing her hips between my legs. Her lips were at my ear, her breath hot, as she whispered, "Why don't you hang up now?"

As her manicured nails traced a path across my collarbone and down into my cleavage, I clicked the phone off and laid it on the bar. Her nails flicked lightly over my nipples, and I shuddered with the strong wave of desire that coursed through me. I reached around to hold her tightly against me, massaging her firm ass and feeling the outline of her thong through her thin, tight pants. I heard her moan low in her throat, and then her mouth was on mine, her tongue pressing hard against mine. I was instantly wet and on the edge of losing control. This girl was hot, and I knew if I didn't touch her soon, I'd go crazy. She must have been thinking the same thing, because she backed away and grabbed my hand, nearly pulling me off the barstool.

"Come on." She was laughing as she tugged me in the direction of the ladies' room. I could see the blatant sexual need in her eyes, and found that my legs were trembling as I started to follow her. Then I remembered the odd phone call and how exciting that voice had been. Who had it been? Was she still here, in the bar? I looked around, and once again didn't notice anyone in particular watching us, but the thought that she might be was arousing in a way I'd never felt before.

"Wait." I stopped my new friend, pulling her in a new direction to a small, unoccupied couch in a dark corner, but not so dark that we would be completely hidden from anyone who was trying to watch.

"Here?" she asked, her eyes widening at the thought.

"Here." I moaned in her ear and put her hand between my thighs, pressing it hard so she could feel how swollen I was, even through my clothes. She sat down on the couch and pulled me onto her lap so I was straddling one of her well-muscled thighs. A shock of heat rushed through me, and I grabbed her by the hair at the back of her neck and held her while I nipped and sucked at her neck, her ears and her lips. She growled as she grabbed my ass and massaged lower and lower, pushing me down on her thigh as her fingertips flicked my wetness from behind. I arched my back at the pure pleasure that was raging through me, rubbing my clit on her leg, making sure my thigh was thumping into her pussy, I could feel her heat and wetness against my leg, and we started a slow, intense rhythm that was bringing me closer and closer to the edge.

Then one of her hands was between us, tugging frantically at the buttons on my blouse and popping open the front clasp of my bra. I almost shrieked as the cold air hit my nipples, and in that second I realized we could be seen and heard here, that I was on display. I looked down to see her wet tongue flick over my nipple, slowly lapping at it, and some primal instinct took over. I gasped out loud and ground myself hard against her thigh. Suddenly, I wanted everyone in the bar to watch, I wanted *her* to watch, that voice on the phone. I reached down into her tank, flicking her nipples, and then I felt myself spin out of control. I rode her hard, thrusting down on her so fiercely I knew she'd be bruised later, begging her to suck my nipples, to make me come. I threw my head back to show off my breasts to anyone who happened to look. I thought about the woman on the phone and whether she was somewhere watching me, wanting me, touching herself. I came harder and more fiercely than I ever had before. I knew I was gasping and moaning loudly, and the thought of being heard just made it hotter. As I collapsed on top of her, the redhead pulled my hips close and began thrashing and gasping herself, bucking wildly against me. I felt her gushing wetness against my leg as she came, and held onto her until our shuddering had stilled.

When we could both breathe again, I closed my bra and top and slowly moved until I sat slumped next to her. I looked around surreptitiously around the room. A few women were glancing in our direction, but no one seemed to be staring or really paying attention, at least not anymore.

"That was fucking hot," my companion declared as she stood and straightened her clothes. "You are incredible! Now, I think my break is over." And with that, she glided back to the bar and back to her customers.

Alone in the tub these months later, I pushed my naked breasts up out of the bubbles, tugging at my nipples while my fingers slid over and over my clit. I was throbbing, and I felt the familiar quivering begin in my thighs. I slid onto my knees and found the jet stream of water, thrusting my pussy into it as I faced out over the city, the suds sliding slowly off my nipples. I imagined the whole city could see me as I came, grasping the tile, my head back, my eyes half closed while I gasped and moaned and finally yelled as waves of release rippled through me again and again.

Friday evening came quickly, and as I showered and got ready for my date, I wondered if a normal relationship would ever satisfy me again. In the past year, my mystery woman had called me at the bar again the next time I'd been there, and she'd asked me to meet her at a nearby movie theatre. At the ticket counter, the grinning usher had handed me a note, telling me to purchase a ticket, sit in the back row, and turn my cell phone on vibrate.

Fifteen minutes into the movie, I'd felt it ring in my pocket. We'd had the most intense phone sex ever. She said she was in another part of the theatre, where she could see me. This time, I didn't look around to find her. I'd slipped my hand into my jeans as we spoke, and afterward I'd licked each finger, listening to her moans in my ear.

We connected about once a month for the next year. She'd call my cell or leave a note at my building. We didn't speak of anything except our most personal details—what we liked, how we liked it, what we fantasized about. I'd never seen her. It was enough that she saw me. She watched me pleasure myself and watched me with other women. Sometimes there would be another woman waiting for me at the rendezvous spot, other times she let me choose my partner. The sex was always in an out-of-the-way but public place. I always knew she was watching, that there was a risk of being seen by others. It never failed to be the most intense, mind-blowing experience I could imagine.

As I passed by the restroom in Simone's and walked up the steps, I wondered what I'd find tonight. I opened the door at the top of the steps at precisely nine o'clock. Inside was a large room, furnished with big, overstuffed couches all draped with white linen sheets. Candles illuminated the room, and a row of windows on one wall looked down at the dance floor in Simone's below. Mirrors on the ceiling bounced my reflection back to me at fifty different angles. The door opened behind me, and two women walked in, each wearing a short, white tank dress that hugged full breasts and an athletic body. They smiled and padded barefoot to the couch nearest the row of windows. The blonde dropped a large, white purse onto the floor next to the couch, while the brunette gestured for me to join them.

I took my shoes off and joined them where they sat. The blonde stood and took off her dress. She was naked underneath, and her body was as stunning as it had seemed. As I watched, she slowly licked her fingers, then flicked her nipples. They hardened under her touch. Then the brunette stood and also stripped, revealing she too was naked and stunning, with large, perfect breasts. Her pussy was shaven, as was the blonde's, and as I stood there watching, the brunette lay back on the couch and spread her long, muscular legs. Her pussy gleamed with beads of moisture. I licked my lips, longing for her taste, for the feel of her coming in my mouth. I stepped toward her, but the blonde softly grabbed my arm, shaking her head.

"You're just here to watch," she whispered, and nodded toward the windows. I realized that anyone glancing up from the bar below would have an exquisite view of these two women, and I wondered why I had never noticed those windows before, from down there.

I sat in an armchair near their couch. The blonde lowered herself to her knees on the floor in front of the couch. She leaned forward and the women kissed, their tongues intertwining, sucking at each other and nipping at each other's lips. I could not look away as I felt my pussy start to pulse. Their hands groped for each other's breasts, rubbing their nipples together and giggling as they touched. Then the blonde's head dipped low, and I shifted my position so I had a clear view of her wet, pink tongue licking the brunette's clit. The brunette began to moan, spreading her pussy open with her fingers. As her hips began to thrust forward, the blonde began slowly thrusting her tongue in and out of the dripping hole, her teeth grazing against the engorged clit with every thrust. I realized I was groaning as I tucked my hand into the waistband of my jeans. The brunette, in between gasps, spoke in a breathless voice, "No touching. You're supposed to only watch!"

It was pure torture to not relieve my own ache as the brunette began bucking against the blonde's face, her hands wrapped in her hair, pulling her closer. She was shouting as she gushed fluid, the blonde licking the streams from her thighs and her ass. I thought I'd gush too, but I managed to hold onto it as the brunette caught her breath before reaching into the white bag on the floor and pulling out a huge, pink strap-on and handing it to the blonde, who immediately pulled it up over her hips, adjusting it so the base lay on her clit.

"Suck me, baby," the blonde commanded, as she turned to face the windows, tugging at her nipples with one hand and pressing the dildo against her clit with the other. The dark-haired woman went to her knees in front of the window, licking the tip of the phallus, rubbing her lips and face over it until the blonde commanded her again, "Please suck my cock now." The brunette complied, stretching her mouth wide to accommodate its girth. As she slid the cock in and out of her mouth, the blonde thrust her hips gently forward.

"God, yes, fuck my face," the brunette gasped. The blonde leaned forward, her hands resting on the window, thrusting as the brunette sucked her hard, running her hand over the length of the cock as she did. Then it was the blonde's turn to come, and she did, loudly, tossing her hair back and bending forward until her nipples pressed against the glass. I was trying desperately not to climax, pressing my legs together, but I was unable to tear my eyes away from these two stunners as they continued to pleasure each other. The blonde bent over the couch while the brunette thrust the cock in and out of her, reaching around to stroke her clit until she screamed. I was almost in tears from holding off, my body beginning to thrust on its own accord, when my cell phone rang.

I knew before I answered exactly who it was.

"Hello," I gasped as I watched brunette hair spread across the firm thighs of a gorgeous blonde.

"Tell my friends to go now," the voice instructed. I reluctantly asked the pair to stop, and they slipped their clothes back on and left the room, smiling as they went.

"Now, give yourself the relief we both need. I need to see you come." And she was gone.

I no longer felt any inhibition at all as I stripped out of my clothes and stepped directly in front of the windows. The bar below was crowded, and I could literally see the vibrations from the loud music in the glass. The coldness teased my nipples, and I knew I was too close to climax to wait any longer. I flicked my clit with my fingertip, gasping as I came hard and bracing myself on the window, hoping all eyes were on me. I didn't look down to see who was watching.

Five minutes later, I exited the room and went back down the stairs. I did not go to the bar for a drink, or even step inside to see who was there. I caught myself smiling at nothing as I walked down the block to go back home, where a tub and another row of windows awaited me.

Tease Me, Please
MJ Perry

I am a police detective, and most days I love my job. Today was not one of those days. The guys and I had a drug bust gone wrong. That made for a bad experience for all involved. Our evening needed improvement before going home to our respected loved ones. We don't want to take the stresses of the job home, so the festivities after work at the local establishments tend to be a vice of the job. The guys needed a drink, and, quite frankly, I did too. We opted for the nearby sports bar. We cheered our efforts and jeered our failures and then we enjoyed our libations. After an hour, the guys went home to their wives and children while I finished my beer. My only mission was to find someone to go home with, no attachments, merely hardcore sex. I looked around for a lesbian and found only drunk, straight women falling over drunker men. I left the bar disappointed, walking to the next establishment, which served alcohol and boasted exotic dancers. At this point, I would even take a good lap dance and call it a night.

I walked into the Men's Night Out and noticed a bouncer at the door who I had busted a few months ago. "I'm sorry, ma'am, you can't come in here without a male escort." He paused a moment, looking at me quizzically, trying to remember how he knew me. He then knowingly nodded at his recollection and continued, "Oh, I didn't recognize you, detective. You're all set."

I love the perks of my job. I thanked him, insisted that I pay my cover charge, to which he eventually gave in. I did a quick check of the area to make sure I didn't know anyone else. A hazard of the job, I suppose. I went to the bar and checked out the bartender, who wore tight, revealing clothing and appeared to be about seven months pregnant.

"Pregnant and working in a strip bar. Now that's class," I mumbled under my breath.

I decided it was best to just order a beer and a shot of tequila and keep my thoughts in my head where they belong.

"No lemon, thanks." I threw down a couple of dollar bills toward the kid's education, then moved to the lower-level platform in front of the dancers and selected a seat at an empty table.

It didn't take long to realize the scenery wasn't much to look at on this Wednesday night. The more shapely, better-looking dancers usually performed on the weekends for the horny college guys. I checked the faces of the patrons once more, breathing a small sigh of relief when I didn't recognize anyone. Relaxing a bit, I looked around at the upcoming dancers who tried to coerce the male patrons into the backroom for an overpriced lap dance before they took to the stage. For the length of time it takes one full song to play, this bar charges thirty-five dollars for a lap dance. The performance on the stage is typically the same and usually costs a dollar or two for a decent dance, more if it's enjoyed and an encore is requested.

My eyes focused on a petite dancer coming out of the changing area. She had a Meg Ryan cut—blond hair cut choppy to her chin. She wore a white, silky bra-like top, covered by a white tank top cut just below her breasts and a thong that left little to the imagination. The outfit displayed her curves, while the white accentuated her tanned body. Her sexuality crowded out all other thoughts in my mind as I contemplated her athletic build. Kudos to anyone who does enough crunches to get abs like hers. I liked the way her muscles moved with her as she strutted across the floor toward the bar. I couldn't take my eyes off her beautifully sculpted body. If I saw her in a gay bar, we would be home in my bed by now. This was my type of woman. She was the one I would fuck all night until the sun came up.

She walked over to the bar and stood close to a man sipping a whiskey. A quick nod to the bartender, and a shot of tequila was placed in front of her. She licked her hand, added salt to the moistened area and slowly licked the salt off. She swallowed the shot of tequila, then bit down on the lemon wedge. I watched as she cleaned up the sticky juices with her tongue, just like a cat, gradually licking from her wrist and ending with her thumb in her mouth. I have never wanted to be salt or a lemon until that moment. If she could arouse me just by licking her own hand, imagine what she could do if she licked my body. I watched as she flirted with the whiskey man, maneuvering herself between his legs, rubbing up against him and leaning into his chest to talk. I could feel my clit beginning to throb. For the first time, I was actually turned on watching a woman seduce a man. I barely noticed the performer on the stage dancing seductively in front of me. When I failed to show her money or attention, she walked away in search of the next dollar.

Please say I didn't miss you dance. My inner voice was at it again. Time for another shot. Just as I stood up, she walked toward the private room with the whiskey drinker attached to her arm. Clearly a job well done on her part. She would be giving him a lap dance. I couldn't help but be jealous.

I spaced out for a length of time that seemed like forever. I kept a close eye on the private room, never watching the dancers on the stage. When a pool table opened up, I went over to play a quick game. After many failed shots at the pocket, I realized I lacked the concentration needed and abandoned the table after one game. I walked back to the bar, eager to find the blond beauty or, at the very least, to get a good buzz.

"Beer and a double shot of tequila," I requested from the pregnant bartender.

Feeling the effects of the alcohol, I walked toward the women's restroom, which doubles as the dancers' changing room. Suitcases filled with glittery clothing and props were strewn about on the floor. I navigated my way to a stall, trying to go as quickly as possible to minimize running into a dancer in "their space." In mid pee, I heard the door open and froze.

I heard two women's voices start complaining about the patrons drooling over them. I suddenly felt awkward leaving my safe place and invading their safe place. I flushed the toilet as fair warning and exited the bathroom stall. I made quick eye contact and smiled as the women moved away from the sink. I washed my hands and scooted out of the bathroom, saying nothing.

Back at the bar, I ordered another tequila and beer, then refocused on the patrons. My sexy blond dancer sat to my right. I moved a few seats closer, the better to hear her voice. When she glanced my way, I blushed at first and then smiled. As my cocky side surfaced, I raised an eyebrow and gave her a quick wink to express my interest. She returned the eyebrow raise with a surprised look of interest, but quickly looked away when a male patron grabbed her waist.

I took a deep breath. She was breathtaking even up close and personal. Turning back in my direction, she smiled. With her back to the guy, she enticed him by rubbing her backside between his legs, all the while concentrating on me. Her piercing blue eyes sent a tingling sensation and immediate rush of blood to my loins. She slowly slid her tongue across her lips. Her smile was enough to pull me in, wanting to touch her lips with my own. Her small waist seemed to beckon my arms to wrap around it, to pull her in close. When I came back to my senses, I looked into her eyes and barely noticed that her movements paused as she spoke to me. "Hey, cutie."

I responded simply, "Hey." I tried to come up with something more clever, but instead asked, "Can I buy you a drink?"

Before answering, she returned her attention to the male who had manhandled her; otherwise known as the newest prospective bill payer. He whispered in her ear, and I cursed under my breath as they walked to the back room. This was a good night for her. I sighed. Maybe if I was a man, she would give me the same attention and seduce me to the back room for thirty-five dollars. I checked out her backside as she walked away. Quite impressive, if I may say so. She looked good from all angles. I just love a woman who takes good care of herself.

Unfortunately, she was clearly interested in men only, but would play up the bisexual angle just enough to get my money once she returned to the dance floor. I shot back the tequila and sat back down with my beer, disgusted with the thought. I tried to stop thinking about her because I was sure she wasn't the least bit interested in women. Right now, all she could be for me was a great bedtime fantasy. I attempted to watch the other dancers, throwing an occasional dollar bill on the stage, though I was unimpressed with what they had to offer. In sheer boredom I looked to my right and saw her getting on the stage to dance.

I fumbled with the money in my back pocket so I could entice her to dance for me. I held out a fiver, but four college-aged guys beat me to the punch and caught her attention. She danced for them, and the ache between my legs grew stronger. I couldn't understand my feelings and couldn't control them. She took two steps to the stripper pole, placing it between her legs. As she leaned backward, her flexible body sent my erotic thoughts spinning into overdrive.

She slid up and down the pole, her thong the only protection from the cold metal. She jumped up, caught the pole higher up and swung her legs into the air, putting her stomach muscles to work and wrapping her legs around the pole like a pretzel. Her thighs tightly gripped the pole, while her ankles and feet secured themselves to the top of the pole. Leaning backward, her abdominal muscles tightening, she slowly waved her arms and moved her waist like a belly dancer. The throbbing between my legs became more intense as she jumped off the pole and danced back over to the guys. I let out my breath slowly. She moved closer to one of the men, touching his face softly as she leaned back onto him. If I were home alone watching this on DVD, I would have come by now. She made eye contact with me and winked. Shivers went through my body. The look she gave me could have melted Antarctica.

She walked over to me, maintaining eye contact. "Are you with him?" she whispered, leaning into me.

I had been so entranced with her, I hadn't realized a man had taken a seat beside me. "No," I said, glancing quickly at him, then returning my gaze to her. "He's not exactly my type."

"What is your type? Is his package too small?" she teased.

"I prefer sexy blondes with an incredible body and no packages attached. I'm all yours, if you'll have me."

"Good, because I want you all to myself," she said, her voice a seductive whisper.

The ache between my legs was so intense, I was pretty sure anyone could see the crotch of my jeans breathing. She stepped back as the dance song changed to a slower, more erotic tune. My body tingled as she danced seductively for me, as though we were the only two people in the room. She moved in closer to me. I suddenly felt as though her power was pulling me in, and I would have joined her on the stage if she had asked. She leaned over, as though she would whisper in my ear again. Instead, I felt her breath light on my neck.

Her voice barely a whisper, she sang along with the words that came through the loudspeakers, "I will be the one to hold you down." I shivered and she continued, "I'll kiss you so hard, I'll take your breath away."

I opened my legs slightly, inviting her in, daring her to prove her words. Her lips grazed my neck, then she kissed the area between my throat and collar bone. I closed my eyes, letting myself get lost in the moment. I realized she had stopped, and I opened my eyes to see her looking at me. She ran her fingers through my hair, stopping at my neck and pulling me in for a very intimate, sensual kiss. Her tongue entered my mouth, dancing with my own. Suddenly, her hand found its way underneath my shirt. She hesitated as she discovered my lack of undergarments. A slow smile spread across her face.

"I like that in a woman," she said.

Those words excited me, leading me to think she might have an interest in women after all. She grabbed my attention along with my left breast, caressing it while continuing to kiss me. For a brief moment, I remembered I was in a strip bar, and then realized I had become part of the entertainment as everyone looked on, now surely jealous of the attention I was receiving. When the song ended, she said "thank you" and winked as she walked away.

I tried to get my head out of the clouds, but was unable to do so. Did that really just happen? I suddenly couldn't remember why work had been so awful, what had happened at the sports bar after work, or even the pool game I had played. I sat there dumbfounded, yearning for more. I could feel the throbbing in my crotch, my heart pounding from the overwhelming desire. It had been at least fourteen months since I'd felt like that, and I realized for the first time how much I actually missed that feeling.

Coming back to reality, my inner voice said, *Snap out of it! She's a stripper! She does this for the money she gets from you and the audience watching the seduction. There was nothing personal in the kiss; it's all an act.*

Having lost sight of her, I opted to leave the bar before I gave up my phone number on a bar napkin. Some redhead was dancing when the announcement came over the speakers for last call. As I stood up to leave, the announcer declared that "Stephanie" had requested one last song for those who were interested. I watched as my blonde exited the bathroom, wearing a short, strapless black dress that barely covered her torso. Once again, she stared at me as though no one else existed, maintaining eye contact as she reached the stage. The music started and I heard the lyrics, "I'm in love with a stripper," and laughed at the irony of the words. I sat back down, watching as she walked seductively in my direction, carefully removing the dress and dropping it to her feet. The strapless bra and tiny thong she wore were cherry red with black lace trim. I couldn't find my money quickly enough.

As it turned out, she was performing for me without the bribe of money first. Carefully removing her bra, she threw it onto my lap. I took a deep breath of excitement and grabbed the bra, balancing it on one finger. She shimmied only briefly on the floor before making her way to the tabletop, sitting on it and straddling me with her legs, using them to pull me closer to her. She took the bra off of my finger and flung it over her left shoulder, discarding it for the remainder of the dance. Leaning over, she took my chin in her hands, pulling me to her for a kiss. She tasted like strawberries.

She slid off the tabletop to sit directly on my lap, and I yearned to touch her in the most inappropriate way. Instead, I continued to kiss her, leaving my hands at my sides so I wouldn't get kicked out for inappropriate touching. Her flowery perfume, mixed with the scent of tanning lotion, filled my senses. Her hand went under my shirt again, touching my bare breast and skin. I moaned as she began grinding her hips against my lap, and I threw my head back in pure pleasure and the agony of wanting more. When she kissed my neck again, all I could think of was how much I wanted to pull her into a private room and finish what she had started.

She sat back on the tabletop and spun around, leaning her head on my shoulder. As I kissed her neck, she pulled my head toward her breasts and whispered in my ear, "Taste me." Not wanting to disappoint her, I took her nipple in my mouth, gently kissing it with my tongue and lips. I looked up and saw the frowning bouncer walking over to stop me. Groaning, I pulled away from her breast, knowing I'd been touching her in a fashion not allowed and sure I would be kicked out. Her hand on my thigh, rubbing up and down and nearing my throbbing center, brought me back to her. I moaned again as she kissed me passionately. Before I realized what was happening, she'd unsnapped my jeans and shoved her hand down my pants, grinning wickedly as she encountered my very wet underwear. My hips rose to her, moving in sync with her hand. I stopped to breathe so I wouldn't moan again. Just as I thought she'd make me come right then and there, the music ended.

Removing her hand, she faced me once more. "Thank you," she whispered.

I struggled to get the words out. "No, thank you." My voice cracked, and my mouth felt dry from breathing heavily.

I watched her walk away, feeling an almost physical pain of dissatisfaction. I was so aroused, wishing for just one more hour, one more chance to have a lap dance and be alone with her in a private room. My mind was drifting and I couldn't concentrate, so consumed was I with impure thoughts of the sexual things I wanted to do with her. I pushed myself from my chair and walked to the bathroom for one last time, but stopped as I approached the empty back room. My heart was beating so fast as I poked my head inside that I staggered into the room. Sitting down on one of the couches, I leaned my head back as I thought about Stephanie. The room was spinning.

I felt someone walk up from behind and was startled when she spoke, "Are you waiting for me?"

I turned toward the familiar voice and saw her standing there in her slinky black dress. Digging into my pocket, I found a twenty dollar bill. "What can I get for this?" I asked, holding it up.

She smiled seductively. "That's negotiable," she said, then led me to the private room, where she closed the door. Turning to me, she asked, "What do you want?"

"Anything you're willing to give."

She smiled at me and took off my shirt, revealing my bare breasts. Holding them in her hands, she kissed first one then the other. She moved her hands to my face and gently kissed my lips. "Sit down," she said. "I want to watch your enjoyment as I dance for you." I obliged, and she turned her back to me, glancing seductively over her shoulder as she licked her lips. She moved her body slowly to the music, swaying back and forth and circling her hips. Still swaying, she turned around and crooked a finger at me, instructing me to come to her.

As I walked toward her, excitement making butterflies in my stomach, she dropped her dress to the floor, revealing that she was naked underneath. Her smooth skin glowed in the dim light; her perky breasts seemed to beckon for my touch. She was beautiful, with curves in all the right places.

"Dance with me," she said.

Pulling me to her, our bare breasts met. My breath caught in my throat, and I could feel the throbbing begin again between my legs, feel the wetness starting there as well. With her right hand on my backside, she moved my hips in sync with hers, kissing me all the while. She walked me back to the couch, unbuttoning my jeans with each step. As she slipped my jeans down to my ankles, she kissed her way across my stomach, stopping briefly at the inner thigh, and then down my legs. Coming back up, she licked my inner thigh, moving my underwear aside with her tongue to reach what she was really after. When her tongue touched my wet spot, I nearly fell over, suddenly feeling weak in the knees. Putting her hands on my hips, she pushed me down on the couch. My jeans and sneakers came off together, then she went for my underwear. I lifted my hips slightly to assist, but she whispered, "No, let me do the work. This is all about you."

She started by kissing my ankles, kissing her way up my legs until she got to my inner thighs, where she licked me, swirling with her tongue, teasing me until she found my wet spot. She sucked my clit, then inserted her tongue inside me. I pushed myself against her mouth as I moaned in pleasure, urging her to continue. She returned to sucking my clit as she inserted one finger, then another, deep inside me.

"Oh God, don't stop. Please. Oh yes, suck me there."

Our bodies moved together as she moved her fingers faster. I was gasping now, moaning and pleading with her to keep on. I could feel I was going to release, and she felt it too. She stopped licking me and kissed her way up my belly, to my breasts, taking one at a time into her mouth, sucking my nipples until I thought I would explode. Her fingers, still inside me, slowed as she rotated them around and around.

"Kiss me, please," I moaned.

She left my breasts and seized my lips with her own, kissing me hard, her tongue plunging deep into my mouth. As my orgasm began to build, she pulled her fingers from me and began grinding against me, rubbing our clits together in an sensual dance. Sweat dripped off of our bodies and the heat between us ignited. Her rapid breathing matched my own, and she kissed me with more intensity. Suddenly, she stopped.

"Are you hungry?" she asked.

"What?" I said, confused, feeling the ripple of orgasm leave me. Why had she stopped?

"Are you hungry?"

Noting the dangerous twinkle in her eye, I understood. "What do you have in mind?"

With a wink, she turned around, moving her body above my own in a "69" position so I could taste her. Breathing in the scent of her, I plunged my tongue deep inside her, feeling her wetness spread across my face. This was heaven. But she wasn't finished with the surprises. Lifting her body up, she crawled down to lay across my legs. Positioning us so our clits met once more, we grinded together until we were both moaning so loudly I was sure others in the club could hear us.

And as good as I thought this was, she showed me once again there could be so much more. Intertwining her legs between my own like scissors, she made our clits touch and I felt our wetness come together, like two waves meeting on the shore, our most intimate parts touching the way only two women truly can. Moving and grinding together, we came at the same time, both of us moaning and crying out. Collapsing together from sheer exhaustion, she rested against me for a short time, then gave me one last kiss.

A man's harsh voice snapped me back to reality. "Excuse me, we're closed now."

I was standing in front of the stage, sweating, my heart pounding at a rapid rate. I was breathless and now irritated.

"You have to leave now," the man said, and I realized he was still looking at me.

I shook my head in disbelief. What had just happened? Or, more accurately, didn't happen. I couldn't believe I had drifted so deeply into my own thoughts, so far that it seemed like a reality. The orgasms may have been fantasy, but my soaked underwear were very real. Damn him for bringing me back!

I never saw where "Stephanie" went and don't know if she passed me as she left the building. It seemed as though she had enjoyed the stage performance as much as I had, and maybe even secretly hoped she could come home with me tonight. Reminding myself that she was a stripper and it was all a show for money, I walked out of the bar, disappointed and sexually frustrated that I could not locate her and would be going home alone, again. I didn't know her schedule, and didn't even know if "Stephanie" was her real name or her stage name. It didn't really matter at this point. I just wanted to bring her home with me, be it for one night, or a few nights. I could be okay with either.

I sat in my car for a while, trying to regain my senses and the ability to drive. I don't know if it was her or the alcohol, but I felt like I couldn't see straight, that my mind was not connected to my body, and that the spot between my legs where her hand had been was more wet.

I checked out the license plates of the vehicles in the parking lot before leaving, thinking I could come back when those same vehicles were here. Or maybe run the plates through the police computer.

"What am I talking about? What am I doing? I really am losing my marbles."

After returning home, I showered, letting the hot water pour over my body and trying to forget the day's bad events and remember the good. I found myself thinking about her again. Stephanie. I remembered what had happened, wondering if I'd only imagined it. Was I really that hard up for love or good sex that I couldn't see past a show?

Finishing my shower, I went to the bedroom, pushed the play button on my CD player, and got into bed, pausing only to grab the vibrator from the nightstand. Thinking about what had happened at the bar, I turned the vibrator on my clit. Visualizing the way Stephanie looked at me, the way she walked toward me, the way her body and hips moved, the more excited I got, and the more I longed to have her here beside me, to push her fingers inside me and feel my heat.

With my body arching in response to my vibrator, I envisioned her in the bed with me, feeling her touch my bare breast again, kissing my neck, making me throb. One orgasm was immediately followed by another as my thoughts were consumed by visions of a lovely blond stripper. I could feel her fingers inside me, smell the scent of her, taste her. Another orgasm, and then I fell against my pillows, utterly exhausted. Smiling, I knew I would have good dreams tonight.

Drifting off to sleep, I thought about my real night with Stephanie, as well as my fantasy night with her. If nothing else, I would always have that. Maybe the fantasy is better than the reality. I thought I needed the real thing, but all I need is my imagination and the fantasy right now, at least until I find the right woman.

Then again, maybe I'll see if she's working this Friday night. And this time, I'll be sure to get a lap dance so she can tease me once more.

Dirty Little Secret
Geneva King

"Marcella! Marcella, come here a moment. I want you to meet Senator Janice Morgan." Robert (secretly nicknamed The Turd) simpered at the woman in front of him. "Senator, this is one of my subordinates, Marcella Graves."

Subordinates? This fool had lost his mind. I smiled politely at the Senator and shook the hand she offered. Her crisp gray suit looked like it cost more than I made in a month. The only spark of color came from the deep green scarf tied around her neck.

She examined me for a moment. "Ms. Graves, nice to see you again."

The smile left Robert's face. "You two know each other?"

"We met briefly at the San Francisco Arena, if I'm not mistaken." She let go of my hand. "I was rather impressed by several of Ms. Graves' ideas."

Robert looked completely taken aback. Served him right, the overeager bastard. He'd been on the job three months longer than me and seemed to think it enough reason to boss me around.

Senator Morgan turned back to me. "Hopefully, we'll be able to talk a bit longer this time. If you're not too busy . . ." She raised her eyebrow a tiny bit. I doubt Robert noticed.

"Don't worry, I'm flexible." I could tell from the pink flush that started around her neck that she remembered exactly how true that was.

She coughed and smoothed back her hair. "I should get going." She shook Robert's hand.

"Good day, Senator Morgan." Robert nodded and walked a few feet away. I noticed he turned to watch us.

Janice grasped my hand and stepped closer to me. "I'm in Suite 2A." I had to strain to hear her voice. "Come around seven." She moved back. "I look forward to speaking with you later, Ms. Graves."

"Same here."

She turned and walked over to a tall, gray-haired man. Almost instantly, the butterflies I'd pushed away fluttered into my stomach. It hadn't been easy staying so composed when the only thing I wanted to do was fuck the serene expression off her face.

We'd met at a football game at the Arena a few months before. My boss had a significant interest in getting a bill passed, so he decided that was the best place to butter her up. As the only single, childless woman without plans, I got the lucky assignment of accompanying him. I think he realized his mistake a few minutes into the first quarter. My ignorance of the game made him wince with shame. Janice took me under her wing and explained everything, saving my boss's pride but giving him precious little time to push his cause. Luckily for me, and probably my skin, the bill passed. I got a raise.

When he congratulated me and asked how I'd done it, I smiled, leaving out the part about the Senator inviting me up to her room for a nightcap. Drinks led to kisses that spiraled into a night of sweaty sex. In the morning, I'd left without exchanging personal information. After all, what could possibly come of it?

The rest of the day dragged by. Robert had no clue how close I was to throttling him at lunch. If I heard him describe the last ten million dollar project he got to manage (five hundred thousand), his excellent evaluation score (average at best, I saw the paper), or his model-esque girlfriend (no comment) one more time, I might dump my bowl of soup over his head.

Finally, seven came. Janice was on the ninth floor, so I took the elevator to eight and walked the final set of stairs. When I knocked, she opened the door almost immediately and yanked me inside.

"No one saw you?" She peered into the hallway.

"I don't think so. It was dead quiet." I took a moment to look around the suite. Her bed was twice the size of mine. The office area was on the other side, with overstuffed sofas and a solid desk facing me. "So, this is what our tax dollars go for, huh? Fancy rooms for our representatives?"

"Yes. Then we invite our lovers to visit. It's what you call trickle-down economics. Want some wine?" She walked toward me, her smile more inviting than it had been that morning. She had shed her business suit in favor of a fluffy terrycloth robe. To hell with the robe—I wanted to see what she wore underneath.

I shook my head. "No."

"I wish I'd known you were coming." She stood in front of me now, her breasts bumping mine through the robe. "I would have made sure I had time for you."

"We're here now."

She laughed and kissed me. "Damn straight." She tugged at my shirt. "Take it off."

"Yes, ma'am." I stepped out of her reach before she could kiss me and started unbuttoning my blouse. I played with the buttons, watching the gleam grow in her eyes before finally slipping each button through its hole.

"God, you're sexy." Her hunger was almost palpable at this point. Her hands rubbed along the insides of her thighs as she watched me. "Get over here."

"Not done yet." I kicked my shoes off and wriggled my pants over my hips. My tease was ruined a little when I tripped, but she merely smiled and reached out to steady me.

"I can take care of the rest." Janice unhooked my bra. Her hands slid over the sides of my breasts as she pulled it off me.

We kissed. Her mouth tasted slightly sweet, like the wine she'd been drinking. I could tell the wait had driven her nuts. One hand gripped my ass, while the other was entwined in my hair.

"Don't make me wait like that again." She bit the side of my neck. "Cunt."

I laughed in her face. "Yes, Senator." I peeled back the lapels of her robe. "Anything else, Senator?"

Janice slapped my cheek lightly. "Don't get smart with me." She kissed me again as she slid her hand between my legs. "Get on the desk, Marcella."

She sat in the large, leather seat and watched me climb onto the hard, wooden surface and put my feet on her armrests. Her fingers stroked my pussy until I started grinding my pelvis against her hand.

"I really should make you suffer first." She blew on my cunt, the calm expression returning to her face. "But that wouldn't be much fun for either of us, now would it?"

I shook my head, hating her composure when I wanted her so much.

Her tongue made a single pass over my clit. "You should thank me."

"Th-thank you, Senator." My hands felt numb from their death grip on the desk.

"You're welcome."

She went to work in earnest, her tongue flicking me into oblivion.

I heard a beep and we looked around in confusion. Then, it sounded again.

"Oh my god, oh my god." She tore away from me and pulled her robe tightly around her. "That's the doorbell." Janice grabbed my arm and shoved me under the desk. "Stay there and be quiet." I heard the door open.

"I came by to get some papers. I'm glad you're here. I need to ask you some questions." The speaker's voice was deep and even.

"This can't wait until later? I was about to take a bath." Janice sounded flustered. It was easy to picture her running her hands over her delicious little neck.

"It won't take long. Why don't we sit down?"

I heard Janice sigh. "Fine. Let's get this over with."

Her legs slid in front of my face. I kissed her knee and she patted me on the head. My fingers grazed the back of her calves until she jumped and pinched my cheek.

"Are you okay, Senator?"

"Just chilly. Now, what's so important?"

The space under the desk was rather cramped. To make matters more difficult, I could smell the soft scent of Janice's cunt from where I sat. How wet was she? Did it turn her on to know that my head was mere inches from her body? And Mr. Monotonous Cunt-blocker, would he discover her dirty little secret? I ran my finger over her hairless lips.

"Are you okay? Your face is red."

"Fine. So about this clause . . ."

I had to applaud her. Even under duress, she managed to pull it together. Her hand covered mine to still it, but I shook it loose and slid my other finger inside her. My mouth wanted to get in on the action, so I took one of her fingers between my lips and sucked it as I fucked her.

"Do you mind if I use your bathroom?"

"No, it's right there."

I heard Monotonous walk away and a door closed. Instantly, Janice pulled her finger from my mouth and pushed back from the desk to look at me. "Didn't I tell you to behave?"

I pretended to think. "No, you said to stay here. Oh, and be quiet."

"You little slut." She tried to look stern, but her eyes were shining. Finally, she gave up and kissed me until my lips felt bruised.

The toilet flushed and she shoved me back down. "I'll try to get rid of him soon."

"Hey, sink down a bit. In your chair."

She hesitated. "You want me to slouch?" She looked horrified.

"Just do it." The door opened, and I scrambled back under the desk.

She parted her legs again and I resumed fingering her. She was still too far away so I tugged on her leg to make her scoot forward. She must have felt like she was at the gynecologist; her ass nearly hung off the chair. If I stretched my neck and tilted my head just right, I could reach her. The first try, I missed and bumped my head on the desk.

The Senator's quick thinking covered my mistake. "My knee."

I wanted to rub my head, but there wasn't room. Her clit mocked me from between her legs. Leaning forward, I tried again, smiling as I tasted my goal. Her hand clenched my hair as I worked. My finger stroked her deep inside.

She began saying less and less to her associate, and I felt her twitch more and more. At least she couldn't accuse me of making her wait, I thought, with a certain amount of satisfaction. Instead, I continued to tease her, feeding off of her subtle reactions. Each shudder was a chink in her armor. Knowing Janice was torn between pleasure and secrecy excited me, even though

I realized she'd punish me for it later.

"Well, I think I've taken enough of your time. I'll see myself to the door."

About time the boring fucker left! I heard his chair push back.

"Good night." She remained seated, but she removed her hand from my head. "See you tomorrow."

When the door clicked, she moved back, dragging me with her. "Don't stop. Don't you dare stop. Oh shit, I'm gonna get you for that. I thought he'd never leave."

Janice yanked my hair, her other hand scratched my shoulder. Then she came, with a deep groan that resonated throughout her body. But my need was still growing. I kissed her stomach, moving upward until I reached her breasts.

"I hope you weren't planning on kicking me out just yet, Janice. I've still got plans for you."

My goading had the desired effect. The satisfied look left her face and the heat returned to her eyes. "Get your ass back on the desk." As I scrambled into position, she reached into the night-stand and pulled out a blue, jelly dildo. "I've been saving this for you." Janice yanked my legs open and rubbed the head against my slippery hole. "Silly bitch. It's time you realized who's in charge here."

"Then stop playing with that toy and act like it."

Her eyes flashed. I felt the thick tip plunge into my pussy. Despite my bravado, my body wasn't ready for the assault. Aided by a thumb on my clit, her thrusts forced the orgasms from me, until I cried for mercy.

Two hours later, I pulled my clothes on and waited while she checked the corridor.

"All clear." She smiled and stroked my cheek.

" 'Bye, Janice."

"Wait." She handed me a piece of paper. "I'm attending a small business convention in Daytona next month. You should ask your boss to send you."

I kissed her hand. "I'll do my best."

The next morning, I saw Robert leave the hotel restaurant with Janice. He sidled smugly up to me. "Guess who just had breakfast with Senator Morgan?" He puffed his chest out. "Stick with me, kid. I'll show you how it's done in the real world."

I rolled my eyes. "Right."

Janice stood by the gift shop, speaking with the gray-haired man from yesterday. With her pressed suit and tight bun, no one would ever suspect she was standing ten feet away from her dirty little secret.

The Tattoo
Renée Strider

My name is Luce.

Way before I loved the woman I love now, there was a woman I will never forget, even though when I think about her I sometimes see her unclearly. Her features and body and dress appear drenched in such bright sunlight that the details are obscured.

I wasn't an early riser in those days, and during the summers I used to jog mid-mornings along the lakeshore whenever I could. I loved that time of day. The sun was high enough by then to cover the cobalt blue lake in sparkles. And on those rare days in early summer when the air wasn't humid, the cloudless sky— if I looked away from the sun—was so blue and so clear and so infinitely deep that it seemed as if I would topple off the earth and tumble into space. Every tree leaf and blade of grass appeared to stand out individually in brilliant greens of lime and viridian. Even the limestone ledges and shelves projecting out above the water were not their normal dour gray, but white and the palest blue in the dazzling brightness.

It was that kind of shining morning.

Tired after a long run, I lay back on the grass, arms bent behind my head. As the light breeze from the lake ruffled my hair, I looked up at the cloudless sky and sighed with pleasure. Looked *into* the sky. I was actually staring, unblinking, *into* the azure vastness. A slight sensation of vertigo made me close my eyes.

Now it was silent—no rustling leaves, no lapping wavelets on the shore. At the same time, I felt my body begin to float up into that infinity above me.

Startled, I opened my eyes and sat up. All was normal—the same shining water, luminous colors and soft breeze whispering through the leaves. The sensation had been so fleeting, I promptly dismissed it.

As usual, I returned home along a street that paralleled the edge of the lake for a short distance. It had houses on one side only, and through bushes and trees on the other side you could sometimes catch a glimpse of the water. The houses were attached—townhouses, high and narrow and built of the local limestone that had lightened over the years. Today, like the rock lining the shore, they too looked bleached in the sunlight, and I had to narrow my eyes against the reflected light.

This particular morning, a beautiful woman I had never seen before was sitting on a low stool on one of the large front stoops, painting. Her small easel was set at an angle so she did not face the sun directly. The houses, with their shallow front gardens, some with clumps of tall designer grasses, and contemporary sculptures, were close enough to the road that I could see her quite well.

The woman was dark-haired and tanned like me, but I'm tall, muscular and solid, whereas she was smaller, elegant and fine-boned. And unlike my short curls, her hair was long and black, gleaming like midnight-blue silk in the sun as it cascaded over her right shoulder to her breast. She wore a loose sleeveless dress, something like a long tunic, which bared her left shoulder. The gown fell in folds of white, ending in a band of palest yellow. The fabric was so delicate and gauzy that I imagined she would feel the slightest breath of air through it. The woman was exquisite.

I was especially fascinated by a colorful swirling tattoo that began at her bare shoulder and flowed down the side of her upper arm. I wondered what it represented and wished very much to see it up close. At this thought, my heart beat faster.

The radiance reflected from the houses almost blinded me. Instead of walking by, I stopped in front of the painter.

"Hi," I said, trying not to squint.

She turned her attention from the low easel to look at me. Her full, red lips matched the deep red of the paint covering the paintbrush in her right hand. Putting the brush down, she smiled as her eyes swept over me.

"Hello. Have you been running?" Her voice was soft and melodious.

For an instant I stood transfixed under the woman's scrutiny. Then I found my voice. "Yes, jogging by the lake. What are you painting?"

"Flowers. Well, actually just one."

"I like flowers. By the way, my name is Luce." I grinned, turning on my considerable charm.

Blue eyes like the sky met mine, also blue—like the lake, as someone had once described them. My stomach fluttered.

"Good morning, Luce. My name is Celeste. Would you like to see?" She gestured at the painting.

Stepping up to the stoop, I stood behind Celeste slightly to one side. Bending, I peered at the painting, screwing up my eyes a little against the brightness of the sun. The woman's scent distracted me—sandalwood, just a hint—as did her hair and naked shoulder, now suddenly so close to me.

It was a wonderful painting. It showed the inside of a flower, with textures and folds and curves all pink and red and purple, and darker toward the center.

"An iris. It's gorgeous," I said.

"Thank you. It's not finished yet, though. You can sit down and watch if you like."

Celeste lifted the paintbrush from the small table beside her and swirled it around in the thick, colorful blobs on the glass palette till the brush was soft and wet again and so full of red paint it was almost dripping.

"This is carmine red," she said, stroking the thick oil paint onto the image on the canvas.

I sat down cross-legged beside her. The fragrance of orange-rind from the paint thinner and the oily smell of the paint itself assaulted my senses. The scents became one with the colors as I gazed at the glistening canvas. And all the while the brilliant sun threw up heat and light from the pale stone around us.

For a long time I sat, almost in a trance, as I watched the flower evolve and unfold more with each pass of the brush. After a while, Celeste's hand moved more slowly, applying light dabs here and there with a delicate touch.

"Is it finished?" I asked. My own voice sounded far away and indistinct.

"Almost," said Celeste. "Just a bit more cobalt violet on this outer edge."

Her voice had broken the spell. My eyes wandered from the flower to the graceful hand resting near me against the edge of the low canvas. My gaze followed the slim brown arm up to . . . the tattoo. I had been so fascinated by the painting that I had almost forgotten about the tattoo. Another iris, it extended from Celeste's shoulder halfway to her elbow. It had the same dark center as the painting, but the rest was even bolder and brighter, and clearer, with more reds and pinks, and only traces of violet and purple this time.

Smiling with delight, I rose up on my knees to see the tattoo better. The full brilliance of the sun illuminated it. I looked more closely. It was like the iris in the painting, and yet it was not.

Suddenly I was deaf and blind as my ears roared and my focus blurred in recognition. Heat rose to my face and surged to my groin. My heart ached in my breast. The tattoo was of an open vulva, a woman's sex. Not abstract, not even impressionistic, each fold and curve and hollow was clearly defined. I was mesmerized and could not look away. Time stood still.

Peripherally, I was aware that Celeste put the brush down and turned to look at me. Still I stared at the tattoo as if hypnotized. I raised my hand toward the satin skin.

"Luce?" Her soft voice penetrated my reverie.

Slowly, I looked away from the beautiful tattoo. For a moment my hand still hovered there, then hesitantly touched impossibly smooth skin as our eyes locked.

She smiled faintly, knowingly. The light of the full sun reflected from her golden face. Her eyes were so very blue. In the brightness, the pupils were only pinpricks. So much blue in eyes that seemed to draw me in. I had to close mine in defense.

I could hardly breathe as soft fingers reached out to touch my cheek, the nape of my neck. The fingers of her other hand came to rest against the pulse beating in my throat. Then those full, red lips lightly grazed my own. I felt the tip of her tongue, warm and wet, insistent. I whimpered softly as it entered and slid against mine.

I stroked the silky tattoo. My other hand found Celeste's breast, and I held its fullness in my palm. She moaned into my mouth. I tasted her sweet breath.

"Luce?" Again she whispered my name as if in question. My head fell back as her hands stroked my shoulders and her mouth caressed my throat.

Our breaths turned urgent, shallow and quick. We burned from the white heat of the sun and from the touches of our hands and lips and tongues. When my mouth tugged on her nipple through the filmy muslin of her dress, I heard and felt her gasp.

"Yes," I breathed, finally answering as desire coursed through me. "I want you."

Celeste pulled away from me to look into my face. "Will you come inside?"

I trembled. "Yes . . . yes."

I was only vaguely aware of following her through the door into the house for I was too aroused, so wet and swollen that I could hardly walk. All I could think about was Celeste's moist, warm mouth, her satiny skin, her hands, the breast I had just been kissing. But just as I started to pull her back and in against me, I suddenly *did* notice my surroundings and paused.

It was just one big space, not the inside of an ordinary house. There were no windows and doorways, no rooms with furniture. The only light came from very high up, pouring through a kind of skylight onto a bed. Around and beyond the bed was only darkness. If there were walls, I could not see them. The bed was large and close to the ground, strewn with pillows and coverings in every color of the rainbow.

Somehow, none of this seemed strange to me.

Celeste removed her sandals and gestured for me to take off my running shoes. Taking my hand, she walked me to the low bed, pulling me down. We knelt, facing each other. My heart beat so fiercely against my chest, I thought she must hear and see it.

Reaching around to cup full hips, I pulled Celeste up and into me, pushing my mound against hers. I groaned as I nudged my thigh into the heat between her legs. She thrust hard against me, and I clasped her to me to hold her still, gasping softly into her hair. *Not yet!* I clenched my jaw, warding off the faint ripple of orgasm. The woman in my arms panted softly and shivered.

"Can we get rid of these clothes?" Celeste's voice was husky as she leaned her upper body away and fingered the white tee I wore, brushing my erect nipples. Her hand moved down my stomach, then slid between my legs. I jerked once, uncontrollably, and almost cried out when her fingers slid under my loose running shorts to dip into the slickness they found there.

"Ah," she said, a smile in her voice, "commando."

I must have undressed myself—or been undressed—in a daze for I'm not sure how I lost my outer clothes and bra. I know only that I was naked, breasts and belly and thighs moving slowly against Celeste through a barrier of soft, flimsy cloth.

"I want you naked, too," I said. My voice sounded harsh and my fingers shook as I untied a drawstring at her waist. As I lifted the white cascading folds, our eyes met and my breath caught. I had never before seen such intense desire in a lover's eyes.

I pulled the gown over her head and tossed it aside. The white, diaphanous fabric drifted slowly in the shaft of light from above, its yellow band seeming to glow as it came to rest among the tangled colors on the bed.

Now Celeste wore just a small silk loincloth. I had only to undo the soft ties on either side. I bent down and kissed her there, my lips and teeth moving across her belly, then up to her breast. She lay back and arched up against me. My mouth found a hard nipple, and pulled it in against the tip of my tongue. Then the same with the other one, sucking it. I was ravenous. I thought I would come.

From deep in her throat came a low keening sound as I moved down her body, my mouth leaving a wet trail shimmering in the radiance from above. Celeste's hands twisted in my hair, pressing down, willing my mouth and hands closer to the apex of her thighs.

I knelt between her legs. My hands stroked her inner thighs, which felt as soft and smooth as warm water. I bent down to kiss the dark, curly hair, soft and damp against my lips. I breathed in the sweet sharp scent of arousal as my tongue stroked gently all along the cleft, barely going inside. Celeste moaned and pushed her hips up for more.

With both hands I spread open the drenched vulva. This time it was real—not a painting or a tattoo. Wet and fragrant folds and silky creases—the labia, the hood, the clitoris, the darker entrance. All in hues of red—crimson, rose and carmine. *So beautiful.* I took her sex into my mouth, licking all along its length.

Celeste murmured, then cried out. "Please, inside me, as I come."

One finger, then two, slid easily into her. I drove them deep into her slippery heat. My lips closed around the swollen clitoris, drawing it in, pushing it out with my tongue, in and out. I moaned as my whole being narrowed down to the taste and texture of Celeste's sex and my own arousal, in my belly, between my thighs.

Suddenly, my fingers were gripped in spasm as Celeste convulsed. For a heart-stopping moment I felt her go rigid, arching the whole length of her body. Her shout of rapture went through me as if it were my own.

Fast losing control, I slid up her body. "Touch me!" Fingers found me, stroked me. I exploded into her hand, my ecstatic cries muffled against her throat. I shuddered once more while Celeste held me fast.

At last I pushed myself up and looked down at her. The ethereal light from above reflected from her face like an overexposed image. Her eyes seemed translucent, the palest blue. I looked at her shoulder. Each line and curve of the tattoo glowed brightly too, but as if lit from within. I was dazzled and closed my eyes.

When I opened them again the sky above me was not as deep and clear as it had been when I first lay down to rest after my run. The azure had become a lighter hazy blue, and a few feathery clouds drifted overhead. The warm breeze had picked up a little, making the grass tremble.

I blinked, and my stomach contracted as I remembered the erotic dream. It had been so real that I was very wet. I remembered the scent of the woman's arousal even though I could not smell her on my fingers. Sighing with regret, I wished I were still in the dream, still in her arms.

With a heavy heart I began to jog home the usual way, along the same street as in my dream. The houses were their normal pale gray in the soft light from the sun.

As I came closer to the front steps where I had met the beautiful painter in my dream, I slowed down and stopped. I had never really noticed the house before beause it was almost indistinguishable from the rest in the elegant row. It looked empty. Probably by next week there would be a for sale sign.

When I saw something red, I walked up to the stoop. As I got closer, it appeared to be a large glistening drop of thick red paint—carmine red. The contrast with the dull gray stone upon which it had fallen was almost shocking.

I touched it with shaking fingers. It was wet. I brought it to my nose, and when I smelled the oily fragrance, all the sensations of the dream seemed to resound in my head—the searing light, the colors and textures and aromas, the cries of ecstasy. I smiled, although my chest ached and my eyes blurred with tears. *Celeste.*

Of course, the dream, or whatever it was, faded with time as dreams do. But ever after, I would associate the color carmine, and the word itself, with the scent and silkiness of a woman's sex and the sound and sensation of orgasm.

And still today, whenever I see an iris, I never see just an iris.

Discovery Baptist Camp
Laurie Cox

You come to my bed one afternoon, waking me from a nap on my twin bunk. The primary kids had just left camp. This was the beginning of our second summer together on staff at Discovery Baptist Camp. Since ninth grade we were high school campers, always in different cabins but seeming to pick the same afternoon activities. Being drawn to you wasn't something I worked at, or chose. It just seemed to happen to me. It just seemed to make sense.

"How many kids did you save this week?" you ask.

"Two accepted Jesus, one recommitted. How many did you save?"

You laughed. "Is that supposed to be a lifeguard joke? You guys stick to your kids so close when they're in the water, I don't know why they even pay me to guard."

This bed was not built for two. I know part of you is hanging off the edge by the way you lean into me, but I refuse to scoot over. My hands are under my head, and your head rests on my elbow. I smell the lake in your hair and the dampness of your swimsuit. As we lie on our backs, I don't understand what I'm feeling. It's torture, being this close to you, but I want you closer. When you speak I wish you would turn your head, brush your cheek against mine accidentally.

"Promise we'll be best friends this summer," you say.

"What do you mean?"

"I know you've got lots of friends, I want to be your favorite."

You are my favorite, I want to say. "I don't pick favorites," I say instead.

You roll over quickly and give me a glare. My entire body wishes you would poke me in the ribs, push me against the wall, hold me against my will like when you pinned me to the floor of the staff room and stuck your wet finger in my ear. Your face is inches away from mine when your facetious snarl turns into a smile. Your breath this close is an agony I don't understand. I'm not supposed to feel this way. What is this feeling?

My body is betraying what I know is right by yearning for what is so wrong. I want nothing more than to live how God wants me to live, except when I am with you. And you won't leave.

You fall back on my pillow, laughing. I look away as images of last summer bombard my thoughts. The last time you laid in my bed, just like this but in a cabin full of our friends, you asked me to tell you a story.

"I don't know any good ones."

"Make one up then," you said.

I told a story about you saving drowning kids in the lake. It was almost funny, and you laughed at the right parts. Everyone in the room eventually drifted out, except for one sleeping counselor. You drew shapes on my stomach as I told tales of your heroics. When I couldn't stand the feel of your touch anymore, when I felt like I would explode, I asked, "What are you doing?"

"Nothing."

You didn't look at me, didn't lift your head, and you didn't stop. I watched your finger, dipping close to my belt, swirling around my belly button, across my stomach to pause at the exposed skin below my shirt. I kept going on with the story but was too distracted to think of more funny parts. You kept drawing. I didn't think I'd survive.

Then there was the time you grabbed me from behind, around the waist, and held me, bent over and threatening to pants me in front of the family campers walking to chapel. You grabbed my shorts with one hand and teased them down on one side. You could see my underwear but hid it from everyone's view. I was embarrassed to be seen in your embrace, embarrassed to struggle and make a scene, embarrassed that you hung on so long.

Now you are back on my bed, asking to be my favorite. Heavy breaths brush my forearm and I see that you are sleeping. I know that I am the only girl in the world who thinks about other girls this way. I know you like boys, flirt with them endlessly, and would stop coming around if you knew how I felt about you.

But sometimes, I wonder how you really feel. No one else is as physical with me as you are. No one else looks at me the way you do. I can't think about that. I cannot allow my mind to go there. Your motives are pure, I am sure of it, and I am misinterpreting things.

I force my thoughts to the Bible verses I am memorizing. Another counselor and I started a contest last week. I know I can learn the chapter faster than she can, and I practice in order to drive you out of my head. It makes me sleepy, but I fear letting my guard down. Where will my hands go if I am not aware of them?

I sit up and look over you at the clock. Dinnertime. You stir and turn toward me, brush your hand against my leg and send goose bumps across my skin.

"We should go to dinner," I say, looking at your closed eyelids.

I'm afraid of another counselor coming in to get me and seeing us here, on my bunk, the look on my face, this feeling in my chest, my legs.

"Okay," you say, curling up against me.

Your breathing returns to sleep mode. I look at your face, lying where my face just was. Your lips barely touch, and your eyes are motionless behind their lids. My back is against the wall, and your arm is across my chest, your hand resting gently on my fly.

Your touch is too much. I need to get up, go somewhere else, be with other people and regain my focus. I am pinned against the wall and I don't want to disturb you. I don't want you to move. I tell myself nothing is happening and that I should relax, enjoy the rest, the closeness of another human being.

The skin of your shoulder is pink and hot from the day's sun on the lake. I don't want to, but I can't stop myself from touching its heat. My finger trails slowly down your arm to your finger near my thigh. What am I doing?

I can't remember what I've memorized. I pray no one comes in to walk me down to dinner. I remove my hand, touching first the hem of my shorts and then the hem of yours. I roll the fabric between my fingers without touching your skin. I should not be doing this. I should be at dinner. I should be keeping my thoughts pure. I should be in control.

I hear a group of counselors walk by the cabin window. Have they come to save me from myself? Should I move your hand? I shift my weight in readiness for their knock. It never comes. They don't know I'm here. I watch them walk away, talking and laughing with each other. They are gone, and you and I are still alone.

I look down to see your eyes now open, watching me. You

glance at my fingers, still holding the hem of your shorts, index finger against your thigh, and you smile. I feel myself blush and try to say something distracting. Your hand rests on mine, its soft pressure flattening my hand across your skin. I need to get up. My life depends on it, but your eyes hold me fast. I can smell your breath. It is warm and sweet.

This is all I can stand, and I break your gaze to roll over. I push myself up, to climb over you, to move toward the door. I cannot think twice about this decision. I cannot stop this momentum. I have to be misreading you. I need to get some air.

Your hand on my hip pushes me down on the mattress. I look at your face, your eyes.

"You look worried," you say with a smile.

"I just . . ."

Your lips against mine stop my breath. I try to pull away. This isn't right. But my body won't move. My eyes close. I feel myself getting dizzy as I lean into you. I am no longer in control. I think I never was. You pull away to watch my face.

"I can't do this," I whisper, my eyes clenched tight.

"Okay," you reply, holding the hem of my shorts. You softly kiss my neck as your fingers against my thigh reach up past my boxers to find the physical evidence that I have been thinking of you. I don't understand—you flirt with boys, you're a good Christian girl, this isn't what girls do.

When you touch me again my head spins and I breathe in quickly. You smile as you close your eyes and lean against my chest. I am surprised at how easily your fingers slip into me. Surprised by the feeling when you slide in and out, over and over again. Surprised at how sensitive I am to your touch, how I cannot get enough of it, how my hips move to be closer, how they want to swallow your hand.

I recognize this moment as the dream I have longed for—the one that I banished from my thoughts. It was not your closeness that tortured me, but the lack of your touch. Your touch, which now moves too slowly, back and forth, tracing the edges of parts of me I didn't know were there. I am tortured again, but in a different way. I don't know what to do or say, or even what I want from you. I need something, and my hips push against you to get it but you pull slightly away.

I open my eyes to plead with you and see a knowing smile. In an instant, I know you've done this before, that every lingering touch, every look, every playful jab has been intentional. You flirt with boys while pursuing me. I had no idea. But at the same time, I knew.

You tilt your head to kiss me, harder this time and with your mouth open. My tongue meets yours, and you groan against my lips. A tremor shoots through my body, and the touch of your hand is suddenly painful. You lie still, hovering over me, and I cannot move. I don't even want to move. I lie partially under you, wondering what just happened. Wondering what happens next.

You guide my hand, using my fingers to move aside your swimsuit. Warm and wet, you let go of my hand when it begins to move on its own. I explore you, going to that place on your body where you just went with me, hoping I am doing it right. Thoughts creep in that I shouldn't be doing it at all, but I move my hand faster before I change my mind. I freeze at your first gasp, afraid I have hurt you, afraid someone might hear.

"Keep going," you whisper.

I am surprised at the pleading tone in your voice. I move again, through the groaning this time, through the bucking of your hips, and I watch your face as your body arches. You grab my wrist, throwing my arm to the side.

"Okay," you say between breaths. "Okay."

This is not okay. I have done something I should not have done. And all I can think about is doing it again. I watch as your face relaxes, your eyes open and you smile at me.

"I thought you'd never come around," you say, after moments

of silence.

"I don't . . . I mean, we shouldn't . . ." I really don't know what to say or what I want to say. I want this to be okay. I want to be okay with it. I am okay with it for now, but I know I shouldn't be.

"I'll show you we shouldn't," you say, and suddenly you are kneeling between my legs. My shorts are off, and in a moment my body is filled with the feeling of your mouth. My mind has no room for guilt, for what should or shouldn't be. For now, I give in, let it go and simply be with you.

Writer's Block
Jane Fletcher

I've never actually faked an orgasm, but I'll admit to overacting on occasions.

For a long time the line lay alone at the top of the page. I stared at it, trying to think of a second sentence, and failed.

I had writer's block bad—really bad. Another long, frustrating evening had driven me to reading fan-fiction on the Web. Some was good, some wasn't, but a common trend ran through them. The sex was always improbably dynamic—dribbling hot love juices, hard-throbbing clits and nipples.

It's like that in books. There are pages given over to astoundingly successful lovemaking, and no shortage of gruesome rapes. But as I sat staring pensively at my computer, it struck me that I'd never seen more than a line or two about bad sex—the mediocre stuff that runs a poor second to a nice cup of tea. Why was it dismissed so quickly? Was I the only lesbian to ever have sex where the earth failed to move? Sometimes it wasn't even worth staying awake for.

My fingers moved toward the keyboard. Perhaps here was my story. I could be the first to write, in agonizing and quite excessive detail, "Bad Sex." I would describe each half-hearted maneuver of each tedious minute. Then I paused. There had to be a reason for the omission. Maybe there was nothing you could say on the subject. I decided to try a few test sentences:

Allison's hand roamed down my body. She hesitated at my stomach, as if unsure, but then moved on. Her fingers combed my pubic hair before dipping down between my legs, probing into the soft folds. She brought her mouth closer to my ear and murmured, "Are you always this dry?"

"Er . . . no . . . it's the time of month. I'm due soon. It sometimes affects me." As did boredom, although I knew it would not be tactful to say it aloud.

I considered the passage for a while, swapping around words. It had potential. I was sure I could get a short story from it. What I needed was a scenario—nothing too involved, just a bit of background. I addressed myself more purposefully to the keyboard and typed:

Bad Sex Scenarios

1) An old friend has been ditched by her lover, she starts off crying on the shoulder of the main character, then makes a play for her. Out of pity, the main character says yes, and immediately regrets it.

2) At her girlfriend's insistence, the main character agrees to act out a scene from a favorite novel. The main character is self-conscious and very embarrassed.

3) At their anniversary dinner, the main character ignores her partner's advice and drinks too much wine. She is feeling nauseous when her partner initiates post-dinner lovemaking, but admitting it would cause a row.

4) Having banged into her ex at a disco, draped around the neck of someone stunning, the main character grabs the first woman who walks by so she can wipe the smile off her ex's face. She has second thoughts on the taxi ride home, but by then it's too late to back out.

I stopped typing. Scenario four was it. My gaze drifted to the ceiling, but not for long. How should I handle the story? Going for laughs would be easy:

Of all the women available, why had I picked Gabby—the worst gossip in town? And it was going to be a disaster. I could feel it. By tomorrow night, Gabby would be gleefully describing my less-than-perfect performance to anyone who'd listen, complete with gestures and sound effects. How bitterly I now regretted the curried beans I'd had for lunch.

I shook my head at the screen. Cheap jokes weren't really what I wanted. However, could I make it serious without slipping into melodrama? I gave it a try:

Susan's hand kneaded my breast through the thickness of my clothes. The action was as sensual as a milking machine. And I was the poor cow. With her thumb, she rubbed a button on my shirt. Maybe she thought it was my nipple. Should I point out her mistake? Maybe she knew what she was doing. She couldn't seriously expect my nipple to be quite that hard? Perhaps, like me, she just didn't care.

I sat back and looked at the words. Then I stared through them, my eyes unfocused. Caring. That was the problem. Eventually, the screen saver sprung into life, multicolored lines bouncing around frenetically. I hit the mouse, calling back the words. My writer's block was mounting a counterattack. I had to write something:

Mary was flopping around on the bed. I closed my eyes. I didn't want to be there. It wasn't her fault—heaven knows she was putting in enough effort. Her hands flowed all over me, but too hard and much too quickly. I could have said something, yet there seemed no point. One of us might as well enjoy herself, and no matter what Mary did, it wasn't going to be me.

The thought suddenly struck me: Was Mary really enjoying herself? She was moaning in what sounded like pleasure, but I was too. Was it possible we were both acting? Perhaps if I suggested we stop and watch

TV instead she'd sigh in relief. And perhaps she'd be devastated. It would be the most awful kick to her self-esteem.

Mary's nail scratched across my clitoris. I caught the yelp at the back of my throat, which wasn't wise. Mary might mistake the sound for a groan of passion and repeat the action. It was my own fault. Normally I'd have no problem asking a lover to be more careful, smiling and making a joke, but I couldn't at the moment. I just wanted to get it all over with as soon as possible.

My thoughts scurried through several ideas. I could go down on her. A dual benefit. It would get my clitoris safely away from her fingernails, and I wouldn't have to work at controlling my expression. I was currently nibbling her ear and trying to ignore the taste of wax. I looked the length of Mary's body. How quickly could I kiss my way down without seeming too hurried? Twenty? Maybe twenty-five kisses along the way? I—

The telephone rang. I stared at it, while my heart tried to crawl up my throat. It couldn't be her, could it? I pried my hand from the keyboard and lifted the receiver to my ear. "Hello?"

Julie's voice twittered from the phone. "Oh hi, it's me."

Of course it was. I closed my eyes, praying her next words would be along the lines of "I had a rethink, I miss you, I'm coming back."

"Are you still there?" she asked.

"Yes."

"Look, I'm sorry to disturb you, but did I leave my green shirt at your place? You know, my favorite one with the cuffs?"

"No."

"Are you sure?"

"I haven't seen it." I was lying. It was under my pillow.

"Oh, right, well . . . sorry to disturb you . . . I'll just—"

"Julie—" I cut off her rambling. The silence grew longer as I tried to find the words I wanted. "Please, could we meet up . . . talk. I promise I'll—"

"There's no point. We both know that." This time it was Julie who interrupted me, the gentleness in her voice only making the ache worse. "I'm sorry. I shouldn't have rung you. If you find the shirt you can keep it. I didn't mean to—" She bit back the sentence. "Look . . . oh . . . bye."

The phone went dead. Slowly, very slowly, I put it back on the hook. While staring blankly at the screen, I massaged the palm of my hand with my fingers, as if it had been strained by holding her voice. Julie had gone and taken all my words with her.

I reached out to the keyboard. With one finger I tapped on the up arrow, getting the cursor back to the list of scenarios, then I moved my hands over the keys:

5) The main character is still desperately in love, but her girlfriend is getting bored with the relationship. Sex had been wonderful. However, even this is becoming mechanical. While making love, the main character is terrified it will be the last time ever. She tries everything she can, yet her girlfriend remains distant. Fear and misery kill any hope of it working. Her actions are artificial, passionless, painful, but when she stops the charade, she knows her girlfriend will say something starting with, "I've been thinking about us . . ." The main character is further hampered by the need to keep her face averted, so her girlfriend won't see the tears.

I couldn't type on. My hands balled tightly into fists. My eyes scrunched closed. For a while I struggled with breathing.

I knew there had to be a reason why nobody writes bad sex. I forced my eyes open, flexed my fingers, and took hold of the mouse. I drove the cursor to the top right-hand corner and clicked on <u>C</u>lose. The dialog box threw back the question at me: Do you want to save the changes you made to Document 1? <Yes> <No> <Cancel>

I hit <No>.

<Shutdown>.

Moving to the Heartland
Bryn Haniver

I was in a coffee shop just down the street from my apartment when I got the big news. The Man himself called to congratulate me. It was a huge promotion, and I knew I should be overjoyed. I'd be the first woman to become a regional CEO for the company. I'd been working manically toward this for the past seven years. Really, for my whole life.

The thing was, the regional office was in a small town in Kansas. The Heartland. Conservative Central. There wouldn't be a beach with rocky headlands and pounding surf nearby. There wouldn't be alternative theatre, Chinatown, or funky concerts. Of course, I hadn't had much time for any of those things these past few years, but they were available if I wanted.

The manager of the coffee shop walked past my table, carrying a heavy box. I sighed, thinking there probably wouldn't even be a coffee shop like this one anywhere near my new workplace. The manager was clearly a lesbian, with cropped hair frosted blond and baggy clothes that didn't hide her muscular physique. She was cute in a boyish way and although she wasn't big, she had an imposing presence.

I smiled as the girl at the counter moved to help her. I was in here enough to remember her name. Aya was a cute young Asian woman, kind of Goth, with medium-length dark hair framing her face. She was twenty-two tops, and soft-spoken. I was pretty sure she was gay too—probably everyone who worked here was gay, and most of the customers as well.

From what I'd heard, the regional office in Kansas wasn't just in the Heartland, it was in the boonies, the centerpiece of what was pretty much a company town. There definitely wouldn't be a coffee shop like this. I stared at my phone, still warm, sitting on the table beside my empty coffee cup. I should be happy. Ecstatic.

I'd have all the power and responsibility I could handle. I'd be making tons more money. I'd worked for this. Hard. At least sixty hours a week for years. I had no social life, never took a vacation—basically just slept and worked, pausing occasionally to eat take-out when I wasn't dining with business clients. I'd busted and rebusted my ass for this promotion. So why wasn't I ecstatic?

Aya appeared in front of me, smiling in her hesitant way. "Can I get you another coffee?" she asked.

Distracted, I mumbled something and she leaned toward me to hear. The top buttons of her coffee-colored uniform shirt were undone, giving me a beautiful view of her cleavage. She had small but exquisitely shaped breasts. Christ, I thought. Why was I noticing this now? You damn well better learn not to be ogling waitresses in the Heartland!

I shook my head. "No thanks. Actually, I need to get home and start packing."

A couple days later, I headed for the coffee shop after working a sixteen-hour day. I'd been out for dinner with an important client and several colleagues, so I was still wearing my best business chic, a wool crepe jacket with a matching dress that showed just enough of my legs to impress people without distracting them.

It was after eleven and the coffee shop was closing. "Can I come in?" I asked the manager. Her name came to me suddenly—it was Sacha.

"Coffee machine's off," she said, her voice gruff.

"That's okay. Actually, I, um, wanted to ask a favor of you two," I replied, trying not to stammer.

Sacha raised an eyebrow but Aya, sweeping the floor behind her, said "Sure."

I'd been going over a hundred different things to ask them in my head, and none of them really seemed right. They were both giving me curious looks—we hadn't spoken much and they probably had no idea what favor a woman like me might need from them.

"I got a big promotion," I said, quickly adding, "I'm moving to the Heartland. To Kansas." They stood there, obviously wondering where this was going. "I, um, I'm not really sure if I'll like it there. I feel like I've been missing out on a lot of life with all the work I've been doing and it'll only get worse there and I . . ."

I was babbling, my skin felt flushed, my voice was fading. I felt an overpowering urge to chicken out and run home. This was it—now or never.

"I want you both to come back to my apartment and fuck my brains out," I blurted.

Aya gasped, but Sacha gave me a very thorough once-over with her eyes. "What's in the bag?" she asked, nodding at the large handbag I was clutching.

My throat had closed and my head was spinning, so I just held it out. She took it, looked inside, and smiled.

"We'll be there in twenty minutes," she said. "Right after we close up."

"We will?" I heard Aya say, but my courage had fled and I was already on my way out the door.

"Be sure to leave that outfit on," Sacha called after me as I reached the sidewalk.

Back at my apartment, I wondered why on earth I was doing this. I'd been married to my work, a social hermit. Well, that wasn't entirely true—I'd been out plenty, to dinners and parties and conferences, but all of them had been related to work. My socializing was always calculated—how could the person help my career? I'd kept everything friendly but professional, refraining from even flirting. People took me seriously, and I was about to reap the benefits—I was being promoted to regional CEO.

In Kansas. In the Heartland. In the here and now though, there was no way that two lesbians working in a coffee shop on the coast could help my career. Yet I had just offered my body to them, something I would never do for a business client or colleague. What was I thinking?

I opened an expensive bottle of wine, poured a glass, and sat on one of the bar stools in my apartment. For whatever reason, I was more excited about what might happen tonight than the promotion. I hadn't had sex in years. I hadn't even thought much about it for most of that time. I'm not sure how long I stared at the wall before the buzz of the doorbell made me jump.

They'd come straight over and I wondered if Sacha had talked Aya into it. Both women were still in the khakis and shirts they wore at the shop. As Sacha had requested—or rather, as she'd demanded—I was still in my business jacket and dress.

"You have a nice place," Aya said, looking around shyly. Sacha didn't say anything. She just dumped the contents of my handbag onto the coffee table. I hadn't skimped. There were two top-quality harnesses, with pockets for small vibrators over the clit. Alongside were three butterfly vibes, one as a spare, two containers of lube and a pack of extra batteries. Gigantic dildos had seemed silly looking, so instead I'd chosen a medium-sized, abstract pair, one purple, one blue. Sacha grabbed the blue one, nodding appreciatively.

Aya's eyes went wide. "I don't know," she whispered. "It's, um, not really my style." God, she was adorable.

"I voted Republican," I told her.

Her eyes narrowed. "Pass me a harness," she said to Sacha.

Sacha grinned. "I'll show you how to put it on, babe," she told Aya, leading her toward my spare room. Looking back over her shoulder, she told me "You stay right here." There was no arguing with her tone.

They emerged without any pants or underwear on, just the coffee-shop shirts half covering their new equipment. Aya had long brown legs, her willowy body a contrast to Sacha's petite but strong frame. I stood, my stomach fluttering madly, as Sacha strutted right up to me.

"Take off your jacket," she said, her eyes intense. My arms moved on their own, pulling the jacket off and tossing it onto one of the bar stools. I never tossed my business clothes. My dress was sleeveless, and cut to flare with my curves.

"You're beautiful," Aya said. Sacha's lip just curled into a smile.

"On your knees, Republican Miss," Sacha said. As my legs bent, I thought that she must be a great manager—she had a way of speaking that made you want to obey. Kneeling on my living room carpet, the naked legs and jutting phalluses of the two women in front of me were much more obvious. I felt giddy.

Sacha stepped forward, holding the base of her dildo. Looking down at me, she nodded, and I knew what she wanted. I opened my mouth and took her in. The dildo was smooth and cool, but I could smell Sacha's warmth. My nostrils flared, and tingles ran down my spine as I licked and sucked her. Aya appeared alongside Sacha, those long legs running up to a trim, dark pussy, partially covered by the harness and dildo.

Keeping one hand on Sacha, I pulled Aya's dildo into my

mouth, sucking her, catching her scent. I heard her make a little noise as I did, and Sacha let out a soft, throaty laugh. I moved between them until Sacha stopped me with her hand in my hair.

"Open wide," she said. "I want to see you take it all." I looked up at her, a bit scared. I wasn't exactly an expert at this. She pushed and I felt the dildo slide past my lips. Trying not to gag, I let it slip farther and farther back.

I gagged and pulled away, tears coming to my eyes. "I can't do it," I said. "I'm sorry." I really was.

Sacha actually looked impressed. "Maybe you're a better businesswoman than I thought," she said. She pulled her shirt over her head, and motioned for Aya to do the same. I'd made sure the apartment was warm.

Sacha walked over to the coffee table and grabbed a bottle of lube. "Now, sweet young Aya here has never done this sort of thing before, so we'll have to give her a bit of practice." She handed the bottle to Aya and told her, "Lube up."

Still on my knees, I stared as the now naked Aya spread lube over her dildo. It was something to watch, especially when I imagined what she might do with it. I felt Sacha's hand on my shoulder.

"Hands and knees," Sacha told me. I went to all fours. "Now flatten your chest to the carpet," she added. After I did, I felt her hands lifting my dress. She worked it right up over my ass, whistling her approval. Then she pulled my underwear down, exposing me completely.

My face, chest and knees were pressed against the expensive carpet, my ass high in the air. I watched Aya, sideways and looking very tall from this angle, as she walked behind me. I shuddered as I felt Sacha's fingers gently open me up.

"Wow," Sacha said. "We probably didn't need the lube."

"What—what do I do?" I heard Aya ask softly.

"Kneel right here," Sacha replied. "That's right. Now use your hand to guide . . . that's it. That's it exactly."

I nearly came as Aya slid into me. How long had it been? I heard her moan as her belly touched my ass, the full length of the dildo inside me now. Sacha's hand caressed my shoulder. "Breathe, business lady. Breathe, or you'll pass out."

She was right. I wasn't breathing. I let out a gasp, and sucked air into my lungs. Little spots shimmered in my eyes.

Aya grabbed my hips. Sacha said, "Pull back a bit, Aya," and I felt a hand for a second. A faint buzzing started—Sacha must have turned on the vibrator nestled over Aya's clit.

Aya started moaning and thrusting, clutching my hips with her long fingers. I couldn't get enough of her, pressing myself back even as she slammed me harder into the floor. In what seemed like a few seconds I was coming, and from the sound of it, so was she. My pussy clenched the dildo, spasming around it, while Aya grabbed my shoulders and we both collapsed onto the rug.

Sacha laughed with delight. "Ten seconds," she said. "Like a couple of high school boys." She knelt beside me and grabbed one of my legs. Before I knew what was happening, she ripped the underwear wrapped around my thighs right off, lifted my leg up over her shoulder and slid her own dildo into me. She paused for a second to flick the vibrator on and a wide smile spread across her face. The she started to fuck me.

I hadn't recovered from my first orgasm and was a bit tender at first, but her steady thrusts worked through that quickly enough. Soon I was panting, twisting my body to meet her strong hips. She deftly spun me so I was on my back, both legs on her shoulders, my dress bunching up around my waist as I lifted my hips to meet hers.

I must have been quite a sight, because Sacha's eyes glazed with lust and her thrusts got quicker and quicker. She angled my hips until the dildo was hitting my G-spot and I was crying out with every thrust. This time, my orgasm took longer, building with each pulse. As I came, Sacha used one hand to press the vibrator against her clit—the result was immediate and frantic. I took it all deep inside, screaming out, yet reaching over to touch Aya, still lying beside me, her eyes wide.

Afterward we took a break, ordering some excellent take-out and finishing two bottles of good wine. I wore the remains of my dress, while the other two removed their harnesses and put their shirts back on. Neither woman did up more than two buttons, which kept me distracted and horny throughout the quick meal. When the food was gone, Sacha mentioned that she wasn't done with me yet, which was just fine by me.

She led me into the master bedroom, where they stripped the wrinkled remains of my dress off, leaving me in just a bra. "Since you specifically requested us both," Sacha told me as she put her harness back on, "you're going to get us both at once." Aya put her own harness on like a pro, and both women removed their shirts. Seeing them naked, erect and eager made me ache.

Sacha yanked the comforter clean off the bed and motioned to Aya. "On your back, sweetie," she said. Aya laid on the bed, her purple dildo jutting upward. I stared.

"Pretty, isn't she," Sacha whispered into my ear. "Those impossibly long legs," she continued, her fingers deftly undoing my bra. Her hands moved to my breasts, finding my stiff nipples. "Those wide, loving, dark eyes," she continued, squeezing. I whimpered and stared.

Sacha let go of me and walked over to the bed, reaching between Aya's legs to turn the butterfly vibrator on. "Straddle her," Sacha told me. Knees weak, I moved to the bed. I lowered myself down onto sweet, young Aya, her almond eyes getting glassy as I enveloped the dildo that jutted up from her pussy. I took her all in and our pubes pressed together. I could feel the buzz of the little vibrator in her harness now, and from her expression, she could really feel it.

I lifted up a bit, relishing the look she gave me and smiling as she eagerly lifted her hips to follow. I pushed back down, pinning her to the bed, the vibrator buzzing deliciously between us.

"All right cutie pies," I heard Sacha say. "Sandwich time. Lean over, Miss Fortune Five Hundred, and get ready to take it up your ass."

The words made me clench, literally and figuratively. My only experience with anal sex had been ten years previous and entirely unsuccessful. I wanted to hide, to refuse, to . . . well the problem was, I really didn't want to get off of Aya. It felt so good to have her in me, to be above her like this. I leaned forward, pressing more of our bodies together. For better or worse, I wasn't going anywhere.

Aya stroked my hair and whispered encouragement while Sacha knelt on the bed behind me. Fingers, slippery with lube, touched my exposed anus, and I whimpered at the frightening pleasure of it. I laid my head on Aya's chest and she wrapped her arms around me protectively as Sacha slowly pushed the cool dildo against my tightened ass.

I couldn't stay tense in Aya's arms. Her soft voice, the warmth of our breasts pressed together, the feel of her deep inside my pussy, was sublimely relaxing. I felt myself opening, felt Sacha push past the ring of muscle, moving deeper, slow and deliberate. I shuddered. It hurt a bit, but I let her fill me up.

When she stopped, I felt so full it paralyzed me. Sacha was all the way in now, her hips against me, the dildo deep inside. My ass twitched uncontrollably, gripping the dildo again and again, while the rest of my body was perfectly still.

"It's okay," Aya whispered. I lifted my head and my eyes refocused on hers, so close. They were warm with concern, and something else. Lust. It burned into me. I smiled a bit, saw her smile, and felt her hips move beneath me. It was a small thrust, tentative, but it banished the last of the pain and apprehension I was feeling. I ground myself downward a bit, shifting both of the dildos that were deep inside me. The sensations made me moan, loud.

"Awesome," growled Sacha, behind me. She'd been waiting patiently for me to adjust, keeping her own lust in check. Now she began to move.

Soon all three of us were moving in sync. Sacha set the pace, reading my comfort and arousal like a pro. She'd obviously done some ass-fucking before. As I became more and more aroused, she increased the power and speed of her thrusting, while below me, Aya looked stoned with lust, squirming fiercely as I ground our pubes together. My last rational thought was, *This sure ain't Kansas.*

The orgasm started in my ass, helpless to resist Sacha's deep, steady thrusting. It split in two and curved forward around my pussy, filling my soaked labia with sensation. It met at my clit, and by then I was completely lost in it, thrashing madly between the two women, the sensations obliterating everything else. I know I screamed because I was hoarse for two days, and I know my orgasm swept them both along with me. Sacha clutched my hips and pumped for all she was worth, smashing the butterfly vibrator against her own clit. Aya arched her back, mashing our breasts together while her hips twitched her dildo spasmodically upward into me.

We all must have collapsed at about the same time, because when I came to my senses I was between them, our naked bodies sprawled on the damp sheets, limbs still entwined. I started sobbing.

They let me cry. "Lots of people cry after anal sex," Sasha said. "It's an emotional release." She didn't need to add I'd been a tightass my entire life. Aya just stared into my eyes as she stroked my hair, looking happy and concerned at the same time. Lying between them both, I cried and cried. It was wonderful.

You're probably wondering if I took the job in Kansas. It's a good question. Did I really need to be a regional CEO, a Master of the Universe, or could I scale back a bit on my ambition and try instead for a more balanced life on the coast? Maybe I stayed, content with my place in the company, giving Sacha free reign to fill me up and satisfy my hungers every now and again.

Then again, maybe ambition really is a big part of who I am. Maybe I took the job, moved to the Heartland, and am the best damn regional CEO the company has ever seen. Maybe I brought Aya with me, and she is the sweetest, most wonderful person I've met, someone who can provide the balance that my life was lacking.

Maybe we live together, discreet but still proud, happy in the Heartland.

Picture Perfect
Barbara Johnson

"Damn," I said as I struggled to carry my purse, two grocery bags, a briefcase and a Starbucks latte while dodging pedestrians along busy Connecticut Avenue. My balancing act failed—the cup of latte fell from my hand, landing with a splat that shot the lid off and sent foamy milk and coffee splashing all over the designer boots of a bleached blonde.

She glared at me over her shoulder. "Clumsy ox."

Just as I opened my mouth to offer an insincere apology—she was, after all, also wearing a fur coat—someone grabbed my grocery bags and said, "Let me help you with those." I turned, fully prepared to refuse, and found myself staring into the most gorgeous brown eyes I'd ever seen. And Lord, that smile and the look in her eyes had my gaydar going wild.

Uncharacteristically tongue-tied, I could only open and close my mouth like a fish. The owner of those eyes smiled at me, making me even more stupid. "Oh," I said finally. Then, "I mean, thank you."

She tugged on the bags gently. I let them go, wishing the sidewalk would open and swallow me up. Making a great pretense of arranging my purse and briefcase, I delayed looking at her for as long as possible. I was afraid I would lose my composure more than I had already. Then, realizing we'd already blocked the sidewalk long enough, I smiled my thanks and nodded. We began walking together.

"Thanks so much," I said. "My name's Samantha. Samantha Rogers."

"Jasmine Jackson," she replied, then laughed. "What do you have in these?" she asked, raising the two plastic bags a couple of inches.

I felt my cheeks grow warm. There was a reason nice people called me curvy, although unkind ones called me fat for daring to be a size twelve. "Ice cream," I said, "and a gallon of milk."

"Well then, we'd best get these home before they melt."

As we walked, making small talk about the weather and the traffic, I kept glancing at her, taking in her creamy milk-chocolate skin and riotous dark curls that had just a slight hint of red. Her luscious lips, shiny with pale gloss, were full and utterly kissable, the thought of which made me blush again. She was taller than me, though not by much, and slimmer. She had a bold, confident stride, one that I struggled to keep up with.

"I'm sorry," she said, slowing down. "Am I walking too fast for you?"

"No," I lied.

"My friends tell me to slow down all the time."

I stopped in front of my brownstone. "My apartment's down there," I said, indicating a small flight of stairs to the basement. She waited patiently while I fumbled with the lock. I was really making a good impression today.

"This is cute," she said, standing in my tiny living room while I took the grocery bags from her, thankful that I had cleaned the place yesterday.

"Can I offer you something to drink?" I called from the kitchen. I quickly shoved the two gallons of cookie dough ice cream to the back of the freezer.

"Hot tea would be nice."

I couldn't believe my luck. She was staying. It had been a while since I'd had an attractive woman in my apartment. Any woman, actually. As the words to *Afternoon Delight* hummed through my head, I made tea, hoping I hadn't lost all my social skills. I put the teapot, along with two cups and milk and sugar, on a tray and brought it out to the living room. Jasmine was standing at my bookshelf, reading the titles. She'd taken off her coat, and I couldn't help but admire her shapely ass, snug in tight blue jeans that tucked into slim, brown boots. She turned around when she heard me, and I almost dropped the tray. Her low-cut, pumpkin-orange sweater left little to the imagination. Her bulky coat had covered up a fine-looking pair.

I must have been staring foolishly because she smiled mischievously and walked over to me, taking the tray from my hands. If I'd had any doubts she was a lesbian, Jasmine dispelled those by holding my gaze and letting her fingers linger longer than necessary on mine and then bending over just enough so I could catch a better glimpse of her generous cleavage.

She placed the tray on my coffee table, then sat on the sofa and patted the seat next to her. I was beginning to feel like a visitor in my own apartment. But that is what happens when you forget your hostess manners. I sat next to her, nervously. God, I'd even forgotten how to flirt. I watched as she poured tea, noticing her long fingers with their pale pink nails. Wanting those fingers to stroke my skin.

"Oh," I said. She looked at me quizzically. I jumped up. "I forgot the lemon."

She grabbed my hand. Her touch affected me immediately. My knees grew weak as a not unpleasant shiver coursed through me. I felt stirrings in my stomach and between my legs, stirrings that made me blush yet again. Her hold on my hand became gentle.

"I don't take lemon," she said softly, letting her fingers caress the top of my hand. She tugged until I sat again, then leaned forward and lightly kissed me. "You're adorable," she said.

I'm sure my blush mode was in full force. Either that or I was having hot flashes at the early age of thirty. I couldn't remember the last time a woman had so boldly flirted with me. I wasn't fond of the bars, and I didn't meet a lot of potential girlfriends at my job as an assistant to a political consultant. It was always boys, boys and more boys. And now I was a speechless idiot.

Jasmine picked up a tea cup and handed it to me. "Tell me about yourself," she said as she settled back against the couch cushions, crossing one long leg over the other. Her smile was warm and friendly, and she appeared genuinely curious.

Stalling for time, I took a long sip of my tea. She'd sweetened it a bit too much for my liking, but I wasn't about to say so. Instead, I said, "Nothing too exciting, really. I work for a political consultant."

"I would think that's a very interesting job."

I rolled my eyes. "Believe me, it's not. One politician in this town is like any other. Although, I did get to meet Tammy Baldwin from Wisconsin. She's very nice." I took another sip. "And a lesbian too."

"Yes, I know her." She laughed. "Well, I don't *know* her, like personally. But I admire her a lot."

She started softly stroking my arm. Her fingers sent tingles all through my body. Oh my, this woman was certainly very bold, and a fast worker. I wondered what her motive could be. I mean, she was an absolute stunner, my very own Tyra Banks clone live in my living room, and I was just an average sort of girl with ash blond hair and green eyes, though I'd been told by an Irish ex that my eyes made her think of her homeland. I took Jasmine's hand and looked at her.

"Jasmine . . ." I took a deep breath. "I don't mean to sound like a prude or anything, but I don't know anything about you, or you about me, and it seems like you're moving awfully fast here. I mean, we met over a spilled latte a little over an hour ago."

She laughed again, deep-throated and sexy. "Not to scare you or anything, but I've noticed you before." She soothed my startled look with a caress on my cheek. "You go to that Starbucks every day at the same time. I saw you the first time about two weeks ago."

"Why didn't you just approach me there?"

"Just waiting for the right opportunity."

Contrary to what I might have felt under any other circumstances, the fact she had watched me all this time didn't creep me out. I was actually flattered. Of course, that could have been my lonely spinster talking. Before I could say anything, she leaned forward and looked at me very seriously. I tried to look serious too, but her enticing décolletage distracted me. I wanted more than anything to plant a kiss between those luscious breasts. I forced myself to look at her face, blushing again when I saw her grinning. I had no doubt she'd read my mind.

"I'm a photographer," she said, "and I'm always looking for interesting subjects. That's why I troll places like coffee shops." She took my hand again. "And I think you'd make a marvelous model."

I laughed out loud. Me? A model? "Oh Jasmine, I'm flattered, but you don't have to lie to me."

She looked offended. "I don't care what other people think, I'm not interested in what you see in magazines and on film. Those flat-chested, skinny girls with bleached hair extensions and a hundred plastic surgeries aren't real. You're real. And very beautiful to me."

How could I not believe those earnest brown eyes? With the way she looked at me, I felt beautiful. And desirable. I wished we could have met under different circumstances—like when I was all dressed up for the Kennedy Center and wearing makeup, not in frumpy business clothes with a nose red from the cold. But I could see from her expression that she was being truthful. Once again I got that tingly feeling all through my body. God, how I wanted to kiss her. And so I did.

Her lips were soft, and she opened them for me, letting me slip my tongue inside her mouth. She tasted sweet. I put a hand on her shoulder, then let it drift down until it rested lightly on her breast. I caressed her through the orange sweater, enjoying the way her nipple hardened at my touch. She moaned softly as I pushed her back against the couch, letting my free hand roam through her dark, corkscrew curls. I traced my fingernails lightly across the back of her neck. She moaned again, and I think I did too.

"Samantha . . ." she murmured against my mouth.

"Yes?"

"We really shouldn't . . ."

Was she really going to stop me? I felt her hands push gently against my chest. With a sigh, I ended our kiss and leaned away from her. She didn't look like she wanted to quit. Her swollen lips glistened beckoningly, her gorgeous eyes luminous and inviting, and her erect nipples strained against the wool of her sweater. Damn, that color looked fabulous on her.

She laughed, but playfully. "You said yourself we don't really know each other. And unfortunately I have to prepare for a gallery opening. But I'd like to see you again. Will you come by my studio on Saturday? I truly do want to photograph you."

Disappointed that we wouldn't get to know each other better that night, I agreed to come to her place. After she wrote down her address and phone number, I went outside with her. She kissed me at the top of my stairs, not caring at all who might see us.

"Don't forget," she said as she took off down the street.

"Not a chance," I said, watching her delightful backside as she disappeared into the crowd.

I don't know how I managed to function at work those three days before our Saturday date. All I could think of was Jasmine and what she'd been hiding beneath the orange sweater and tight blue jeans. And listening to her sexy voice when she called me on the phone each night only made me desire her even more. But Saturday did come, and I dressed carefully that morning in black jeans and a black and white sweater that accentuated my curves. I also put on a surprise underneath—a black-lace–trimmed purple bra and panty set that I hoped wouldn't stay on long.

I found her place without any trouble. She lived on the ninth floor of a corner building in an expensive part of town. A doorman let me in, and security called up to Jasmine's apartment to make sure I was welcome. My whole apartment could have fit into the ornate lobby. In mere moments I was escorted onto an elevator for a short ride, until the elevator door opened with a silent whoosh and Jasmine stood waiting for me. She was as beautiful as I remembered.

"You look lovely," she said as she led me into her apartment. It was so bright, I blinked. An enormous skylight took up most of the ceiling, and the windows on the far wall were practically floor to ceiling. "I need the light for my work."

"I thought you were a photographer."

"I am." She took my coat, then laughed. "Oh, I see. You think only painters need studios like this."

"Don't you worry about glare?" I asked as I eyed the enormous velvet-covered sofa against one wall. Just the idea of that sensuous fabric against my bare skin made certain body parts begin to tingle. Several cameras on tripods stood before it.

"Not at all," Jasmine answered as she took my hand and led me to the sofa. She brushed my hair away from my face, kissing me softly on my eyelids, then my mouth. The effect of her touch was immediate. I could feel my breasts swell, their nipples harden, while between my legs a rush of fluid made me squirm uncomfortably. Her kisses became more demanding as she grabbed my hair and pulled my head back, leaving my throat exposed to her teeth and mouth. In no time at all, she had my sweater off. I fumbled with the zipper of my jeans, wanting to help her along. She took off my boots, then my jeans and socks.

She stood before me as I lay sprawled on the couch, clad in only my bra and panties. The look of appreciation and hunger in her eyes made me catch my breath.

"You have a gorgeous body. Wonderfully voluptuous," she said, grinning.

I waited for her to come to me, to take me in her arms and ravish me, but she stepped back behind a camera, leaving me severely disappointed. A quick click of a remote and the hot, pulsing beat of Heart's *Barracuda* filled the room.

"Samantha, pose for me," she commanded.

Surprisingly, my normally shy self had not come along that day. Whether it was the music of Heart or the way Jasmine looked at me or both, my inhibitions fled as I performed and posed for her. Recalling images of Marilyn Monroe and Jane Russell and Ava Gardner, I stretched out, letting my breasts thrust forward as I ran my fingers through my hair. The camera clicked as I twisted and turned, looking at Jasmine over my shoulder, running my hands over my body. Sitting. Laying. Click. One knee up. Running my tongue over my lips. Click. Hands caressing my breasts, traveling down over the soft curve of my belly and between my legs. I could feel how wet I was through my satin underwear. The music throbbed, making my clit throb too. Click. The warm rays of the sun streamed through the skylight, heating my body and making me glow.

"Yes, that's it," Jasmine said. "Just like that."

I took off my bra.

"Oh, yes," she said.

Next came my panties.

"Oh, God."

Click. I arched my back and took both my nipples between my fingers. Click. I leaned against the velvet, spreading my legs. Leaving one hand to play with my breast, I let the other wander down to play with the curly hair between my legs. Click. I ran two fingers through my hair, over my clit, and between my labia. Click. I was slick with wet, my clit hard. I stroked myself slowly, feeling the flutterings of pre-climax begin. Mere anticipation had kept me on the verge for three days. Click. Not wanting to come yet, I left my clit and dipped my fingers briefly inside me, hearing Jasmine gasp as I then brought them glistening to my mouth.

With a groan, Jasmine was suddenly between my legs, pushing them farther apart as she pulled me to the edge of the couch. Her hands roamed up my thighs, followed closely by her lips. I moaned as I grabbed hold of her head, guiding her mouth to my molten center. Her tongue licked me, stroked my clit. She opened me with her fingers, letting her tongue dip first before she thrust her fingers inside me, whether two or three I didn't know. I was so wet, they slid easily and deep.

"Jasmine," I said, "please don't stop."

She laughed softly, a low humming that vibrated against me. I pushed against her mouth and fingers, pulling on her hair to bring her closer to me, feeling her coarse curls graze my thighs. She sucked my clit, harder and faster. "Oh, yes," I moaned, feeling the orgasm build. Her tongue fluttered over me. "Oh, God. Yes!"

I bucked against her as she withdrew her fingers so she could hold me down with both hands. Her mouth and tongue didn't stop their exquisite torture. Waves and waves of orgasm swept over me. I called out Jasmine's name again and again before the waves subsided and I fell back limp and panting against the couch. I could feel the velvet damp beneath me.

"Mmmm," Jasmine was saying as she continued to nuzzle me.

I pushed her gently away. "I don't think I can take anymore," I said, smiling.

She looked up at me, her lips swollen and her eyes shining. She came to me when I reached for her, and as she hovered above me I pulled her shirt off to find her braless. "Oh, my," I said before I took her full breasts in my hands and sucked a taut nipple into my mouth. She moaned loud and long, letting me suck first one, then the other. She stood up and quickly stripped off her pants and underwear. When she leaned over me, I twisted so she was lying on the sofa and I was above her.

"Samantha," she breathed, "make love to me."

"My pleasure," I said as I ran my fingers along her arms, across her hips, and down her legs.

I kissed her mouth, then her neck, trailing my tongue along her collarbone and down to the indentation between her breasts. She smelled like gardenias, and she was oh so soft. She arched against me, urging my hands to make their way back up her thighs to her moist center. She was clean shaven, the unfamiliar smoothness a new sensation to me, but my fingers glided over her silky skin to find her wet and ready. I played with her while I teased her nipples with my tongue, alternately licking and biting and sucking. She moaned and wriggled beneath me. I smiled, knowing full well what she craved, but wanting to make her wait.

Our bodies slid together, damp and glistening in the hot sun. Jasmine's hands caressed my back, finding their way down to my ass. Her nails pricked me, making me squirm, but I didn't let it distract me from her breasts, her nipples, her flowing wetness. I ran my fingers between her swollen labia, dipping deep inside her, then out again. She writhed on the sofa, pushing her hips against me.

"Please, Samantha," she pleaded, "don't tease me."

"What do you want, sweet Jasmine?"

"Make me—"

I smothered her answer with a kiss. "Do you want me inside you like this?" I said as I thrust two fingers deep into her, letting my thumb rub and play with her clit.

"Yes, oh yes!"

I felt her begin to contract around my fingers. I moved quickly downward, taking her clit in my mouth and sucking on it hard. She cried out as she began to thrash under me. She squeezed my fingers tight, and I felt a gush of warm liquid flow around my hand. She let out a long, long sigh and relaxed into the sofa cushions. I withdrew my fingers, but continued to lick her, loving the smell and honey-sweet taste of her.

I looked up at the touch of her fingers in my hair. She was smiling, her brown eyes dark with desire. The sun brought out the red highlights in her spiral curls.

"Wow," she said, "you are something."

"You're not so bad yourself," I said, feeling myself blush at her praise. I sat up, wanting to just look at her. This time she blushed. Unselfconsciously I strode naked over to her cameras. "Is there some trick to how these work?" I asked. "Or are they like ordinary cameras?" I'd played her game, so it was only fair for her to play too.

"Oh, they're ordinary all right," she said.

"So come on, pose for me. I want to capture you on film like you did me." I grinned. "Tit for tat, no pun intended."

She laughed. "That'll have to wait for another day." I pouted. She laughed again. "Only this time, I'll put film in the camera."

Dear Diary
M.C. Ammerman

Saturday. Saw her again, out in her garden. Buck naked. That's three times now. God, she's so hot. That sounds so juvenile, I guess, but it's the honest truth. That's why I started this diary. I had to tell someone, but if I tell my friends, they'll all be over here! Thank God I never took down the tree house when I bought this place. Thank God I was inspecting it the other day when she was out there the first time. I've got a clear shot right into her back yard. It's the perfect spying spot.

Sunday. Shit! I think she saw me today. But maybe not. The leaves are pretty thick on that one branch. I don't want to make her mad or upset her. She was really nice when we met. She's just so friggin' gorgeous, I can't help myself. The day she moved in I took one look at her long, soft hair and those amazing brown eyes, and I was hooked. The fact that she has a figure a Vegas showgirl would envy didn't hurt, either.

Monday. She was out there again, weeding her little vegetable plot. I could stare at her luscious ass for hours. Actually, I did. It was hot today, and I guess the little breezes weren't making it past all those high hedges of hers, 'cause she actually turned the hose on herself once. She should've turned it on me! Watching her shiver under the cold spray made me feel things between my legs I haven't felt in years. I keep thinking I should be more neighborly, and do something decent like take her a damned casserole, but I don't cook so well, and by now I'm afraid she'll see it in my face that I've been watching her. Shit. I bet she's smart and funny, too. I'll invite her over once I get myself under control. I promise.

Tuesday and Wednesday. I had to work late both yesterday and today, and it was dark by the time I got home. But tomorrow I'll make it a point to get home on time. Oh, yeah.

Thursday. Damn rain!

Friday. God, that was worth racing home from work for! She was just lying there on a blanket, sunbathing. I drooled myself dry. Geez. Her skin is so smooth, her tan a perfect light, golden color. And her boobs! Well, hell, words can't describe those. At least, mine can't. My hands were itching to touch her. She was like a golden goddess, a woman in her prime, and reveling in it. Every once in a while she'd reach up to stroke her breast, sort of lazily. It made me crazy! I kept hoping for more, silently begging her to go further, but no. Does she know what a tease she is? I ended up stroking my own breasts instead, until I had to stick my hands down inside my pants and take care of things, right there in the tree house. I probably scared the squirrels, but I don't care. It was only a fantasy, but it was great.

Monday. Oh, boy. Yeah, there's no entry for Sunday, but damn, no one would ever believe it. I still don't.

I heard her screen door bang late in the afternoon, so I knew she was out there. I ran to the tree, climbing up the pieces of wood nailed to its trunk. There's one tricky part getting onto the platform where I'm always worried she'll see me, 'cause I have to look at where I'm going and I can't keep an eye on her. Well, I hauled myself up onto the platform and looked over her hedge. And there she was—naked, beautiful, and looking straight at me. Oh, shit.

I couldn't tell if she was mad or what, but she crooked her finger at me. I could see she meant business, so I climbed down again, slowly, trying to figure out what to say. By the time I got inside her back gate, I'd decided to try to bluff my way out, but one look at her face told me that wouldn't work.

"I thought you were watching me," she told me. Her lips kind of quirked a little, like she was trying not to smile. "So what am I going to do with my Peeping Thomasina?"

I swallowed. Her face looked like my cat's when it notices a spider scuttling across the floor.

"I think it's only fair," she purred, "that if you got to see me, I should get to see you."

Huh? Whoa. She wanted to see me? Naked? I shook my head and found my voice. "Don't do that to yourself," I croaked. I meant it, too. I'm no slouch in the fitness department, but at forty-eight, a few things are saggy, lemme tell ya.

She just laughed, at least at first. Then she got serious. "Strip. Now. You owe me, don't you?"

I was going to protest, but I realized there were a lot of gardening tools around, some of them kind of sharp and pointy. I didn't really think she'd use them on me, but I decided not to risk it.

I pulled my T-shirt off over my head, feeling the goose bumps rise on my shoulders as a faint breeze caressed my skin. The bumps got bigger as I unhooked my bra and watched her eyes light up when my breasts slipped out. She then stared pointedly at my crotch. My hands dropped reluctantly to the button on my jeans. I had to wriggle a little to get them over my hips.

My boobs were jiggling all over the place, and I silently cursed myself for buying tight jeans just to show off my ass. I glanced up to see a look on her face I can only describe as both amused and hungry. No one had ever looked at me like that before, and I started to breathe faster. I pulled down my underwear and stepped out of it. She looked me up and down, making me shiver with sudden arousal, wondering if I was lucky or doomed.

"C'mere," she whispered. Her tone was almost taunting. I'd already lost any resistance to her I might have had, so I went. Scared shitless, but I went. She ran the back of her hand up and down my arm as she spoke. "I know you did more than look." Her voice was so low I had to bend my head to catch it, noting with surprise that she was shorter than me. "You wanted to touch me, didn't you?"

I nodded, feeling vaguely like a guilty child.

"Well, maybe you'll get a chance." I looked up, startled. "But only if you're good," she finished.

My stomach had tensed, and I was starting to squeeze my thighs together to ease the ache that had begun growing between them at her commanding tone. She dropped her hand, letting her fingers graze my nipple. I gasped. With a feral grin, she lowered her head.

"Hands off," she ordered, just before clamping her hot mouth on my left nipple and sliding her tongue around it. My legs nearly gave out, and my hands started to come up, but the fear that she'd stop made me drop them again.

She pulled away. "Don't you like that?"

I nodded vigorously, breathing too hard to speak.

"Hmm. I didn't hear any moaning. I like moaning, but no talking." She gave me a stern look, and I nodded again. By this time I would have walked naked into the street and kissed the mailman if that was what she wanted. She smiled. "Good. Let's see if you can keep it up."

Her mouth went to my right nipple, her tongue teasing the

very tip. That moan she wanted escaped without any prompting. Her hand came up to caress my left breast with a gentle, yet firm, touch. Her mouth released me, making me whimper.

"I knew your breasts would be this good," she said. "I can always tell. I've been watching you, too."

A little thrill of fear and anticipation shot along my spine, but it didn't last. Her fingers were pinching and twisting both nipples, and she watched in undisguised delight as I cried out in pain and writhed in pleasure. She let go, palmed my tortured nipples a moment, then pinched again. I don't know how long it lasted, the alternations between pain and soothing caresses. All I remember next is my knees giving out and my head clearing a little as she helped me to a blanket spread out on the grass near the roses.

"Kneel here," she said, guiding me down from behind. "Bend forward, all fours."

I did as she bid me, aware of the trickle of juice running down the inside of my thigh. She pushed my knees apart, and I felt her kneel between my legs. A strong arm wrapped around my hips. Her fingers stroked my labia so lightly that I shuddered uncontrollably. The featherlight touch ran up the back of my thigh to my butt, tracing a swirling pattern that left my skin tingling, the fire following her fingertips back between my legs. I felt one finger slip between my soaking folds, then another followed. I cried out as both fingers suddenly plunged into me even as she pulled me back against her, ramming her fingers deeper inside. Again and again she thrust and pulled, jamming her fingers deep into me. Each thrust forced a small cry past my lips. She was relentless. I felt her hand pounding against me, her arm solid around me, and I knew I was hers. Over and over she rocked me in an overwhelming mix of pleasure and helplessness.

As she leaned forward, I felt the warm, gentle weight of her breasts against my back and her long hair tickling my shoulder.

"Don't come," she whispered in my ear over my panting

cries. "I'm not done with you yet." I just panted harder. I could feel the sweat running down my face. She stopped thrusting and shifted her arm to my chest, pulling me up onto my knees, her fingers still wedged inside me. I groaned as her fingers moved, exploring my vagina eagerly, her other hand fondling my breasts. I felt a fluttering in my gut. She was flicking my cervix, making my uterus vibrate deep within me. I moaned and leaned against her, my pelvis rocking on its own.

"Oh, please, please," I begged. "I can't hold on."

"Shh. You have to now. I said no talking, so now you have to wait."

She released me, her fingers pulling out, leaving me cold and empty. She laid me on my back. I tried to catch my breath, but it was useless. She forced my legs apart. Before I could register anything, her mouth was on me, her tongue burrowing through the folds to find my clit. I cried out sharply as her tongue touched it, a shock running through my body. I was shaking with need as her teeth raked across it. I scarcely noticed when two fingers entered me again, but a pressure on my anus caught my attention. I'd never been entered there, but I was powerless to stop it. I didn't know if I wanted to, but I couldn't say a word, or she'd never let me come. My juice was everywhere, so her thumb slipped in easily. I gasped at the odd sensation, but I liked it. Abandoning my nipple, her free hand stretched toward my face, then she pushed her middle finger against my lips, forcing it into my mouth.

"Suck," she ordered, then lowered her mouth to me again. I sucked for all I was worth, my mind reeling. She'd filled me, taken me by every orifice, controlled me completely, and I loved it. Her arm was pressing down on my breast, her mouth was warm, and I rocked and gasped, desperately trying to relax, to wait like she wanted. I was whimpering, desperate little sounds leaping from my throat. Her mouth released me briefly.

"Now you can come."

For one second my breath stopped as my mind processed this, and then I screamed out against the finger in my mouth. I rocked and struggled against the explosions I thought would split me in two, catching me again and again. Her fingers in my body kept thrusting and teasing, forcing shudders out of me long after the greatest waves were over.

Finally, I lay there, spent, limp, her fingers still filling my mouth, my cunt, my anus, with her head resting on my thigh.

"You've been very, very good," she whispered warmly. "I knew you'd be responsive, but never like this. I'm not releasing you until you promise to come back tomorrow night and pleasure me. You're too tired now to do it the way I like, but I can wait. Promise me."

I was again sucking her finger gently, soothed by the action, but I managed to get the words out willingly. "I promise."

Slowly, one by one, she pulled her fingers out of me, then sat up to look at me with twinkling eyes.

"We're going to be great neighbors," she said with a grin. "I knew it the minute I laid eyes on you."

I grinned back and she helped me up and into my clothes, sneaking in little caresses that set my head whirling again. That night I slept like I never have before, dreaming of my hands on her exquisite body.

That was yesterday. I'm due over there in a few minutes to keep my promise. I still really can't believe it, but she called to remind me, so I know it's true.

Ya know what? I have a feeling I won't have time to write a diary anymore.

Paris, 2003
Maggie Kinsella

I've always had a thing for French women.

It's their chic touch-me-not way of looking down their noses as they sip a coffee, legs crossed at the ankles and their pants pleated just so. It's the way their hair falls artfully across a manicured eyebrow, and their nails are always short and clean. It's even their unshaven armpits, where the hair grows lush and long.

Yes, I've always had a thing for French women, but I never had a chance to do anything about it until I met Célestine.

I'd flown to France on vacation. Two weeks of café society, and tourist sites in Paris, followed by a hire car to Nice and the burning sands and scorching women of southern France.

I met Célestine on my first night in Paris when the jet lag rendered me so tired I could barely function. I was staying near Charles de Gaulle airport at some cheap hotel—my bedroom could have fit into my closet back home. My flight had arrived mid afternoon, and not wanting to waste a moment, I'd dumped my bag on the bed and headed out to find a café for coffee or something stronger, and to savor actually being in France.

I wasn't looking for a woman. Really I wasn't. Not yet, anyway.

Stumbling through my order in night-school French, I received strong black coffee in a tiny cup when what I wanted was something larger and white, but I didn't care. I'd made it here, and Paris burst into life in front of me. The traffic whirled past, and the women . . . yeah, there were women. I did notice.

I was halfway through my second coffee when a beautiful brunette plonked herself down in the empty chair beside me.

"Bonjour ma petite Américaine!"

She must have seen my labored look of incomprehension because she laughed and said, in singsong English, "Hello, my sweet American. You are alone and lost, and your face is falling into your coffee."

"Bonjour," I replied haltingly. *"Je m'apelle Diane."*

"Célestine." And she swooped in and, before I could gather my breath, kissed me swiftly, once on each cheek.

One hand pushed aside my coffee cup and the other signaled the waiter. *"Deux Ricards, s'il vous plait!"* She turned back to me. "In France, you drink the French way."

Two tumblers appeared, with a clear, strong-smelling liquid. Célestine added water to hers and pushed the carafe over to me. I eyed her cloudy glass doubtfully, but added water all the same. The fumes from the strong aniseed liquor made my eyes water.

"Santé!"

Excitement warred with my jet lag. Here I was, in Paris. ME, in Paris, and already a gorgeous woman was sitting with me, flirting as she poured me liquor. But the jet lag was winning. After another of the licorice-flavored drinks, Célestine leaned over. Her hand settled on my thigh and traced up and down the seam of my jeans. Her lips caressed my cheek, touching the edge of my mouth.

"*Tu es trop fatigué, ma petite Diane,*" she said. "You are too tired for me now. I will meet you tomorrow. There is a café called Les Deux Magots near the Arc de Triomphe, on the Champs-Elysées. I will meet you there at three o'clock. Don't be late." And then she kissed me full on the mouth, her tongue darting out to flicker over my lips and push between. "*Au revoir.*"

And she was gone, leaving me with a glass of cloudy *pastis*, and the tab.

I didn't wake until eleven the next morning, and immediately I panicked. I didn't know how to get to the Arc de Triomphe, or where to stay. Luckily, the concierge spoke English and he booked me into a moderately priced hotel, a short walk from the café where I was meeting Célestine. One over-priced taxi ride later, and I was ready to go.

By ten to three, I was installed on the terrace of the café Célestine had mentioned. I ordered a tumbler of Ricard; I was determined to acquire a taste for the stuff.

At 3:01 exactly, Célestine plopped herself onto the corner bench next to me. She wore black Capri pants, a tailored white blouse and sunglasses so dark I couldn't see her eyes.

"You don't like this," she said, pushing my Ricard aside and loudly summoning the waiter for a bottle of wine. The red wine from Bordeaux settled sweetly on my tongue. Célestine regarded me narrowly over her glass. "You are over your jet lag, *oui?*"

I nodded, although that wasn't quite accurate; it was only adrenaline keeping me going.

"Then I think we should do the sights, *oui?* It is what you are here for."

Maybe. But maybe I was here to meet Célestine.

"*La Tour Eiffel, l'Arc de Triomphe, les musées . . .*"

She grinned at me, and her thin face shone. She had a dimple. My eyes fixated on it, and how it appeared only with the widest smile. I wanted to kiss her lips, slide my tongue between them, and then tease her dimple. My eyes slid down to her modest cleavage, to where her olive skin disappeared into the white blouse. Tiny breasts. Pert. I guessed she'd have large, dark chocolate drop nipples.

"All in good time."

She'd seen me looking, and it was as if she read my mind. I flushed.

Célestine slid closer to me on the bench, letting her hand curve over my thigh. She leaned in and kissed me on the side of the mouth—a chaste, sweet kiss. "Before you have me, you must have Paris."

Our first stop was the Eiffel Tower. We rode to the top, crammed into the elevator with other tourists, mainly Britons and Germans, red-faced and sweating in the September heat. At the top, Célestine dragged me away from the oohing and aahing group that admired Paris spread out beneath us.

"It's there," she said, dismissively. "It's always there. But I am not." And she crushed my body to the metal railing with her own, kissing me hard, reaching up to hold my face between her two small hands and bring my lips down to hers. Her arms pinned me to the railing, her pelvis rested against my own—such heat where we touched. I kissed her in return, and my hands started my own exploration—down her slim back to her nicely rounded yet taut buttocks, cupping them and pulling her tightly against me.

Her hands were moving too, exploring my body, running under my blouse, mapping every square inch of skin she could reach. I breathed into her kisses, my fingernails tightened on her ass. She tasted of strong coffee and faintly of aniseed. Just as my hips started to press back against her, my pelvis grinding into hers, she pulled away.

One manicured hand gestured expansively at the view below us. "*C'est Paris. Et maintenant*, we leave."

Our next stop was the Louvre museum. We walked around for an hour or so, Célestine's arm tucked companionably into mine as she chattered about the various exhibits. Every so often, she would let her fingers drift up to tickle the side of my breast, a quick, delicate caress that was over before it began. And she'd lean over, her hot breath tickling my ear, raising the delicate hairs on my cheek.

"You are hot for me, hmm, yes?" she'd say, or, "I wonder if your breasts are softer than the skin at your waist?"

It was too much. Between the Rembrandt and the Renoir, I pulled her into a niche by a fire exit. It was brightly lit, as was all of the gallery, but unless anyone came round the corner into this area, we wouldn't be seen.

My mouth swooped down her neck as my fingers fumbled with the buttons down the front of her blouse. Underneath, her small breasts were encased in a sheer bra, red with black embroidery, its half-cup lifting her petite curves. I bent and pressed my lips to her cleavage, letting them trace the upper line of her bra. My hand snaked down her belly, to the top snap of her pants.

Abruptly she grasped a handful of my hair and pulled me off her. "Wait," she said sternly. "You Americans are so impatient. You fuck with no finesse. You must wait for me, but for now, this is what you have."

I didn't think she had so much strength in her wiry body. With one swift movement, she reversed our positions, slamming me back against the wall. My head bounced back, hitting the partition. Then her hands were on me, unfastening my blouse with sure fingers and pulling it out of my jeans. My body jerked in anticipation, waiting for her touch. But she didn't stop there. My bra wasn't as delicate as hers—I'm more of a white cotton sort of gal—but she opened the front fastening, exposing my breasts to the cool air.

Her fingers palmed my full breasts. "Beautiful," she said, her breath hot on my skin. "I want to taste."

I moaned in anticipation, "Touch me. I want to feel your mouth on me."

Her lips descended, sucking one nipple while her free hand pinched its companion to quivering erectness. A red-hot haze drowned my senses. Each tug of her mouth was a direct line to my clit. Each pulse took me spiraling higher as the ache in my belly grew. I grabbed her hand and tried to push it down to my needy cunt, but she resisted.

"*Pas encore*, Diane." Not yet.

My breath came in sharp pants; I was caught in her finely spun web of sexual desire. "Please," I gasped, and still I tried to direct her fingers to where I wanted them most. "Oh, God, please!"

I could feel her lips curve against my breast. "*Non, pas encore.*"

They were the cruelest words I'd heard in a long time.

I crossed my legs, squeezing my thighs tightly together—clench, release, clench, release.

I must have looked the very picture of sexual heat with my face red, my mouth open and gasping, damp tendrils of hair clinging stickily to my forehead. And Célestine, with her mouth and fingers on my body, manipulated me to a fever pitch, even though she had yet to reach my cunt.

Just as I was gulping air, climbing to the peak, she stopped and moved away.

"Cover yourself, *chérie*." Her lips curved in amusement at my plight. "There's a security guard coming our way."

Hastily, I scrambled to button my blouse, trying to ignore the heavy feeling between my legs.

"*Bon*. There is no guard, however. But we will leave anyway."

My fists clenched in frustration, but Célestine was in charge in this wild rocket flight through gay Paris, and all I could do was scurry along in her wake.

I don't remember the Arc de Triomphe; all I remember is Célestine's hips pushing into me from behind, pushing my clit against a metal railing as I gasped and tried to angle my pelvis for better friction, while all the while trying to look for the families and children around us as if I were merely admiring the architecture.

And each tourist attraction was punctuated by another street café, where Célestine would watch me through hooded eyes as we sipped our tumblers of Ricard. I was determined to acquire a taste for the stuff. And indeed, as my head started to spin from the pungent spirit, the liquid began to slide down more easily.

The twilight was well advanced before Célestine called a halt to our mad whirl through the city. I'd lost count of the highlights we'd seen, just as I'd lost count of how many Ricards we'd drunk. Now we ambled slowly along the banks of the Seine, arms entwined around each other's waists. The brilliant leaves in their fall colors above our heads were echoed in the reflection on the gray-green water beside us; only a pair of graceful swans disturbed the mirror. Around us, Parisians swarmed in their thousands, socializing at street cafés or heading home after the working day.

Célestine steered me away from the river, through a tangled maze of small streets, before stopping at a bright pink doorway in an older stone building.

"Here is where I live," she said. "Now we do the business, *oui*?"

My arousal had muted during our final walk, but her words brought my clit jumping to sharpness. *Now*, I thought, exultant. *Now.*

Her fourth-floor apartment was small and neat, very much like Célestine herself. There were fresh flowers on the windowsill, a bunch of vivid fuchsias, and a view over the tiled rooftops and tree-lined streets. But I didn't have time to admire the view.

Célestine grabbed me by the shoulders and pushed me against the windowsill. It bit into the back of my thighs, and the force of her body bent me back until my shoulders met the pane. She followed, pressing her slight body against my more solid one, her breasts flattening on my chest as she wound her arms around my neck.

And she devoured me. There was no other word for it. Her tongue pressed into my mouth, and her lips moved on mine— hot, insistent, damp and tasting of Ricard. Hands moved from my neck, down over my shoulders to my sides, insistently tugging at my shirt until it slid out of my jeans and she could touch flesh. When kissing me was no longer enough, her mouth moved to the crook of my neck and shoulder, lapping at my skin, tasting me and then biting with sharp nips.

Four stories below, the traffic crawled in a river of light through the darkness. The height made me dizzy—that and the knowledge only a thin pane of glass kept me from tumbling down to the street.

Her hands moved again, ripping my shirt open and removing my bra. Her small mouth and sharp little teeth engulfed a breast, sucking hard on a nipple until I was writhing on the edge of pain.

"Please," I gasped through the crimson haze of pleasure. Although the feelings were so intense that I wasn't even sure what I was begging for.

Célestine ignored me. It seemed she wanted to stay the aggressor, the giver of pleasure. When I tried to touch her, she shrugged my hands away.

"Later," she said. "First, I want to watch you come."

My jeans disappeared, dragged down my legs with such force that my skin felt abraded and raw. My panties went too. It was already warm in her apartment; the humid September air was all cloying moisture, but now it was scorching. Célestine's fingers trailed up my inner thigh, touched my cunt lips gently, and then retreated to my thigh. On they went—advance, retreat, advance retreat, a soft, sly dip inside, but never staying where I really wanted them. Each gentle touch of a fingertip fueled the fire, brought me closer to the edge. I gripped the wooden sill, letting the momentum build.

She lulled me into a false sense of serenity. I was expecting these skillful touches to continue until the tickles became a storm, but Célestine surprised me again. Another advance of those fingers, then a sudden, abrupt withdrawal. But not for long. Suddenly she was kneeling on the floor in front of me, her thighs spread wide for balance, her jaunty Capri pants taut over her toned legs. And she lunged for me; there was really no other word for it. Her hands gripped my thighs so hard I knew there'd be fingerprints in my flesh. She gripped, she spread, and her face pushed up into my cunt.

She knew what she was doing. Her tongue felt firm and strong—almost like a miniature cock—as it pushed its way inside and the dance of advance and retreat continued with a new focus.

My clit pulsed, hot and swollen, in time to her fucking. Now her firm friction was unbearably beautiful. My belly quivered, and the first molten waves of orgasm erupted.

"Oh God!" I wailed my pleasure as my cunt convulsed. I seized her short hair in my fists, holding her in place, although she showed no inclination to move away, and came hard, grinding myself against her face.

My rigidity passed as the aftershocks quaked away, and I eased my death grip on her hair. A final sweep of her tongue sent me buckling on the edge of pain, my shoulders firm against the damp glass, then she rose to her feet and moved up to kiss me. She tasted of me, salty hot and warm.

Pulling back, she unbuttoned her neat blouse, taking it off and folding it smartly before placing it on the back of a chair. She kicked away her sandals and slid her short pants down her legs to join the blouse in its orderly resting place. Hands on hips, she faced me; her red and black bra vivid against her olive skin. She was trim, slender to the point of fragility, with a tiny waist banded by a strip of black and red lace. Her legs and arms were firmly muscled.

"Well," she challenged, "are you simply going to stare, or are you going to do something?"

Pushing away from the window, I stepped purposefully to her and pretended to consider my options.

"I could tie you up," I suggested. "Bind you to the bed and fist you until you screamed."

A tiny smile. "I stay in control. No bondage."

"I could lead you naked into the street with a collar around your neck."

A full glare. "*Non.* I do not do that." And then a sweet smile. "And neither do you."

She had my measure. "I don't," I agreed. "A bath then, slippery with oil and steaming hot."

"I have only a shower."

"Then I'll just have to return the favor, won't I?"

"Of course. That is what we both want, *n'est-ce pas?*"

I eyed her kitchen counter—marble, cool, and waist height. Taking her hand, I led her over. Grinning, she hopped up and spread her thighs wide. Mahogany-colored hair curled around the edge of her tiny lace panties; it seemed that not only her armpits were *au naturel*. I licked my lips.

Opening a drawer, I found a small, sharp knife. Taking it out, I hooked the slim blade through the side of her panties, making sure she felt the cool touch of the steel against her smooth skin.

She gasped, then warned, "You cut them off, you replace them."

The knife sliced cleanly through the delicate fabric and fell away, exposing her pussy to my gaze. Her breath caught in her throat. I smiled as I observed the glitter of anticipation in her eyes.

"I'll buy you two pairs." Even though they were French lace and would probably cost a week's salary, I figured it was worth it.

Her bush was abundant and lush, a darker shade than the hair on her head, and it hid a moist and shining treasure. I leaned over the counter and parted her labia with a finger that slid easily into her clasping heat. My mouth followed, running along her inner thigh. I could smell her—rich and warm like a Paris *boulangerie*. I tasted her gently, slowly. In contrast to my urgency to reach this point, now I wanted to take my time. My lips moved leisurely over her, my tongue licking, and when I found her hard clit, I circled it carefully even as she tightened under my mouth, while her hands tried futilely to direct me closer.

My belly tightened as my own arousal built again. My senses were filled with Célestine, and I wanted to stay there forever, my face in her cunt.

"*Merde!*" she gasped, and her hands tightened in my hair. "Diane, you suck pussy like a Frenchwoman!" And then her words disintegrated into soft moans, as my tongue lapped at her clit.

I teased her for a few minutes longer, but after all, we both wanted the same thing. Softly sucking, I finally gave her what she craved. It only took a few more super-charged seconds before her hips bucked under my hands and a gush of fluid filled my mouth.

I rested my head on her thigh, and we relaxed for a few minutes. But the kitchen counter was uncomfortable. Célestine sighed once, then pushing me gently aside, she lowered her feet to the ground.

"I have wine," she said, "and salad and cheese with fresh, crusty bread." She smiled at me, the lights of Paris twinkling through the window behind her. "And in the morning we will buy croissants for breakfast."

I never did get to Nice.

Strangeness on a Train (and a Bus)
Crin Claxton

Until the train swished slowly to a halt, the only eventful moment of the journey had been being covered in hot coffee just outside Peterborough. The train had veered sharply, and I had looked up to see an attractive but disturbingly startled and unbalanced woman hurtling toward me, a steaming stream of brown froth pouring into my lap and all over my briefcase. I jumped up as Ms. Hot-Coffee gushed an apology, tried to mop at it with half a napkin, realized where she was about to put her hands and continued apologizing instead. I'd grimaced and excused myself to the bathroom. I had only just dried out and cleaned up my briefcase when the train slithered to a standstill, causing everyone in my carriage to look around and wonder why we'd stopped outside this particular turnip field in Lincolnshire, the flattest part of England.

Minutes later an announcement informed us a power cable was down on the line ahead, and we would shortly be continuing to Grantham where we would get off the train, get on a bus, be driven across country to Doncaster and get back on the train. Everyone without exception laughed aloud at the news and a merry carriage we were. But not so merry walking along the platform at Grantham as the high and bitter cold wind whistled around our ears and the skies opened, throwing icy rain down on our heads. England, oh England, such a little country, so full of weather.

I scuttled along with the best of them, clutching my briefcase, glad I'd chosen my wool suit. Outside the station it was like a coach package holiday nightmare—long, shivering queues of passengers standing outside rows of buses. The drivers, miserable to a man, seemed reluctant to open the bus doors until the person at the front of the queue was blue around the lips. I joined a shuffling queue and found a seat. I was watching sorry-looking people dart about outside when I heard someone ask "Is this seat taken?"

I looked into the smiling face of Ms. Hot-Coffee-in-your-lap. It was a very nice face. Now that I wasn't distracted by a searing pain in my crotch, I could see she was a pretty, smiley, friendly looking thing. I must have mumbled that the seat certainly wasn't taken because she sat down next to me, smoothing down her skirt a fraction of a second after my eyes had flickered over her thighs. Well, my, my. Something told me she was a lesbian. There was something about the way she grasped the material of her skirt and let her eyes meet mine for a blink of a moment. Body movements are a dead give away, and this woman was setting off my gaydar. As I glanced at her, she rested her arms in her lap and tapped out a silent tune with her fingers, then turned and smiled. I smiled back, thinking she seemed vaguely familiar.

The bus was driving past field after field of vegetables. It was fen country, so flat the horizon rolled on endlessly. Bold green brussel sprouts glistened in fat chunks on their long stalks nodding toward perky turnip tops swaying in the driving rain. I looked out of the window for a while, thinking I could enjoy this unscheduled bus tour if I let myself. I tried not to think of the meeting carrying on without me at the Leeds office. Results from the first trial were in, and I was eager to go over them. Gradually, I was aware of a warm leg against my leg. I ignored it at first, thinking she'd realize and move her leg away. After five minutes I had to admit this must be intentional. I tried pressing back. Her leg pressed unquestionably into mine. Casually, I turned to her. Her eyes flicked to my lap.

"I hope I didn't make you sore."

"I beg your pardon?"

She was definitely a lesbian.

"The coffee. I do hope it didn't burn you."

"No. Well, not really. It's fine," I said stoically.

"And there doesn't seem to be any stain." She was now staring at my crotch. Staring far longer than necessary to ascertain the extent of any staining. I could feel my muscles contracting, and yet the rest of me didn't seem to be able to move. This stranger was hitting on me! On a bus, in a hailstorm, traveling across Lincolnshire.

"I was wondering how to pass the time on this journey," she told me, snuggling in a little closer. "Bumping into you again has given me an idea." She made it sound like we were old friends.

"Have we met?" I blurted out, trying to place that elusive smile.

"I've seen you around," Ms. Hot-Coffee confided. "Babe Delicious . . . the Candy Store . . ."

Of course, I must have noticed her on the scene. Rubbing shoulders at gay bars and clubs, the same faces crop up.

"I've got something here you might like," Hot-Coffee whispered into my ear.

I was sure she had. And I would. She was digging in her bag. I used the time to check out her breasts. They would go down nicely with a can of whipped cream. She came out of her bag with a clenched hand, smiling suggestively, and uncurled her fist to reveal . . . a tiny mobile phone. I frowned, not quite sure what this meant.

"That's a lovely coat," she exclaimed, spreading it over my lap. "Feeling warmer now?" she asked, unzipping my fly.

"Um-hummm," I kind of murmured as I felt her fingers underneath my shorts, and then cold, plastic around my clit.

"You've got a mobile, haven't you honey?" she breathed into my ear.

"What?" I realized what she'd said. "Yes . . ."

"Can I see it?"

This was a strange time to be assessing my hardware, but I gave her the phone anyway. She dialed a number and seemed to be leaving a message for someone. I guessed it must have been very important. I looked out of the window, wondering if this was her idea of foreplay. Seconds later I realized who the message had been for. Me. As her phone vibrated silently against my clitoris I breathed in so sharply, the woman across the aisle looked over.

"It's a breathing technique," Ms. Hot-Coffee-in-your-lap explained to her. "Relieves stress."

I smiled, clenching my teeth to stop involuntary noises escaping out of my mouth.

"It's a miserable day," the woman across the aisle remarked pleasantly.

"Terrible . . . terrible," Hot-Coffee agreed, fingering my phone with lightning speed. "You don't mind if I finish this text while we talk, do you? It's rather important."

Dear God, I did . . . As another message bounced off several satellites and thundered across my clit, I struggled hard to keep my face neutral. Unfortunately, the effort forced a small groan from between my lips.

"Travel sickness," Hot-Coffee explained, pressing resend.

"He does look rather pale," Aisle Lady decided.

I glared across at her, but as the third message arrived I was forced shut my eyes and concentrate on my breathing so I wouldn't shout at the top of my voice, *I'm about to come, stop texting me*.

"We're at Doncaster," Hot-Coffee informed me.

"What?" Disorientated, I looked around and confirmed that the bus had indeed stopped outside Doncaster station.

"Off we get." She sounded like a teacher on a school trip.

Alarmed, I realized everyone was getting off. Just as I was about to retrieve her phone, she snatched my coat off my lap. "Can I wear this?"

"Well . . . yes, sure." How could I refuse?

Doncaster greeted us with hail. Hot-Coffee had my overcoat on, while I had a hard, plastic object knocking about in my boxer shorts. It was a uniquely strange experience. We had to wait ten minutes for a train. Hot-Coffee wouldn't let me go anywhere to remove her phone. She texted me a couple more times, though. We were sitting in the waiting room, out of the arctic conditions. She was wrapped in my coat, her legs crossed, smiling a between-the-sheets grin in my direction. In between messages, she subtly teased me. Whenever my eyes flickered her way, she was feeling herself up through my coat, fingering through all my pockets in a strangely exciting way.

As soon as the train pulled up we got on, and I pulled her into the nearest bathroom.

"I think this is mine." She had my fly open and her hands in my shorts before I had the door locked. I was pushed up against the door and determined to find the lock, preferably before I lost concentration altogether. I felt my trousers drop to my ankles as I pressed the lock button and cold air around my naked arse as she dropped my shorts.

"Spread 'em, baby," she said, her breath warm on my neck, causing all the hairs to lift. I did as I was told, giving her plenty of room to work. She pressed her whole body against mine as she slid into me. I was wet and open, and she did me hard and fast, pushing me against the door. I rode her fingers and thought *I do think there are advantages to train travel. I certainly couldn't do this in a mini cooper on the M1.* We were thrown about a bit by the train, but we just incorporated the thrusts and turns. And in the end I didn't know if I was coming or going, until I was suddenly very sure I was coming, with her thrusting away right to the last pounding wave. Immediately, I was very aware my trousers and boxers were around my ankles and I was pushed head first into a toilet door. After I buttoned up, I turned to her sweet, satisfied smile.

"So. How you doing?" I inquired.

She answered me by unzipping her top to reveal rock-hard nipples that had me lifting her onto the sink and popping them one after the other into my mouth. Sucking hard, I slipped both hands underneath, spreading her buttocks and slipping up inside her. She pushed herself onto me, making hardly any sound, her deep cunt swallowing my fingers. I wanted my harness . . . I almost suggested it, but Hot-Coffee bucked and bounced till she was sliding on my wrists. I was scared the little sink would come clean off the wall. As she came, she reached down and bit my ear lobe, panting.

As her breathing slowed, she moved off me, rearranged her clothes and drawled, "Come sit down with me a while."

I followed her happily into a carriage, where we sat in silence for a while, watching rain fall from dark clouds over the dull landscape. Watching the rain made me very relaxed. It also made me need the toilet, and I headed back to the scene of our liaison. She said she'd stay and watch our bags.

I was washing my hands, smiling down at the sink fondly when I remembered exactly where I knew her from—Organic Skin Care 2005, Madrid. Damn! The little plastic badge on her ample breasts swam before my eyes: Organic Body Company. I ran back to the carriage to find her going through my briefcase.

"You think I'm stupid enough to leave anything in there?" I told her, anger curling in my gut.

"I was looking for my phone . . . You didn't give it back to me you . . . naughty thing you." She tried to wriggle out of it. "But this did rather distract me . . ." She held up last year's best-selling organic lubricant: Nature Juice.

"There's nothing in there you can't buy on the open market," I told her, coldly.

Startled, she closed my briefcase with a snap.

I looked at her. "You're wasting your time. Any information of value's in here." I pointed to my head.

"Well . . ." She was up and collecting her things. "There seems to be some kind of misunderstanding."

She was good, I gave her that. All the same, I grabbed her wrist and uncurled her fingers.

"I was enjoying our little meeting," she said.

She smoothed my tie with her other hand as I took back my memory chip. I watched her walk out of the carriage.

Industrial espionage is a dirty business. The formulas to organic skin creams are valuable commodities. I'm not allowed to carry electronic or paper information. Seems Ms. Hot-Coffee was nothing but a spy. I guessed she was after the secret ingredient to our youth serum. *Well, she wasn't the first . . . but possibly the most inventive*, I decided, as I licked the secret ingredient off my wrist, shrugged into my coat and left the carriage.

In the Garden of Eden
Scarlett French

I've been working at the emporium for five years now, maybe six. The whole of my adult life, I haven't managed to hold down a job or a flat or a relationship for longer than a year, but for some reason I've just kept working at *Eden Women's Erotic Emporium*, part time, year after year after year. When I was new to London, I started working there to meet women, whether for friendship or for something more visceral. *Eden* turned out to be my red carpet into the London lesbian scene. I had made many friends and a little love. And here I was, five years later, with several other jobs, four flats and few short relationships under my belt, but still at *Eden*, stocking shelves with a smile on my face.

The shop focused on women's sexuality. Men were only allowed if they were "accompanied" because women's and couples' pleasure was our business. Our ethos was about information and empowerment for all women, rather than pushing a product because it had more markup, or showing the expensive stuff to someone who looked like she had lots of money to spend. We worked tirelessly with our customers to make sure they got just what they needed. Sometimes that was just a cup of tea and a listening ear, sometimes it was three-hundred pounds' worth of dildos, harnesses, butt plugs and bondage tape. I guess that's why I was still there after five years; the place had integrity and I felt like feminism was put into practice there, even in this post-feminist world. I think that somehow the pro-porn and anti-porn camps of the 1980s got caught up with their positions and lost the focus of women loving their bodies, loving whomever they wanted to, and feeling powerful and wonderful about their sexuality. To me, *Eden* was pro-sex feminism in action. And, apart from the friends made and the great vibe (excuse the pun), some of the customers were hot, and getting paid to flirt while you sell sex toys ain't that bad. Then, one rainy Saturday afternoon, my job satisfaction reached a whole new level.

It was cold and gray outside, but the shop was lovely and warm, the heaters coupled with the bright colors of the toys dispelling any gloom. The music of Marvin Gaye, Madonna, Barry White and Prince alternated chilled sexiness and straight-up-horny from the speakers. It was a steady day despite the weather, and we had a pretty constant stream of customers as the rain beat out a staccato rhythm on the concrete steps outside.

I had just sold a straight couple some anal toys—one of my favorite sales combinations—when in walked Marlene. I had first met her through friends, at some club as I recall. I remember thinking how hot she was the first time we met, the meeting of our eyes, the sharp edge of desire communicated back and forth and back again. There was a palpable heat between us every time we saw each other, but I'd been briefly seeing someone on that first meeting, and while I'm serial, I am a monogamist. Then, when I was available, she'd been seeing someone. She'd been away for a while too, visiting back home I think. I figured it was just one of those things—some connections aren't meant to happen, and hey, sometimes it's better that way. I remember fulfilling a fantasy once with this musician I met, and although she was irresistible, the reality was undeniably a disappointment—for both of us. We were a complete mismatch in bed and I regretted having not kept her as the potent wank fantasy that she had been. I'm sure she would agree with me—perfect fantasy connection, bad sex connection.

"Hello Emma," said Marlene as she walked toward me across the shop floor.

I felt a little flutter in my belly. "Marlene! Hey there," I said, going for the friendly approach.

When she reached me, we leaned forward to kiss-kiss each other's cheeks, European style. Her blond hair contrasted against her tanned skin, her floppy-fringed short hair falling over her blue eyes so she was constantly brushing it out of the way in a definitely flirty manner. Marlene had come here from Germany ten years ago, just for a change of scenery, then decided to stay.

"And how are you?" she asked, her intense look somehow melting away my clothes.

Dropping my nonchalance, I decided to go for playful. "I'm great, thank you. Just been selling beautiful silicone anal beads. Ergonomic design. Can I interest you in some?"

She smiled broadly, not taking her eyes off me for a second. "Perhaps another time. Today, I'm looking for a new dildo." Her clipped accent punctuated each word.

I twitched a little. The thought of her wearing a strap-on caused a clench of pleasure between my legs. I can't be sure, but I think she noticed. "Okay," I said, with a now fixed smile on my face, "Follow me."

Marlene grinned, revealing dimples in her lean cheeks. I led her over to the dildo display, checking that the other customers were being attended to by my colleagues, that there would be time to spend with Marlene. Relieved to see only two other customers, both of whom were being helped, I turned back to Marlene with a grin.

"Got a new girl, then?" I asked her.

"No, not specifically," she said, her eyes sparkling at me from underneath lowered eyelids. "I just like to update my collection. I've been wanting a bigger one for some time now.

Marlene was smirking, the result of suppressing a smile. She was being flirtatious but cautious, I thought. No one likes to be rejected, after all. That was what I was doing too, trying to hold back how fucking, mouthwateringly sexy she was. God, it was hard to concentrate. I was just doing my job, of course, but this felt like foreplay. If we were in a room alone I would have wrenched her jeans down—just wrenched them right down—and buried my face in her pussy, licking and flicking until she came on my tongue. But anyway, here we were, in the shop, and I'm a sales assistant, and I'm selling her a dildo, just like I would any customer who wanted one. I needed to ask her what size she wanted.

"Do you know how much bigger you want to go?" I asked, that smile creeping up my cheeks.

"Well, I've always liked these," she said, lifting a large, thick one off the "generous range" shelf. It was called *The Spiral* because of the undulating coils of the shaft, like a long Mr. Whippy ice cream. The one she selected was the color of black chocolate and gold dust, a galaxy of swirls on its surface. Our new dildo maker was creating some of the best colors and designs I'd ever seen.

"Well, that's from our generous range, so it's definitely not for the fainthearted," I said, relishing the idea of her wearing it.

"Do you think it's too big?" she asked, her head slightly cocked to one side, just like her grin.

"Well, it depends a lot on the preferences of the person it's intended for," I said, trying to focus on our famous customer service, "but one functional thing you have to think about is the kind of harness it's going into. If it's sturdy, you'll be fine, but if it's a light one, the dildo may be too unwieldy in it."

She was listening intently, her eyes shining with bad intentions. "How will I know? My harness is roughly standard I think."

I had a sudden idea for prolonging this transaction. "Well, why don't you go downstairs and try on this harness," I said as I grabbed our standard harness from the rack beside the dildo stand, "put the dildo in, and if it's too heavy for it, you'll know you probably need to invest in a sturdier harness than the one you've got." I raised my eyebrows at her.

"Well, that sounds sensible," Marlene said. "But could you come with me, in case I'm not sure?"

We locked gazes. "Of course, I'm sure I can help." I looked over to Anya then, a fellow *Eden Grrl*, who pulled a face that said, "You're *so* hitting on that customer—but go and flirt with her, I'm fine up here."

I took the harness downstairs. Marlene followed behind, carrying the spiral-pleasure-galaxy she had her heart set on. It really was a stunning dildo, if a little on the large side for my personal taste.

There was no one downstairs as I led her into our one ample changing room. It had a chair in the corner and a large mirror on each wall. *Eden* management had thought about making the changing room into two smaller ones on account of the occasional couple getting overcome with desire and shagging in there, but it seemed mean-spirited somehow. So we continued to have a big changing room that a couple or friends could occupy for trying on outfits, collars, whatever. Sometimes people needed time together to be sure of the aesthetic.

I stepped into the room with Marlene. It would have been rude not to since she'd requested my help. Before I could think, she pushed me up against the wall, her face so close to mine that I could have kissed her by simply puckering my lips. Her face filled my visual field, and I could feel her breath on my mouth. Putting my hands on the back of her head, I guided her face that remaining inch to meet mine. Her lips were so soft that my mouth spontaneously fell open to envelope them, smooth on smooth. I slid my tongue between her teeth, grazing the interior parts of her lips, reaching in until our tongues met. She brought my hands around, took them in hers, our fingers interweaving, and pushed them above my head, pinning my arms to the wall. A little sigh escaped me, but she stopped it with her tongue, leaving the sigh to build inside me. Kissing her was intoxicating. I wanted to climb inside her mouth and kiss her from the inside out. The taste of her mouth, the smell of her skin, all of her, was utterly erotic.

Finally, I said between breaths, "So, let's see how you like the feel of the spiral, then," as I managed to pull myself away from her momentarily, still conscious that I was supposed to be working. Barely. An extended mix of Madonna's *Justify My Love* was playing in the shop, wrapping around our arousal, making it dreamlike and expansive. I began to feel like we weren't anywhere. But at the same time we were everywhere. This changing room could have been any place. We were untouchable, except to each other.

"Yes, let's see about the spiral," she said. She was silent as she kicked off her shoes and slid her jeans down, her boyshorts coming down with them. Our policy was, obviously, that items must be tried on with underwear, but right now I wasn't going to object. She stepped into the harness as I stood watching, my pussy drenched, my heart racing. This had never happened before, I swear—not to me anyway. And if I was going to get fired for it, well, in this moment I wasn't really thinking straight.

Marlene inserted the dildo through the harness ring. Its sheer weight made it droop down a little. I could see that the harness just needed a bit of adjustment. "Let me . . ." I got down on my knees before her and put my hands on her hips to direct her to turn her back to me. Oh God, her arse . . . so beautiful, so firm, and yet with the sweetest curves and a dimple on either side of her coccyx. Resisting the urge to run my tongue over them, I paid attention to the matter at hand and adjusted the straps on either side of her arse cheeks, to pull the harness firmer into place. I felt her shiver as I brushed my hand across her tanned thigh. I put my hands on her hips again and turned her in the direction of the mirrors so she could admire herself.

"How does it feel?" I asked as I stood up.

"It feels fine to me. What do you think?" she asked, raising her arms to grip the pole above her, which served to push her pelvis out, the huge dildo extending from it invitingly. I smiled and stepped forward, not taking my eyes off hers, which glinted, challenging me to make the next move. I gripped the cock and pulled it slightly toward me. She murmured an "Mmm" as her pelvis was pulled forward by the force of my hand. "So far, it feels like it's a part of me," she sighed, her eyes baiting me, "but the question remains, what do you think?"

In the corner behind her was a box of lube samples that no one had found time to put out on display yet. I felt a momentary flash of fear that we'd be caught, but the absolute fucking need was just incredible. In the next instant I made my decision. I grabbed a lube sample and tore the lid off, squeezing the clear gel into my palm.

I resumed my *Eden Grrl* mode, as though this was perfectly normal, just a regular day on the shop floor. "Well, with dildos this big, it's important to lube up, even if your partner is very wet indeed," I instructed her as I slathered the cock with lube, stroking my hand up and down to make sure it was well covered. I could smell her arousal, smell her want—my own had already overtaken me. There was no going back now.

"It's important to go very slowly to start with," I advised, as I finished the lubing and slipped my hand under my skirt to smear the remainder on my already very wet pussy. The heat of my arousal noticeably warmed the center of my palm. I imagined my desire for Marlene had made my cunt a branding iron by which she would be marked. Marlene pushed me up against the mirrored wall again and lifted my skirt as she slid her hands up my thighs.

"Oh fuck, you're not wearing underwear!" she gasped, as her hand pushed between my legs. She smoothly buried three fingers in my pussy and brought her thumb up to rub my clit, her ministrations producing a squishing sound heard only by us, concealed as it was by the sounds of Madonna moaning as she was having her love justified.

With each thrust of her fingers, I was propelled up the wall a bit, until I was on tiptoe, and then back down again. As her fingers began to lightly tap my G-spot, she pressed her mouth to my ear and hissed, "I knew it would be like this with you, Emma—you all wet and up for anything. Would you like to feel this cock inside you? Would you like me to fill you?"

As she moved closer to hear my answer, the dildo banged against my thigh, making my pussy clench around her fingers at the thought of it. I'd never had anything this big, and yet, I was sure I could take it. Anything attached to Marlene was right—I just wished I hadn't waited so long to find out. Suddenly, I knew what I wanted and how I wanted it.

"Sit on that chair," I told her.

Marlene grinned as she stepped back and sat down on the chair. Her legs were toned from physical training, the muscles defined. The leather harness straps were tight, black strips across her sun-carameled thighs.

Rather than straddling her as she expected, I knelt down in front of her and parted her legs. As I looked up at her, I saw her smile. "You have something else you'd like to do first," she said, more a statement than a question.

"Yes," I said, "something I have wanted to do since we met. Something that gets me very wet."

With that I buried my face in her pussy, pushing the harness straps apart with my tongue. I licked her as though my life depended on it. I licked up under her clit, teased the tip of my tongue into her opening, just a fraction, and felt her quiver. I sucked her labia into my mouth ever so gently. I felt her twist and turn under my tongue as I drank up every bit of her sweet, musky juice. I finally lifted my head, leaving her teetering on the edge of orgasm. I wiped my face with my fingers and watched her sigh as I sucked on them, unwilling to part with even a drop of her come.

The taste of her, the scent of her in my nostrils, had gradually made me wetter and wetter until I was slick to my thighs with desire. Now, I was ready. I lifted my skirt and placed my legs on each side of hers to straddle her. I hovered above her as she held the spiral at its base, rubbing it back and forth, the helter-skelter curves slipping and sliding against my hardened clit. I slowly lowered myself down, thinking that if I could ever manage something this big, it was now. The slick head of the dildo pushed its way between my folds, deeper and deeper, the walls of my cunt expanding to accommodate its girth. I took great pleasure in the ever-increasing sense of fullness as I slowly pushed myself all the way down to the base. I paused, enjoying the feeling of sitting on Marlene's lap, filled with her enormous cock.

"How does it feel?" she asked, as she stroked my hips. I could tell she was eager to thrust.

"Incredible, like it's filling an enormous want, pacifying it," I whispered.

We kissed then, deeply, passionately. Her artful tongue played within my mouth and danced along my lips. Then she began to slowly bump her pelvis up and down, banging my clit against her pubic bone as she moved.

"Ahhh!" I cried, as waves of pleasure flowed through me.

The more we bounced like this, the more I wanted to be fucked hard by Marlene, no matter what. I began to move my pelvis too, matching her rhythm so the dildo slammed into me with each thrust. I worked myself up and down its shaft, suffering the bereavement of withdrawal so I could experience again the sensation of being filled. Marlene's hands were on my hips, guiding my movement. As I felt my orgasm build, I noticed that Marlene was panting faster and faster with the approach of her own climax. Ever since I ate her, I think she'd remained on the knife-edge of orgasm.

It began in my toes, like pins and needles. Then it gathered momentum in my feet before coursing up through my veins and tissue, converging in my belly where it built, each muscle clenching and unclenching until finally it broke inside me like a rainstorm, every synapse, every nerve ending dancing with release. As I sighed deeply, Marlene clamped her hand over my mouth and then clamped her mouth over the same hand, muffling her own groans as she twisted beneath me, her orgasm shaking her as mine still rocked my body. Madonna was done, too, and Prince began singing about cream and sugar.

"Emma," I heard Anya call from upstairs, "I need you up here."

"I'm coming!" I called back.

I looked at Marlene and we laughed into each other's shoulders, before trying to calm ourselves. As the fog of my orgasm began to subside, I was jolted back into reality—I was sitting on the merchandise. Which was attached to a customer.

"Shit. I have to get back upstairs!"

I slowly—and carefully—extracted myself from the firm anchoring on Marlene's lap and began to pull down my skirt, a little uncoordinated as my legs wobbled and my arms flopped like a rag doll's. Marlene followed my lead, standing and removing the dildo and harness, both of which were slick with lube and sex juices. As I smoothed my hair down and prepared to re-enter the world of the shop—and explain why I'd taken so long in the changing room with a customer—Marlene handed me the strap-on and said curtly, "Well, thank you for your help. I think this will do nicely."

Unselfconsciously, she threw the curtain open, then beamed at a straight couple hovering by the handcuffs who, by the furtive looks on their faces, had heard us and lingered to listen. I stepped out of the changing room first, saying for effect, "I'm glad you're happy with that combination. Let me wrap it for you."

We ascended the stairs, with me trying to conceal the juice-drenched strap-on from other customers, when Anya appeared at the top of the stairs. She had obviously guessed something was going on.

"Counter's free," she said, before ushering a customer over to the corsets. I slipped around to the till and quickly got Marlene's purchase into a bag and rung it up.

"Thank you very much for such good service," said Marlene, with a perfectly straight face.

"It was my great pleasure," I replied, taking her money and giving her the change.

"Well, I'd better go. I see you have other customers to attend to," she said, without a hint of irony.

I stepped out from behind the counter and we kiss-kissed good-bye, European style of course, then Marlene headed toward the door with her purchase, a certain swing in her step. She paused in the doorway to find her umbrella. I walked over to hold the door open for her as she opened the brolly and prepared to step out into the rain.

"Thank you again," she said. "Perhaps next time I *will* enquire about those beads you so highly recommend."

With that, she turned and left the shop, and me with some explaining to do.

Monster Mash
C.L. Crews

It's impossible to drink or eat anything with a Halloween mask on, but I really need some liquid courage and anxiety dead-ener, so I move into an almost pitch black corner of the back-yard, raise the mask halfway up my face, slam a sixteen-ounce cup of some lukewarm keg beer, reposition the mask and move back among the partygoers. I've been lurking on the fringes of this party trying to be inconspicuous and waiting for you to arrive for about thirty minutes. I decide I'm only going to wait another half hour. If I wait any longer, I'll likely be tossed out on my ear anyway. The mask and my lurking about not talking to anyone is beginning to draw attention and wary glances, even at a Halloween party.

You told me in an e-mail a few days ago that you planned to attend this party, among a couple of others. I did some pretty creative investigative work to find my way here, and up until now I was feeling quite proud of myself for that, but I'm getting increasingly nervous and considering the possibility that you've decided not to come. You have no idea that I'm even in town, so I'm certainly the last person you'd expect to see tonight. I could have just called you and saved myself this trouble, but if it pays off, that wouldn't be nearly as exciting. Plus, I really didn't think I'd have a chance to see you because I'm not exactly here on vacation.

My uncle's had a stroke, and I was the closest family member with the common sense and resources to come out and assist with the decision-making, initial caretaking and whatnot. He's doing better, though, and one of his friends offered to uncle sit and thus ordered me out to find some fun for the evening. He even hooked me up with a room for tonight at the hotel he manages, which is where I probably should be because I've been bunking on my uncle's lumpy couch for a week and could really use some sleep. Anyway, that's how I've ended up here, at a costume party in your fair city, presumably in the company of your friends and dressed as a werewolf.

Hey, it was last minute—what else was I gonna do with what has been my standard caretaker and hospital-wandering attire of jeans, T-shirt over a white, thermal, long-sleeve undershirt, Timberland work boots and denim jacket? Hairy hands and a hairy mask were the easy and perfect costume solution—not to mention one of the only three costumes left in the store I popped into—and, okay, I remembered that you were supposed to be Frankenstein and your girlfriend the Bride this evening, and what with my love of classic monster flicks and stupid sense of humor, I just couldn't resist the thought of us possibly starring in our own sequel to *Frankenstein Meets the Wolfman*.

I've got fifteen minutes left before I head for the door. If I'm going to leave without seeing you, I might as well leave with a buzz. I head back to the keg. I'm knocking back my second round when I hear the unmistakable sound of your laughter somewhere in the crowd behind me. I quickly slip the mask back into place and position myself close to the keg. If I know anything, it's that you'll be over here soon.

I watch you make your way through the crowd, which is easy enough, because you have a green, square head and you're wearing platform boots to augment your already considerable height. Sure enough, not five minutes pass before you've made obligatory chit-chat with a dozen or so people and find yourself face-to-face with a wolfman. You did a great job with the costume, and I catch myself before I say as much. Smiling slightly in my direction in that uncomfortable way people do when they're being stared at by a masked person, you busy yourself with getting beer for yourself and, I am assuming, your girlfriend, since she's just walked up behind you and placed her hand on your ass. The fact that she's sporting a wedding dress and four feet of hair on top of her head is also a pretty good indication that you two are together.

What the hell am I doing? You glance at me again, slip your arm around the Bride's waist and head back into the throng. Now what? How stupid was this? I'm so sleep deprived and I've been so stressed out with my uncle's issues that I never thought this out realistically. I've been stuck in fantasy mode for a week, and now I realize there's no way this can go down the way I had so naïvely imagined it. There is no way I can get you away from your girlfriend without exposing myself to both of you. There's no way we're going to be able to play out in real life the fantasy sequence that's been replaying in my head for a week, where I draw you into one of the bedrooms in this stranger's home, back you up against the closed door and kiss you blind while we play tiddlywinks under each other's shirts and you gasp with the realization that your request has been granted and I've gone commando for you (which I do about seventy percent of the time anyway) and my hand likewise finds its way into Frankenstein's trousers, only to discover, oh my, this is not a boy monster at all!

My moans are jarringly loud against the muffled din of the

party as you slip two fingers in on the ground floor. We are jerking each other in a simultaneous rhythm, my senses alive with our raspy, gasping breathing, the rustle of clothes, intermittent moans and whimpers, the feel of you, the smell of us. I imagined it all so vividly. And now . . . And now, what? How the fuck am I going to get you aside to let you know who I am and even if I do, then what?

I'm so lost in my thoughts that I don't notice you walking back to the keg and, by proximity, me. When you finish refilling your beer, you look at me and take a step in my direction. My eyes are darting wildly all around as I try to pinpoint your girlfriend's location. Shit, I don't see her anywhere. She's probably behind me and she's going to bash my furry head in. You come right up to me and peer into my eyes.

"Hey, do I know you?" you ask. I look at you and nod my head. I'm suddenly feeling in character and almost howl. Apparently encouraged, you smile and continue, "There's something so familiar about your stance, and your eyes. C'mon tell me. Who are you?"

I start to make a saucy retort like, "Are you attracted to the eyes of the Wolfman?" or some such nonsense as that, when I spy the Bride heading our way. I'm out of time. "I'm staying in town with my uncle for a few days, but I have a room tonight. Call my cell if you're interested, Frankie. No pressure." I watch your face as my voice registers and you realize who I am. Your stunned look is priceless. I squeeze your arm quickly and head for the exit.

My phone rings a few minutes later. It seems the Bride's not feeling well, and you two were planning to leave the party and call it a night anyway. You report that you'll meet me at the hotel after you tuck in your woman, remove the bolts from your neck and scrub off the green. Meanwhile, I have no idea where the fuck this hotel is and only a very tiny idea of where I am right now, so by the time I find my way to the hotel and get into a room I've only been there for five minutes when you arrive. Just long enough to have turned on the air, stripped off my bra and started nervously flipping channels on the television.

You said you might cry the next time we saw each other, but you're not crying. You're practically swallowing my face, but you're not crying. I take your overnight bag, toss it beside the bed and start removing your clothes. Finally, fantasy and reality start to merge as I back you up against the closed door and kiss you blind while we play tiddlywinks under each other's shirts, remove each other's shirts and then you do it, just like I imagined. You actually do gasp with the realization that your request has been granted and I've gone commando for you.

We drop trou and fall on the bed together. We're exhausted. The headiness from years of buildup to get to this moment and the realization that it's arrived is overwhelming both of us. We are kissing and giggling and kissing and laughing. I am in love with the feel of our skins together. I need to explore all of you. My fingers walk around your body, investigating the landscape, followed by my lips, tongue and teeth, taking small nips of flesh. I am so hungry. You are so beautiful. Your body is so soft and lush, sinuous and responsive, so utterly feminine. I look at you and you smile awkwardly, but obviously happy, and pull me in for a breathtaking kiss, full of emotion and need. We take a few minutes to dig in your bag and pull out some toys. I busy myself with lube and a plug while you strap me into an unfamiliar harness and attach your favorite ride, your fingers "accidentally" slipping off course while you work. We don't say much. We're both afraid to break the spell I guess, but each time we make eye contact, it's like a gut shot.

Once you've got me locked and loaded, you pull me back down on the bed. A hot and heavy make-out session follows. Your butt's wiggling all around the bed, but you're getting no part of what's between my legs—not yet, and no time soon. I stroke the length of your pussy lightly with the back of my fingers, bring them to my nose, inhale your essence, and immediately move my face between your legs, lick the length of your lips so lightly that it tickles, and alternately nip the sensitive insides of your thighs. The smell and taste that is you has been haunting my memories for years and I'm lost. I push your knees back to your chest and trail my tongue down your slit, from just below your clit to your flowing hole, and then push my tongue inside. How badly have I wanted to be here again? When will I have another opportunity? I've been starving for more than a decade, with only your words to sustain me. I feast.

I back off and my tongue continues its journey, circling backward until I reach your ass, where the circles that my tongue draws become tighter, but no less delicate. I lick so lightly that your sphincter quivers and spasms under my tongue. I slowly add pressure, drawing ever tighter circles until I feel you relax and allow me access. I tongue fuck your ass for a few moments, your breathing beginning to morph into a pant, and I head back up the way I came, taking time to review all past material. As I make my way back to your clit, I lick the very underside with increasing intensity and then suck it into my mouth suddenly and vigorously as I simultaneously guide the warmed and lubed stainless steel egg into your ass. Your fingertips digging into the base of my skull let me know that I'm doing something very right, but I'm not nearly ready for this to end—it's taken far too long to get here. I release your clit and head back up to look into your eyes. I crave that connection again. I need your assurance. I need to know that what I'm feeling isn't one-sided and that this isn't just about popping off. It isn't. You get so far into me with one smoldering look that my chest constricts suddenly, painfully, with feeling and regret, but we've had plenty of time to explore that and we'll have plenty more. We kiss hungrily and you start rocking your hips.

"Take it," I tell you. "Take what you want."

Without hesitation, you reach down and unceremoniously

stuff the head of the dick into your hole. Then you grab my ass and try to push me deeper, but I lock my arms on either side of your head, lock my hips in place and hold tight. That's all you're getting right now. You look at me in puzzlement and frustration. There you go, that's what I'm after. I can't get enough of those eyes. I slide all the way in, immensely enjoying your ensuing groan and your unwavering gaze. We begin a slow, grinding fuck. You claim my breasts with your hands, rubbing the nipples with your thumbs and then tugging and pumping them with your thumbs and index fingers. I'm helpless, completely lost in sensation as you watch me intently, a flicker of amusement in your eyes. You're enjoying your moment of power, very aware that every movement of your hands is dictating the rhythm of my strokes between your legs. We're reaching critical mass. I bring your right leg up and prop it on my shoulder. I take your right hand, kiss and suck your fingers, thoroughly wetting them, before placing them on your pussy. You immediately begin to pull and rub your clit. I reach around and twist and tug the egg, reminding you of its presence in your tight hole as I continue to fuck you, upping the tempo in response to your incoherent cries, my excitement and the flight of your fingers across your clit when, at last, between the two of us, we trip your wire and I pull the egg just as you cross over. You are so open and so beautiful. I am overwhelmed, swept away by your vulnerability, the gift of you.

After a moment's rest and some delicious, lazy, after-party kisses, I shuck the harness and take another journey down your beautiful body, swirling my tongue lightly around your still sensitive nipples, taking a quick dip into the whorl of your belly button and then finding myself back at your frothy slick center, where I delicately tongue your tender swollen folds, while manipulating my own with my right hand until I scream my pleasure, misery, love, regret and happiness into your cunt. You are my oldest and dearest friend, my closest confidant and again, finally, for this second first and last time, my lover.

The Temp
Jen Cross

We're in the middle of an actual heat wave. Temperatures in the city have hovered around ninety degrees this whole week. When I moved here from Massachusetts, my friends promised me it never got like this in San Francisco. I can't believe I have to go to work today; I'd so much rather take my skinny butt to the beach.

Temp jobs are killer. The only reason I keep showing up—you know, besides the need to keep a roof over my head—is the knowledge that I'll get to see you. You, whose shock of dyed red hair is always a wake-up call far more effective than the sad attempt at coffee that awaits me in the office kitchenette. You, whose sweet strong eyes catch me like a fish on a hook every morning as I walk across the office. You—well, my crush on you—are the only thing that makes this fucking filing/photo-copying/telephone answering job bearable. It's certainly not the pay.

Although the firm has a business-casual dress code (all employees must wear at least one item that is beige, in other words), it's impossible for me to be subtle when it's this hot. Rifling through my closet, I choose a tightish blue-and-orange striped shirt and a straight skirt that comes down just to my knees. This skirt is my favorite because it manages to hug what little butt I actually have, giving me a bit of curve. Clunky black platform sandals finish off my outfit, and after a little breakfast and the barest attention to my messy mop of hair, I'm out the door and into the heat. Dampness immediately darkens my underarms and beads along my upper lip.

It's too hot to care about anything much today. I ignore the sour face of the elderly woman on the bus when she notices the moist tuft of hair peeking out from under the sleeve of my shirt as I hang onto the bar over her head. I disregard the snapping, smarmy comments from hopeful day laborers on the corner where I get off the bus. And, as I yank open the office building's heavy glass doors, I prepare, once again, to take no notice of the sidelong glances and condescending sniffs of my supervisor's supervisor, a woman who has "worked harder to get where she is today" and feels I don't present a professional enough image or take my job seriously.

No kidding.

"You'll never get hired full-time looking like that, sweetie," she informed me last week, in an oily attempt at camaraderie, commenting on the Hello Kitty T-shirt I wore not so discreetly under a secondhand men's tuxedo shirt that was unbuttoned to about midway down my chest, both over a red-and-yellow plaid skirt, and black Mary Janes with white socks.

Like I would want to get hired permanently to this seventh circle of hell. Like I wouldn't rather shove my head into the shredder.

I take the elevator to the ninth floor and shove into the offices of Burlington and Burke, Attorneys at Law. I make my way to

Reception, drop my politico-button-addled surplus army knapsack at my (temporary) desk and pick up my coffee cup (which pushed unofficial office moral codes with its straight-line smiley face and command to "Have a day"). I make a beeline down the hall.

Hustling into the kitchen, my thighs sticking together a bit, mostly from the heat—at least this goddamn office is air-conditioned—I manage to run smack into your cart stocked with garbage bags, cleaning solutions, dusting things, a broom. You look up, shocked and immediately apologetic. Then you see it's me, and your face melts into that phenomenally wide grin. My knees buckle and my heart rate doubles, although all I do is nod before extricating my hip from the wet cloth bucket at the cart's edge.

"Good morning, ma'am," you say with a conspiratorial grin, like you realize we're just two people pretending to be adults in these jobs. "Sorry about that." Under your (unsnapped) maintenance uniform shirt you're wearing an old *Never Mind the Bollocks* Sex Pistols T-shirt over cuffed jeans too big for you and held up with a studded belt. And those work boots that we briefly discussed last week.

You pull back, easing yourself and your cart back through the doorway and into the kitchen so I can get through the door.

"Good morning," I respond, holding your gray eyes with my green ones as long as I can, until I feel my face begin to flush. "No problem. My own fault for trying to walk when I'm not awake." Still not quite looking away from you, I grab the pot out of the silver-gray industrial coffee machine. I begin pouring absently, but find that some asshole decided not to empty the pot, and the leftover coffee has burned and thickened into sludge.

"Goddammit," I say, slamming the pot on the counter. You lean back against the cart, pressed up next to the side of the refrigerator, and fold your thick, strong arms across your chest.

"No coffee yet this morning, huh, lady?" you ask as I fumble with giant packets of what looks like pre-chewed and desiccated coffee beans, dumping the grounds into a bedsheet-sized, bleached white filter and shoving the thing into the grounds holder, which I then slam back into the machine. I thrust a new, sort of empty orange-handled pot of once-was-decaf into place and press the button that reads "Brew" and means rescue.

"Nope," I reply with a grin and an attempt at a sexy flip of the hair, which ends up just looking like I tried to crack my neck and failed. "That obvious, huh?"

You purse your lips at me in a tight, sweet smile and we move into that part of our every morning's interaction that is uncomfortable silence while each frantically tries to think of something to say as an excuse to stick around and keep looking at each other.

"Pretty hot out there today, huh?" you say, running your thick fingers through that funky red hair. "I was drenched by the time I got in this morning."

"Do you walk?" I ask, managing to pull my attention from the muscles in your forearms.

"Ride my bike."

"Cool," I say. "Street?"

"Nah—I wanted a mountain bike, but they're too fucking expensive. You know," you say, with an abrupt change of tone and a glance away from me in such a feigned act of nonchalance that I almost giggle out loud, "that coffee's gonna take a minute or two. Are you into bikes? You wanna see mine?"

Are you kidding? I think to myself. But then I quit thinking and say, as brightly as possible and with as much forced casualness, "Sure." I follow you (without your cart) through the office corridors and warrens of gray-walled cubicles, remembering too late that I've still got my *Have a day* mug clutched in my left hand.

Babbling like an excited kid about your bike, improvements

you've made, accidents you've been in, and so on, you speed ahead of me and I'd have to trot to keep up. I don't though. I like being a little behind you and watching the swell of your shoulders shaping that oversized blue-gray maintenance shirt, your round, hard ass, as well as those strong, biking thighs.

The maintenance room is back by the rear office bathrooms and the Emergency Exit stairwell. You finger one of the many keys on the chain you keep clipped to your belt loop, open the room to me, usher me in, flip on the brash fluorescent overhead light and shut the door behind us. I notice a fairly battered and heavily stickered bike leaning against the far storage shelves, which are lined with rolls of toilet paper and huge bottles of different cleaning solutions.

"There she is," you say, a little breathless, pulling me toward the bike by my wrist. It's the first time you've touched me, and my skin burns. There's a green light flashing at the edge of my vision.

"Uh-huh," I nod, and reach behind you to switch off the light again—I think I mentioned that it's just too hot to be subtle today—and lean in to kiss you. Your lips press, hot and heavy and dense, against mine as if drawn magnetically; there's none of that missing and hitting my nose or eyes, fumbling around in the dark. Your body draws close and I have those hard arms finally under hand. I squeeze hard, wanting to bruise you from the get-go, wanting to transmit the desire I've had for you all these months.

But then I move on. In these brief, few minutes, I want to feel everything. If I'm going to get fired for fucking maintenance staff, then goddammit, I want it to be good.

It's quiet and stifling in the room, and our sighs and moans are amplified in the trapped air around us. The smell of your sweat and musk combines with mine, which together much improve the chemical aroma of cleaning supplies. I wrap my arms around you, clocking you with the goddamn mug, which you immediately remove from my hand and shove onto a shelf behind my head.

"I can't believe this," you whisper, finally, in my ear. "I've wanted you ever since you started working here, that day you came in wearing those pink Pumas with your good-girl temp suit."

I shudder to think you noticed, and feel your grin against my skin. You nibble down from my earlobe to my neck, and I clutch hard to your hair, thrilling in the shivery sensations that your soft lips and sharp teeth send resonating down my back and legs to my swelling cunt.

Your hands ease under my little striped shirt and cover the unencumbered breasts you find there, which brings me to near collapse against you. Your body, hot and strong, holds me up. Pushing my shirt up under my chin, you move your mouth from my neck to my tits, and your hands stroke along my belly, over my hips, and then grip my ass. Pressing the fullness of your lips around my breast, you stroke the tip of your tongue gently and firmly across my already hard nipple. I chew on my bottom lip to keep from moaning as loud as I usually do.

Then your hands slide down to the hem of my skirt, which you begin to gently shift up my thighs toward my hips. This takes a certain amount of patience, and I am grateful that you don't just tear through in the heat of this ratcheted moment. Your hands ease my body back and forth, rocking the material up until it's bunched around my hips and then you drop down to a squat in front of me.

I lean back against stacks of brown-paper wrapped replacement paper towels while I push my own pink panties down, bending down to ungracefully yank my foot out of one of the holes so my legs can be spread.

You place your hands on the insides of my moist thighs and press, encouraging me to spread myself wide open for you. The scent from my cunt mixes overwhelmingly with ammonia and bleach, and I feel faint with arousal when you release your hot breath all over my soaked fur and flesh.

"Hmmmm." Your voice floats up through my engorged labia, and I get a little loose with vertigo, clutching your head to steady myself, which you take to be encouragement and a request to move faster. All of a sudden, the hot muscle of your tongue is splitting through the furry cleft of me and bringing a shout up my throat, which becomes a desperate moan upon release only through sheer force of will. You taste all the flesh there, licking and sucking along my labia and the tender skin at the top of my thighs, then returning, without warning, to my clit.

I try not to tear your hair out, but you don't seem to mind. This is just too hot to be worrying about bald spots, or the bruise forming at the small of my back, pressed against the edge of the shelf, or the fact that I'm about to lose my job.

First, oh first, I get to lose control. And when your tongue works into the opening of my cunt and releases all the trapped flood of wetness there, it's your turn to groan. Then there are two—or is it three?—fingers pressing into me, and I drop down a little on my thighs, reflexively fucking myself onto your hand, holding your face hard against my cunt. You suck the whole small globe of my clit between your lips while you move your fingers deeper into me. My breath comes short and sharp, and an orgasm like the hard slam of a wave clenches me to breathlessness and then releases into wave after wave of sensation. I bite my lip so hard to keep from screaming that it's going to be swollen later.

I ease up off your fingers while you reach behind me and grab something. You rip open one of those packages of paper towels and I hear you wiping your hands, then feel the rough paper against my thighs and cunt. My ragged breath surrounds us, and I don't know whether to fall into you and keep this momentum going, or whether I should maybe ask you your name.

"Look, you," you say, your voice tight and thick. "I'm gonna turn on the light so I can find the sink without breaking anything."

I laugh, but it sounds more like a croak, which makes you laugh too. I'm sure the grimace that contorts my face in response to the evil fluorescent brightness is singularly unattractive.

"Sorry," you say, when you find I've clamped my eyes shut, still unable to move from where the orgasm left me—my little bare ass making an imprint in the rest of those paper towels. The thought of you finding it later makes me grin.

"What is it?" you ask, noticing my smile, while applying now-dampened paper towels to my damp and disheveled body.

"Oh my god," I say, my mind gone blank. "I have absolutely no idea."

We both start giggling a little hysterically, and when I open my eyes finally and squint through the brightness at your face, so attentive to your cleaning, a renewed rush of arousal weakens my thighs.

"Will you come see me wherever I end up temping next?" I ask as you lift my foot to get my panties back on and then start working my skirt back down my legs.

"What?" you say with concern, looking up at me with raised eyebrows.

"I mean after I get fired." You chuckle then, relieved, going back to work.

"You're not going to get fired, lady." Rising gingerly, thighs obviously sore, you toss out the paper towels you used on me, then wash your hands and face. I wonder what, if anything, you'll do about the smell of sex, of me, in the room.

Drying your hands, then your face, you look around for something. Eyes brightening, you reach up for a clean, new coffeepot.

"Here," you say, handing it to me. "That other one looked cracked, and you don't wanna leave caf coffee in a decaf pot."

I try to respond, and find myself lost in the gray depths of desire in your eyes. I clear my throat, and take the pot from you. "Good idea. Thanks." We look at each other, and you take my cheek in one firm hand and kiss me with so much tenderness and lust that both my eyes and cunt get wet.

"Sure," you say as you pull your face from mine. "See you later on, okay?"

"Of course," I respond, my voice still a bit froggy.

Opening the door, I'm smacked with a rush of chilled air, which makes me shiver.

"Wait!"

"I've got to get back—" I begin, turning to find you holding my coffee mug out to me.

"Have a day," you say.

"Oh, I've already had one." I return your big grin, then head back up the hall, letting the door fall shut behind me. The cold air feels so good against my feverish skin that I find myself pleased with the goose pimples that rise up all over, like some mark you've left on me.

I return to the kitchen and swap out the coffee and pots, wondering how many decaf drinkers are going to be up until two a.m. after getting a bit of the real thing. I hustle toward my desk then, passing my supervisor on her way to get her own coffee.

"Well, good morning, dear. Didn't want any coffee this morning?" she asks with a raised eyebrow and a nod at my empty cup.

A hot flush colors my neck and cheeks, and I duck my head, hoping she doesn't notice. "Oh, well, the pot was empty. I'm brewing a fresh one now." I turn around a third time and walk with her to the kitchen, where I am nearly, once again, run over by your cart, rushing out at us.

"Oh, do be careful, please," my supervisor says in her snotty voice, stepping aside to let you through. "Um—Jacqueline, isn't it? Aren't you usually through this area by now?"

"Yes, ma'am," you say with a straight face and not one glance in my direction. "I had an unexpected cleanup in the back this morning."

She's not listening, though—has dismissed you already and turned her attention to the decaf. I take the opportunity to stroke your ass with the back of my hand as you pass, whispering "Bye, Jack," which brings a little gasp that you immediately cover up with a cough. We don't look at each other, and I take my turn after my supervisor to fill my cup.

Metro Heat
Therese Szymanski

I walked into the empty station, noticing for the first time ever just how cavernous and empty the Woodley Park Metro is this late on a weekday night—especially with the snow that began falling just a few hours before. I should've remembered how snow could shut down the nation's capital.

Even still, I was amazed when I got onto the red line train, and I was the only one in my car.

I was exhausted at the end of a long, hard day as a desk jockey. My head was spinning from the number of reports I had read and all the Excel spreadsheets I had been studying, and so I discovered I actually enjoyed being all by myself in the train car, even though I thought I could practically hear my own breathing echo throughout all the empty space.

I wondered if the snow would affect the movements of the train, even though it was underground through the District, because, after all, to get to Silver Spring, I'd have to stay on it for a while above ground as well.

I sat back and, deciding I was safe because I was alone, and unlike the New York subway, the D.C. Metro didn't allow you to switch cars while the train was in motion, closed my eyes, enjoying the rest and relaxation after a particularly trying day at the office.

That was when I began to notice that the movement of the train over the rails wasn't smooth, in fact, sitting on the seat wasn't too much unlike sitting on top of a washing machine while it churned away. I smiled to myself. If no one else came into my car, this could end up a pleasant ride home.

The train's next stop was Dupont Circle, and when the doors opened and no one got in, I thought it really might be my lucky night. It appeared that all the Washingtonians were buried under their blankets during what they must've considered a blizzard.

But lady luck was not with me tonight for, just as the doors were about to close, two women came flying in.

"Whew! Just made it!" one said, quickly glancing about the car. She was tall, maybe five feet eleven, with short, black hair. She was wearing jeans, a flannel shirt with a white T-shirt underneath it, a pair of heavy work boots, and a black leather jacket, decidedly ostentatious with its rows of fringe all along the sleeves and in a V down the back.

I said a silent prayer, hoping they would not sit near me, and I'm not sure just how successful it was, because although they didn't sit next to me, the seats they chose were only three rows in front of me, albeit on the other side of the aisle.

"God! I am so drunk!" the other woman exclaimed, laying her head back against the top of the seat. She was wearing a skirt and pumps, with only a jean jacket covering her over what appeared to be a rather sheer blouse. Her partner wrapped an arm around her shoulder and pulled her in. "I think that was the best holiday party ever!"

Just what I needed, yet another reminder that Christmas was

upon us, and I'd be spending the long weekend alone in my apartment, with only my tiny turkey, mashed potatoes and veggies to keep me company.

Oh no! I'd forgotten the cranberry sauce again!

"I hope you're not too drunk for what I have in mind tonight," the taller woman whispered into her partner's ear. Or, she said it in what she probably thought was a whisper, but reality to a drunken mind is far different than reality to a sober one.

I wished only that loud-mouthed drunks didn't always have to disturb my after-work, wind-down period.

"I was thinking 'bout giving you a little pre-Christmas Eve surprise tonight," the tall one continued. She unwrapped her arm from the other woman's shoulders and reached down, as if taking the other woman's hand and doing something with it. I wondered what exactly was going on.

"Oh, Sandra . . ." the femme moaned, "you know how hot it makes me when you pack. When did you put that on?"

"Just before we left the party, Katie. I didn't want everybody to know all the details of our lives, after all. But I did want to give you something to fantasize about during our ride home."

Katie turned to Sandra and gave her her mouth and the two kissed. Deeply.

I nonchalantly moved across the aisle for a better view.

"Do you know what I'm gonna do to you when we get home?" Sandra asked. When Katie didn't reply, she continued, "I'm gonna take off this jacket of yours . . . then I'm gonna peel off your skirt and panties . . ."

"Oh, baby . . ."

"What else are you wearing?"

"Blouse and bra."

"You know what I mean."

Katie gulped. "Stockings with a garter belt. I had been hoping we might have a chance for a little adventure during the party."

"Hm. So then I'll take off your blouse and bra, leave you

wearing only those incredible stockings, garter belt and heels, and you'll like that, won't you?"

"Baby, you know I'm yours."

"You like being naked when I'm still clothed, don't you? You like showing me your pussy and tits, especially if I make you show them to me. You like teasing me, but most of all, it makes you feel naughty—it makes you feel so bad, it's good."

I suddenly realized I was just about caught up in the middle of an episode of phone sex. Sandra was turning Katie on with her words as a sort of foreplay.

I wondered what such a careful and creative lover would be like in bed. After all, if she was willing to play like this just to get her partner good and wet, what else might she do? What else might she be planning?

"Then, if you've been very good . . ."

"Oh baby, please, you know I'm always good . . ."

"If you're very good, I'm gonna let you get down on your knees and open my zipper."

"Oh yes, please baby, let me suck it, let me show you just how good I can be."

"I knew you'd want to blow me, want to suck my cock."

What? I had been sure these were two women—what was going on?

"Baby, let me do it now, let me suck you, right here, right now."

"Katie, we're in the Metro!"

"We're alone!"

"No we're not," Sandra looked over her shoulder at me, and I pretended to be deeply engrossed in something I was reading.

"She's busy," Katie countered.

Hold on, Katie had said Sandra was packing something she had just put on. Sandra must be wearing a strap-on dildo!

Sandra again looked back at me, but even though I was thoroughly into my pretense of reading something I wasn't actually holding, I realized she knew I was hanging on to their every word and action. The only thing she didn't know was how much I was also enjoying the movement of the train.

We stopped at Farragut North. I prayed even harder than before that no one would join us. I really, really wanted to see Katie suck Sandra's dildo. I wanted to hear Sandra's zipper being lowered, I wanted to see Katie drop to her knees . . .

Suddenly some little guy with short brown hair, dressed in a dark blue suit, with a red and blue paisley tie and dark green trench coat sat down right in front of me.

I almost cried. They'd never do it now, with this boy watching!

But then I heard Sandra's voice again, as if she were deliberately taunting us, "Baby, I'm gonna give it to you so good tonight, I'm gonna spread you out on the table like Christmas dinner and then I'm gonna fuck your brains out. I'm gonna ride you like a cheap whore, like your pussy's only there for my cock to sink into, and I'm gonna make you come like there's no tomorrow."

All of my sensibilities were on fire—I wanted to scream at them about how rude and crude this all was, and how I couldn't believe she was saying such things to the woman she loved, let alone planning on doing any of them, except that, well, I didn't think my legs would hold my weight, and I didn't want to help anyone notice what I was sure was an increasingly wet spot on the back of my skirt.

I couldn't believe it, but I wanted to experience such penetration. I wanted to be taken and ridden and used.

Just my luck that some guy had gotten on the train and spoiled my personal, private little show. He turned his head ever so slightly, as if aware of my presence, as if aware of what was being shown to us, and I realized he wasn't bad looking for a male: His features were rather well-defined, and his chin and cheeks were incredibly soft looking and clean shaven. His eyebrows were neatly divided into two.

He raised an arm to rest along the back of his seat in one of the male ways of marking territory that I so detested. I could imagine him doing such a thing regardless of how crowded the train was. He probably sat with his legs splayed wide apart, taking up as much room as possible. No one would dare try to fit in next to him during rush hour, but yet he wouldn't mind sitting next to someone like me and taking up all of my room, squishing me, with his desire for space.

Suddenly, I heard a zipper being drawn down, accompanied by a peal of girlish giggling. I looked forward and saw Sandra sitting with her back against the outside wall of the train, her body apparently strewn on the seat in front of her.

"Oh yeah, oh yeah baby," Sandra began moaning. "Take it all, all of it."

The man in front of me looked over his arm at me, taking in all of my body, as if assessing how it would feel under his hands, as if wondering what I would look like naked, and how my mouth would feel on his dick.

I have never given a blow job in my life, and at the tender age of twenty-eight, I had no intention of starting. I couldn't understand why a woman would want to suck another's dildo, or what joy having one's dildo sucked could give to the wearer of such apparel.

But I did know that thinking of Sandra with her pants unzipped on the Metro, with Katie's mouth taking it in and sucking on it, really sent a flush running through me.

"You enjoying the floor show?" the guy in front of me asked. His voice wasn't as deep as I expected.

I looked away, pulling my palm pilot out of my briefcase, as if I had important notes to review and agenda items to plan.

"Oh, God, Katie, Katie!"

I knew my face was flushed.

"So it does turn on the ice goddess, huh?" he asked, his voice a low purr as he obviously referred to the antics of our fellow passengers.

I made incomprehensible notes on my palm pilot.

I didn't know where we were, and I wasn't sure where we had stopped. All I knew was that we were cruising through a long, dark tunnel when the light flickered and the engine's roar ceased. We were coasting to a stop, and then all the lights went out.

The conductor's voice, in its garbled Metro-speak, seemed to advise us to stay calm, everything would be okay.

I didn't believe a garbled word of it. But still I rearranged myself, trusting the darkness to keep safe the secret of just how turned on I was.

It had been eight long months since another woman had touched me, since I had made love to another woman. Eight months without sex or affection. And even longer than that if you considered how long Amy and I were breaking up before we finally broke up. She claimed that I thought my career was more important than she was, and for once in our so-called relationship, she was right.

I knew she couldn't deal with a long-term partnership, and I was just starting out. When things began to fall apart, I knew the only sensible place for a Capricorn to focus her energies was on work. I might as well succeed in at least one of my endeavors.

Still, my bed and apartment were awfully lonely each night now. As a congressional aide, many offers were made each day to fill such places, but by males. At this rate, I would eventually take one of them up on it, because nothing better was looming on the horizon, and I would go nuts if I had to keep going on waking up by myself, if I never had anyone to hold and be close with.

"Oh, Sandra, Sandra . . ."

"Are you as cold as I am?" the man's voice floated back to me, as if from over an abyss. It held none of the cockiness or abrasiveness I had become accustomed to hearing from males, but maybe that was because of the faint drawl that coated his words.

"It's cold," I replied. My good Midwestern upbringing had taught me that this was nothing, although the heat in the train had obviously stopped along with the lighting, but still, I had been a Washingtonian for several years now, and was unaccustomed to such coldness, especially when I was sitting still. I was shivering.

"I wonder how long this will last," he said, apparently referring to the train's stoppage. I sensed him moving back a row and into my seat, but fortunately, he wasn't the space hog I had assumed him to be. He kept neatly on his side while I stayed on my side. "I don't think we'll get much company from them," he said, referring to Sandra and Katie, "although they are a good bit of entertainment."

I merely grunted my reply. I would've preferred to be left alone in the car, or maybe alone with the other two women, so I could fantasize, but now he was not only in the car, he was encroaching upon my space.

"By the way, my name's Cyndi," he said.

"Cyndi?"

"Yeah, Cyndi. You have a problem with that?"

I was speechless. I had long ago learned that it was better to hold your words than to stick your foot in your mouth.

"Oh, shit."

"What?"

"Did you think I was a guy?" I could almost see his mouth turning up in a wicked grin. He had me figured out and was playing me.

I wouldn't give him the pleasure of a response.

"You still think I'm a guy." I thought about his fine features, his soft-looking, clean-shaven skin, and how delicate his hands looked . . .

I didn't reply.

Then I felt his hand on my shoulder, his hand working its way down my arm to my hand. I wanted to pull back, repelled, but I was stunned. He took my hand in his own, incredibly soft, one, and placed it between his legs.

"Do you still think I'm a guy?"

I was appalled and scared out of my mind. Someone on the Metro had just put my hand on her crotch!

"Do you?"

I yanked my hand away, but not before I realized that whoever this person was, s/he didn't have a penis.

"Well?"

"Okay, fine, you're a woman."

"Good. I'm glad that's settled. Now, will you tell me if those two getting it on up there is turning you on as much as it is me?"

This was the worst pick-up line I had ever heard. "Not at all."

"You're lying." She paused, as if wanting me to say something, then she continued, "by the way, I didn't catch your name."

"That's because I didn't give it."

"And I thought the air in here was cold." She seemed to shiver a bit next to me. "I'm sorry, I just moved here from Texas, so I'm definitely not accustomed to temperatures like these. I can handle a good hundred-degree day a lot better than this."

I refused to let her drag me into any sort of a conversation. I just sat back, closed my eyes, and tried to focus on the sounds coming from just a few seats farther up in the car.

"I just hope the snow's stopped," she continued, as if oblivious to my silence. "I didn't expect much today, and I've actually never driven in it before."

"Then I hope you're not planning on learning how to do it tonight," I said. I had driven in snow all my life, and knew that it was nothing to fool with, though all too many folks around the D.C. area didn't think the same way. They'd drive around thinking snow was like rain, or thinking they knew how to drive in snow when they didn't, and cause accidents throughout the entire metropolitan area.

"I wasn't planning on it, but I drove to the Metro, and I live up in Burtonsville, which is so far away, there's no way I can walk home."

"Then you should get a cab."

"I hope I can find one this late. But I'm sure I'll be all right."

"Oh, yeah, you're one of those who thinks you're invincible. You think you're all rough and tough and stuff, but do you realize that snow isn't rain? And have you thought about all the people you could injure along the way?"

"I said I'll try to find a cab."

"It's cold out there, so you don't want to end up stranded, plus, the snow will further decrease your ability to see, along with the night." I knew I was being a little intense, but I hated idiots who tried unsuccessfully to drive in the snow. And I just knew this woman's type, and knew that she'd try to do it regardless.

"Hey, sweetie, will you calm down if I *promise* to catch a cab?"

"Mmmm, baby, I love you," Sandra said to Katie.

"I'm not your sweetie," I told Cyndi.

"Okay, okay baby, just calm down."

"I'm not your baby either. My name's Kirsten."

"Well, Kirsten, it's a pleasure to meet you."

I couldn't believe I had told this . . . this woman my name. "Listen, I'm just not into your entire scene, so you can just cool it with this pick-up routine, okay?"

"My scene? Just what sort of kinky stuff do you think I'm into?"

"Well, you know—like them, up there."

"Oh, I get it now, regardless of what you're wearing, you're one of those andro-dykes."

"I have to dress this way for work!" I said, then realized what she had said. "And what do you mean, *andro-dyke*?"

"You're into that entire androgynous scene, wherein all lesbians are supposed to think, act, dress and talk alike—and thus your contempt of my so-called scene."

"I don't like labels," I said, deciding to get right to the heart of the matter.

"But what is a label but a badge of self-recognition? Lesbian, feminist, woman, sister, mother, Catholic, queer, dyke, Jew, marketing professional, development person, differently-abled, geek, techno-nerd—they're all labels, and all means through which we can identify ourselves, and others who are like us. They're modes of self-identification and understanding, and, sometimes, a means for others to discriminate against us, and at other times, words to show our strength, as in via the reclamation of language."

"I don't need a lecture on your beliefs. And I don't like being called an andro-dyke."

"And yet without even knowing me, you're labeling *me*. Even if it is a label I gleefully accept."

I suddenly realized she wasn't the macho idiot I had thought her to be.

The lights flickered on and the train suddenly started moving again, and I saw that a wicked grin wound its way across her face. I realized with a start that she really was a woman, and I couldn't believe that I hadn't seen it from the first. I would definitely not call her beautiful, or even pretty, because neither word really described her (and I was sure she wouldn't like either term anyway), but she really was handsome in a feminine way.

"Of course, I guess butch/femme could be considered a sort of role-playing, a sort of scene, because although it is oftentimes an equal partnership, it is a sort of play as well." She let her eyes trail over me, and suddenly I didn't find her gaze too repulsive. "I know most of my girls can do almost anything, but they make me feel good by asking me to do the mechanical and heavy work, whereas I make them feel good by praising them, by treating them like the beautiful women they are. It's a sort of mutual admiration society. We each do by our strengths, and we love those qualities in each other."

Sandra stood up, zipped her fly and looked over at us. "I can always trust Cyndi to try to recruit new members to our society whenever she has the chance." She grinned at the two of us. "Did you enjoy the show?" she asked me.

"W . . . Wha . . . What?" I stammered.

Cyndi stood up, walking to stand near Sandra in the aisle. "Kirsten, I'd like you to meet my bud, Sandra. Sandra, Kirsten." I noticed the bulge in Sandra's pants where she obviously had "packed" her dildo, and to my embarrassment, I found my eyes flickering over it.

When I held out my hand to shake Sandra's outstretched one, she quickly bent and kissed my hand instead. An unaccountable shiver ran through me.

"And this is my lovely wife, Katie," Sandra said, indicating Katie, who was now standing next to her.

I felt distinctly at a disadvantage, and so I stood as well, but fell back onto the seat when the train came to a stop in Takoma Park. No one else got on, though.

Cyndi sat next to me, and Katie and Sandra took the seat directly in front of us. Cyndi looked out over my shoulder. "Oh shit," she said with feeling.

I glanced over my shoulder and realized that, incredibly enough, the weather people had been right on the money—we had a full-scale blizzard on our hands.

"You definitely need to get a taxi," I said to Cyndi.

"Great, just great," Sandra said. "I told you we ought to just stay at our place," she said to Cyndi.

"Your place isn't even big enough to turn around in," Cyndi said. "And I saw your idea of a Christmas tree—whereas I've got a real one, a real tree in my living room, with all the accoutrements. As well as a real turkey dinner planned."

"I just hope the taxis are running in this," Katie said.

"They've got to know people won't want to drive in this," I

said. "So you're all spending the holiday together? That's nice."

"Yeah, if we can get there." Sandra was still staring out the window. She glanced over at Cyndi, "Just remember the two of us haven't driven since moving up here, and we have about as much experience driving in the snow as you."

I wished I could join them. I wanted to spend the time with friends, with other people. As it was, I was just going to mope around my lonely apartment alone, trying to appease myself with a single-serving turkey, no cranberry sauce, and a two-foot fake tree with only its meager tinsel and lights to keep me company.

"Yeah, we are," Sandra said, as the train came to a stop in Silver Spring. The wind was blowing enough so that even the covered deck had quite a bit of snow accumulated on it.

"I guess I'll see you around," I said, walking toward the north exit.

"Where are you heading?" Cyndi asked, stopping and looking after me.

"I just live a few blocks away, over at the corner of 16th and East-West Highway." I wasn't looking forward to the walk home through the cold wind and several inches of snow.

Cyndi shivered. "Still too far to walk on a night like this. Come with us and we'll have our cab drop you off on the way."

"It's not on the way." I didn't want to impose.

"Honey," Katie said, "these two like taking care of girls. What will it hurt for you to take advantage of it?"

I gave up on all my morals and followed them. Men always try to take advantage of women, so it seemed like something of a payback to save myself a trudge through the beginnings of a very white Christmas.

When we got out into the snow-covered lot, we had to make our way up the steps to where the taxis waited.

"Oh, shit," Cyndi said, probably echoing all our feelings. There wasn't a cab in sight.

"Maybe if we just wait a few minutes," Sandra said, glancing at her watch.

"I'm sorry," Katie said to me, wrapping a sisterly arm around my already shaking shoulders, "it's my fault you just didn't head home."

I accepted her warmth, and it was only from her I'd accept such behavior. "It's okay," I lied, knowing I'd be halfway home by now.

"Listen," Cyndi said, stamping her feet for warmth as she wrapped her arms around herself, "there are no cars out on the road, so how much trouble can we get into if I try driving?" Her voice was trembling along with her body, but still I thought about how cold they'd get if they got into an accident along the road home.

"Where's your car?" Sandra asked, and Cyndi pointed her head toward the main lot, as if she didn't want to expose her hands to the weather.

"R-right o-over th-there . . ."

There was a single, black, Toyota Forerunner in the lot.

"It's got four-wheel d-drive . . ."

It was a good vehicle for this sort of weather, but I'd guess more than six inches had already accumulated, and it was still driving down like a sheet of rain. It really was a blizzard.

Sandra looked at her watch. "I-I'm thinking the cabs have given it up. We were the only ones to get off the train, and it was the last run of the night."

Cyndi silently nodded her acquiescence. "We'll drop you off first, though."

I decided to put her in her place. "Do you have a spare room?"

"What?"

"Do you have a spare room? I don't see a cell phone among you, and I don't like the idea of you facing this."

"And you think you can do better?" Cyndi asked.

"I grew up in Michigan. I've driven through worse than this.

In a Plymouth Sundance."

Katie squeezed my arm. "You go girl!"

Sandra looked down at me, then over at Cyndi. "I think we can add one more to our party, don't you?"

Cyndi grinned at me, then pulled her keys from her pocket. "Just so long as you allow me to clean the windows," she said.

Her idea of *scraping* the windows was to try rubbing them with a cloth she had in the back. I even had to stop her from using a screwdriver on them. "We can wait while the defrost does its job," I said. "Even though I can't believe you don't own a window scraper."

"I just moved here!"

With her fully-loaded vehicle, complete with front and back wipers and defrost, it still took several minutes for the car to warm up enough to start to melt the snow and ice off the windows. I had to keep telling everyone that the heat wouldn't do any good when I first started it up, but they still had to try it for themselves, not believing the *andro-dyke.*

The roads were treacherous, with bits of ice hidden beneath the snow, and on more than one occasion I was thankful for the vehicle's four-wheel drive. I had to focus all my concentration on the road, and finally asked for music, because it was as if everyone else believed they couldn't even speak for fear of distracting me from the drive.

I never got above twenty miles per hour the entire way, and only saw a few other cars on the road. At least Cyndi gave good directions, letting me know ahead of time when I was to turn off of 29, and then onto another side street.

When we finally pulled into her reserved space, I gave a sigh of relief and noticed just how tense my muscles had become. I'm always far more careful driving when there are other people in the vehicle.

The townhouse was warm and homey when we entered. Cyndi had left a few lights burning, because she obviously knew she'd come home late.

"I've got a treat for you all," Cyndi said, quickly taking off her shoes and coat and heading toward the far wall. I realized what she meant when she lit the fire, then turned on the lights on the eight-foot Christmas tree that stood in one corner.

It had been a long time since I had been near a real fire, or real Christmas tree. I could smell the pine penetrating the entire space.

"Make yourselves comfortable," she instructed, heading toward another wall. "What can I get y'all to drink? I have beer, wine, port, soda . . . ?" She turned on her stereo system and immediately the sounds of The Carpenters Christmas album filled the room.

I kicked off my pumps and rubbed my feet against each other to kick off the snow. "A nice cold beer sounds wonderful."

Within a few minutes we were all tucked under afghans in the living room, around the fire, with drinks in our hands, in a neat conversational circle that was imposed upon us by the arrangement of furniture. I rested my head against the back of the couch I sat on, enjoying the release of tension from the drive.

"Thank you so much for driving," Cyndi whispered in my ear, placing an arm along the back of the couch. "Once I saw how bad a time you had driving through it, I was glad it was you and not me."

Her nearness was a comfort to me. I wanted to curl up into her, but withheld myself. I reminded myself that it had just been too long since I'd had any intimate contact with another woman.

I looked over at the love seat where Katie and Sandra were curled up together, necking, and I remembered the promises Sandra had made to Katie on the Metro. I wondered where Sandra's hands were wandering underneath the afghan that covered them.

Cyndi stood up, facing me, and removed her blazer, then her tie. She undid the top two buttons of her shirt so I could see the white T-shirt beneath peeking out, and then she dropped her suspenders down. I expected her to unzip and pull forth something, but instead she said, "That feels much better. I love ties, but there is a joy to taking it off at the end of the day." She looked down at me, then continued, "Will you excuse me for just a minute?"

I smiled, nodded, and took a deep sip off my beer. Someone else must've been drinking from it, although I had held it the entire time, because it was suddenly empty. I got up and went in the direction of the kitchen for another.

Cyndi was apparently an immaculate housekeeper, because the kitchen was as tidy as could be, and the refrigerator was better stocked than mine.

When I returned, Katie was sipping from her glass of port, sitting forward on the love seat and Sandra was leaning back right next to her, sipping from her beer. Both were looking at me.

"Did I do something?"

"Not at all," Katie said, "we just didn't want to be poor hostesses after you helped us out so much." She walked over to me and wrapped her arm around mine, turning me away from Sandra. "Please tell me you don't have some hot butch waiting at home for you."

"No, I don't go in for that sort of thing."

"Really?" she asked, looking me up and down.

"I have to dress this way for work."

"There are other ways to dress like that without looking like that."

I pulled away from her. "It's easy for me, okay?"

"Sorry. Do you have a girlfriend waiting for you at home, then? I mean, from what Cyn's said, she has plenty of turkey with all the trimmings . . . and it'd be the least we owe you." She leaned in close to me. "I wouldn't've wanted either of those two, or me, behind the wheel tonight, if you know what I mean."

"Uh oh, are we in trouble again?" Cyndi asked, coming downstairs. She looked the same as before.

"What do you mean by that?" I asked.

"Oh, nothing," she said, with a wink to Sandra. A barely perceptible wink, but one nonetheless.

"I've figured this out," Cyndi continued, leaning against the couch. "You two can have my bed," she said, indicating Sandra and Katie, "Kirsten can have the futon and I'll sleep on the couch."

"I don't want to put you out of your bed—or futon."

"Hon . . . Kirsten, I'd rather sleep down here than where I would've, in the car. It's fine. And it's actually quite comfortable. I sometimes sleep on it just for the hell of it." I felt like a . . . fourth wheel?

Sandra walked over to Katie, who laid back against the wall in front of me. She ran her hand through Katie's long hair, and then pressed against her, their bodies tight as two pennies in a jar. Just before their lips met, she turned to look at me, leaving Katie leaning toward air. "So, did we turn you on in the train?"

I pushed myself back against the wall, not wanting to be a part of their kinky fantasies.

Cyndi walked around the furniture to come up in front of me. "Don't worry about them, they're newlyweds."

Out of the corner of my eye, I saw Katie's hand creeping down to cup where Sandra had the dildo in her pants.

"You want it baby? You want it?" Sandra asked, putting her hand over Katie's. She guided Katie's hand up and down the length of it. "Then ask for it. Tell me you want it."

I was strangely mesmerized by the show they were putting on. I shifted my legs apart just a bit, wanting to rip off my confining pantyhose.

Katie got down on her knees and unzipped Sandra's jeans, then slid down her boxer shorts and pulled out a long, thick, dark-green dildo. Sandra pushed her crotch forward, putting the dildo into her lover's face.

Katie began licking the dildo, running her tongue up and down its shaft, then slowing pulling it into her mouth while they both groaned in pleasure.

"Are you . . . are you two sure you want to do this here?" Cyndi squeaked, staring. "There's a bed upstairs for you. An entire bedroom."

There was a tingling between my legs, radiating up and down. It was all I could do to keep from moaning out loud. I pulled away from the wall, and was aware of Cyndi watching from behind me.

Sandra stopped with her hand on the back of Katie's head, holding Katie in place with her dildo deep in her throat. "She has a fantasy about being watched, in fact she has several fantasies about public sex, as well as being watched and joined." She pulled out of Katie's mouth, then reached down to help Katie stand up. Katie didn't look at us, instead she continued fondling the dildo, running her hands lovingly up and down its hardness. "If you don't want to watch me fuck her, you should go upstairs."

I wondered what Katie was wearing underneath the skirt, and then I wondered how wet she was. I knew I was wet.

I watched as Sandra went down on one knee so she could reach up Katie's skirt and pull off her panties. Katie stepped out as if she was a lady, as if she had not just been on her knees giving Sandra a blow job, and wasn't about to get fucked in front of others.

Sandra pulled Katie's mouth to herself, kissing her deeply, then she started kissing her neck and ear while she started fondling her breasts. She untucked Katie's blouse.

I could tell Cyndi was right behind me. I could feel her hot breath against my ear. I wondered what her hands would feel like on my body, on my breasts, against my bare skin.

I knew I should leave, I should modestly go upstairs (and most probably masturbate), but I was riveted. I wanted to see what Katie looked like naked, I wanted to watch her get fucked—and, after all, I had already seen and heard quite a bit from them, and they had said they wanted us to watch.

Sandra unbuttoned Katie's blouse, then dropped it to the ground. She reached up behind her and, with a deft snap of her fingers, undid her bra, dropping that to the ground as well, and revealing Katie's lusciously full breasts.

At first Katie tried to almost shyly cover them, but Sandra said, "Oh, baby, but this is what you want, isn't it?" She reached up to palm those incredible, white breasts, and then she took each of the already hardened nipples between her thumbs and forefingers and, lightly at first, and then harder, began to squeeze them.

"Oh, God," Cyndi groaned from behind me, and then I felt her press against my back and rest her hands on my hips. I felt something hard back there, and realized that when Cyndi had gone upstairs, she had put on a harness and dildo, probably like what Sandra was wearing.

I wondered what it looked like.

Sandra was again kissing Katie's neck and ears, still fondling her breasts. Katie moaned her appreciation, and directed Sandra's head down to her breasts, obviously wanting to feel her mouth and teeth on her breasts and nipples.

Sandra was only too willing to oblige.

Cyndi's hands began assessing the shape and feel of my hips, going up and down, then she reached up to cup my breasts, giving them a hesitant squeeze.

I couldn't help myself, I moaned out loud.

Sandra unzipped Katie's skirt, and it dropped to the floor at their feet. Katie was left wearing only her garter belt, stockings and heels. She pressed up against Sandra's dildo, rubbing her body against Sandra's.

"Oh, baby, I need you so bad right now."

Cyndi began gently massaging my collarbone around the top

of my blouse, then I felt one hand begin to unbutton my blouse. Her lips and tongue were warm on my ear, gently massaging it. I wondered how they would feel on my body, I wondered what her dildo would feel like *in* my body.

I barely knew any of these women, so I shouldn't let Cyndi do this. But I barely knew the two different women I'd slept with at Michigan.

I barely knew these women, and who was to say that I'd ever see any of them again, so why should I care?

I took one of Cyndi's hands and placed it in my bra on my breast.

Sandra put her hands under Katie's hips and lifted her up onto the dining room table, where they continued kissing, where she continued examining Katie's body with her hands.

Cyndi unzipped my skirt and let it drop to the floor as well. A part of me was thankful I was still wearing my undergarments, but another part of me wanted to be naked. A part of me wanted her to take me upstairs, while a part wanted her to take me right there.

Katie's legs were wound around Sandra's hips, and then Sandra pulled away slightly, exposing Katie's hot wetness to my greedy eyes. Sandra reached down to finger her girlfriend, to slide her fingers up and down her lips and circle her vagina. Then she slipped a finger into her.

I groaned with Katie.

"You like what you're watching?" Cyndi said her first words to me for a while. "You want me to do that to you?" She undid my bra and let it drop to the floor. When I tried to cover my breasts, she eased my arms down to my sides. "It's not like they're watching you."

She hooked her thumbs into my underwear and pantyhose, then pulled them down and off my feet, which I lifted for her, one by one.

I was now completely naked in a room with three other

people, and I couldn't decide if I wanted to hide my bareness, or enjoy it right where I was.

Sandra reached down between her legs and guided the long, thick shaft right up into Katie. She slowly guided it up into her girlfriend, then looked at me, "You like that?"

I could feel the desire welling up in my belly, it was like a hollowness there, whereas between my legs it was an urgent need. I only felt in from the inside out in my belly when I was really turned on, when I was turned on from my deepest parts.

Sandra already had her eyes on me, and then Katie turned her eyes, swollen with desire, upon me as well. Cyndi ran her hands up from my thighs, over my hips, to cup my breasts. She squeezed my nipples between her thumbs and forefingers, and then she squeezed harder and harder.

I had seen nipple clamps at the women's bookstore, and, for the first time ever, I thought about just how good they would feel, how they would fulfill my need to have my nipples clamped hard.

I arched my groin under the gaze of the women. I couldn't believe I was being so exhibitionistic, and that I was enjoying it so much. I knew I was wetter than I had ever been before.

While they watched us, Sandra slowly pulled out of Katie, regaining her girlfriend's attention, then she started fucking her—pushing it back in, then pulling out and thrusting back into her . . .

I wanted to get fucked like that, ridden like that, I wanted to take it like that and be taken like that.

Cyndi slid her fingers into my wetness, focusing my attention back on myself. Her fingers felt so good, but I wanted more, a lot more. I put my hand on hers and tried to guide her inside of me.

"In a hurry, huh? What, aren't you enjoying the show?"

"Cyndi, please," I finally moaned.

The smell of pussy surrounded me, and I wasn't sure if it was Katie or me or both of us.

I was arching against her hand, helping it to slide up and down my swollen lips. The muscles in my thighs were tight as I rocked back and forth. Under my guidance, between my own legs, Cyndi finally let a finger slip inside me, starting to explore within me.

It still wasn't enough. She slipped another inside of me, then a third.

"God, you are so fucking hot," Cyndi moaned.

"Sandy, Sandy, SANDY!" Katie screamed, arching and bucking as Sandra fucked her hard. She suddenly wound her legs tight around Sandra and held on, holding her inside her as she all but collapsed with her arms around her lover.

"You want me to do that to you, huh honey?" Cyndi whispered into my ear. One hand was between my legs, the other still squeezing a nipple, hard.

"Y . . . yes . . ." I moaned, not wanting to say it, just wanting her to do it.

"Then make me want to," she said, releasing me and leaning against the back of the couch. She opened her zipper, reached inside her black silk boxers and pulled out a large blue dildo. Like Sandra's, it was thick and long, tapering off toward the top. It had little black markings on it, as if some sort of art nouveau.

She held it like a real dick, and I knew what I was supposed to do.

I wanted it inside of me so badly I'd be willing to do almost anything. I dropped to my knees and hesitantly ran a tongue along the length of it, like I had seen Katie do just a bit earlier.

"You've never done this before, have you?" Cyndi asked, slowly caressing my hair.

I shook my head no. I had just seen Katie do it, but it seemed wrong, and I was confused. I looked up at her and into her understanding, caring, deep brown eyes. She ran her soft hand across my hair, gently brushing it back.

I leaned back toward the dildo, running my tongue along its

length. She wasn't forcing me to, but I wanted her to do something for me . . . I glanced up at Katie and Sandra, who were both watching me. Sandra was casually running her hands over Katie, and Katie, in turn, was running her hand over Sandra's come-soaked dildo.

Katie stood up and came over to me. I felt her hand on my back, and her bare breast against my arm. The nipple was hard. Her hand slipped into my hair.

"Enjoy it," she whispered to me, "imagine it inside of you, think about how you want it there and enjoy it, and Cyndi, for the pleasure they will give you." As if to emphasize her point, she ran her tongue up the side of it.

Katie guided my head up to the tip of the dildo, then guided it into my mouth.

I imagined this was a bit like S/M was—being forced into service for the pleasure of another—except I wasn't being forced, I was being asked.

And then I heard Cyndi groan as I took more of it into my mouth. She began to push it in deeper, and it was an incredible feeling, knowing that I could cause such pleasure just with my mouth. I never would've believed such an inanimate object could pass along such sensations as Cyndi was obviously experiencing. Her hand tightened in my hair, urging me on.

I had been holding the base of the dildo in both my hands, but now Sandra guided my left hand from it and down to her own dildo. I could feel Katie's slickness still on it, still able to lubricate my hand's movements along it, up and down its thickness.

"Oh, yeah, baby," Sandra whispered into my ear. She had one hand on my back, and with the other she began playing with one of my tits while her mouth and tongue were occupied with my shoulder and neck.

Meanwhile, Katie had given the dildo over to my loving attentions and was now busying herself by almost mirroring her girlfriend's actions, except instead of being on a breast, one of her hands was running up and down my thigh, growing ever closer to my wetness.

Suddenly, Cyndi's hand tightened in my hair, pulling my head backward, away from her dildo, off of her. "You want it, don't you? And you're ready to give it to me, aren't you?"

"You want her to fuck you?" Sandra said in my ear, placing one hand on my breastbone to push me away from Cyndi, while her arm on my back helped guide me backward.

Only when I was lying on my back with my legs open did I realize how exposed and open I was. The lights were on and three people could see all my intimate parts.

Cyndi laid on top of me and slowly guided herself into me.

"Oh . . . God!" I screamed. I had never had something so big inside of me before, but I wanted it, I wanted to get . . . fucked. Hard.

"That's it, baby, that's it," Katie cooed into my ear.

Cyndi began slowly fucking me, in and out, slower than I wanted or needed, but at least she was inside of me.

"Yes, please, faster," I begged, arching up against her.

Cyndi raised herself up on her strong arms, looking down at me while Katie and Sandra availed themselves of the opportunity to nibble and tease my breasts.

Sandra reached down between my legs to finger me while Cyndi fucked me. "I think she wants more," she said, her fingers sliding along my wet clit while Cyndi thrust into me, then pulled out.

"Have you ever taken a whole fist?" Katie whispered into my ear.

"That's an idea," I heard Sandra say. I closed my eyes and lost track of whom was doing what to me, I was just getting fucked harder than I ever had.

Cyndi thrust into me, and I felt her come to her knees between my legs, forcing my legs ever farther open.

"Sit up," Sandra commanded, helping me do so, even though doing so pulled me from Cyndi's hard cock.

I had three sets of hands on me, and had lost watch over whom was doing what, who was touching me where with hands or mouths. I opened up my eyes, and saw Cyndi pouring lube all over her right hand.

"I . . . I'm not sure if I can . . ." I said, inching back against the wall.

Cyndi entered me, a finger at a time, one, two, three, four . . .

"You're gonna enjoy this, honey," Katie whispered, "just relax and open up. You're so wet she doesn't even need any lube, you want this . . ."

She kept talking, urging me on, preparing me, and I watched while she fingered my cunt, toying with me, while Cyndi shoved . . .

. . . her entire fist . . .

. . . up into me . . .

"Oh God!" I screamed. I was out of breath, my legs were as open as they could be and I felt her presence throughout my entire body, from my shaking limbs to my stomach to my arching pelvis. I could feel her moving around inside of me, and, looking down, I could see her wrist penetrating from my cunt. She moved around inside of me and I could feel every movement reverberate inside of me.

I could feel her and see her.

Then she began to . . . fuck me . . . with her fist—pulling it out and thrusting it in and the sensation was overwhelming and she was taking me with my legs open and two other women with their hands and mouths and tongues on me and . . .

"Oh my fucking God!" I screamed, feeling myself tense around her fist, holding it tight and tighter within me.

"Drink this." I felt Cyndi holding me in her arms, and then putting a sippy bottle of water to my lips. I gratefully latched onto the nipple, pulling the refreshing liquid deep into my parched mouth and throat.

I didn't know who was touching me, but pleasant sensations were running throughout my body. I was curled on my side, and I moved to better open my legs again, wanting the sensations to continue.

I looked away from Cyndi to see Sandra between my legs, slowly blowing on my wetness.

"Hmmmm!" I moaned when her tongue touched my clit, when it began to work me over.

"Not so easily this time, don't make her come so quickly," Katie softly commanded.

In my foggy mind I briefly wondered how they could fuck me any better, how they could do it more intensely, and then I saw that both Cyndi and Sandra were inside of me, I saw both their fingers plunging into me.

"Oh God, oh God, OH GOD!" I screamed, bucking them around. I twisted till I was on my back and curling into Katie, who held me close.

"This is a fantasy come true," Cyndi said, looking at me. I suddenly realized that I had curled up into Katie's lap, her still hot cunt inches from my face.

I pushed myself up and looked at her. I couldn't believe what I was about to do. I eased her legs out from the Indian-style position they were in until they were fully extended along either side of me. And then I dipped my tongue into her.

Her scent surrounded me and her taste filled me. I lay out in front of her, and she slowly went to her back from me. Cyndi moved upward to caress her breasts, to squeeze and nibble on the hardened buds while I ate her out.

Then I felt my own legs being spread open again. Sandra curled her hand up toward my pussy from under me, fingering me again, and then I felt a drop of what could only be cold lube on my butt. I shuddered to think what that meant, yet I didn't want to stop what I was doing, didn't want to stop running my tongue up and down Katie's exposed lips, dipping into her wet hole, tasting her wetness, and running my tongue over her hardened clit. Back and forth and she squirmed under my tongue.

Sandra's thumb entering me from behind caused me to arch into the ground, almost away from it. She began moving it around inside of me, causing me to grind against the floor, then her finger entered my cunt, and I was penetrated in both places.

I spread my legs farther, all the while beating my tongue harder and harder, causing Katie to squirm ever more frantically, until she began to arch under my tongue, pushing herself harder into my mouth, clutching my hair to her with her hand, begging me for release . . .

Katie came under my tongue, her sweet juices all over my face. And I wanted more, yet again.

When Sandra withdrew from me, I moaned my frustration, and I saw Cyndi gently caress Katie's hair, grab a pillow from the couch for her head, and then stand while Sandra helped me get up onto shaky legs.

I felt her hardness first against my back, and then Cyndi approached me with her dildo still bobbing up and down from the front of her pants.

I didn't know if I could take it, but I wanted to try. I helped guide Cyndi up into my greedy cunt, even while I knew Sandra was lubing herself up behind me. The cold shock of the lube against my behind almost pulled me out of it, but the ache of my want and need overcame that, and I felt her slowly shove that thick cock up into my asshole.

I was a sandwich, with two women taking me at the same time.

They ground hard against me, both fucking me at the same

time, invading me totally, and I would grind front and then back, urging them both on, wanting them both, and we all found our rhythm, with them only occasionally invading me at the same time, and what glorious times they were, I pushed my legs farther open, almost losing my footing, but wanting them both, wanting it all, wanting both holes filled and fucked and taken and . . .

That night we slept on Cyndi's king-size bed with its over-sized comforter, butch-femme-butch-femme.

I don't know about lesbians, but the butches and femmes of this world have one hell of a recruitment plan.

Aural Pleasures
Stacia Seaman

Before we get started, let me make one thing clear—this is all Jill's fault. If she'd just stayed out of my private life like I asked her to, none of this would have ever happened. But no, she had to pry into the details of my (mostly theoretical) sex life, and she had to send me the CD, and she had to tell me about the author reading. Which, I might add, turned into the sexiest, most exciting, most embarrassing moment of my life.

And now I'm sure you want details as well. No doubt you've already heard rumors, and you're not sure if they're true so you've decided to come to the source. Fine. I can understand that. Let me get you a drink, and I'll tell you the story.

Jill and I were out having dinner one night. Pint night—cheap beer and half-price appetizers. We had a couple of beers, she told me about her latest hookups, and then inevitably the conversation turned to me.

"So, you getting any?"

Yes, she actually asked me that. Jill is nothing if not direct.

I just looked at her.

"Didn't think so," she said. "So I got you this."

She handed me a CD. On the cover was a photograph of a naked breast. Just a hint of a soft filter blurred the outline, and a warm color wash brought a golden luster to the skin. The result was absolutely gorgeous, and I found myself tracing a finger over the nipple in an unconscious caress.

"Stop analyzing the damn picture," Jill said, impatiently taking the case from me and turning it over. "Here."

There was another, smaller photograph on the back—a portrait of a woman with lustrous dark curls and sparkling brown eyes, dressed in a low-cut, deep burgundy sweater. "*Girls' Night In*," I read. "Aliza Paran reads a collection of her most popular work."

"Well?" Jill was almost bouncing in her seat.

"Well what?" I said. I mean, yeah, the cover was fabulous, but . . .

"You have no idea who she is, do you," Jill said. "Should have seen that coming."

I frowned.

"Never mind." Almost as an afterthought, she added, "Just be sure to listen to it at home the first time, not the office. Or the car."

That got me curious. Jill generally doesn't advise—or exercise—restraint (please note the singular here; I'm sure you know her reputation with regard to the other). I could understand not listening to this CD at work, but what could possibly be on it that I shouldn't listen in the car?

Later that night, I found out.

The sun had already set by the time I got home, but the temperature hadn't dropped any. There was nothing worth watching on TV, so I decided to take a nice long bath and cool myself off.

Schubert's Unfinished Symphony played softly in the bathroom. The tub was full, the water scented with eucalyptus, and I was just about to get in, Neil Gaiman novel in hand, when I remembered the CD from Jill.

I had no idea what was on it. In hindsight, it should have been obvious—Jill's not exactly a deep thinker, and there was, after all, a naked (perfect) breast on the cover—but I wasn't expecting what I heard when I settled into the tub and pressed Play on the remote.

The voice alone was incredible. Low pitched and steady, with no obvious regional accent, the S's sometimes almost shading into Sh's. Each word was clearly enunciated, although there was clearly no special effort involved in it. Aliza Paran had a beautiful, clear speaking voice, almost soothing. In other circumstances, I could have easily dropped off to sleep under its influence.

In other circumstances.

The first sentence was innocuous, just a description of a woman. By the end of the first minute, though, the words had gone from descriptive to evocative, and from there to erotic.

As I listened to that first story, my body flushed, a delicate pink tingle that I told myself was caused by the heat of the bathwater and not the words. My nipples were hard where they peaked out of the water, but that was obviously because of the breeze from the air-conditioning, not the voice coming from the speakers. Yeah, right. I tried to relax as I listened to the voice, tried to ignore the rising heat within my body.

The second story began. It was more descriptive than the first, and as I massaged fragrant bath gel into my skin in an attempt to distract myself from the images my mind was forming, I found myself acting out what I was hearing. I trailed my fingers up my arms, then my legs. When I cupped my breasts, I suddenly became aware of what I was doing and stopped, shocked and more than a little embarrassed at how aroused I'd become. Deciding to ignore it, I closed my eyes and listened as the voice told me what she planned to do to me: gentle caresses, teasing bites, firm strokes.

I could feel the touches, could hear the water ripple as she made love to me. My hips moved in time with her rhythm, and my legs opened as the heaviness between them increased. Finally, I could take no more. I teased my nipples with one hand, rolling and pinching them between my fingers, and with the other hand I massaged my clit. In no time at all I came, a long series of convulsive waves that left me gasping and breathless.

I turned off the CD player and lay there in the cool water, not quite sure what had just happened. I'd read erotica before, but it had never had that effect on me. It was just words on a page. But this—this was something completely different, although I wasn't sure how or why, or if it was a one-time thing, the result of months of celibacy and a boring fantasy life.

I didn't listen to the CD the next day, or the next. I avoided Jill for a week, certain she'd take one look at me and know what had happened (which, now that I think about it, was probably her plan all along).

Then I had a really bad day. The kind where you fill your car in the morning and your hands and clothing reek of gasoline all day, so you have a headache that you can't shake, so you go to take some Advil only there isn't any because your coworker had the world's worst cramps last week and took your last four caplets and you forgot to bring more in.

I came home, stripped off my clothes, filled the tub, climbed in, and hit Play. That voice filled me with warmth. Once again I imagined her touching me, teasing me. This time I didn't hold back.

I caressed my own breasts, not bothering to be gentle. My body was too ready. Even beneath the water I could feel the heavy silk of my arousal when I slid two fingers inside myself. My thighs were spread wide, my head lolling against the bath pillow at the end of the tub.

Moving my fingers in and out, the other hand working a counterpoint on my clit, I lost track of what the voice was saying. Like my hands on my body and the water against my skin, it was another caress, rising and falling, increasing in intensity and passion, building to a crescendo that my body echoed. My clit throbbed, once, twice, and with a rush of wetness I came, hard, even harder than I had the first time with her. Then I lay still again in the water, enjoying the final spasms that gripped my fingers as the voice ended its tale.

After that, listening to the CD became almost a ritual. I was usually in the bath, although sometimes I was in my bedroom, lying naked atop the quilt. As I listened to Aliza Paran's voice, I'd touch myself slowly and gently, then fast and hard, sometimes reflecting the actions she spoke of, sometimes not. I'd work myself up to incredible climaxes, her voice soothing as I returned to myself.

One day it occurred to me that perhaps the author had recorded more of her stories. The next time I met Jill for drinks, I asked her. It's not that I was tired of the CD I already had—far from it—but there was a part of me that wanted more.

"So you really like it, then," Jill said with a saucy grin. "I thought you might."

I tried desperately not to blush.

"I mean, you're always talking about 'ooh, isn't her voice amazing' and 'who is that singer, that's the sexiest voice I think I've ever heard'," she continued, "so when I saw that CD, I knew it was perfect for you. High-quality audio porn."

My face was on fire. I ducked my head, hoping nobody had heard her, telling myself the snicker behind me was completely unrelated to our conversation.

"But wait till you hear this," Jill said. "Aliza Paran will be in town next week. She's doing a reading and book signing at Turn The Page." She waggled her eyebrows. "You can listen *and* watch. Maybe even tape it and listen to it later."

"I don't think so," I said. "I'm not really into that. I mean, I've never even read any of her books and—"

"Tell me you don't know all of those stories by heart," Jill said.

"I don't." And I didn't. As many times as I'd listened to them, I hadn't focused on the words as much as the voice, the imagery, the responses of my body. "I'm serious," I said as Jill shook her head at me.

"Next week," she said. "Turn The Page. You should go."

I thought about it every day. Should I go or shouldn't I? I'd only seen the one picture of the author, the one on the back cover of the CD. What was she going to read? For how long? How many women would be there? The CD was a private ritual, my private ritual. I wasn't sure I wanted to share that experience in such a public way. Little did I know . . .

The day of the book signing arrived. I'd gone back and forth all day, and ultimately decided that I would go. I had nothing better going on, and what if there was a new CD for sale? I walked into the bookstore late, just as the author was thanking the bookstore owner for her kind introduction. I sat in the last row of folding chairs, beside an empty chair, wanting to preserve as much as possible the illusion of being alone as I listened to the reading.

Aliza Paran began to read the first selection, an excerpt from her latest novel. Her voice was exactly as on the CD: smooth, clear and steady. Though low in pitch, it carried well and somehow managed to convey a sense of intimacy. If I closed my eyes, I could imagine she was speaking just to me, alone in my living room.

The excerpt was a romantic scene, full of emotion but not at all erotic, so I was unprepared for my body's reaction to it. Zero to sixty in two pages. I was completely turned on—which made no sense given what she was saying.

I tuned out her words, focusing instead on her voice. Once I got used to hearing her speak, I could get my body under control, right?

Wrong. As her voice rose and fell, the tone gentle and loving, my body's reaction grew stronger. My nipples ached to be touched, and I squeezed my thighs together in an attempt to stave off the growing pressure between them. I made it through the first excerpt and halfway through the second without too much escalation—until a teasing note crept into her voice, resulting in a flood of arousal that dampened my bikini panties.

Obviously that wasn't working, so I switched tactics: I focused on her words.

Mistake number two. She was reading an erotic short story that was not on the CD. I hung on every word as it created vivid images in my mind: a lush, curvy body and its responses to my touch. The author didn't just read the words, she brought them to life. Every gasp was a gasp, every moan a moan, and I was simultaneously in heaven and in hell.

She finished the story, much to my relief, and took a sip of water while she waited for the applause to subside. Then she introduced the next selection. It was my favorite story on the CD, the one where her voice most closely matched her writing style. It was slow and erotic, fevered and languid at the same time.

I closed my eyes and listened as she read. This time there was no visual; instead, I could almost feel hands moving on my body, as I had so many times while listening to this story. A thumb and forefinger pinched my nipples into peaks, then tugged at them, sending bolts of fire to my clit until my hips rolled with the sensation. I was incredibly wet, and my head turned to one side to allow her access to my neck. Her breath was hot on my skin as she kissed me, nipped me, made her way to my mouth, which she took in a hungry kiss, her tongue dancing with mine, her fingers tangling in my hair.

She moved down my body, stopping at my breasts to suck

them, spreading my legs and positioning herself between them. I sighed at the first touch of her mouth on my inner thigh. She burned a trail of fire up one side, then down the other, before I felt the flicker of her tongue on my clit. My hips bucked and she pushed me down with one hand. With the other, she parted and entered me in one smooth thrust.

I bit my lip to keep from moaning as she moved in and out, speeding up the strokes of her tongue to match the rhythm of her hand. The pressure built steadily within me. Her fingers moved inside me, her mouth was on me, and her voice was in my ears, urging me toward climax. I wanted to come for her, was desperate to come for her, and finally I did, shattering, an explosion of glory that ended in absolute silence.

Confused, I opened my eyes and Aliza Paran was looking straight at me, not quite smiling, and the women around me reacted enthusiastically, clapping and catcalling and shouting for more. A couple of people in the row in front of me turned around and looked at me quizzically. I sank into my seat, not sure whether to be embarrassed, not sure of what was real.

My breath returned to normal right around the time the applause finally died down. I stayed put for a few moments, until I was sure my legs would support me. Then I skirted my way around the crowd of women to the front of the bookstore, to a table that had stacks of books written by Aliza Paran. I picked one up and read the back cover. Much as I had enjoyed the CD, I'd never even considered buying the books. It wasn't that I didn't like her writing—I did—but reading her words on paper just wouldn't be the same as hearing her say them. I was here, though, and it was a book signing, and Jill's birthday was only a month away, so . . . I looked at a couple more novels before deciding on a collection of short stories, many of which were on the CD.

The line was shorter now, but I was going to be waiting a while, so I opened the book and started to read. Big, big mistake.

As I looked at the words, I could hear her voice reading them to me. I could feel her breath warm against my neck. My nipples tightened. I tried to keep reading, but my body's reaction was too strong. I was already wet and throbbing, and every word, every image, was making my body more insistent.

The line moved at a steady pace, thank God. After a few minutes, there was only one woman ahead of me. She bounced a little, hugging her book to her chest. "Are you as excited as I am?"

Oh, you have no idea. I nodded. "Sure am." I watched as she bounced her way to the table to get her books signed.

Then it was my turn. I stepped forward nervously and placed my book on the table.

Aliza Paran looked up at me with a generic public-appearance smile that turned genuine when she recognized me. "And to whom shall I sign this one?"

That voice. Speaking to me. I melted. "Fiona." So much for Jill's birthday present. Then I blurted out, "You should sell your other books on CD."

That earned me a grin. "Well, Fiona, I'm glad you enjoyed the reading," Aliza Paran said. She signed first the book's title page and then a bookmark, which she tucked just inside the back cover, and handed me the book with a twinkle in her eye. "See you at the next one."

"Right," I said. "Thanks." I walked away from the table and ducked behind a bookshelf to see what she'd written in the book. There it was: *To Fiona: you made this reading a pleasure. For both of us.*

My humiliation was complete.

So that's it. That's my story. Much as I'd love to stay and have another beer, I have to go. Taxes, you know. I always wait until the last minute. Oh, and if you see Jill, be sure to tell her I said thanks. Seems I made a bit of an impression. The bookmark in the back of the book? I'm going up to Seattle next week to visit Aliza—for a Girls' Night In.

About the Authors

Marie Alexander lives in Northern New Jersey with her wife Toni, their son and their four cats. She runs a local toy shop when she's not busy writing. Her short story "Best Friends" can be found in Bella After Dark's *Wild Nights Anthology*. She is currently at work on her second novel.

M.C. Ammerman was born and raised on the East Coast and now lives in Los Angeles, where she works, hikes and grumbles about not having enough time to write. Her last short story, "Rose-Colored Glasses," appeared in the Bella anthology *The Perfect Valentine*. She's still grinning about that.

Victoria A. Brownworth is the award-winning editor of numerous books, most recently *The Golden Age of Lesbian Erotica: 1920–1940* and *Bed: New Lesbian Erotica*. She teaches writing and film at the University of the Arts in Philadelphia.

Rachel Kramer Bussel (www.rachelkramerbussel.com) writes the Lusty Lady sex column for *The Village Voice*, is senior editor at *Penthouse Variations*, and hosts *In The Flesh Erotic Reading Series*. She's edited or co-edited thirteen erotic anthologies, including *He's on Top and She's on Top, Caught Looking: Erotic Tales of Voyeurs and Exhibitionists, First-Timers: True Stories of Lesbian Awakening, Glamour Girl: Femme/Femme Erotica*, Lammy finalist *Up All Night: Adventures in Lesbian Sex, Sexiest Soles, Ultimate Undies* and *Naughty Spanking Stories from A to Z 1* and *2*. Her work has been published in B*ookslut, Bust, Cleansheets, Cosmo UK, Curve, Diva, Girlfriends, Gothamist, Mediabistro*, the *New York Post, On Our Backs*, the *San Francisco Chronicle, Time Out New York, Zink* and others, as well as in over 90 anthologies, including *Best American Erotica 2004* and *2006*. Her first novel, *Everything But . . .* , will be published by Bantam in 2008.

Crin Claxton writes novels, short stories and poetry. Her first novel *Scarlet Thirst* was published by Red Hot Diva Books. She has had short stories published in *Girls Next Door* (Women's Press), *Va Va Voom* (Red Hot Diva), *Lessons in Love* (Bold Strokes Books), *Extreme Passions* (Bold Strokes Books), *Road Games* (Bold Strokes Books), *Diva Magazine, Carve* webzine and *Suspect Thoughts* webzine. Her poetry has appeared in *Naming the Waves, La Pluma* and *A Class of Their Own*. Crin is working on her second novel. More info on www.crinclaxton.com

Laurie Cox is an emerging lesbian freelance writer. She is currently editing an anthology of stories by ex-ex gays and writing a humorous memoir about growing up gay and Baptist. Laurie is also a member of the Bent Writing Institute, a queer writing group in Seattle, Washington.

C.L. Crews is a paralegal in a Denver law firm, mom to the smartest four-year old girl in the world and partner of fifteen years to a most supportive, generous and loving woman. They flee the suburbs with their two dogs to hike, bike, snowshoe and snowboard the Rocky Mountains as often as possible.

Jen Cross's writing can be found (some under the name Jen Collins) in such anthologies as *Best Fetish Erotica, Back to Basics, Glamour Girls, Nobody Passes* and the forthcoming *Best Women's Erotica 2007*. She is currently working on two book-length collections. For more information about Jen and her work, visit www.writingourselveswhole.org.

Having escaped the chaos and concrete of London, **Jane Fletcher** lives in southwest England. Her novels have won a GCLS award and been short-listed for the Gaylactic Spectrum and Lambda awards. She is author of two fantasy/romance series—the Lyremouth Chronicles and The Celaeno Series.

Scarlett French is a short story writer and a poet. She lives in London's East End with her partner and a pugnacious marmalade cat. Her erotic fiction has appeared in *Best Lesbian Erotica 05, Va Va Voom, First Timers: True Stories of Lesbian Awakening, Tales of Travelrotica for Lesbians* and *Best Women's Erotica 07*. "In the Garden of Eden" is dedicated to Sh! Women's Erotic Emporium for what it stands for and all the joy that it brings.

Bryn Haniver, a nature lover and sexy B-movie aficionado, writes fiction from islands and peninsulas whenever possible. Anthology credits include the upcoming *B is for Bondage and D is for Dress Up* as well as *Garden of the Perverse, Rode Hard Put Away Wet, Taboo, Down & Dirty 2* and *A Taste of Midnight* as well as a couple noteworthy shorts on Desdmona.com.

Nairne Holtz is a Montreal-based fiction writer whose first novel, *The Skin Beneath*, will be published by Insomniac Press in

2007. Her short fiction has appeared in literary journals such as *Harrington Lesbian Fiction Quarterly, Blithe House Quarterly, Velvet Mafia, Other Voices* and *Matrix* as well as in various anthologies. She has also created an annotated bibliography of Canadian lesbian-themed literature in which she has reviewed close to one hundred books (see www.canadianlesbianliterature.ca).

Karin Kallmaker is best known for more than twenty lesbian romance novels, from *In Every Port* to *Finders Keepers*. She has also earned a naughty reputation with novellas, novels and erotic short stories, including *18th & Castro*. In addition, she has a half-dozen science fiction, fantasy and supernatural lesbian novels (e.g. *Seeds of Fire, Christabel*) under the pen name Laura Adams. She likes her chocolate real, her Internet fast and her iPod very loud. You can find out more about her work at www.kallmaker.com.

Geneva King (www.genevaking.com) has stories appearing in several anthologies including: *Ultimate Lesbian Erotica 2006, Best Women's Erotica 2006, Ultimate Undies, Caramel Flava* and *Travelrotica for Lesbians*. She intends to publish a book, if her professors ever give her enough time to do so.

Maggie Kinsella is an ex-nurse, living in the west of Ireland. Her work has appeared in *Best Lesbian Love Stories, 2005 and After Midnight: True Lesbian Erotic Confessions* and is upcoming in several anthologies in 2007. Maggie sells Wexford strawberries by the side of the Sligo road, which gives her plenty of writing time.

Cate Lawton is mild-mannered, cubicle-bound attorney for a large state agency by day, lesbian erotica writer by night. Although this is her first publication, her previous writings have helped free the wrongfully accused, defended constitutional rights and generally tried to make the world a better place.

Joy Parks began her career by lying about her age to the editor of her hometown newspaper to get a part-time job and started publishing poetry and reviews in literary magazines at the age of fourteen. She was a columnist for *The Body Politic,* Canada's infamous (and long defunct) gay newsmagazine and has written for many GLBT and mainstream publications including the *San Francisco Chronicle,* the *Boston Globe,* the *Toronto Star,* the *Ottawa Citizen,* the *Globe and Mail, Gay and Lesbian Review Worldwide,* the *Advocate, Lambda Book Report, Girlfriends* and *Publisher's Weekly.* "Sacred Ground," her erratically scheduled column on lesbian writing, can be found online. She began writing fiction as a fortieth birthday present to herself and since then, her short stories and erotica have appeared in quite a few anthologies. Every time she writes about a fantasy, it ends up becoming real, so she has to be very careful about what she wishes for.

MJ Perry: I'm MJ (Pisces), living in Southington, Connecticut. I'm a police officer by night and writer by day. My therapeutic outlets include reading, writing and many forms of athletic activities (take that as you will!). I enjoy traveling, flirting and spending time my friends, family and Dante and Diva (my cats).

Ren Peters lives in the Northeast with her partner and two big, beautiful Ragdoll cats. She retired from teaching English and now, instead of correcting high school essays, she edits much more interesting lesbian fiction and poetry. She enjoys reading, cooking and baking, and most lately, trying her own hand at writing.

Radclyffe is a retired surgeon and full-time author-publisher with over twenty-five lesbian novels and anthologies in print, including the 2005 Lambda Literary Award winners *Erotic Interludes 2: Stolen Moments* ed. with Stacia Seaman and *Distant Shores, Silent Thunder,* a romance. She has selections in multiple anthologies including *Call of the Dark*, *The Perfect Valentine*, *Wild Nights*, *Best Lesbian Erotica 2006* and *2007*, *After Midnight*, *Caught Looking: Erotic Tales of Voyeurs and Exhibitionists*, *First-Timers*, *Ultimate Undies: Erotic Stories About Lingerie and Underwear*, and *Naughty Spanking Stories 2*. She is the recipient of the 2003 and 2004 Alice B. Readers' award for her body of work and is also the president of Bold Strokes Books, a publishing company featuring lesbian-themed general and genre fiction. Her forthcoming works include *Erotic Interludes 5: Road Games* ed. with Stacia Seaman (May 2007), *Honor Under Siege* (June 2007), *Winds of Fortunes* (Oct 2007) and *In Deep Waters: Volume 1*, an erotica collection written with Karin Kallmaker (2007).

Jean Rosestar: Jean has stories posted online and is a book reviewer for *Lambda Book Report*. She was in the U.S. Army in the early 1970s, but unfortunately, she didn't realize she was a lesbian until after she got out. She lives with her partner, Vic, and mother-in-law near Dallas, Texas.

Stacia Seaman has edited New York Times and USA Today bestsellers and numerous award-winning books, and has herself won a Lammy with coeditor Radclyffe for *Erotic Interludes 2: Stolen Moments*. She edits everything from textbooks to popular nonfiction to mysteries and romance novels. She lives with her cat, Frieda, and enjoys being silly.

Nell Stark is a graduate student of medieval English literature in Madison, Wisconsin, where she lives with her partner and their two cats. When she is not teaching, writing or teaching in the Writing Center, she enjoys reading, cooking and any sport that involves a lot of running around maniacally. Her first novel, *Running With the Wind*, was published by Bold Strokes Books in March of 2007. She has recently started work on her second novel with BSB, an urban fantasy titled *Free to Fall*. She can be reached at nell.stark@gmail.com, or by visiting www.nellstark.com. Nell would like to thank her partner, Lisa, for her continued support, encouragement and inspiration.

Renée Strider lives in Ontario, Canada. Besides writing lesbian stories, some of which have also appeared in the Erotic Interludes anthologies, she writes about art and translates poems and stories into English from an endangered minority language. She can be reached at reneelf@cogeco.ca.

KI Thompson began her writing career when her first short story, "The Blue Line," was included in the Lambda Literary Award winning anthology *Erotic Interludes 2: Stolen Moments* from Bold Strokes Books. She also has selections in the subsequent anthologies, *Erotic Interludes 3: Lessons in Love, Erotic Interludes 4: Extreme Passions, Erotic Interludes 5: Road Games, Best Lesbian Romance 2007* by Cleis Press, and Fantasy: Untrue Stories of Lesbian Passion by Bella Books. Her novels, *House of Clouds*, an historic romance set during the Civil War, is forthcoming from Bold Strokes Books (October 2007), to be followed by *Heart of the Matter*, a contemporary romance, due out in 2008. She can be reached at www.kithompson.com or www.boldstrokesbooks.com.

Eva Vandetuin is a religious studies graduate student. She sees sex and spirituality as being closely intertwined, and the relationship between the two inspires much of her fiction. She has recently been published in *Extreme Passions: Erotic Interludes 4* and *Ultimate Lesbian Erotica 2007*, and has a story upcoming in *Road Games: Erotic Interludes 5*.

Anna Watson is an old-school femme and a hip mama to two groovy boys. She can often be found driving to sports games in the femme-mobile, hastily applying lipstick in the rearview mirror. Her work has appeared in *Mothering, Unsupervised*

Existence, Best Lesbian Erotica 2007 and *Suspect Thoughts'* anthology on drag kings, among others. She has been in a long-distance relationship with her butch beau for the past three years, which gives her plenty of time to dream up smutty stories and commit them to paper.

About the Editors

With German as a first language and a childhood steeped in homophobic and misogynistic messages, **Barbara Johnson** did not seem destined to become a bestselling author of lesbian novels, short stories and novellas. Her first serious attempt at writing came at age ten, when she wrote an award-winning essay entitled "What It Means to Me to Be a Good Catholic." Her second effort, at age nineteen, was a tad more controversial—a semi-autobiographical, coming-out novel for a creative writing class. With that, nature overcame nurture and the budding lesbian-feminist writer was on her way.

Although today's college students can major in LGBT Studies, Barbara grew up at a time when lesbianism was still the "love that dare not speak its name" and there was little in the way of popular literature for a woman-loving audience. A voracious reader of Regency-era novels (Georgette Heyer was a favorite), Barbara decided to write her own version, only this time the handsome Lord and elegant Lady would be a handsome Butch and an elegant Femme. That novel, *Stonehurst*, and the mysteries *The Beach Affair* and *Bad Moon Rising* and the romance *Strangers in the Night* were all published by Naiad Press. Barbara's short stories have appeared in anthologies from Naiad Press, Bella Books, Alyson Publications and Hawthorne Press, and she is part of the successful quartet, along with Karin Kallmaker, Therese Szymanski and Julia Watts, who write the *New Exploits* series from Bella Books.

Fantasy: Untrue Stories of Lesbian Passion is Barbara's second editorial collaboration with Therese, the first being *The Perfect Valentine*.

Therese Szymanski is an award-winning playwright. She's also been short-listed for a couple of Lammys, a Goldie and a Spectrum, as well as having made the Publishing Triangle's list of Notable Lesbian Books with her first anthology.

She's edited five anthologies for Bella After Dark (BAD): *Wild Nights: (Mostly) True Stories of Women Loving Women*, *Back to Basics: A Butch/Femme Anthology*, *Call of the Dark: Erotic Lesbian Stories of the Supernatural*, *Fantasy: Untrue Stories of Lesbian Passion* and *The Perfect Valentine* (the latter two with Barbara Johnson). She's written seven books in the Lammy-finalist Brett Higgins Motor City Thrillers series (in order: *When the Dancing Stops*, *When the Dead Speak*, *When Some Body Disappears*, *When Evil Changes Face*, *When Good Girls Go Bad*, *When the Corpse Lies* and *When First We Practice* (*When It's All Relative* is due out in 2008)). The first book in her new mystery series—*It's All Smoke & Mirrors, the first Shawn Donnelly Chronicles*—is due out later this year. She's part of the foursome who created (and write) the bestselling/Lammy-finalist Bella After Dark (BAD) New Exploits series, which include *Once Upon a Dyke: New Exploits of Fairy Tale Lesbians*; *Bell, Book and Dyke: New Exploits of Magical Lesbians*; *Stake Through the Heart: New Exploits of Twilight Lesbians* and the forthcoming *Tall in the Saddle*. She also has a few dozen short works published in a variety of books.

Reese generally works a day job as a writer/editor, and also sidelines as a designer/typesetter and sometimes edits on the side as well. Interestingly enough, in the past two years she's made money as a copywriter, an editor, a security guard, a newspaper editor, a writer, a graphic designer, production manager of a newspaper and serving subpoenas. Among other things.

She tends to find inspiration for her stories from her everyday life.

COYOTE SKY by Gerri Hill. 248 pp. Sheriff Lee Foxx is trying to cope with the realization that she has fallen in love for the first time. And fallen for author Kate Winters, who is technically unavailable. Will Lee fight to keep Kate in Coyote?
1-59493-065-1 $13.95

VOICES OF THE HEART by Frankie J. Jones. 264 pp. A series of events force Erin to swear off love as she tries to break away from the woman of her dreams. Will Erin ever find the key to her future happiness?   1-59493-068-6 $13.95

SHELTER FROM THE STORM by Peggy J. Herring. 296 pp. A story about family and getting reacquainted with one's past that shows that sometimes you don't appreciate what you have until you almost lose it.   1-59493-064-3 $13.95

WRITING MY LOVE by Claire McNab. 192 pp. Romance writer Vonny Smith believes she will be able to woo her editor Diana through her writing . . .   1-59493-063-5 $13.95

PAID IN FULL by Ann Roberts. 200 pp. Ari Adams will need to choose between the debts of the past and the promise of a happy future.   1-59493-059-7 $13.95

ROMANCING THE ZONE by Kenna White. 272 pp. Liz's world begins to crumble when a secret from her past returns to Ashton . . .   1-59493-060-0 $13.95

SIGN ON THE LINE by Jaime Clevenger. 204 pp. Alexis Getty, a flirtatious delivery driver is committed to finding the rightful owner of a mysterious package.
1-59493-052-X $13.95

END OF WATCH by Clare Baxter. 256 pp. LAPD Lieutenant L.A Franco Frank follows the lone clue down the unlit steps of memory to a final, unthinkable resolution.
1-59493-064-4 $13.95

BEHIND THE PINE CURTAIN by Gerri Hill. 280 pp. Jacqueline returns home after her father's death and comes face-to-face with her first crush.
1-59493-057-0 $13.95

18TH & CASTRO by Karin Kallmaker. 200 pp. First-time couplings and couples who know how to mix lust and love make 18th & Castro the hottest address in the city by the bay.   1-59493-066-X $13.95

JUST THIS ONCE by KG MacGregor. 200 pp. Mindful of the obligations back home that she must honor, Wynne Connelly struggles to resist the fascination and allure that a particular woman she meets on her business trip represents.
1-59493-087-2 $13.95

ANTICIPATION by Terri Breneman. 240 pp. Two women struggle to remain professional as they work together to find a serial killer.   1-59493-055-4 $13.95

OBSESSION by Jackie Calhoun. 240 pp. Lindsey's life is turned upside down when Sarah comes into the family nursery in search of perennials.   1-59493-058-9 $13.95

BENEATH THE WILLOW by Kenna White. 240 pp. A torch that still burns brightly even after twenty-five years threatens to consume two childhood friends.
1-59493-053-8 $13.95

SISTER LOST, SISTER FOUND by Jeanne G'fellers. 224 pp. The highly anticipated sequel to *No Sister of Mine*.   1-59493-056-2 $13.95